That a Man Can Stand: The Evolution of a Nation

AN ANTHOLOGY OF COLONIAL FICTION

Created by the 7th and 8th grade students at
Decatur Discovery Academy
Indianapolis, IN
2008

With support from:

Mr. Robert Schutte, Ms. Sarah Weimer, and Ms. Abby Wilfong

The 7th and 8th grade Facilitators

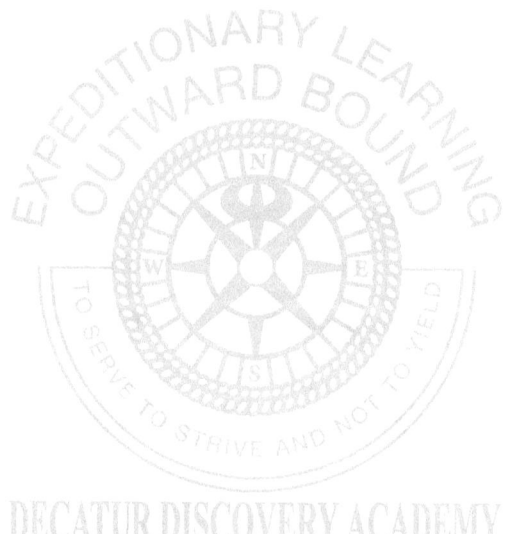

DECATUR DISCOVERY ACADEMY

Published in the United States by

Decatur Discovery Academy

5125 Decatur Blvd. • Suite D

Indianapolis, IN 46241

Phone 317-856-0900

Fax 317-856-0143

http://decatur.discovery.schoolfusion.us

ISBN 978-0-578-01173-8

Acknowledgments

Thank you everyone who aided us during the course of our expedition and in the creation of this book:

- ❖ To all of the parents who volunteered as chaperones or experts, and to those who helped their children accomplish this monumental feat.

- ❖ To our Captain Kevin Leineweber for his belief in us and his dedication to adding 7th and 8th grade to our school.

- ❖ To the other facilitators at DDA for their patience, aid, and cooperation during this crazy process.

- ❖ To Tom VanWinkle and Deb Otto at Expeditionary Learning for all of their help and support over the past five years.

- ❖ To the Parent-Facilitator Organization who provided us with supplies and goodies over the last few months.

- ❖ To the staff at Connor Prairie Living History Museum in Fishers, Indiana, particularly Nancy who scheduled our fieldwork and coordinated our experts.

- ❖ To Ryan and the rest of the staff at the Learning Curve at the Indianapolis Marion County Public Library for all of their support and help with the blogs.

Table of Contents

Massachusetts

Rhode Island

Connecticut

New York

New Jersey

Part II: Letters Between Friends and Foes

Part III: Scenes of Colonial Life in Silhouette

Part IV: Student Acknowledgements and Dedications

Introduction

"I never thought I'd be doing this!" could be the battle cry for the authors of this book. When Decatur Discovery Academy, or DDA, welcomed its first class of middle schoolers, they were told that great things would be expected of them. They were told to expect that they would be pushed to accomplish things they would think impossible. They were told that *this* school was different from *other* schools.

The students all heard this speech, acknowledged that they heard it, accepted that the staff believed it, but failed to believe it for themselves. I know. I was there with them- both physically and mentally.

As a brand new teacher at DDA, I knew just about as much of what was to come as they did. Oh sure, I had the benefit of a few days of planning time to give me the slight advantage of knowing what we wanted to have happen in the days to come. But if there was one lesson that I had learned in my many years of teaching before coming to DDA, it was that there is a profound difference between what is *planned* and what is actually *accomplished*. I had heard the "company line" and was prepared to begin my new assignment with what I thought was an open mind, but deep down, like the students themselves, I still had doubts.

So, even as I helped deliver this speech on Day 1, I too needed to be convinced. Like the students, I was willing to go along with "the plan," but I was also not going to be surprised if things were not quite what I had been told. Boy, were *we* wrong!

I have taught in some capacity at every level of education from elementary to college. I have spent most of the last decade teaching at the middle school level. I am no stranger to teaching. That said, teaching at DDA has turned out to be different from most of my experiences. I'm sure our first class of students would say the same thing. DDA is different from most other schools.

For the last few years, I have been struck by the amount of apathy I witnessed in my students. Each year, I have welcomed a new class and each year, I watched as many of my students went through the motions of being a student. I used to tell my students that I was different from other teachers they had had. Once they were a student of mine, they would always be a student of mine. (To this day I do my best to check up on any number of my "former" students.)

Each year, I would spend countless personal hours doing my best to connect with each student; trying to share with them a vision of hope that I saw in each one. As the year would go on, I would find that some of the students would "buy in" to what I was trying to teach and encourage. I would also find that there were just as many that would not. This was to be expected. This may sound pessimistic, but no one teacher can be all things to all students. So while this bothered me, it did not consume me. What did consume me was the "middle group" that kept appearing to get larger and larger- the students who just remained unaffected. I had a hard time reconciling the notion of apathy in people so young. What possible hardships had they been forced to endure by the age 12-13 that could make them so jaded?

As the school year would progress, I would have others accuse me of "being crazy." I didn't see myself as such. I thought I was just doing what I had been taught in college to do. I would do my best to create what I thought were innovative lessons using techniques that I thought would wake up my students; shake them from their metaphorical slumber. I would spend more than the required 1 hour a day "overtime" to make sure I was there for my students. Not that I was some exceptional or great teacher- I know a great many teachers who are better at teaching, are able to accomplish in a "standard day" what it takes me hours of "overtime" to accomplish, and are just as dedicated to the idea of awakening students from their apathy. It just always seemed to me that there were fewer and fewer of us that not only believed in the goal of ending apathy, but also thought it was possible to accomplish it.

Each year, I watched as the staff were told about how our students had not performed as expected on standardized tests, not lived up to behavior expectations, etc. Each year, we were asked to do more to make matters personal for students and encourage them to "raise the bar." The more I tried to "think outside the box" and "shake things up" for my students, though, the more I was told, "You can't do that." More than once I began to wonder if I was cut out to be a teacher- I obviously wasn't from the same mold as other teachers, as they never seemed to get this criticism by doing what they had always done. Slowly I began to understand my students' apathy. Why "think outside the box" when all that gets you is negative attention? If you leave things alone, people will leave you alone. But, I'm not the type of person who can do that!

When I came to DDA, I was worried about this. I had heard that DDA believed in things that *sounded* good, but would they really *be* that way? Would I be able to find another teacher who believed as I do? Imagine my surprise as I found not *one* teacher who believed as I do, but *an entire staff*!

I am certain that our students walked in with the same hopes and fears as I did. Our "Captain" (principal) had told us all that DDA was different, that there we would find "something special." He was right. I have come to realize that our Captain has made some very deliberate hiring choices. I can honestly say I am surrounded by some of the best and most caring teachers I have had the opportunity to work with. In finding these "like minds," we (for nothing in EL so far has been a solo experience) have been able to not only plan innovative lessons, but have actually been encouraged to take them further! (It turns out that some of the lessons/techniques that I had thought were "innovations," aren't as innovative as I thought. They have names and are the very heart of the fabric of what I've come to know as Expeditionary Learning or EL.)

As I have learned, so too have our students. That process too, had its obstacles to overcome. We had to develop trust, set high expectations, and teach our students the principles of EL teaching/learning so that they too could buy in. Slowly they have.

That doesn't mean there haven't been bumps in the road. Piloting a program at a school new to me, for a grade level new to the school, using techniques that are new to the students (and, in my case, to teachers as well) is not an easy task. The middle school staff of DDA has probably learned as much from the experience as the students themselves. But the bottom line is, we ARE learning.

We began this expedition with trips to historic Conner Prairie here Indianapolis. Our students began with the idea that this was a field*trip*, but soon came to understand that it was field*work*. They had to conduct interviews with the staff, write down observations, and draw conclusions. They had to take that information and apply it to later lessons. We did not do it for them.

As our expedition progressed, they had to use their interviews with historic re-enactors to design their own "colonial characters." The characters were not given to them or designed for them. As a result, each character is as unique as the student author who created them. While some of these characters' histories may contain errors in fact, language/grammar, or personality, they are based upon the work of the students themselves.

We challenged our students with activities of which they were neither comfortable nor familiar; frozen tableaus, creating silhouette busts and scenes from paper, blog writing, reader's theaters, spirit reads, protocols, rubrics, reflections, portfolios, etc. As we challenged them, we had more and more of them shake off their fear and apathy and rise to our challenge. Before long, it wasn't just me who was saying, "I can't believe we did that!" Or, "I never thought I'd be doing this!" It was all of us.

As we went into our first writing lesson, I was shocked by what I perceived to be a lack of skills. I began to worry that we would never be able to get to our goal of being able to publish a book about Colonial America. As the students and I went through *our* first writing workshop, I began to see significant improvement in some of their work. As we began to design characters and create our first blogs, I once again doubted whether or not we could reach a point where these writings could be published. I am positive that the students did too. I am sure that they had been told things like "We're going to publish a book" before, only to have it fail to come true. As we entered our first period of heavy revision, one could almost see them thinking, "Why bother? It's good enough. It'll never get published anyway."

A few months (eighteen short weeks) later, here we are. We did it. Some of us have come further than others, but we made it. Our book has been sent to the publisher and we are now published authors.

As part of the EL process, there is a lot of self-reflection both for students and for teachers. I have read a number of student reflections on this entire process. Most of them contain a variation of the battle cry. "I never thought I'd be doing this!" They have become believers… and so have I.

So, if you had asked me back in August of 2008 if I ever thought I would be writing the introduction to an anthology of student work; teaching with a group of outstanding, caring teachers; and achieving some of my greatest goals for my career, I'd have said, "I never thought I'd be doing this!"

Robert Schutte
DDA 7th/8th Grade Facilitator

Part I:
From Colonial Thoughts to American Dreams

New Hampshire

CHAPTER 1:

ALICE MCDOOGLE'S CONFUSION

By: Karlee Nielsen-Baker

About Alice McDoogle

December 9, 1708

Dear Journal,

    This is my first entry so I will tell you about myself….

    I am Alice……fourteen year old Alice McDoogle of Strawberry Banke, daughter of the shopkeeper Richard the second and Helen McDoogle, older sister of Georgia, Annie, Mary, Hanna, Elizabeth, and Felicity, Granddaughter of Richard the first and Patricia McDoogle, also Granddaughter of Maria and Benjamin Smith; Great Granddaughter of Augastice and Eleanor McDoogle. I never met my great grandparents from my mother's side nor any of my aunts and uncles or cousins from any side of the family. See all I know is my pa's side of the family came with the first settlers to Strawberry Banke in the 1630's when John Cabot allowed people to settle here, Great grandpa Augastice had opened a shoppe known as McDoogle Shoppe, it has been in the family for almost three generations now and he left that to my grandpa Richard the first. Grandpa Richard gave it to my father knowing he was getting to old and might pass soon but he is still alive and kicking. Do to the fact that my parents didn't have any males I am the one who gets to inherit the shoppe when Pa and Ma passes and all the land and other processions until I am married then my husband gets it all.

    There are eleven of us living in our decent sized two room home, me and five of my sisters sleep in the barn with the cattle, horses, sheep, and chicken. Mary being only a year and a half old sleeps in the house with my parents and grandparents from Pa's side.

    Since my ma has been ill I have to tend to her, my grandparents and my younger siblings. I also do all of the cooking, sweeping, laundry, dishes, and sewing. I also have to feed the farm animals, milk the cows, collect the eggs, shave the sheep and clean the animal feces. I also have to tend the garden. My sisters have no choice but to have to help. I also work in the shoppe every day. I have to sweep, put things on shelf, help unpack boxes, handle costumers, and make sure all tabs are paid. My days are so very tiring.

I am so tired, and my body aches, the air in the barn stinks and is quiet cold. Right now, oh how I wish winter would end, me and my sisters are all bundled up in the hay piles with only 3 wool blankets trying to keep our body temperature at normal. I guess there is a plus side though about winter, tomorrow is Sunday and after church we will be skating on the pond because all chores end, all the shoppes and schools are closed. But sadly, everything picks back up on Monday.

I want to go back to school so badly. I did once when I was five up until I was eight and I got a pretty good education I can read and write a lot of words and I know a lot of math, some of my younger sisters are attending school now but that is because they are so young, Pa says he is going to take them out in a few years. See if I was back in school I would be getting a better education and then I wouldn't be doing all of these chores, but I can't complain, I guess.

So I guess that is all I have to say......I need to get some sleep so I can get up early for church.

The Three Soldiers

December 13, 1708

Journal,

Church was a few days ago and that is when I heard the news, we girls me, ma, grandmother and my six sisters were at home while the older males were at town meeting. Me, ma, and grandmother were preparing dinner while the younger ones played with their rag dolls and played hand clap games, when pa and grandfather came in bursting through the door. Pa said angrily that three British soldiers are coming to live with us. He said if we don't allow them to then he will be put into jail and our family will have to pay a fine. I am going to have to cook more do to the fact we have to feed them. Pa didn't say anything else about the matter except that we girls will have to move into the attic so that they could live in the barn.

Early today when I was walking around town I heard some people saying they are having the soldiers come to protect us from the Indians. That is ridiculous, we have lived in piece with the Abenki tribe for years now and we know they wouldn't pull anything.

The soldiers will arrive in nine weeks. Pa told us that when the soldiers are here that we should continue with our chores nothing will change too much.

February 23, 1709
Journal,

It has been months since my last entry so I want to catch you up on some things. The snow is slowly melting, even though it is still cold out Pa says it will time to plant soon. Ma hasn't been getting better, she is much worse, her skin is so pale you can see her veins, and she is so skinny she can't keep anything down, she bruises easily, is losing chunks of her hair, and her bones are like paper they break so easily and she can't walk; she can barely even move. We had a doctor come and he said there was nothing he could do, I pray she gets better. Pa has added another room onto the house; the shoppe has been doing so well lately that we could actually afford the supplies to do so. Pa says he didn't want to have to move the animals from the barn to make room for the soldiers. There are three hay mattresses in the room that I have sewn myself, and a fire place and a few lanterns, it's the smallest room in the house thought soldiers seem to like it though, one even confessed that he did.

Yes, the soldier have arrived just a few days ago, two of the three soldiers are rude and obnoxious, they come in and out without saying a word, all they do is eat, sleep and give us dirty looks. I believe there names were Edmund Jones and Francis George. Edmund has dark curly hair and evil dark eyes, as does Francis but Francis has straight bronze hair that is always pulled back, he is slightly taller than Edmund. Honestly, they both scare me. The other soldier is named Edward James; he is polite and is quiet a gentleman. Edward has an odd blue shade of eyes sort of grayish and he has black sloppy hair. He is probably the nicest man I have ever met, he even helps me with my chores, and Pa seems to like him best. The other day he helped me feed the animals and we talked he is only sixteen but everyone else thinks he is eighteen, and today he helped me out in the shoppe for free. He refused to accept the small amount I offered for his assistance.

Truthfully I don't mind cooking or cleaning up after Edward which he always helps with anyway but I don't mind because he is thankful. As for the other two, Edmund and Francis if it were up to me I would kick them out and tell them to eat dirt; they are such unhelpful, ungrateful donkeys!

Excuse me that is not lady like, well I guess I will have to live with them. I've got to go now. I have to wash the soldiers' clothing.

Fears...

February 25, 1709

Dear Journal,

This is terrible, terrible indeed Ma wants to see me marry, and to be a proper young lady. Before she passes! Ma isn't going to pass, she will get better, she has to get better don't know what I would do without her. Anyways, I can't marry and be a proper young lady, I am Alice for Pete's sake, the Alice that climbs trees and hunts. I am not the type of person who sits and weaves all day and makes candles. It just isn't me. Sure, I am to a point but otherwise I was built to do hard labor. And besides that I am only fourteen, how can I marry? I can't I am to young, right? Oh lord, marriage? And you think Pa would side with me, Oh but he didn't he sided with Ma. This is the Pa that taught me everything I know, he is the one who technically taught me how to hunt and fish, he forced me to do hard work and not cry over splinters or mud, and all of the other things. And worst then being married it's who I might be married to, it might be an arranged wedding! How can this happen?

To top that off, I got little sleep last night because I keep having these horrible dreams about the shoppe burning down. Then it almost happened. Since I got little sleep, I sort of fell a sleep in the shoppe while waiting around, then I knocked over a lit candle. Thank God it only burned some of my dress and now there is a big black spot where the floor caught on fire, Edward is the one who putted out the fire. Thankfully, because I was in such shock, I couldn't move. I could have burnt to death.

Then earlier I was talking to Pa and he said that if the shoppe does burn down we would have nothing. What if I would have burned down the shoppe? What would we do? What if someone burned down the shoppe? I can't even imagine how horrible that might be.

Right now it seems that the shoppe is the least of my worries, the whole wedding ordeal keeps popping up in my head, I can't imagine my name as anything other Alice McDoogle, I can't imagine living with a husband and then having kids. I could act lady like for Ma, that wouldn't be that hard, right? Maybe if she sees me being lady like, then she wouldn't want me to marry. Oh who am I kidding, once mom puts her mind to it, it gets done. Why can't she wish that one of my younger siblings was more lady-like? Why, I mean she has seven daughters she could have just picked Mary, or Georgia, or Felicity. But no she wants me to be lady like. I guess I will have to deal with just to make her happy.

Whittling

February 27, 1709

Dear Journal,

I have been quiet frustrated lately and I found the perfect activity for me when frustration comes about, it is called whittling. I have seen many older men whittling just to pass time and truthfully it seemed really dull. But today when I finished my chores I had nothing to do. The shoppe and house were completely swept and clean, the beds were freshly made, all the laundry was washed, hung and dried, folded and left in the trunks; the animals were fed, the sheep were shaved, the cattle milked, and the chickens' eggs were collected and dinner didn't have to be on for awhile. I began to walk around when I saw Edward leaning against a tree. I walked over to him and saw that he was whittling, he was making a duck. He told me it's a fun activity when you are bored or frustrated so he taught me how.

All you do is find a nice stick or piece of wood, and then you take paper thin shavings out of the wood very carefully with a sharp blade, like a knife. I cut my fingers a few times with the sharp blade; my wood was almost completely dyed red. I didn't make anything but a pile of shavings and a toothpick, but I must say it is the best toothpick ever. I guess if I practice then I will get better at making things.

Sugar Act!

April 5, 1764

Journal,

It has been decades dear journal of mine, your pages are a tainted a deep yellowish tan, my old writing is smeared, your edges look as though they have been nibbled on by mice, and there is still straw in the creases of your pages from the spot in the hay mattress I hid you in years ago.

Well journal I am now sixty-nine years of age and you have missed so much. First, I did marry before ma had passed, to Edward and I was fifteen at the time. I then had three children the oldest being named Benjamin who I see everyday, I don't really see the other two that often do to the fact they left and hardly ever visit, I also have seven grandchildren and two great grandchildren that I know of. Since ma has passed pa had remarried to a younger women and he had his first son, Abraham, and since then I haven't stayed in touch with pa, I moved out of Strawberry Banke with my husband to raise our family. I saw no point in staying there, I mean Abraham has pa's shop now, and his land and all of his possessions, nothing belongs to me. I do wonder how my sisters are doing every now and then. Well, Edward and I live with our oldest son and his wife and child who soon will be old enough to move out. I do miss Strawberry Banke.

Today while walking with my grandchild, Anna to get cloth I saw aggressive people gathering around the general store yelling at Mr. Bartley the store owner. He tried to calm down the people, "This is not my fault people, and I can not control the King's orders. I am sorry." He stood on a bucket telling the people.

"Excuse me, good sir." I said to a random man that was running away from the crowd.

He stopped, "Yes ma'am?" He asked jaw clenched.

"What is going on?"

He starred at me in confusion. "Parliament placed a tax on sugar and lumber," he said in an angry tone.

"On sugar?"

He nodded.

"But, we need that."

"That's the point. End of the war and the home land ain't gettin' enough from our taxes, so they place the act." The man walked away.

It is times like this that it makes me wonder about pa's store and the troubles they are going threw, if anything probably having to stand on a bucket and yell to the crowd just as Mr. Bartley, they are probably getting a low income. Me and Anna went to the fabric store and got what we need then left. We came back home and that's when I found you, in a box with my sewing supplies.

They Seem Pretty Tolerable To Me...

June 22, 1774

Journal,

    We all gathered around the table after a long, tiring day of anger and work to feast upon a small roast that had been on the spit all day. My daughter in law, Mary was just about to sit the wheat bread onto the table when there was a rapid knock on the door. "Who can that be?" she asked curiously, as she took her seat.

    "Just ignore them," Benjamin said bowing his head like the rest of us preparing to say grace. "Dear Lord...," he began.

    "By order of the King open this door!" a loud voice boomed continuing to pound on the door. Ben cursed as he got up and walked quickly to the door. He pulled the door open furiously.

    "I am Henry George, commanding officer of these soldiers." I stared out the door past Ben and Henry to see three men in red coats and tan pants, "I need quarters for these men."

    "And what would you like me to do about it?" Ben said with a clenched jaw.

    The officer smiled, "Well, you see sir, as rule by Parliament you must allow these soldiers into your home or I have all rights to take control of your home or anything else I need to shelter these men." He ended his sentence with a grin.

    Ben's face began to turn a bright red from anger. I stood up and walked slowly to the door, "It's okay honey." placing my hand on Ben's shoulder, "Come on in fellows," I said smiling. "We were in the middle of saying grace before a feasting."

    The men bowed their heads and filled into the house. Ben moved out of the way and his face began to go back to its normal tan shade. We all gathered around the table as Ben took his normal seat at the head and Mary rushed to get the three men that were joining us a chair.

"Dear Lord," Ben began, "Thank you for this wonderful meal we are about to eat. Thank you for keeping our family together, and thank your for keeping our health well, Amen."

"Amen," we all said in unison as Ben began cutting our small roast that was big enough just to supply our family.

"Sorry, men," I said to the soldiers as Ben gave me a small piece of the roast, "The meat was big enough just for our family, didn't expect company, so we all just get a moiety piece." We all ate in silence.

Just a little while later, Anna, little Luann Mae and I went to get some ingredients for our pottage we will be making tomorrow. "Why grandmother would you allow those soldiers into our house?" Anna asked, watching Luann skip."

"Because Anna if I didn't we would have lost our home. And not just that I grew up having soldiers living with us, it's not that bad."

"I know but grandmother they're evil." She had sorrow in her voice.

"They are not all evil," I said calmly.

"Grandmother a British soldier killed my husband," she yelled.

Luann stopped skipping and turned to look at her mother "That's evil."

I nodded and said, "Do you think Edward is evil?"

"Grandfather? No."

"Well your grandfather was a British soldier." Her eyes grew wide in shock. That was something Edward never did tell them.

"I never knew," she said shaking her head back and forth. When we got to the store the sun was beginning to set, purple clouds were splattered across the orange-ish pink sky.

"Where's Mr. Bartley?" Anna asked as we walked into the store where Mr. Bartley's son, Pete, stood cleaning up the shoppe.

"Oh evening Miss, Mrs., little lady," he smiled. "My pa is at home under to much stress with all the notices and all." He shook his head back and forth, "There are too many notices anymore, people are getting sick of it, and the one that came out today sat him off."

"It's sad. The soldiers get by with so much because of the Administration of Justice Act and now they get to live with us folks," Anna said.

"This is the forth act this year. I can't even imagine the pain Massachusetts is in right now, with their ports being closed and no choice of government officials. The people must be outraged," Pete said keeping their conversation going. I decided to keep out but listen.

"Well ladies the shop is bout' to a close." he smiled.

"Oh, yes" Anna said, grabbing up sleepy Luann. We began walking out the door and down the dirt road.

"Anna, that boy is head over heals for you."

She looked at me. "Grandmother your nuts, we are just friends."

"Don't call me nuts, young lady."

There was yelling coming from behind us in the town square. "We can't take this!" some one hollered.

"Go away!" another shouted.

Who were they talking about? Who were they talking to? Everyone came running toward time square. "The King is running us down!" people yelled.

Me and Anna looked at each other and began jogging the way home, I ran as fast as my old legs could go. I don't know what went down in the town square I am just glad we didn't get caught in the middle of it. These acts that came out this year earned a new name, the Intolerable Acts.

Colonial Notices

I am very confused. I am a very old woman and there is not much more I can take, I will die soon and as I get older the less I understand. Why are we rebelling? Why can't we just stay under England's rule? Why so many wars? Who are the evil ones, us, England, the Indians? I have grown up under the rule of the king and I may have questioned some of his decisions, but I got over it, and I didn't rebel, not once. But the laws and the notices and the congress, and the "are we Americans or are we Brits thing", it just got confusing and overwhelming. And the notice that was posted all over the place, that people gather around and argue and get angry all about, the notice about how we are not allowed to export to England, well won't our economy lose money? I think this just ridiculous, why can't we just stay like we were before? I am too old for change.

Today while shopping with my daughter in law, Mary, I heard a few men wearing dirt coated clothing talking in angry tones. Usually I walk by and ignore them but this time I didn't since my gut said listen.

"King George won't respond, the people are getting angry," said one man.

"Something needs to be done," another added.

"If it's a war he wants it's a war he will get." another man growled.

War? It was the only word going through my mind as we walked down the dirt road to the fabric shoppe. If the Continental Congress is there to help us then why is war necessary? People will get hurt! These people don't know what they are doing. What is wrong with the King?

Tea Act

Dear Journal,

Today, while the sun shined high up in the cloudless, blue sky, me and my granddaughter Anna Maria and her child, little Luann Mae walked to the general store down the road. Luann stopped and picked flowers every so often making it a longer trip then it needed to be, which was a good thing really since the day was so nice, men around my age sat in their front lawn whittling and young boys and girls skipped threw tall grass and the people that had enough money to afford tea drank it with there porcelain tea cups enjoying there herbal drink.

By the time we got to the general store Luann's basket was full of colorful flowers that now sit in an empty jam jar on the dining table. Mr. Bartley, the store owner helped us find what we were looking for.

"Have there been any more notices?" I asked as he added up the math of the price of our goods.

"Yes ma'am," he said sadly with a hint of anger in his tone. "One just came out to day, about the tea." He frowned looking at me.

"What about it?" Anna asked watching little Luann admire the maple candies on the counter sitting next to Mr. Bartley's arm. Mr. Bartley handed her a piece and smiled along with her as she said "thank you," in her childish whisper, and began nibbling on it.

"It's just nonsense really," he said looking at me and Anna. "It is costing less for the motherland to send us tea, making it seem as though tax has gone down, but it really hasn't. The people are outraged around here and feel as though they are just trying to trick us to make us pay."

I nodded along with what Mr. Bartley said because I know how these people feel. I do wonder how pa's shop is doing, are they people angry around there too, I bet they aren't making a very good income.

They Signed it....

Dear Journal,

I don't know to feel right now, I am a bee hive but instead of bees, a swarm of emotion. Today while sitting in the lawn drinking some coffee with Anna watching little Luann Mae, people walked down the road hitting pots and pans with large wooden spoons and they screamed and hollered with bright smiles. Luann marched around the yard and played along.

"They signed the ticket to our freedom, ladies!" a man yelled to us leaning over the fence.

"Oh, Lordy," Anna smiled and began clapping her hands with a large smile on her face.

"Freedom!" the people cheered.

I felt ill. My heart beat wildly and I couldn't breath, I thought I was going to die. We are free, I should feel happy right? Then why am I so scared about what is going to happen not just to us, but to the signers? I know something bad is going to happen to them, they just stabbed the King in the back; he will be furious. Everyone is so happy but I am upset because I know the King wanted to fight us, or be rude to us, we were just away for him to make money. I know that they have sent olive branches and he didn't respond, but I fell as though there was something else they could have done. I hope nothing bad happens to us. Oh I pray nothing bad happens or at least nothing bad happens to my family. I do hope I die before anything does though, because I do not want to be killed in a war over something I did not partake in.

CHAPTER 2:

A TIME IN THE LIFE OF JOHN CHAPPLEN, THE INNKEEPER

By: Hunter Thompson

About Me

I am an inn keeper in New Hampshire. I have my own house with two kids and a wife. My name is John Chaplin I live in the southern part of New Hampshire. It is a big town named Concord. Our inn is right on the docks so we get lots of people that come to stay. We are the closest inn for miles.

The Three Soldiers

One afternoon the governor came to my house and he said, "You will have to live and eat with three soldiers. If you do not your father will be put in jail the family will have to pay a big fine".

The three soldiers were well educated, well mannered and they were very thankful that we were taking care of them. I think it was just as hard on them as it was for us; staying with people they did not know. They were away from their families and friends for a long period of time and they needed to feel like a part of a family again. Over time we got to know each one of them and they became a part of our family.

We were able to learn a lot from them. At first I was very scared when I found out strangers would be living with us; not knowing if I could trust them, but as time went by they became my friends. When it was time for them to move on it was a very sad day for my family and me but we promised each other we would keep in touch. After this experience I had made new friends and learned that not all strangers are bad.

Fears

My sister and I are having little classes with our mom and dad. My sister is with my mom being taught how to be a wife of an innkeeper and what kind of responsibilities it takes to keep the family going. I'm with my dad being taught how to run an Inn by myself and what responsibilities it takes to run an Inn. I am learning things like where to keep the money, and should I keep it in a lock boxes with a combination, what to have in the Inn and what to have upstairs in the rooms, and things like what to have in the dinning room. My sister is learning how to cook meals and how to start the fire place and how to clean and how to make and change the beds. It will be hard if my sister and I had to figure it out by ourselves.

The Stamp Act

I hate the Stamp Act because l lost a lot of money. It is a time of low income and high unemployment. I hate the King because not a lot of people travel much anymore because it costs a lot of money so I am getting no one in or out of the Inn. Now that l have no money it is hard to buy food, tea, bedding and wax so l can make more candles. I need to find fabric so l can make hot pads and I have no money so I cannot really pay for anything anymore. That's why I hate the Stamp Act.

Hands-On

Several years later…

When I woke up today I was thinking of making some flap-jacks for breakfast and when my kids woke-up they asked the same question they do every morning, "What are we having for breakfast, dad?"

I answered, "We are having flap-jacks." They love flap-jacks. That is their favorite meal for breakfast so we all sat down at the table and we prayed.

My kids asked, "What are you doing today?"

I said, "Your mother and I are making candles for the guest so they can carry some light to their rooms when it is dark out. Tomorrow we are making hot pads for the kitchen."

One afternoon me and my wife decided to make two things; one candle and another hot pad. The first thing l made was a candle and how I made it was with wax, some string, a pot of hot water, a pot of cold water and a rod. How l made it was I dipped the candles in the hot wax and I held it in there for about two seconds. Then I took it out and put them on the rods and let them dry. After thirty minutes I then took the next candle and put it in for the same amount of time; dipped the next candle and held it in for the same amount of time, and then I took the candles and put them in the cold water. So I did that for about one whole day then I had many candles. I made a hot pad the next day. I weaved the extra fabric. I made that with string, a loom, and a needle. I put the string on the loom and took the needle and went under and over. I did that for a while and the old string became a beautiful hot pad.

The Tea Act

I hate the Tea Act. I think it is the worst act out there. This is not fair that the British don't have to pay taxes for tea but us colonists have to pay triple the price on tea. The export tax on tea that the British had goes to us and this is a really bad thing for me now that I have to pay more taxes on tea. Me and my family and guests drink tea at lunch and at supper. Because we go through two boxes of tea everyday that shows you how many guest I have again. We get new people every day and our busiest days are on the weekends because that's when all the ship's come in with new people from Britain and other colonies. On the weekends is when I use about three boxes of tea. So on Monday mornings I have to go get about 16 boxes of tea from the market down by the ports. If you go early you get the best pick of the litter but they charge you a fortune for the tea. So, that is why I hate the Tea Act.

The Intolerable Acts

I like the name the press is giving them, "The Intolerable Acts". That includes the Quartering act, the Massachusetts Government Act, the Administration of Justice Act, the Quebec Act, and the Boston Port Act. The Quartering Act gives the Kings army the authority to take your home if you do not let them live in it. The Massachusetts Government Act says something like this, "We the people of England do not like the people you are picking. So, from now on we will pick who will rule you over there."

The Boston Port Act says we can not ship any thing in or out of the Boston ports. The Administration of Justice Act says that, "If any of our soldiers get in trouble there you will not trial them, and we will trail them here in Britain." And those are the Intolerable Acts.

The Boycott Against Great Britain

We are boycotting goods from Great Britain because we were sending them letters that were saying things we don't like, but they were not sending them back to us. So, we are boycotting Britain so when they send their stuff over we will not buy their tea, food and any other things they send over. We boycotted for a while and they would not leave us alone so we stepped up and we said this is were we draw the line. We should become our own country.

Meeting the Signer James Wilson

I am so happy that the signers did sign the Declaration of Independence but I am also sad because I will lose money too. All of the people that stay at my inn are English people but sometimes people from other colonies come and stay at my inn.

I heard the door open and the person behind it was one of the signers of the Declaration of Independence. His name was James Wilson. I was surprised but I gave him a room, and after he settled in we went over to the fire and had some tea. We talked for a while until dinner and then he asked me what we were having. I answered, "We are having some cranberry pie for desert and for the main meal, creamy potato soup and mashed potatoes. For the appetizer we will have some potato skins with bacon bits and cheese."

After the three days he left and said our Inn was one of the best places he had ever stayed and then I said, "Thank you and have a nice day."

CHAPTER 3:

THE LIFE OF A BLACKSMITH'S APPRENTICE

By: Maurice Jones, Jr.

About Me

My name is Jon H. Smith and it's just another day at the blacksmith shop learning how to use a vice and how to make a bradawl. My brother and sister got in trouble and my parents made them clean the whole house. In the morning I have to do work around the house before I go to the blacksmith shop. I go to school only when the master wants me to, which might be once or twice a week. The master says I can be very helpful to him. On Sunday I don't go to work I go to church with my family and my master.

Soldiers

Today the government sent three British soldiers to my house. They said that we had to do everything they said or they would make my family pay a fine and put my father in jail. There was a short one, a tall one, and middle sized one. I had to feed them and let them sleep in my bed and use my things. The next day I was late to work and my master wanted to know why I was late. I told him that the government sent a letter that said they would send the soldiers. They're still at my house right now; they kept me up all night. When I got home my parents asked me how I felt and I told them that I didn't see why this had to happened to us or anyone.

Fears

My fears about becoming an adult are the dealing with the government, getting a house, and getting married. My expectations about it are to be a good father to my kids and to be a good husband to my wife and to be a good worker.

Hands on Experiences

I did some silver smiting today. I made a coin. There is a long process to doing this. First you have to make the mold. Then you have to heat the metal until it melts but not for too long or the metal will separate. Finally you have to pour the metal in the mold. It may take a few tries for it to work.

Sugar Act

I got a notice sent to me saying that the parliament started a new act. As a result of the seven year war, expiration of the Molasses Act and the economic depression happening right now. In these British colonies that has prevented the mother country from receiving enough money in taxes from colonies. So I have to pay more for the things that I use every day.

Stamp Act

Today I got a notice saying that the Stamp Act was passed. It said that the end of the Seven Years War resulted in an increase of our national debt from £75,000 before the war, to over £800,000,000 now. This was also because of a lack of income generated from the Sugar Act in 1764. As a black smith this makes it very difficult for me to earn a living because I have to pay more for stamps if I have to bill people. Now with the arrival of this additional tax, I may have to go out of business.

Boston Port Act

Today I heard about the Boston Port Act. They said that whereas dangerous commotions and insurrections have been fomented and raised in the town of Boston, in the province of Massachusetts' Bay, in New England, by people seeking to subvert his majesty's government and that within said commotions, they did seize and destroy valuable property {tea} belonging to the East Indian Company {EIC}. This is bad; I have goods coming from Boston that I need for work. Without them I can't work.

Last Notice

Today I got a notice but not from the British. It was from the colony. First the British, and now the colony. Man this stinks. I think they should stop with the notices already. If I could I would just start my own colony.

Declaration of Independence

Today is the day of the signing of the Declaration of Independence. It has finally happened. We now have our freedom and independence from the British and that King. They thought they could come over here and give us these taxes we wouldn't say anything about it. They thought wrong. Now it's time we fight back. Today I'm going to see this happen. There may be a bigger war after this. If there is, I'm going to be there. I want to fight for my freedom and the right to be an American; not a British slave.

CHAPTER 4:

BLACK BEAR

By: Anthony Vaughn

Soldiers

Today I wake up by smelling the delicious breakfast my mother made. "Good morning Black Bear, you slept forever," said mother.

"Where is everyone?" I say.

"Your father has already eaten, as well as Little Bear," says mother. "Your father is helping the chief build new homes and Little Bear is playing with his friends."

"I'm going to go outside to play as well mother," I say.

"OK, watch your brother," says mother.

As I walk outside, I feel the cool, morning breeze and then I see something, it's a small spec, then growing larger and it is three British soldiers and then I think they're here to attack, so I run home to tell mother.

"Mother! Mother! There are three British soldiers!" Mother runs out of the house to see and they're even closer to our home.

I go to father and tell him the news. As father comes home, he talks to the soldiers because he's the only one who can speak English. I can't understand and I'm very nervous that they might hurt us.

Then he finally says, "They aren't here to harm us and they are tired and injured and they're hoping they can stay with us until they get better."

"Are you going to let them?" I asked.

"They should stay," said father, "and they will be provided food as well, plus the government might harm us if we don't take them in." I feel awkward, but we are nice and giving people and they should stay.

As I look at the soldiers, their big, bulky bodies scare me, as well as their dark green uniforms. I wonder all of the things they had to win to get those metals? Did they have to kill someone? I have to try not to think of the worst about them if they're going to live with us and who knows, maybe I'll become good friends with them.

Hands on experience

Today, I would like to tell you about my leather band I made. The eagles on it represent the time when I rescued a baby eagle from its nest because it was abandon by its mother. The sun represents how hot it was that day. I rescued the baby eagle from the heat and the donkey (which represents the rode), is the animal I used to get the baby eagle and to ride home. The beads and my name on the leather band are for looks.

April 5, 1764

Today I heard that the British just passed a new law. I am shocked because of the new law and if we want to trade goods for other goods, we have to pay tax! I don't even know how the money system works! Also, I am afraid that the chief of my tribe might not let us Native Americans trade with the British colonists. The chief may not even let us go near the British colonists. Hopefully he will let us trade with them.

I am very angry with the new law because we have to pay extra money to trade! I know my fellow Native Americans are angry as well. This has been a really hard time for my tribe and myself. Hopefully, we will get through this horrible tax law.

March 22, 1765

Today, when I went into town to trade, I saw that there was a new tax law and it is called the Stamp Act. I am very upset about this new tax law because the British are charging the colonists and us Native Americans to trade or to buy things. I also heard that the reason why the king approved this law is because the colonies are experiencing an economic depression, which means they have high unemployment and low income. This is a very horrible act and I wish it would end. I really hope the British will banish the Stamp Act. I also just want to know, why did these laws have to be made in the first place? This makes me very upset!

This new tax law effects all of the trading that I do and I'm just sick and tired of it! Why should I have to pay for tax if I'm not even a colonist! I guess I just have to sit here and suffer while the British make even more laws. Even if I try to do something about it, they will probably just laugh in my face. Now, I feel like the British are just toying with the way us Native Americans trade! I now hate the British more than I ever have before.

Encounter with Josiah Bartlett

Dear journal,

Today some thing amazing happened! When I traded with a colonist, (who for some reason was very excited) I tried to pay him the tax money, but he told me that the Declaration of Independence was just signed today. I asked him what that was and he told me it was a declaration for independence and freedom. It also means that some taxes were over and one of the taxes that got canceled was the tax I had to pay! So I had to pay no tax!! I was so happy and excited that I told my whole tribe. They, too, were excited.

After the trade I did I went deeper in the town to trade some more. I saw a poster and on it were the people in New Hampshire that signed the Declaration of Independence. Then I thought to myself, "If I could meet one of the three people that signed the Declaration of Independence, that would be amazing!"

So, I kept walking and I accidentally bumped into a male colonist, "I'm sorry sir," I said.

And then he said, "It is alright."

When he turned around I froze and this is because it was one of the signers, Josiah Bartlett! I was shocked, thrilled, and humbled when I saw him. I asked him a couple of questions and he gladly answered them. After we finished talking, I ran to my tribe having the thoughts of trading way back in my mind. After I told them about my meet with Josiah Bartlett, I thought about all of the acts and how I was furious at them. Also, I think about all of the changes my colony went through. Now that the Declaration has been signed, I expect nothing but good things to happen in the thirteen colonies.

Until next time,

Black Bear

CHAPTER 5:

ABIGAIL

By: Ashley Hall

About Me

Dear Dairy,

My name is Abigail. I am 14 years old and I live in Hampton, New Hampshire. My dad is a doctor and he wants me to be a proper lady. So I have to go to school and study on good manners and on how to be a proper lady. I enjoy having afternoon tea with my friends; they often remark how outgoing I am. In my free time I help my mom make cloths. MY religious values are Christianity.

Goodbye until next time,

Abigail

Hands On

Dear Dairy,

Today was a great day. First I watched my mom make candles after awhile of watching her I picked it up. It was pretty simple all you did was tie a string to a stick and hold the stick and dip the string in to the hot wax and then dip it in to water to dry faster then you repeat. Later that day I after my classes on how to be a proper lady, I was told to weave my mom a pot holder. That was easy to make you gust weaved it under and over and the opposite way the other time until you wear dun. Then you weaved it all too together. My day was filed with lots of making stuff I made lots of candles and weaved a pot holder.

Goodbye until next time,

Abigail

Fears

Dear Diary,

Imagine living your whole life having the fear of your mom died and you had to take on the mom role. It sounds really horrible doesn't it? Well I've had that ever since I was 10 years old, mom was sick and as if that wasn't enough my older brother told my that if she ever died I would have to do every thing that she dues and every thing I do. I had never really thought about something like that until he told me that. That was not the first thing that he had told me made me fear about. When I was 6 years old and I was eating super and my mom and dad was talking about the government. I had never had of the government so I caked my brother about it and he told me that all he knows was that if we didn't do what they what us to do that they will take my dad away. I fear about that almost every day.

Goodbye until next time,

Abigail

Colonial Notices

Dear Dairy,

I thank that it is a good idea because maybe we can have a rite to speak are minds. I don't like the idea of a war even though I support their ideas. That is all I will say about this subject.

The war will affect me financially very good because we will not be controlled by the king and his stupid soldiers.

Goodbye until next time,

Abigail

Declaratory Act

Dear Diary,

I'm happy that they stopped the Stamp Act. I believe my self to be an American colonial. I believe that the issues between Great Britain and the Colonies will be resolved. I believe that the best possible solutions for these problems are that the British should stop trying to take charge of the Colonies.

Goodbye until next time,

Abigail

Intolerable Acts

Dear Diary,

Today I read about the multiple new notices. What where they thinking when they made these! They are not fair! Also the newspapers are starting to refer to them as the "Intolerable Acts"! The name fits perfectly nobody can stand it, I hate it. My parents told me that they side more with England and the mother country. I don't know what the rest of the people in the area are siding. As I walk down the street I can hear people talking about how badly they affect are colony. They were saying how we are supposed to eat and buy clothing if they close the ports.

Goodbye until next time,

Abigail

Soldiers

Dear Dairy,

Two weeks ago I found out that my family had to take in and feed a few British soldiers. If we didn't the government threatened to put my father into prison and make my family pay a fine. I was not happy sharing my home and food with people I don't know.

Yesterday the soldiers arrived at my house. They ware vary dirty and vary mean to my family and I. Their names are Joseph, Andrew, and Christopher. They were big, powerful and vary controlling.

After the first couple of days we war ready fore them to leave. I was tired of how they demand my family to do get them stuff that they don't want to get by themselves. And they are so messy and they don't pike up after themselves. I only have couple days left and I can't wait for them to leave.

Goodbye until next time,

Abigail

CHAPTER 6:

JOHN'S STORY

By: Corey Dodson

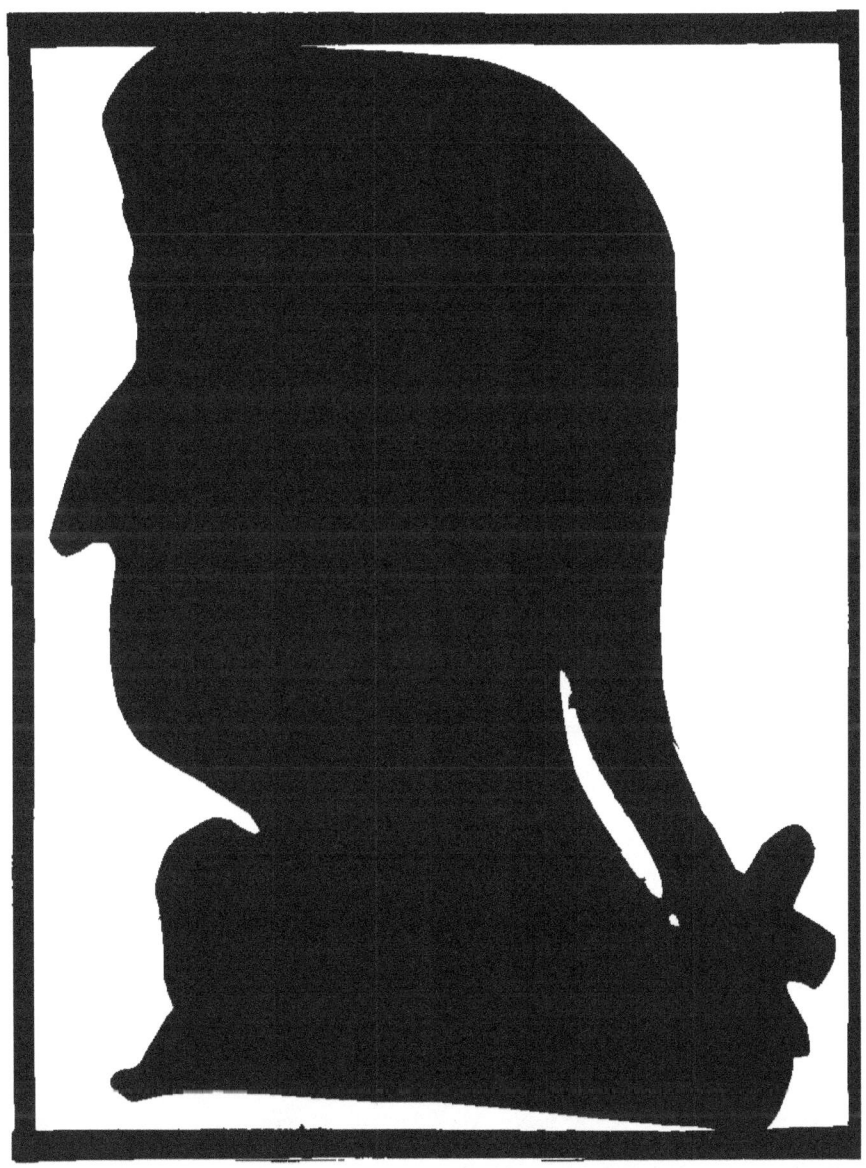

About Me

My name Is John Smythville and I own an Inn here in Concord, New Hampshire. Today is June 6, 1776 and I can't go to my Baptist church because I need all new furniture for my brand new inn where the richest people come to stay. So I'm going to go to the bank to cash my check. When I got to the bank I saw a huge guard standing in the doorway asking me what 2+2 is I said it was 4 then he moved. When I got my 200 pounds I left and went to my favorite store. It has all my favorite high quality stuff cause that's all I like. I went to the clerk and asked how much 10 tables, 35 chairs, 3 couches, and 2 end tables were. He said it was all 275 pounds then I just walked out. I then went to another store and he said it was 245 pounds. So I walked back to my Inn and thought forever and ever. Then I just remembered that my neighbor is selling all those items for 150 pounds. So then I walked over there and bought them and put them in my Inn. My papa said that I get two days off so now I can go to church.

The Store

Today I'm going to the store to get some groceries for my dad's tavern. When I arrived at the general store there was a man standing there in front of the door. He asked me if he could take him to my house because he was left from the army when they camped out here. He said to think about it when I get all my groceries and come out. I snuck out the back of the store and went home and asked my dad and he said no. I went back to the store and went in the back and then I got my groceries and went to the clerk and bought the items. The man came up to me and asked again and I said that I'd have to sneak him. Then we got to the Inn and I gave him a room and some dinner. The next day my dad asked me why a man from the army is in the hotel. I told him that I snuck him in from the store and now he won't leave. Well I'll call the cops. The cops then arrived and they got the man back to his camp.

In Six Years

Today is the day in six years that I get the Inn to myself. So I'm starting easy training. Today I will have to serve people. I'm scared right now cause what if I screw up some body's order and they get mad and shove the food in my face an there's hot sauce in it? That would really burn. Or tomorrow I do the check-ins and stuff. What if I mess up and my hotel gets ripped off? Or maybe I do some cleaning and get the cleaner in my eyeball? Oh my gosh! I am so scared. Well maybe those fears will change in six years.

Candles

Today the innkeeper and I were making candles. They were about 6" long and wide enough to fit in a candleholder. I think it was so fun except for the part when I accidentally dripped steaming hot wax on my hand. We had to get a small rod made of wood and put a string on it. Then we dipped it in the wax and pulled it out and hung it up on another rod to dry. Some other people got theirs more perfect then mine but over all I had fun. So now I have more candles for my dad's inn.

The next day my dad and I had to go through the steps of making an oven mitt. Step 1 is to gather the material. Step 2 is to weave and weave. I thought this was fun because I like weaving a little bit. We had to get a loom (this is a square wood piece) and a whole bunch of used bands that I got from the storekeeper. Then we put them on and wove them through. It was a whole bunch of fun because I made it for my family and friends and of course I saved some for my dad's inn.

Sugar Act

"JOHN, GET DOWN HERE NOW!" When I finally got down stairs my mom said to get the mail. So I went to get the mail, I opened it up and it said the King had enacted a new act of Parliament. It's called the Sugar Act. You cannot export molasses or lumber to anyone other than our mother country, Britain. To stop smuggling, all ships' captains are required to have detailed manifest of their cargo and the paper will be checked before anything can be unloaded from the ship. If you break this law you will be tried in vice-admiralty court rather than in jury trials in the local colonial courts. That's really going to suck because I can't get molasses or sugar to my dad's inn. That is going to mess with all the sailors.

Declaratory Act

I was walking to my inn when I saw an enormous crowd pushing and shoving into the town hall. When I went to see what the racket was I heard the town crier talking about a new act that was called the Declaratory Act. It said Ben Franklin's speech about internal taxes on internal colonial transactions, like the stamp act called for, but not internal taxes or duties laid on important commodities were gone. This act is making me and my fellow Colonials madder. I consider myself as an American colonial now because from all the Brits taxing. I think these taxes will continue. I also think there is a way to resolve all this madness. They should raise taxes in the mother country rather than here.

Intolerable Acts

Today I don't have to go to my dad's inn. I was just going to breakfast at my friend's house when I saw a letter flying with the wind. I picked it up and read it. It said, "To the king, we need four new acts they are called the Quartering Act, the Massachusetts Government Act, the Boston Port Act, and the Administration of Justice Act." When I read this it really wasn't pretty what I said. This is really going to screw up my life because what if people start fighting and they come to where I live? The people are calling it the Intolerable Acts. Most people in my area are going more towards the side of the men of Boston and New England.

George Washington

Tonight I'm going to my friend's house to have some of his wonderful herbal tea straight from china. But first I have to go to a town meeting. Finally when I got settled in my seat the town crier started to speak. He said two or three things. One was about the Continental Congress, the hostilities and outright war, and the last one was that the French and Indian war hero, George Washington, has been appointed General.

Then the town crier said, "Dismissed".

Then we all got up and left. Now that we heard about this whole thing about the war it seems like my colony is disappointed because my colony thinks we should fight not talk about it. At this point in this hostile economy I stand at the top cause I refuse to get mad. Now that I've already made the decision that I won't get mad there will be nothing that will change my mind because I don't want to be killed by the king. My friends also take my side on this one because they don't want to be killed ether.

Congress

Today I woke up to a wonderful smell. It was the smell of some meaty bacon and delicious chicken eggs with some of my mom's wonderful fresh milk; fresh, as in made this morning fresh. After breakfast I went to my dad's inn but before I could get inside I heard a huge crowd coming down the street. I wondered why until I heard two couples talking about the Second Continental Congress. Wow this is a shock for me I can't believe it. I really didn't think we would get our independence so soon. Couple days ago I met William Wipple, one of the signers. He said that when he went up to sign he was hoping it would start a new beginning.

Massachusetts

CHAPTER 7:

A LITTLE CORNER OF COLONIAL HISTORY;
MISS ELIZA MAY CARTER

By: Dara Turner

About Eliza May, A Lawyer's Daughter

January Twelve, Seventeen Sixty-Four

I have been told by my Mama Jean, that some day my personal life story may be of interest to later scholars. So my calligraphy assignment of current day is to record, at the least, a portion of my life. So I am to tell this object, in writing, about myself.

My birth name is Elizabeth May Carter, but I am most often referred to as Eliza May. I was born in on December fifth, seventeen fifty-six. I am a female living my life in Salem Massachusetts

My family is a family of four persons, not including the mares. My families names are Henry White Carter, my Papa Hen, Jean Louise Carter, my Mama Jean, my infant brother, Ferguson Lee Carter, and me, Eliza May.

I enjoy my stitchery and afternoon tea. But I do not enjoy all this writing. Sorry Mama Jean. Cooking and baking are other hobbies of mine.

My Family religion is Catholic, as am I. But I'd rather be dressmaking and baking for afternoon tea than sitting in a blazing church house.

Until Later,

Miss Eliza May

The Sugar Act

April Fifth, Seventeen Sixty-Four

The Sugar Act. Placing a new tax on molasses and lumber! Thanks to the expiration on the Molasses Act and the Seven Years War. As they put it, we are in need of money, in debt, from the seven years war. So naturally, after the expiration date of the molasses act, they basically repealed it and remade the act with a new name. Adding a tax with it (lumber).

How does lumber have anything to do with sugar? Or molasses for that matter? And when will we ever finish paying off this war? I thought that we had the money for it in the beginning.

So no one may export molasses or lumber to anywhere except our mother lands. And to prove that our ship men aren't smuggling, they must produce a document detailing at least the contents of their cargo. What do they expect? Even if they make it harder to smuggle, if they continue to tax our simple goods, we will continue to find other cheaper ways to get our goods. Legal or not.

I don't mean to be rash, but it just infuriates me. Although my family is going to be fine, our income levels are as low as ever. And the families that could barely make it before, my heart aches for them. We are headed for rough times if we continue on this way, I tell you. I can only hope that the King comes to terms before we do.

Until Later,

Miss Eliza May

My Week's Studies

January Sixteen, Seventeen Seventy

My home lessons are getting quite complicated. In the past few days I have learned how to dip my candles, weave a potholder, and being a hostess to a tea party. The candles and weaving took only a day of lessons. But the Tea is taking almost three days!

To dip a candle you must first purchase the bees wax from your general store. And once it comes in and you bring it home, you melt it in a big pot. But not a cauldron, no one uses those since the Witch trials. Anyhow, while the wax is melting you can go find a fairly straight twig. You'll need one for every two candles. Once you have your twigs, wrap a piece of soft twine around the twig with a little more that the length of the candle hanging off. When the bee's wax is completely melted, you can start dipping the twig with the twine into the wax. It might help if you have a bowl of cool water to dip the candle in in-between dips in the wax. It seems to help cool the wax off faster. You must wait for the wax to completely dry before you dip the same candle back into the melted bees wax.

Keep dipping and cooling until you have the desired fatness. I made four candles when I first learned.

Then to weave is really quite simple. All you need is the yarn in the colors you wish and the loom. Once you have that just loop the yarn across the loom one way. And while you loop it the opposite way you must weave in and out between the other strings you placed on the loom a while before. Although it does take a while it does help in cooking on the stove or oven.

Mama is also teaching me how to be a hostess to an afternoon tea party. It is all quite complicated really. It isn't at all easy. There are just so many rules and etiquette tips to take note of.

Such as don't actually stir your tea, instead make up and down arcs in your tea cup. And remember to point the spout of your teapot toward you. Never take more than two lumps of sugar. Don't ever appear to be greedy, always thank your hostess before you leave the party.

It is so hard to remember them all. If I don't mama Jean will come to believe that I don't care about her teaching me.

Mama has told me that we are to start a tea dress, and it is also to be done before the winter season. Can you believe that? A tea dress! And I have to make my own recipe for tea and biscuits starting tomorrow. I only hope I can make it as good as mamas.

Until Later,

Miss Eliza May

When the Soldiers Came

January Twentieth, Seventeen Seventy

Oh no! My papa got an official letter from John Winthrop, our Governor, today. He said that there are a few soldiers that are going to be staying at our house for a while. And if we refused them then papa will have to go to jail!

And we'll have to have a fine paid! Not that that will happen. Mama Jean's hospitality is too good to let that happen.

But now they will come and drink all of our tea, and I will have to wait on them! What if I am to sleep in the barn with the mares so they are to use my room? And no doubt that mama will tell me to help clean after them. How I detest cleaning.

Our House is not small, but it is not made for unwelcome guests. I suppose that papa hen will be in an angry mood every day after he gets home related to the guests. Mama Jean says that she is going to have to work with me on my hospitality skills. That it is an important part of my studies and is something that women everywhere use. But no matter what happens I will always stay polite and cordial, as young ladies should always be.

They will arrive tomorrow about noon, unpack, and then afternoon tea will take place.

Whoever decides to read this is going to have an important part of my life to read.

Well, I'm off to attend to supper.

Until Later,

Miss Eliza May

January Twenty-First, Seventeen Seventy

I have just finished my afternoon tea with our new house guests. They seemed to be very interested in my interests and me and as they persistently questioned me on my personal opinions. In fact, I almost omitted my tea this afternoon when William, I think, countered my opinion on hospitality! Who was he to question such a subject when they themselves have barged into such a lovely home?

They do seem nice, nonetheless. And I don't have to share my room and sleep with the mares, as supposed before. They, in fact, offered to sleep in the barn with them! But of course, Mama Jean wouldn't see to that and shooed the thought away; instead insisting that they take the nursery. Ferguson's cradle bed is to be moved into mama and papa's room, and he will sleep there for now.

Anyhow, I'm to tell you about the soldiers now. First is William, my favorite.

William is an older soul who feels complete, as he spoke it, belonging with all the soldiers. But he does miss his family, undoubtedly. He is strong and tall, and enjoys deep conversations.

Then there's Harry. Harry is as old as William, or appears to be. He's also extremely quiet. I'll say, "All he did during afternoon tea today was stir and stare at his tea." All the while everyone else was discussing various subjects.

The last one is Albert. I don't care for him as much, but I will not repeat that, nor, show it. He tends to question ones opinions and thoughts, yet doesn't engage in the conversation following.

Well, I'm off to attend to dinner.

Until Later,
Miss Eliza May

Plans for the future...

January Twenty-Fifth, Seventeen Seventy

I've just finished a discussion on my future and the things I must do. Like I am to wed, I am to bare children, and yet I must stay cordial. There are other things too, but I was too shocked to take not of them all. Why am I to grow up into a woman so quickly? I did decide to be polite throughout the whole ordeal though. I didn't want to have another lesson on what polite ladies do.

But I've got my own things to accomplish like, getting rid of my head bugs, and perfecting my biscuit recipe, and finishing my winter ball gown before the winter season arrives. How am I ever to finish all of these things?

I must take a few days to think, collect my thoughts; clear my head if you will.

Until later,

Miss Eliza May

January Twenty-Seventh, Seventeen Seventy

I have collected my thoughts and life plans, and am ready to put them to words.

First I will work to finish my ball gown and biscuit recipe. This will be completed in the late fall months. While I am at the ball, I will look for possible men to wed. But papa has already said that he must approve my choice.

After I find my mate and companion we, as a couple, will have a house built soon after the wedding

Six months after we've lived together, we will try for children.

Whether or not things will work out this way, I am not sure. But I need to appear organized for Mama Jean and Papa Hen.

I am off to afternoon tea, and am in a better mood that before.

Until Later,

Miss Eliza May

My First Tea Party and in Trouble with Mama

February Sixth, Seventeen Seventy

I went to my first tea party today. It was at Miss Millers. I was to think it was going to be much fun. But Mama Jean ruined it. She just had to sit right beside me and rudely remind me what to do, what to say. I disliked it so. I already knew of everything to do!

Once I almost spilled my tea when she startled me saying, "Now Elizabeth, remember to hold your smallest finger up, delicately, while you sip your tea." What a mess that would have been if I did happen to drop the tea cup, for

Miss Miller had all of her dishes imported in straight from England! And she said that it took months to come in.

But I managed to remember my manners and stay polite the whole time. Even through Mama Jean's ranting on. I never realized how Lady Sanford talked so. She ranted on for hours about politics and town gossip. I never want to hear about the King the way she described him again!

I just do not understand why on earth Mama thought I required the reminders. When I said something to her about why she was acting like that she got extremely upset and things, well, got a bit out of hand.

She asked back, "What action are you speaking of Elizabeth? You should be asking me that question if I recall correctly. Where on earth did you hear to take five scones and dip them into the jam, hm? Not only was it rude, you could have made a mess with it. And everybody was starring!"

I was getting upset at this point. I had held my poise until then, and no longer. I spoke firmly, "My dearest apologies Mother. But I must say, I would rather have had ladies starring at me, than being as unsocial as you were. It might have seemed, from afar, that you were shy. And I know from experience that you can steal the role as hostess at any occasion. For you did that very thing at Madam Browns Evening Gala last year."

I knew as quickly as I said it that, I shouldn't have. For Mama Jean gasped and replied shakily, "I did no such thing. Don't talk like that. I should punish you. But now that you have made me aware of my embarrassing you, I will remember to leave you behind the next time we have a kind invite asking for our presence; I will have to give my apologies for your absence." This time I gasped.

We walked in silence for a while. Then as we passed the general store, I pulled the hood to my cloak over my head and said, "I have just remembered an important errand I forgot to take care of at the general store."

As I walked away I remember Mama Jean saying, "If it was so darn important, it must just be a coincidence that you forgot. Be sure to be home before dinner. And pick up a ginger root and some sugar for me. Just charge it to papa's account." She drew her cloak closer to her for warmth and walked away slowly with her head down.

I pursued walking to the general store tearing up at the last events as I walked in. I grabbed what Mama Jean asked for and as I charged it Smith, the kind man that runs the store, asked softly, "Is everything alright of late Miss Eliza May?"

I responded sweetly, but sadly, "Everything is alright; just a little quarrel with Misses Carter is all."

"Well I hope everything smoothes out. And have a great dinner," he replied. I thanked him and walked the rest of the way home.

When I arrived Mama asked for the items from the store like nothing happened. But her face was red from crying, and I felt horrible for offending her like I did. I only hope she won't pursue the punishment she gave me. And I hope that the next tea party I go to will be better.

Until Later,

Miss Eliza May

The Tea Act

May Tenth, Seventeen Seventy-Three

The Tea Act. I will write only shortly, in hope of not maddening myself again over this act. They say that this tax money will go to supporting the protection that England provides us, and it will somehow go to the colonies also. Whether that will happen, or it is completely what is said on His Majesty's agenda, I do not know. But that, that is what we are supposed to believe.

I can make no sense of it. Maybe I just can not understand it. But I am at a loss. You see, why take money from us just to give it back?

Until Later,

Miss Eliza May

Intolerable Acts

June Twenty Second, Seventeen Seventy-Four

Four new acts of Parliament have been enacted! And over such a short period of time! They're considered the intolerable acts because of how ridiculous they are. They are The Boston Port Act, The Administration of Justice Act, The Massachusetts Government Act, and The Quartering Act. I'm getting tired of simply all the crude remarks about it. I am tired of hearing of the matter, on the street or even at the dinner table!

It is extremely maddening that the king won't just hear us out! Isn't that what a good king would do? I've heard that things in Boston are still stirring though through gossip and the Gazette. It seems to be getting a little out of hand.

Although things in Salem are still very hush-hush. People are mad, but since things in Boston are, well, as they are, we figure that we can't help any, and if we do try it will only cause more trouble for the King, causing more acts. So all we have to do is wait and be angry and hope that there won't be anymore acts.

Although I didn't and still don't for that fact, agree with the sons of liberty's act of rebel, I do agree with their cause. The taxes are high! I only wish there were other ways to reason with his majesty and his poor decisions. Like not being aggressive. I had my faith in the old king, but now, I'm thinking otherwise. Mama jean doesn't say so, but i can see it in her eyes. He is acting the part of an unfair parent! Not to be so treason, but honestly!

I do have faith and hope for the future of our colony, and others. If things go on, we will run into dark times. Oh, I do hope things improve. Hopefully mama jean is right in that someday someone in the future days will find this then old battered and dusty journal of events and read it. Maybe people from the future will learn from these horrible mistakes.

Until Later,

Miss Eliza May

Illegal Actions

June Twenty-Second, Seventeen Seventy-Five

The colonies are talking action of the tax situation on their own. But according to law, it's really illegal! And I'm so worried for my colony, all the colonies! What will the king do when he finds out? How will he punish us this time?

His Majesty just will not listen to us. We've sent bunches of letters to him, but he won't respond. We want to stop being punished for silly things. We want to be part of the decisions made for our colony. We want the King simply listen to us!

I have said continuously that if the good king didn't listen to us, we were headed for trouble. And there are even whispers to detach ourselves from England and become another country. But the chances of that are rare. That would be a lot of effort and a big chance to take. I don't think that they are willing to take that chance.

And we have people in charge of these issues and how to resolve them. That is an illegal act! We are not to have organized meetings, clubs or appoint figures of authority. I only hope that the King won't find out!

Until Later,

Miss Eliza May

The Declaration of Independence!

July Fifteenth, Seventeen Seventy-Six

Oh I am just overjoyed at this new accomplishment of our colonies, I mean country, I mean states. Even my own confusion will not ruin it. We are free! A real, free country! No more unnecessary taxes. And someone in my own colony, I mean state, got to sign the declaration! His name is John Hancock. I've met him only once. But he seems the sort to do the duty of his people. He says what other men only think.

I think the king is very mad because I heard in town that if any of his men see any of the men that signed the declaration then they must capture them and they will be hung. I think this scares the men a bit, but for the sake of our new country, they don't show it.

I am a bit worried for the men that signed it and whether or not our states will be forced to be colonies again. But we'll have to wait and watch. And until then, there is not point in worrying.

Oh no! I've been so excited this whole time, I've forgotten to use my manners. I hope mama jean doesn't read this! She will have a fit!

Until Later,

Miss Eliza May

CHAPTER 8:

THE STORY OF JAMES; A BLACKSMITH FROM MASSACHUSETTS

By: Calin Johnson

About Me

Hi, my name is James and this is my first journal entry. I'm a 15 year old who lives in Charleston. I had my birthday just a few months ago. My birthday is on the 9th of March, and I was born in 1750. For my birthday, my dad (Eli) made me my favorite blacksmith tool, a set hammer. In order for him to make my hammer, he had to make the head of the hammer first, and then purchase the handle at the carpenter shop. My mom (Jan) gave me this journal to write my thoughts down. My sister (Elizabeth) gave me a new bible. I needed a new bible, because our church requires that we have an undamaged bible. I think it's stupid that our church leader makes the Puritans have undamaged bibles, or you can get a fine.

Ever since I was a little boy, my dad has taught me nothing but how to be a blacksmith. My dad's trade is a blacksmith. I think the only two skills I have are running fast and blacksmithing. Before I became my dad's apprentice I used to go out into the woods and have fun adventures. I'd also play with the animals.

One time I stayed in the woods too long and it became dark. When I couldn't find my way home, all the trees and bushes started to form distorted, scary faces! Soon after that, I started hearing ghostly sounds! I got scared and started running. I finally made it home! I told my parents what happened in the woods. After I was done with my story, all my parents did was tell me to go to bed!! So I went to bed mad at my parents for not believing my story.

When the Soldiers Came

Last week we got a letter from the local government stating that three British soldiers were coming to live with us for a maximum of 3 days. It also said that if we refuse to do what it says, they would send dad to prison and fine our family! Today, they arrived. There were three tall men wearing redcoats, big black hats, and stupid white wigs. They didn't have any problem coming in without being invited. This made me hate them already. They sat their bags down, and started inspecting the house. After they were done, they said the accommodations were poor!!! The soldiers told us to get out, and then literally kicked us out!!!

I was so mad, I planned on going in there, grabbing a gun, and shooting all of them!!! I mean, who cares what the local government says!?! My mom saw how irritated I was, and said that it's only for a couple of days. Elizabeth went to our stockpile, which we keep in the workshop just in case of problems like this one. She returned with food, water, and blankets for everyone.

When we woke up the next morning, to our surprise, the soldiers were gone. Boy was I so happy! But when we went inside the house, it was destroyed! My mom picked up a broom, and said we should start cleaning. Mom swept out all the trash, while Elizabeth washed the dishes. Dad and I fixed an hole that was in the roof. When we were all done, we got ready for bed. After today I think we all deserved a nice, restful sleep.

The Kitten and the Act

Today as I headed to my friend John's house I saw a kitten in the street. It looked skinny and you could see its ribs. I felt so bad for it. I thought how mom probably wouldn't mind having it around, and how Elizabeth would just adore it. And Dad has been talking about rats. It came over to me and rubbed against my leg. So, I picked it up and started heading toward John's house.

When I got to John's house, the kitten stayed in my arms. It must have been tired, because it fell asleep. John came out of the kitchen, and saw me. He got this worried face, and waved his hand trying to tell me to get out.

Then his mom came out from behind him grabbed my arm and started half telling, half screaming about the new tax, "Our molasses and lumber if sold correctly can make up a large part of our income. Selling all of it to Britain really makes me mad. They don't ever give us that much money for it. Soon we will just get poorer and poorer. Without that money and the extra tax besides, we will just fade away. We really have to do something about this. The question is what should we do? I'm sure someone will find a way to do something without breaking the law."

After she was done she stormed back into the kitchen. John came and apologized, and said that I should probably go. I thought that was a good idea, and left. When I got home everybody seemed really happy about the kitten. I've got to go now the candle light is hurting my eyes.

Growing Up

Today dad told me it's time I prepare myself to become a man. He told me that it's time that I start saving money, and thinking about finding someone to be my wife. Man, was I scared! After I calmed down, I realized dad was right. I didn't have much time until I was a man. I'm 15 right now, and when I hit 17 I'll be an adult, which means I only have a year and a half until I'm around that age.

So I went to my room, and pulled out my box. The box holds all of the money that I've ever saved. When I opened my box, it was empty!!!!! I must have stood there for at least 10 minutes. A soft sound came from my mouth, and grew. Until I finally yelled at the top or my lungs!!! I ran to workshop, and found dad. I asked how to make money and fast. He told me that there were a lot of ways to make money. He me that I could go to neighbor's, and see if they had work I could do for money.

As I ran to other people's houses looking for work, I started to think about the future, like how my life would be, and things like taxes. Would the recent boycotts affect my soon-to-be blacksmith trade? Would a war take me from my wife, and would I ever have a wife? After a long time of asking people for work, I gave up and went home.

When I arrived home, dad was waiting for me. I was so caught up in the future, that I forgot about the present and helping dad out in the shop. My dad told me to take a seat, but instead of getting mad he told me that he understood how I felt. He said that I still have a year and a half to go, and that I didn't have just one day to work everything out, so I should take my time. I am so tired from today; I think I'm going to bed now.

The Act, My Friends, and My Pride

Today after I feed the kitten a saucer of milk I went outside. Once outside, I started heading to John's house. After a little while I stared thinking about the kitten. The little kitten, now known as Rose, has already gotten rid of our rat problem! For such a little kitten, it is a very ferocious eater, and catcher.

When I arrived at John's house, John was so mad. He started telling me about the newest Act, "The tax is supposed to be on any skin, parchment, permit, commercial contracts, newspapers, wills, pamphlets, dice, and playing cards. Apparently, it applies to all things that are paper. The things that really made me mad were the skins, and the dice! Those have nothing to do with paper at all!" When he was done he went back into his house. I decided I should probably leave him alone so I started to head to my next destination.

When I got to my friend Samuel's house, he was upset too. He started talking about the same thing John talked about. He worded his feelings differently though. "Not only that, but the National Debt has rose from £75,000 to £8,00,000,000!!! James, if they keep this up we're done for! I know a lot of friends who need to buy these materials each day to make their living. Someone needs to stop England! If someone doesn't then, well, it's not going to be good!!!" He was right and he knew it. I decided to head on to my last destination.

I meet my last friend Isiah, and he was mad too. He started telling me about the new act, "In order to pay the taxes people will have to raise the prices on everything. But, if the prices go up we won't be able to afford to buy things that we need. Pretty soon none of us will have any money to buy things or pay taxes. I hope that someone does something about this, and quick! You know what? I want to be one of the people doing something about this!!!" Isiah has all ways been ready to fight. Since I was done with my chores I decided to go home.

As I walked, I couldn't wait to get home and eat; until disaster struck. I tripped, and landed in some mud. If that's not bad enough then hear this; the mud splashed on a chicken. The chicken was so startled that it just jumped every where. Feathers went flying, and landed on me. With the mud on me, the chicken feather stuck to me and I look like a giant chicken. The real problem is that the feathers didn't get on my face, so as I ran home everyone laughed, and they knew who they were laughing at. What a day!

My Average Day

Today my dad told me to get a move on! This day started out so weird. Dad never rushes me. I thought maybe someone was in trouble. I ran to the shop as quickly as I could to find dad very happy in the shop. I ran to him and asked who was in trouble. He said no one was and then he told me that we have an important order to make. This was a rare event! We had not had an order of any kind let alone a special order in days!

I quickly got to work. I started with getting the furnace ready. When we are done with work at the end of the day, we leave a couple of coals so that we can just re-heat the coals to get the fire going again. After the fire was started, I started working on a piece of metal by heating it. Then I started hammering it. Our job was to make 16 horseshoes!

First, I had to pound the metal to make a big "U". When they were finished I put one on each of the horses' feet one by one. I nail the horseshoe to their feet. This is painless. Once dad and I were done, the man came right on time to get the horses. He paid for the work and left. Dad said I did a good job. I am so tired from the work that I'm going to bed earlier than usual.

James and the King

When I woke up this morning, I heard shouting. Dad, mom, and Elizabeth were all yelling. I asked what was wrong. They said that the King issued four new acts already this year! Then dad said, "I hate the King so much!!!" All he does is boss us around!!!"

Dad told me about the first act. "One of the acts is called the Administration of Justice Act. Its purpose is to make sure we have no freedom of the courts! It makes sure that only King George III can rule! The King is the worst! We're pretty much his slaves!"

Mom told me about the second act, "The second act is called the Boston Port Act. This act says that all vessels can't leave the harbor!! No matter what size the ship, it will stay until repayment has been made for the loss of their property; the tea. Those Brits have gone far enough! They need to be taught a lesson!! I can't wait till I have my chance at them."

Elizabeth told me about the third one, "The third act is called the Massachusetts Government Act. It says that we no longer elect our government officials! Only the King can decide who serves in our government! I can't believe this!"

Then they all at once told me about the last act. The last act is called the Quartering Act. It says if barracks are not available for British troops they have the right to stay with town folk! It means that we have to give up our homes if British soldiers want it!!!

When they were done, I went outside and tried to have a normal day but it was hard to concentrate after what my family told me.

To War or Not to War

Today I woke up very early to make sure that if they decided on a new act, then no one would yell at me this time. When I got to the kitchen, everyone seemed all right. They did seem a bit taken aback though. I asked if everyone was all right. They said that they have called for a Second Continental Congress! I was stunned! If they have called for a Second Continental Congress, and, they agree, that means our whole country will go to war with the most powerful country in the world!!

Of course we would win, and it's about time we got rid of these pests once for all but so many lives! Of course there have already been a few battles. That was just a little rebellion, but this is just flat out war! I told my family I needed to go to the woods and left.

Once in the woods, I thought long and hard if I should join them. I guess it didn't matter really, if we lose, we would all die. So I decided that I would fight, but only later in the war. I went home and went to bed.

The Last Journal Entry

Today, after I had put out the fire and went to the woods, I went into my Ma's house to see her running everywhere. I asked her what she was doing. She said that she was busy trying to cook dinner. I quickly realized that tonight was the night dad and his friends played cards. I asked if I could help, and a second later, I had my arms full with a list and a burlap bag for the store.

As I walked into the store and picked up all the supplies that Ma needed, I saw someone out of the corner of my eye. It was John Adams! Probably sensing someone staring at him, he turned to find me doing just that. I didn't know it at the time, but I was starring wide eyed and my mouth was gapping as wide as it could be. As soon as I noticed my poor manners, I quickly shut my mouth.

My next words were so stuttered that he couldn't understand a single word. I said, "Y- Y-Your J-J-John Adams!" Just like that. He smiled, and shook his head yes at my statement. I asked if he signed, and he shook his head yes again. A smile must have crossed my lips, because he frowned.

I said simply that, "I smile because we are at war."

His next words were so loud and angry that I was just glad no one was around to hear it. He told me of the lives taken and families mourning over lost loved ones from the war. He said some more things but the words were too big for my vocabulary. After he was done, he said, "Therefore, my young man, what gives you the right to be so happy?"

I believe my next words not only surprised him but impressed him as well. I said, "I smile because from here on out, all those people fighting, in pain, dying, dead, or those suffering over loved ones, are no longer suffering."

Some people wouldn't have understood what I had just said, but John Adams raised his eyebrows like he understood me. He told me goodbye, and that he wouldn't be disappointed if our paths ever crossed again. With that, John Adams left the store.

As I walked back to my parents' home, it was dark and dad's friends had probably already left. Mom was probably going to kill me, so I took my time. As I walked, I thought all about what Mr. Adams was talking about. Many have died, and many more will die. I thought about what I said. In the end, this war was going to be tough, but through it all we should be happy and proud to be fighting for our freedom. This proves that a man can stand up! Oh no, I'm all out of paper! I guess this is the end.

CHAPTER 9:

A STORY ABOUT A MASSACHUSETTS STOREKEEPER: JOHN BRENT GOES THROUGH THE ROUGH LIFE OF BEING A COLONIST.

By: Bobby Rose

About John Brentt

John Brentt, I'm 13 and I was born June 23 1750. Dad works at the town's General store. I come in and help him all the time. Today I had to go work all day so Mom schooled me when I came home. I work there all the time. So I can't do the school hours. I'm really good at helping Dad with stocking items on the shelves. Sunday I went to Catholic Church with my family; my Mom, Dad, sister and brother. I know the shop assistant at the General store; he and I joke a lot. He always laugh's at my long black hair. One day I and my family went to the capital of the colony of Massachusetts, Boston. There are a lot of shops there.

Sugar Act

April 5, 1764.

At last the Seven Years war has ended! But now the British government thinks they can tax us to repay the stupid money they lost and for their idiotic mistakes they made during the war. Me and my Dad Joshua Brentt have been running the General store well. I love working there and he always goes on about how it will be mine some day. I can't wait to take it over and have the best general store in Massachusetts.

I'm sick of all this conflict over a stupid war that I thought was just unreasonable. I think the British should keep to themselves.

British Soldiers

Today the British government demanded for us to have three British soldiers to stay at our house. I talked to one of them and he said that they will be there for about a month. One day I snuck into their room and as I was tiptoeing as quietly as possible, I heard the sturdy wood floor screech. I was glaring at a powdered wig on the chest when I came across a note. It was a letter by King George the III. It said, "My British men, I order you to slay all thee who do not obey your beckoning. Those Filthy Catholics will pay if they do not treat thee soldiers like gods." It was signed with a signature by King George the III.

I ran and went to my dad's study where he usually reads. I saw him rocking in the sturdy rocking chair. He said, "Quiet! I don't want them to know what were saying to each other."

I screamed with fear, "DAD!"

He said "Shhh.. Son they're right outside." So then I quietly whispered our situation. Then he said, "John don't worry just be careful and respect them."

So after a month of misery they left. We were allowed to live our normal lives.

Life Decisions

Today I was thinking about my future, wondering what I'm going to do when I grow up, and honestly I don't know. I'm scared that I will slack off and not have a future. If I do get a good job I don't what it'll be. Will I take over the general store from my dad? Will I find a new hobby/job? I don't know, but I guess I'll just work at the general store and when my adulthood comes I'll choose.

Being an adult sounds kind of scary; having to do so much hard labor, stressing over work and family, hunting or cooking dinner every night... Well, I guess that's life. I don't know, just take a path and go wherever it brings you. I talked to Dad today asking him what it was like to choose his future when he was a kid. He said that he also worked at a shop with his father and that one day his dad was hunting deer and never came back. He doesn't know if he died or ran away from the family. All he knew was that he then had to take care of the store for his dad and keep food on the table for his family.

Lowering Tea

Today the British Government lowered the export tax on English tea. This is good but I personally think the British are scamming us to paying more taxes. I hate the British; they always take advantage of us Colonists.

The new rule that's accruing is called the Tea act. It is okay but the British are filthy scammers.

Tea Act

May 10th, 1773.

The Sons of Liberty dumped all of the British Tea into the harbor. I'm so incredibly happy because they finally got what they deserve. But then again I'm angry because now were going to be fined until all the money is back. I'm sick of this. I'm not a part of the Sons of Liberty; its not my fault that just because the British are over controlling our colonies' and make us pay tax whatever they want. I almost wish that the sons of liberty would just behead King George the III.

The Quartering Act

Today, the British have told us again that if there are ever any British soldiers without quarters then they are allowed to stay in my home for as long as they want. If I say something about this I'll be sent to Great Britain and go on trial for questioning authority. I'm sick of this.

CHAPTER 10

THE LIFE OF A MASSACHUSETTS CABIN BOY

By: Darrell Plymate

A Normal Day of Benjamin Pymer

"Watch out!" said the captain. A rock went flying right by my head and hit the sail making a hole in it. I quickly got the sail down and tied it to the pole with the help of some of the sailors that lived on the ship with me. A crate came out of the cargo hold and flew up and hit the captain in the head. The captain was knocked out because there was heavy lumber in it. I'm scared because this is the first time that the captain was knocked out during a storm.

I'm also mad because I'm treated as a slave. I don't get paid, I'm treated horribly, and I hardly get fed if I want a good meal I have to do something when we aren't doing anything to get money or catch some fish and cook it. When a sailor that I hate told me to do something, I had to do it because I'm not a sailor. I was sent here as a permanent punishment.

Some of the rain and the sailors woke the captain up. He was dazed at first but regained full consciousness. He quickly took control of the ship again. The captain said, "Benjamin Pymer go help batten down the hatches, but first go get the cargo, put it back in the cargo hold, and shut the lock the door."

When we were done with the hatches we went down to the sailors' quarters and shut the door. Everyone was in the quarters but the captain, who was up sailing the ship into the eye of the storm, the middle of the storm. The reason he sails into the storm is it's the only way to sail if you don't want the ship knocked over by the waves. Another reason to sail to the eye is the eye is the calmest part of the storm. When we were waiting for the storm to stop I started to write to my mom:

Dear mom

I miss you a lot. I'm in a terrible storm and I got scared because the captain was knocked out but he's ok now. I wish I could see you right now I will make another letter when the storm is over.

Love,

Benjamin

CHAPTER 11:
THE STORY OF A FREEDMAN

By: Demi Brown

About Me

My name is Alaya Nicole Freedmen. I don't really mind my last name! I love to smile and laugh but not about my past. I really do try to stay happy now that I'm free. I was a slave and I escaped and now I'm called a freedman. I had to do a lot of stuff for other people and not much for myself. I had to listen to whom ever I had to slave over and serve.

I really don't have much meat; I'm skin and bones because I don't get much food. My hobbies are cooking, cleaning and knitting. My birthday wasn't celebrated at all; I don't really know the day or year.

Now I'm fine and doing pretty good. I think I'm 15 years old. I don't really have much family. I do have a friend that's dear to me; she is also a freedman. She run away at the same time I did. Well that's all about me.

Always,

Alaya Freedmen

Leather Work

One cold breezy day I was on my way to have a fresh walk to get away from all the riots, and I just happen to run into a native family member of mine. I haven't really thought about any of the past but I thought I had barely any family left. After I had chatted for a while I headed on to where I ran into another native friend of mine making moccasins.

I sat down and the smell of leather was flowing through the thin cold air. I got a piece of leather and cut it to about six inches and took some tools so I could engrave names and letters into it so I could explain myself. When, "Ouch!" I hit my hand with her mallet I was using to put letters on my leather bracelet. It was getting really chilly outside.

Pretty soon I had my name, Alaya Freedmen; well, not my whole last name but half of it. But how will I let people know how I describe myself? Or how will they know I once was a slave and am now a freedman. So, I got some blue beads and a string and put them on and found a way to connect the leather bracelet to it. Now I have a leather bracelet with my name and half of the last, some blue beads, and the sweet smell of leather. I say goodbye to her, and head off back to my house.

Alaya Freedmen

The Sugar Act

This isn't fair. How are we supposed to get stuff like molasses and lumber? I'm not from the mother country, I'm from Massachusetts. I think this will be a big struggle and a very hard time for all of us especially my colony, Massachusetts. I'm very mad about this and, what captain? Why? Where? What? Why would the paper be checked before they load the ships? I'm confused right now on this act.

Alaya Freedmen

3 Soldiers

I'm frightened not only as a freedman but about being a slave once again. I will do whatever they tell me whenever they tell me to do it. I don't want my family to pay for what I have done or not done. I have very little family anyway. I will not feel safe in my house, knowing I have three strangers in my house treating us like slaves when I am a freedmen; I was a slave once and now free. I'm a kind person and I'm good at taking orders so I hope everything will be okay and no one will get hurt. I don't want to go back to my master and how it used to be when I was a slave so I will just have to do every command they tell me and live in a poor environment, and not live very wealthy until things improve again. Well I have to head out. They're calling me.

Alaya Freedmen

Smuggling

John Hancock shouldn't be aloud or able to smuggle. All he's going to do is start a fight, no more like a riot. I just know there's going to be a big bloody riot!

I'm afraid and worried of what might happen or go down at any time. I think people will do it because they will disagree with the law.

Alaya Freedmen

The Tea Act

I think that they are trying to trick us as well. Why would we have something this good? We need time to think things over as a colony but I don't really support much on this. I understand it's not going any higher on taxes but what if they where tricking us in some way? I mean the tea is delicious but I'm not so sure. I think my colony will think the same as me and try to understand much of it. I'm not sure what to say. I just hope they don't try to trick us and they're staying with their word.

Alaya Freedmen

Fears

I hope these acts calm down. At first I thought everything would be okay. It was just one act but now we have so many I don't know what it will be like. And what if we get so many acts that there are bad consequences? What about my money and my few family members that live with me? How will I take care of them with a job or two on my hands, with these acts, and a husband and children? I think it will be a long hard life but hopefully things get better and these acts get better. I have a few years till my life is full; not that it isn't already I'm just scared and nervous for my life. Well I must be going now.

Alaya Freedmen

The Continental Congress

Why is everyone fighting? Why are the British and New England doing this? I think everything will go downward now that this is going on but I'm hoping and hoping that George Washington of Virginia helps being the General at this point. What about my colony as a whole? They will be very upset with this act. I am a freedman. I will not stand for this and not being a freedman anymore. I was once a slave and I will not be ever again. I don't think there is anything that could change this because they have already made their decision along with me and there would be way too many issues within this as it goes. My neighbors are probably in the same ship I am; along with my family and friends their upset. Hopefully this doesn't go on and we start new.

Ayala Freedmen

The Declaration of Independence

This is something I cannot believe! This is one of those speechless moments; you know the ones we have when something fantastic just happens. It sounds like freedom to me. I think it is just mind-blowing now that we have a Declaration of Independence and I can be free! Me being free. As I used to be a slave, I cannot wait to let my few family members and friends know. Now I will not have to slave over anyone, and hopefully this is a really good act, maybe one of the best of them. Finally someone was thinking right. I cannot explain how I feel about this; just signing a piece of paper. Could it make me feel so glad and excided with joy? This might just be a new start and the end of the riots and fights arguments and all the stuff we hate?

Alaya Freedmen

CHAPTER 12:

JOHNATHAN THE CARPENTER

By: Austin Williams

About Me

My name is Jonathan. I am 15 years old. I live in Massachusetts in a little town that you've probably never heard of, Stevensburg. There are not many people that live here. I was born on 7/24/1755.

I work as a carpenter's apprentice. His name is Paul but I usually call him master. He is a very nice man but can be mean at times. I don't know my family. My mother and father both died, but I will tell you more about that later. I live with Paul, and his family is like my own. I have a fancy for his daughter Elizabeth. She is the most beautiful girl I have ever seen. I love the way her eyes look in the midday sun. I hope to some day work up the courage to ask her out.

I am a very aggressive person. I am also not patient, but I am kind and trustworthy. I am also very strong, but I am not very fast. When it comes to wrestling I always win, but when it comes to racing I don't do very well.

Soldiers

I don't think the soldiers should be allowed to come in our homes. We shouldn't have to give them shelter and food they should have that provided to them.

Fears

Fears in the future are as follows. I am afraid that I will not make enough money. I am also afraid that I will be robbed or stuff will be stolen. I am also afraid that I will not have enough help and the store will be forcibly closed. People may not like the work I do.

Hands On

I was woodworking and it was fun. We made faces in the wood and carved the wood. Some people got hurt. It was a good experience and I will look forward to doing it out of school.

Tea Act

I think the Tea Act is horrible. It makes me mad that the British would try and trick use like that. It will take a lot of arguing to get them to get this act taken back. I think its only going to get worse from here. I know my master is very angry at the British making all these taxes on us.

The Townshend Acts

I think these taxes are stupid. They say its to help use but its not. All of those little taxes equal big taxes. We have been paying these taxes for years now! My whole family is irate, and so am I! It is crazy to think that they thought they could get away with this.

Others

I think all of these acts are stupid. I feel we should leave the mother country. I wish we would do it soon too. I think most of my neighbors feel the same way but there are a certain few that think we should stay with England. Now I think the whole colony would want to be a new country by them self.

The Boston Port Act

I think this act is stupid. We did not do anything illegal. We are getting punished for having a protest. I think things are going to get rough here in the next year or so. I feel we are soon going to have a full war with Britain. It is not fair that they would give us all of these taxes and punishments.

Letter

Dear David,

I think the new act is in fact intolerable. They have given us too many taxes that we already have to pay. I yelled at the tax collector yesterday and I didn't even mean to. I think we shouldn't have to be paying these taxes!

Jonathan

CHAPTER 13:

AN INKEEPER'S DAUGHTER

By: Mercedes Preston

Soldiers

Dear diary,

This week has been very interesting, three soldiers came to my door all scarred up with blood all over them. I felt bad for them so I let them in. The first soldier to greet himself was 17, his name was David Dixon and he was one of the British soldiers. Now the second soldier didn't like to talk much but David told me a little about him. He was 15, his name was Michael Thomas and he is one of the British soldiers. The third soldier was quite a gentleman, he stepped forward and said, "Hello ma'am my name is Jacob Hampton, I'm 18 and I am a British soldier."

After hearing their short description of themselves, we all go down to the cellar and I show them to their beds. When I went back up stairs I filled up a big bucket of water and put it over the boiler for a second. Then I got a cloth and put it in the water. Going back down stairs I trip and the bucket of water fell every where. Tumbling down the stairs I see the boys laughing. Embarrassed I stand straight up and ran up the stairs. Later, forgetting about what happened I went back downstairs to serve the boys some fresh corn. Then I left the boys so they could get there sleep.

The next morning I woke up and saw Michael sitting outside alone. I hurried up and got dressed to go see what he was doing. Going outside I decide to sit next to him. Trying to start a conversation, I asked him how he was. First time he didn't say anything so I asked him again the next time he just stared at me with a blank look on his face, trying my luck I ask him again. I guess my luck wasn't that good, because he did not say anything. When I got up to leave he grabbed my ankle. Puzzled I just stood there waiting for him to say something. He just stood there silent like he always was. So I just left him outside, alone.

A few days past and it was about time for the soldiers to leave. On the last day I thought it would be nice if I went out and got them a going away gift. I got David a pocketknife, because he likes to hunt. I gave Michael candle with his name craved in it, and I gave Jacob Hampton a hat. Finally saying goodbye I gave them all hugs and I said my farewell.

The Inn

My goodness, I can't believe my dad is going to make me own the inn. Really I just want to live my own life, and make decisions for myself. The weird thing is that I have two older brothers which are capable of owning the inn, except my dad thinks they are rough-housers. I am so confused on what to do, because really I don't want to own this inn.

I just wish that Jonathon and James would get serious and act their own age.

Candles

Dear diary,

Today I went to my first candle dipping class. All of the candles were so pretty and some of them even had color to them. The candles were so simple to make, all you had to do was dip string into a bucket of wax. That's a lie; it is difficult, at least the way my teacher was teaching it. Ok first you had to measure the string to an even length. After that boil the wax, it can't bubble it has to be at medium. Then dip the string in there and wait 3 seconds, take it out for about 5 seconds smooth it out then keep doing the same process over and over. After a while it gets fun, I just can't wait until I get to make colored candles!

Intolerable Acts

Dear diary,

       This is terrible, as I was walking through the town to get some fire wood. I saw tons of little papers pinned on just about everything. When I tore one off it had listed that they were called the Intolerable Acts. One of those acts was called the Massachusetts Government Act. The thing that brought my eye upon this was that it had the name of my colony so this is really to the people of Massachusetts. Anyways they literally said that we are not grown up enough to pick our leader. My husband will probably not like this; he usually participates in picking the leader. Yeah I don't think he will be very happy when I tell him the news.

Rhode Island

CHAPTER 14:

RHODE ISLAND'S DEVOTED

Delilah Hrica

By: Lindsey Kurucz

About Delilah Hrica

Dear Diary,

May 23, 1770

I am Delilah Hrica, a young daughter of a local farmer, just outside the reaches of Providence, Rhode Island. I am thirteen years young, excuse my grammar, but I am not yet old. By the likes of my grammar, you may think I have but a second grade education. I have just graduated from the seventh grade; I will not go to high school though.

Earlier, closer to the end of the year, I begged my father, John Hrica, and my mother, Valeria Hrica to let me work instead of going to school. I convinced them that it would be more profitable if they did not have to pay school fees and I was home to help make money. It took many hours of careful thought, but finally my parents let me stay home and work. They know how responsible, intelligent, and handy I am.

On a typical work day, I wake up at dawn to feed the chickens and gather eggs from the coop. Then, I go to the barn to milk the cows and goats. I was not allowed to sheer the sheep for fear they would be too closely shaven. Next, it was time for a hearty lunch. After lunch, I proceeded to the stables to groom the horses, Midnight and Luna. I must say, Luna is rather hefty. I would know, she stepped on my little toe... Anyway, the rest of my day is spent in the field picking corn and wheeling it to the silo. I work everyday except Sunday. On Sundays my parents, my brother, Rachel Connaway, Stephen Connaway, and I ride into town together, like a wagon pool. We all go to the Providence Quaker Church. Work is absolutely forbidden on Sundays anyway.

Aside from work, I like to sew, sing, and wrestle with my brother, he usually wins though. Every shipment of corn made from the farm, my father pays me a dollar to spend and a dollar for my bank account at Ye' Olde Bank. I usually end up buying cloth, thread, and things of that nature. I like to sew dresses for all occasions, whether it's for work, play, or a party in town. I have a passion for using my beautiful voice, not to be conceited or anything. I am good at cooking, but I do NOT fancy it, but I will do it if I must.

Now that you are all caught up…

- Delilah Hrica

P.S. My last name is pronounced "Hor-it-sa"

Three British Soldiers

Dear Diary,

May 24, 1770

Today has been hectic. Let me just say that. Three British soldiers are trampling mud into the cracks in our floors. I know they are going to clean that up, Mama will throw a fit. They have no respect for our belongings either, a plate has already been broken!

Around three o' clock this afternoon, three soldiers came to out door with a government warrant that said:

Hrica Family,

I am sending three soldiers that are to be presented a bed each and full meals. If you chose not to comply, Mr. John Hrica will be sent to prison and you will pay a fine.

Sincerely,

Your Governor

We had no choice but to offer out hospitality to the brawny soldiers, even though we hated the thought. They trashed our house successfully in two hours. My mother almost began to cry when the men came in carrying guns and grenades. The government did not say we had to be nice. Mama confronted one of them and said "If anyone of us is harmed, I will use your own weapons against you!" The tall, broad man with a scruffy chin nodded at my mother and walked on. The other two were confronted also, but by my father. One of them was skinny and clean shaven and the other was shorter and heavier.

I have to end my Diary entry now; the soldiers want to talk to us all together.

Delilah Hrica

Fears

Dear Diary,

May 25, 1770

Oh dear, I don't know what to write first. Conner and I just had a talk with Father about who will inherit the land, when I thought he was going to say Conner; he looked straight at me and said "The land will go to you." I stared right back at him, awestruck and dumbfounded.

"B-but a woman can't…" I stammered, "A woman can't own land!"

"You can because I am giving you permission, and the land will remain under my name," he said deviously, shooting a look at both me and my brother as if to say 'DON'T TELL ANYONE!!!' I couldn't believe it, and I still can't! I looked over at Conner and he gave me a huge grin and wrapped his arms around me tight and then let me go. "Now, you know, taking care of a large farm is a lot of work, you must till, plow, seed, and water the land and harvest the corn all by yourself." My jaw dropped. "How many hands you wish to hire is not my concern, but I will help you get started. You will also receive the full payment."

I am still in awe, but now I know am destined to be a land-owning farmer. My father is calling, time for my first lesson, farewell.

Delilah Hrica

The Sacred Bookmark

Dear Diary,

May 26, 1770

Today my father gave me an unusual bookmark. He said it was to help me prosper, now that I am in total control of the farm. The bookmark is a small slab of black leather, a hole in the top renders a leather string with turquoise beading between knots in the string. My father also gave me a paper, such an old looking thing, the paper read:

Cut a piece of leather and punch a hole in the top. Proceed to tie a knot at the end of a piece of leather string and thread the knotless end of the string through the hole. Slip on one bead, and then tie a knot. Slip on another bead and continue the pattern until you run out of string. (Make sure to end with a knot.) Next find a metal pattern and pound it with a rawhide mallet until the imprint is shown on the dark leather. You may add good luck feathers, if you wish to perspire.

-Wampanoag tribe

All of this had to have been translated at some point, but it was still very old, the edges have browned and shriveled a little, the ink perfectly smudged. Anyway, my father told me that my great-great-grandfather passed this bookmark down and it has been passed down to the next generation farm owner. When my great-great-grandfather owned the farm, the Indians attacked and tried to take the farm, but they eventually agreed on a pact, written on a bookmark. The pact states that there is an alliance; one does not take from the other, so long as the other does not take from the one.

I am guessing the instructions were made to tell you how to make it, so if you had a similar experience, you could make another pact. This bookmark, is not only said good luck, it is the key to my past and my future as well.

Delilah Hrica

Tea Act

Dear Diary,

I am SO very tired of all these new acts being passed. The Tea Act is supposed to seem as if things are getting better, but the existing tax is still in effect (Townshend Act). Now that they dropped the other taxes Parliament must think people are going to stock up with tea and in the end they are going to make

EVEN more money. I am smarter than that, let me assure you. I see right through Parliament this time! I have to boycott buying any tea right now, and it pains me so. I will miss having a nice cup of hot tea after a hard day's work on the farm! Do I not reserve the respect of Great Britain, as I ship my goods to them for a small fee? Not even a cup of tea to brighten the day?

Can you keep a secret? This evenin' after work, I went in to the cupboards to get a spot of tea and….there WAS none. We had run out of our last supply. This is worse of the matter, I immediately ran up to my room and threw myself on my bed and let the waters flow freely. Oh dear, now I'm quite embarrassed, I really cannot believe I cried almost for an hour and a half. If my brother or someone ever got into my secret drawer under my bed, I don't know what I would do first. Nothing good anyway.

I cannot think of anything to say but that I'm just so disappointed. While I'm not givin' up, I feel as though I should soften up a bit and just start begging almost. What this colony has come to is so sad that I have just withered away inside and I need the mortar to harden, so to speak. I have decided I can stand strong and bore through this verbal battle with my fellow colonials, although they are mostly loyalists. I know only a few patriots here in Rhode Island and I feel like I should be more connected with them, maybe then I can regain my strength.

Delilah Hrica

Townshend Act

Dear Diary,

A new act has been passed saying that shipments by ship have to be accounted for on parchment. There is also a tax on important artifacts like glass, lead, paint, tea, and paper. The Sons of Liberty may not be very jolly chaps when they can no longer write their newspaper, they are simply unpredictable. Although this act does not affect me much, it really angers me that Parliament dare be so rude. Let us live in New England, yes, but pull our finances from under our wobbly legs? What exactly has this world come to? Why can't we all just get along and talk about things like rational, mature adults. Well, I have a hard tomorrow; I'll be plowing the crops so, until next time I suppose. I am frightfully sorry I cannot write any more, there was SO much I wanted to get off my chest.

Delilah Hrica

Intolerable Acts

Dear Diary,

Delilah Hrica here, have you forgotten who I am? What with all of these acts, anyway. My farm is doing pretty well for Providence, although feeding my family is getting tough. They really are overpowering me and my lifestyle, these acts; all of the things I like to do are becoming more and more expensive. It's like they know…

March 31, 1774; The Administration of Justice Act clearly states than an attempt to overthrow the government has been issued. Quote-" An attempt hath lately been made to throw off the authority of the Parliament of Great Britain over the said province (Massachusetts's Bay, New England.) and, "Resistance, by open force, has taken place." And another, "Officials and soldiers attempting to reestablish lawful authority throughout the area have been discouraged from their duties, apprehended, questioned, and brought to trial by persons who do not acknowledge the validity of the laws." A whole new government, what say you to that my dear friend? So you see, in fewer words, these 'persons' are reinventing the wheel, so to speak.

March 31, 1774; The Boston Port Act claims that the ports of Boston (including Massachusetts Bay) is closed to all vessels, regardless of size or cargo until the obstruction debt has been lawfully paid off. Really now, are they trying to starve us all? Now much grows here in Providence, Rhode Island. I enjoy eating corn, but I can't eat it and nothing else! Sons of Liberty hear thee say, "Intolerable

Acts they are!" How dare they rob me of my hobby, this means no more fabric for a long time! As I do love dearly the thought of making myself a new dress...

May 20, 1774; The Massachusetts Government Act implies that those of Massachusetts are no longer under a democracy. They now are not allowed to elect ANY government official, His Majesty will decide for them. This is ridiculous, and I can not describe it in any other way, I am struggling through word-loss.

All of these acts, and now they want to invade my home again? Soldiers, always "needing" something. Hath thou no respect for thy home? They have places to stay! If there is one thing I hate more than soldiers, it is spies. June 22, 1774; The Quartering Act.

Now that I have explained the intolerable, I feel my fellow colonials are feeling the wrath of Great Britain, maybe even more than I. I wish New England was Act-Intolerant...or rather, retardant. Anyway, I cannot say much for my fellow colonials in Rhode Island, they are mostly loyalists, and while they ARE feeling His Majesty's wrath, they refuse to accept that. I just don't understand why they didn't stay in the mother country sometimes. And sometimes, I even wonder if there are spies...all around me.

I shall blow out thy candle now, if I should want to get any sleep after thinking about all of the commotion.

Delilah Hrica

Colonial Notices

Dear Diary,

I would write to you, mood: apathetic, but I can not because it seems these notices make me very, very angry! I've been calm and patient with these acts and the depression, but nobody informed me of this mayhem! Today, I found out for myself at the General Store, where my friend Alice works. There were notices posted all about. Don't get me wrong, it is very good that the colonies are taking action, but His Majesty is being just plain stubborn.

Calling all possible delegates…get your buttocks' over in Philadelphia! I'm not all for one and one for all if 'all' doesn't do his part, you see, we need harmony. Personally, His Majesty's setback isn't…fooling…anyone. We have built houses here, we have lives here, and we're NOT coming back. Under His reign, overseas is bad enough. Back to the all for one, and one for all matter, if women can't have a say in government, then gentlemen may you be on your toes. You can call me childish and stubborn, but I like to think of it as being American and doesn't anyone dare tell me different? And I dare not say American is childish and stubborn, I just want what every other patriot wants…freedom. I swear it, if I could meet His Majesty, I would fall onto my hands and knees and BEG for him to just end this, and it is wearing everyone thin down to the core. I have that feeling that I could just go to sleep thinking about it at any given moment. What I'm saying is no one needs this exhaustion. If the soldiers are here to keep peace, did they ever think of keeping peace of mind in the colonies? The MOST powerful kind of peace.

That is another issue; the biggest, most important issues are overlooked by Great Britain, such as them abolishing some of our most important laws. We ARE under their reign still, and rebelling against us (in a way) they are just pushing our buttons to get us to claim freedom. As my Native American friend once said, "The King may actually be good, in a sense that he is putting us to the test to see if we can really become something more."-Rajanigandha.

Delilah Hrica

William Ellery and the Declaration of Independence

Dear Diary,

Today I rode into town in my Sunday best to go to church. On the way, my brother Conner and I had a subtle discussion about politics while Ma and Pa carried on their own conversation with the Connaways. Somethin' 'bout Stephen getting a job at a tavern in town somewhere.

During my discussion with Conner, he brought somethin' up 'bout a declaration of some sort that was to be sent to King George III claiming our freedom. As he explained it in depth to me, we pulled up to the church in our wagon. Our conversing stopped abruptly as Conner's eyes swelled up with excitement. I then followed his gaze and saw a wealthy-looking man. "William Ellery!" he exclaimed in a whisper. (Yes, making that actually possible!).

"What? I suppose you know him!?!" I asked with a chuckle.

"Yes, yes…he is going to sign The Declaration of Independence!" said he. I just nodded and returned my gaze back to the elegant man; what a true American! The next thing I remember, he walked up to the wagon and ever so kindly, helped me out of the thing. Oh, and Luna even whinnied a little!

"Do I know you folks?" he asked.

"No." said my father, interrupting.

"Oh, well it is good to meet you fine sir…ma'am…miss…young man," he said nodding in each of our directions. "I am William Ell…"

He was cut off by Conner, "We know."

"Well young man, I suppose you too know that I, William Ellery, am going to sign The Declaration of Independence?" he asked with a kind, smug look.

"Oh yes, I keep up with every bit of news, sir," he told him, expecting praise. *"What a sack of potatoes!"* I thought to myself. I am twenty-five and I don't know half the news. I don't have time to know the news really. Anyway, we went to church and went shopping after service in the market as a family (for once). I had an amazing time and I think William…was kind of……nice.

All in all today was very exciting. I got some cloth and I am going to make a new dress! I want to get started right away, as I have to work tomorrow.

Delilah Hrica

A Husband

Dear Diary,

I don't mean to seem rude, but please bite your tongue. I can't believe it! I'm getting MARRIED!!! I don't particularly want to get married but my father says I must get married so my "generation" can go on. I've exactly seventeen days to find a gentleman and hopefully fall in love, but I don't understand how that will work because if I don't fall in love, if it's the wrong person I choose, what will happen? Will I be forced to marry, even if I don't love the man? I am twenty-five and I think I should be able to decide my own future, what are true Americans for if we cannot express ourselves uniquely? What is this Liberty without making our own decisions? Pish posh, I won't have any of that nonsense from father, I am old enough to decide for myself.

My only concern is I am wondering if my father will look down on me for standing up to him. I can't quite be sure whether he will congratulate me for becoming American or slapping me for talking nonsense and he expected more of me blah blah and blah. Growing up is so confusing, I feel like a little kid, though, not understanding how it will all work.

Anyway, I have heard there is a line of handsome young men seeking my hand in marriage. Of course, these ~~handsome~~ young men had to go through my father. Yes, I am saying that my taste is most likely much different than my dad's. I do not believe that my father would choose the wrong selection on purpose, and maybe I can reason with him. After all, he gave me something very few women have had before…land. Yes, now I am quite sure of it, my father will understand, he always has been as reasonable as permitted by His Majesty and more. May he have the best of luck in his new American ways.

I see it now, the glory of becoming free, and let it be so, real quick like. I'd wish to go on but my heart is overwhelmed and I shall rest now. The flame of my candle flickers under my breath, dying for sleep. So for now, farewell my sweet, sweet Diary whom has listened to me so understandingly, and been undyingly patient.

Delilah Hrica

CHAPTER 15:

MAGASKAWEE: A NATIVE AMERICAN GIRL

THE LIFE AND TIMES OF A NARRAGANSETT GIRL LIVING IN COLONIAL RHODE ISLAND

By: Anna Scott

Prologue: The Beginning

Dear Diary,

Today was a very sad day for our tribe. My mother, Kimama, died of the smallpox plague. Our whole tribe turned out for the burial. While my father, Sachem Massaoit, helps the pale ones through the harsh winter, our people perish. He does not show any emotion or sign of missing my mother. Always wanting to be like our father, my brother Metacomet continues to do the same. During her life, my father did not speak to her often. In all of my sixteen winters, he has barely spoken to my sister Ayashe and I. In fact, except for his council, he does not speak to anyone much. There is one time he spoke to me that I vividly remember. I was singing to Ayashe by the river one day when he came up from behind and said just one word: "Magaskawee". That was six winters ago. It has been my name ever since.

Part 1: Mysterious Visitors - December 14, 1764

Dear Diary,

It has been eight days since my dear mother died. My father and brother continue to show no sadness for our loss, while Ayashe and I cry ourselves to sleep every night. Metacomet thinks that our tribe is in peril. Three men have arrived from the pale village. My brother thinks that they were sent here to drive us out and claim the land for their leader. My father has become familiar with one of the men, and they say that they are lost and have been mildly injured on their journey. They cannot find their way home to their town in "Rhode Island", as they call this land. While Metacomet does not trust them, I think we should let them remain in our camp. If they are hurt, then they will be powerless to harm us. My friends, Kachina and Anpaytoo disagree. They have listened to Metacomet and think that we will be forced to be slaves for the pale ones. They have ceased speaking to me until I have joined my brother's way of thinking. If the white men do not take our land, then their presence shall surely tear our people apart.

Part 2: Peter - December 21, 1764

Dear Diary,

Now being of age to marry, my father must choose a husband for me. Although I trust his decisions, I do not wish to have an arranged marriage. As you know, three men from the pale village have been staying in our camp. Against my brother's wishes, I have befriended one of them, named Peter, and he has told me of his homeland. Like us, he lost his mother to the smallpox epidemic, and his father died of grief soon after. He has no family left anywhere. When he turned eighteen winters, he decided to join the army. Peter calls me a name of his village, Meg. Peter has befriended Ayashe, too, and he calls her Amy. Ayashe and I keep our friendships a secret from our father and brother. We do not know how they could react. Metacomet is very powerful and could very well harm Peter and most of the tribe would not see his actions as unfair. If only Metacomet would get to know the white men, then he would see how wrong he has been.

Part 3: Tales of the Leather - January 4, 1769

Dear Diary,

Today Takchawee taught us how to work with leather. We had to stamp shapes into a piece of leather to tell a story about our lives. Since I couldn't stop thinking about it, I decided to tell about Peter. Peter was my best friend, He was supposed to not trust Natives, but he befriended Ayashe and I anyway. My brother, Metacomet, did not trust the villagers. He thought that their only purpose was to steal land and capture us as slaves. Most of the tribe believed him, and he formed an army to drive the soldiers out. The other two soldiers got out in time, but Metacomet's main target was Peter. I guess he found out about our friendship now that I think about it. Peter was captured and "set to be made an example of" the next day. Feeling desperate, Ayashe and I helped him escape before dawn. Metacomet didn't find out who helped Peter, but it's been two moons, and Ayashe and I still miss him. I think Metacomet still resents us for being friends with Peter in the first place. I still think of Peter. I will always remember him, and how I learned the meaning of friendship: TRUE SACRIFICE.

Part 4: Letters to Peter; Part 1 - May 10, 1767

Dear Peter,

Communication has been slow lately. I won't be able to write as much as I would like. I see difficulty in writing in your letters, too. Since June and the renewing of paper taxes in The Townsend Act, doing anything with paper will be difficult. Although it is unheard of for women to say what they think in your colony, I feel compelled to having my opinions and speaking them out loud. Parliament has gone overboard with the new taxing of glass, lead, paint, AND tea. Also with the law of every ship captain having to write manifests on their cargo before they leave the port. People have the ability to lie in writing. If Pariament is going to make a law, they have to at least make sure there are no loopholes.

Your outspoken friend, Magaskawee

Part 5: Letters to Peter; Part 2 - May 20, 1773

Dear Peter,

I can't believe it has been nine winters since I have seen you last. All that is happening in the colonies eludes me also. The past issuing of The Tea Act removes all the taxes on England, renews all tea tea taxes, and also proclaims that New England should still support Britain, correct? I have once said this before, but I am compelled to speak my mind. This act makes no sense. England steals all of the colonies money, yet still expects to be supported by the colonies? I am finding it difficult to agree with you that this is fair. Have you forgotten that these taxes also effect some British soldiers?

Your frustrated friend, Magaskawee

Part 6: Letters to Peter; Part 3 - May 2, 1774

Dear Peter,

It seems like all we write about these days are the unjust acts of Parliament. The rate at which the acts are being issued is unbelievable. Four acts in four months is unnecessary. Two on the same day is…well…intolerable! But even though you're a British soldier doesn't mean that you have to agree with the king just to be loyal, does it? Some of these acts, if not all, are unfair. Some do not come close to making sense! For instance, The Boston Port Act in March. Technically, the ship of which the colonists dumped the tea belonged to Britain, "great" or not. Legally, Britain is supposed to pay for the tea, not the colonists. Therefore the closing of Boston Port is inadequate. I'm sure the other acts are unfair somehow. And that includes the past four acts of this year.

Your concerned friend, Magaskawee

Part 7: Defiance in the Colonies - October 29, 1774

Dear Peter,

It is amazing how willing the patriots are to take charge of their own problems. Ceasing to export is a big step toward their horizon of this "independence". They seem to be getting more organized by the month. They actually have true demands now. To tell the truth, I agree with them. The Quartering Act was going a bit too far. This Second Continental Congress, what happened to the first one? Is it as powerful as Parliament? I suggest that the King should reply to the colonies requests. At least give them an answer! It's strange how the King seems to not care. It's like he believes this is just a phase that a child is going through and this will just end at his command. This will not end until the patriots have won and are satisfied.

Your enraged friend, Magaskawee

Part 8: As the Tension Grows - July 14, 1776

Dear Diary,

I think you should read Peter's latest letter. I wouldn't show anyone Peter's letters, including Ayashe, if this weren't important. Well, here it is:

Dear Meg,

I write with the saddest of sorrows. Just last week, on the noon of July 4th, the colonies distributed a so-called "Declaration of Independence", supposedly "freeing" themselves of His Respectable Majesty King George III. I have redeemed this information through a very reliable source within the colony of Pennsylvania, the residing home of inventor Ben Franklin. The inventor had no-doubtedly taken part in this tyranny, if not written the Declaration himself.

This document is also said to have been signed by John Hancock himself. He was obviously forced by men of an evil, deceiving manner. Poor unfortunate souls, the men who signed that death warrant. 'Twas always a pity when respectable men are forced to defy our King. 'Twas a greater pity for Hancock. He was such a useful ally to His Majesty, too. Judging from your most recent letters, I would think that you had been misguided also if I didn't know you better. Those Patriots think that they will get their freedom without a fight! Well then, they will be unpleasantly surprised. There will be a war. You better just make sure you are on the winning side.

Your friend,

Peter

Personally, I don't know what to think. Part of me knows that the patriots are right, but the other part of me longs for Peter's friendship more. Maybe I should consult with Ayashe on this one. She knows Peter just as well as I do. She may be younger, but she is a good decision-maker. So is Metacomet, but I definitely wouldn't go to him. I really need Ayashe's opinion on what I should do.

CHAPTER 16:

NATHAN THE BLACKSMITH

By: Tyler Hoffman

About me

Hey this is my 1ˢᵗ day writing in a journal and becoming a blacksmith, oh my name is Nathen. Today was just me moving in with the blacksmiths family, boring. I'm bold, active, and very irresponsible. I like to do everything right, kinda like a neat freak. My dad is Joe, my mother is Sally, and sisters are Peyton and Sindy. My dad is a doctor, my mom is a stay at home my sisters aren't old enough to leave the house there only 10, so they help my mom.

I live in Newport, Rhode Island, a nice place. I was born 03/4/1757 mom was 18 dad was 23. I was homeschooled by my parents until 13 now I am going to be taught by the blacksmiths wife. Right now I can read, write, some math, and will be learning to make good trades. I am catholic by birth. I like the religion but I have some uncles that are Puritans don't like that religion. Well I got to go master is calling.

Soldiers

Dear Journal,

Well today the governments made 3 British soldiers come to our house to live with us for a little while. We have to feed them and give them a sleeping place. Beds are being made by the carpenters. I have to put blacksmithing aside the soldiers leave or are close to leaving. We are having a town meeting about these new soldiers. Going to be getting rid of them or making money for everyone to have to pay each others that refuse the soldiers.

If this plan fails I have to get a job and no more blacksmithing. These soldiers are very rude, and think they can get whatever they want. Worst part is that if we don't listen we will put in jail along with the fine of $300 dollars. An added bonus is that the taxes are being raised because of the war. Well I got to go the stupid soldiers need us for work/helping them move in.

Dreams

Dear Journal,

Hey again I can't believe when I get older I'm going to be a master blacksmith woot. Only that I have to make a lot of metal objects like weapons, hammers, etc. My master has a lot of burns like I will one day. But on the good hand I will be making a lot of money.

I'm hoping to be the master of my town one day or at least the master blacksmith. In about 10 years I will be able to teach another student the blacksmithing arts. I just have to worry about a New England blacksmith taking my spot. So I will study and learn the most that I can so I won't be replaced. Well I got to go need to learn my lessons for the day.

Skills

Dear Journal,

Today I leaned how to make and use a mold. I have to use plaster to make the molds. All we do is carve the design into the plaster. Then I get a flat piece of plaster and put them together and pour metal into the opening.

After it cools in like 2 minutes I pull them apart and see if the design came out right. If it doesn't come out right I will re-melt the old design and try again. My design was a sword with two arrows over lapping the sword. I want to make it right so I could change it into a pin I could wear. Oh man I got to go master wants me to try and make the mold again.

Sugar Act

Dear Journal,

Hey again it's Nathan from Rhode Island in Boston right now. Guess what the Brits made another tax the sugar and lumber act, hard to believe, right? We will have to pay for are sugar and lumber we cut. So if I buy sugar for 10 cents the Brits will tax it so I have to pay more. If I want to make a house I have to pay for the lumber I use.

I mean I do all the work they make the money and we don't even get a say in it. I think we need to send some people over to GB in the House of Lords so we have a say. Once we get a person over there if the Brits don't listen we can revolt some more. For now the Sons of Liberty can plan for the worse and if a war does happen let's hope the colonies win.

Tea Act

Dear Journal,

So the Brits aren't lowering the actually tea just the other cost it comes with. They're now shipping the Tea directly from Great Brittan to the colonies. There also having no more exportation taxes on their tea. The bad thing about all these new taxes is that smuggling has gone way down. Smuggling may be bad, but it helped the Sons of Liberty with resources.

If the Brits don't stop soon with all there taxes I believe we will have a big problem on our hands. My opinion is completely with the Sons of Liberty. We should throw or try to get rid of all loyalists. If all loyalist are gone we colonist can revolt with out any people ratting us out.

Intolerable Acts

Dear Journal,

So when I woke up this morning I knew it was going to be a bad day. I got out of bed and fell on my face trying to get dressed. Then when I was leaving to do some errands and dropped the money and it blew away. Then to make matters worse the Brits made four new acts, the Massachusetts colony are calling them the "Intolerable Acts". I'm so happy I'm leaving Boston in a week or so. But on the bright side I live in Rhode Island so only one of these acts shall affect my colony. This act is the Quartering Act so most people will have to have one or maybe even more of his Majesty's pigs of troops living with them.

These acts and others are making the Sons of Liberty thinking of becoming our own country not part of G.B. I would help but when I'm back in Rhode Island I can't help much because most people there are loyalist. All my family are loyalist besides my Aunt Sally and Uncle Jim plus there son Adams, but there the people I'm visiting so they have felt the pain I have and some even worse. My parents and my siblings are loyalist because Rhode Island has not felt the wrath of King George III and his taxes. My last stand before I leave is me and some friends are going to go and beat up some tax collectors. Bye guys my friends just showed up and I heard there are a few tax collectors down the block.

Loyalists

Dear Journal,

I can't believe the war has actually started between BG and the colonies. Rhode Island is a mostly loyalist colony which stinks for me. But I will be able to join the Army. On the bad side I will need to be extra careful because most people in RI are against me, and they could always rat me out.

The thing I can't bare is that my families are mostly loyalist. So I am going to explain why I am doing these acts of rebellion, if it doesn't work I'll have to leave RI. The worst thing that could happen is I join the army and get moved to RI, so I might have to turn in friends and family or even worst kill my loved ones. I won't think about that unless my family wont believes me. But until then I must try not to get caught in these acts of freedom.

The Declaration of Independence

Dear Journal,

I knew today was going to be a good day. When I went to Mr. Green's market I found £10 in the street. Then the 2nd Congress made the Declaration of

Independence. The colonies finally agreed on something, which was to declare are independence from GB. But my greatest dream would be if I could meet somebody from the 2nd congress. The person that I would chose would be Sam Adams. This great man created the idea of a D o I, so the colonies in America could be free.

I really can't believe it's been so long nice I first started out as a blacksmith apprentice and there were very few taxes. Then things started getting worse when the Brits taxed the colonies so heavily. It took America way to long to do anything about the tyrant King George the III. I just can't wait a until I get to join the army and fight the Brits. I'm going to join the army in 1776. Even if everyone says I should just stay home because I'm walking into my death by joining the army, I will fight for my freedom no matter what. If and when we win and I live threw the war I will go back to RI and be the master blacksmith I am supposed to be.

CHAPTER 17:

A SLAVE'S LIFE

By: Kaitlin Spears

Five years ago…..

Five years ago today, aboard the ship, Lady Luck, I experienced the worst nightmare of my whole entire life. I was on a slave ship, had one pair of clothes and one pair of shoes at the time. I also had this journal that my mother gave me before I left Africa. When she gave it to me she said, "Take this Liza, and one day I hope you will have learned enough of their language to write about your journey."

I got on the ship hoping that it wasn't going to be as bad as the mothers in the camp said it was. I handed the man at the door of the ship my bag and he looked through it to make sure there wasn't anything dangerous in it. When he was satisfied, he threw it at me and I dropped it and he kicked it onto the ship. I ran in and sat down with the others in a….. Oh drat! I will have to write more later because Joan is calling me.

-Liza Franklin

Ok I'm back… I sat down with the others in a room. It was dim lighted and there were cots and each one had a pillow and blanket. I tried to talk to another girl that looked my age but she just started to cry. I spent the rest of the trip doing what I was told and staying out of trouble. When we got to the shore, we were kept on the ship someone bought us. I was lucky to get bought by Mrs. Holt to take care of her fourteen year old daughter, Joan. Now, five years later, she has given me an education, nice clothes, and anything I want to a certain degree. Now I'm fulfilling my mother's wishes to write about my journey. I love you mama, always and forever.

-Liza Franklin

Oh No!!

Today I'm setting a couple goals for myself. Number one: Do my chores faster to impress master and missus. To do this, I'm going to get up earlier every day. Number two: help Joan with more things. To do this I will do number one so I have even more time for Joan. Then master wants me to help Gladys with getting the milk and helping with the cooking. I'm pretty sure that I'm going to have to do my morning chores then help Gladys, and then do my afternoon/evening chores then helping Gladys again to pull this off. I'm really scared that I'm not going to be able to do all of the things I'm being asked to do AND the things I want to do for myself.

-Liza Franklin

A Sticky Situation

I'm so mad! We have to have three British soldiers live with us and we have to feed them. That means more work for me. When master told me I didn't think it would be that bad, but I was wrong. They have been here a week and already I despise them. They eat all the time and Gladys is getting tired of cooking and cleaning every 5 minutes. This morning I was walking down the hall to Joan's room to help her with her morning routine, and one of them came by and pushed me against the wall and stepped on my toes while doing it.

When I walked into the room limping, Joan asked me what was wrong and I had to lie and make a joke of it and tell her that I stubbed my toes while getting out of bed. She laughed and told me to be careful. I said I would be and helped her get ready. By the time we got downstairs, Gladys was making a second breakfast for me, Joan, master, and missus. The soldiers had already eaten their food and were gone into town. I was grateful. Now I could get my chores done in peace. I got done in record time. I was using the privy when they came back. Of course, one of them had to use it, so the whole time I was in there he was banging on the door and yelling at me.

When I opened the door, I thought he was going to hit me he was so mad. He said that I was taking entirely too long. I stood there to wait for him to go around me or something but he just looked at me. I said, "Excuse me sir".

He said, "I don't move for a slave".

I said, "Ok then, I'll just get out of your way".

He said, "You better or you'll be sorry you ever messed with me".

I ran back to the house and told Mr. Holt what happened. He was mad, very mad. He told me that I was part of his family no matter what color I was. I was very touched at the words. I felt my eyes start to water so I excused myself to go see if Joan needed anything. She said she didn't. So later that night when I came down to dinner, the soldiers weren't any nicer, but they weren't mean either.

Declaratory Act

Dear Diary,

I don't have much time to write so this is going to be a short entry. I have to help with dinner tonight. There was another act passed today. It's called the Declaratory Act. I think its blackmail. I know no one will stand up for us, but everyone will want to. I think we should all come together and stick up for ourselves. I also think we should defend ourselves. But that's probably not going to happen. And if and when someone does try that, they won't succeed. I'm an American, and this isn't right.

The issue we have with Great Britain will go away. There will definitely be more fights, more acts, and more taking over. But we shouldn't let that discourage us. We need to keep rebelling and fighting for ourselves and break off from Great Britain and become independent and free. We need to fight back! Ignore their ignorant acts… and they'll stop doing it because they won't have any money that they stole from us. Ok, well I have to go now. Bye.

- Liza Franklin

The Tea Act

Dear Diary,

This morning I was serving Mrs. Holt breakfast when Mr. Holt came barging in and banged his fist on the table. I was too scared to ask what was wrong so I just stood there staring wide eyed like a newborn deer at them. And a little while later I heard them whispering about something in the parlor. I was getting tea and Gladys, the cook, was mumbling under her breath about something. I poured the last of our tea supply into a pot to boil.

I was just pouring it and about to take it up to Joan when Lucas, the boy servant, came in with the fire wood. He seemed distressed about something so this time I asked what was wrong. He said something about King George and I didn't want to press the matter so I said okay. I wrapped my coat around my body to hold in the warmth that I had.

I walked out the back door because we slaves aren't allowed to go out the front. I stepped out of the warmth of the house and turned to face the bitter wind and started down the street. I stopped when I reached Mr. Potts general store. There was a mob outside his store gathered around a post with a piece of paper on it. I walked over there to see what it said and got pushed 3 times before I got close enough to read the paper. I got schooled with Joan, my mistress's daughter, and I can read and write fairly well.

I was reading the paper and it said something about Great Britain (King George) passing a tea act. But it's not actually a better deal because it took a tax away from England. That means we have to pay more money to buy tea. Now I know why Master was so mad.

I walked into the store and went down the usual aisle where tea is, but it wasn't there. I walked to the counter and stood there while Mr. Potts was helping someone else. He finally turned to me and asked what he could do. I asked why there was no tea. He said he was keeping it in the back because people were stealing because of the new act. I made my purchase quietly and went back home.

I was pretty mad. I put the tea away and went to my room. It connects to Joan's in case I'm needed right away. I sat down and started writing this journal entry. I know that I am just a slave but I do have an opinion even if I can't share it out loud. One day, I guarantee you, I have a hunch that this will all go away.

-Liza Franklin

Intolerable Acts

Dear Diary,

Well, they've passed four new acts! The townsfolk are calling them the Intolerable Acts. You can say that again! They are dumb. And they passed them all within 3 months; Two of them in the same day. The Justice Act basically says that the British don't trust our government anymore so they are taking their soldiers and other officials back to England to try them in court. If they want to be rude, let them. Our courts are just as fair as any other. Well, I don't know if we would be if there was a soldier on the stand. But they could at least give us a chance and not be mean.

Then there's The Massachusetts Government Act. Now we can't pick our government. It's because we've been "bad". They are now going to put British soldiers in those spots. I think this is not very good because they will be unfair. I don't care for these acts at all so far. They are unjust.

The next act was the Boston Port Act. This doesn't affect me but I still don't think its right. Is Britain that greedy that they don't want anyone to get anything but from there? It's uncalled for.

The last act was the Quartering Act. It says that if we don't feed and house the soldiers, they can take our house and use it for them. This is the craziest act of all. They cannot take our house. It's stealing! Well, I am going to stop now before I get too upset.

-Liza Franklin

CHAPTER 18:

AN INNKEEPER'S DAUGHTER

By: Sara Everman

About Me

Good morning. My name is Providence Walsh. I am nine and I am the daughter of the folks who own the local inn and restaurant. I live in the colony of Rhode Island. My birthday is December 15, 1755. I am being schooled by my mother to learn how to look after the inn and restaurant long after my parents are gone.

I am kind and willing to help take care of people. Because I am schooled to learn them, my top two skills are cooking, and cleaning. My family is half Christian and half Catholic. My family and I have a lot of friends. Most of them are previous costumers of the inn and restaurant. I meet a lot of kids my age at the inn and restaurant as well. And I don't really know the rest of my family. The only other family I know of is my brother down in Georgia. I know our family is kind of friends with the King as well.

Sugar Act

Today is Tuesday November 24, 1765. Yesterday I went over to Jimmy's house for dinner. After we were done eating we headed into town. There was a giant gathering in town and we couldn't get past. I heard a man yelling out something. I wasn't sure what. I tried to hear, but couldn't. I got closer. A tall thin man was standing atop of a small crate. He was speaking of the British and about how they had set a new tax on molasses and lumber. I turned looking at Jimmy, his mouth was wide open. I turned back towards the man. I heard the words "Seven Years War" and listened again.

He said that the new taxes were brought on by the end of the seven years war. I again looked at Jimmy, but he was gone! I ran back to his house. He was there telling his mother and father about what we had just heard. So I said good bye then ran home to let my mother and father know. My father was angry. My mother was somewhat upset, but my mother and I both know that we would have to live through what we called the Sugar Act.

Stamp Act

Today is Friday December 10, 1765. Earlier today I went to Amy's house to see if she was there. She was, but she was upset and crying in her bedroom. I went up, knocked on the door. With no reply I opened the door. She was sitting on the bed under the covers with her face buried in the pillows. I sat down on the bed. And asked her what was wrong. She sat up. She wiped her eyes. And then with a sniffled nose she told me what had happened. She said that there was a new act out called the Stamp Act. She also said that it made any legal papers without stamps illegal.

She said that with this motion many people would loose their jobs. Then she broke out in a quiet sob. I hugged her until she calmed once more. Then she said that her father was one of the many to lose his job. I hugged her again and, trying to calm her, I said that everything was going to be okay. Though I wasn't so sure of it. I said bye then headed back downstairs. I said that I was sorry to her father, then left. With my heart in my boots, I headed home. I could only hope that my father hadn't lost his job.

When I got home I told my mother what had happened. She said that that had been happening a lot lately.

Townshend Act

Today is Wednesday October 5, 1767. A couple days ago I went to Jane's father's shop to see if she was working that day. She was, but there was something wrong with her. I knew it. I asked her what was wrong, and she pointed to a flyer on the far wall. I walked over to it then read it. It said that there was to be a new tax on glass, lead, paint, tea, and paper. I turned to Jane, her eyes were pleading for help. I could tell she was worried so I said, "Don't worry, we'll get through this."

She said, "I can only hope we will."

I gave her a hug and ran off to tell my parents. My mother was worried. My father was not surprised. He said that a few of his friends had warned him about it. He said that at first he didn't believe the rumor, but then he started getting warnings from the whole town and figured it must be true. Even though he knew it was coming, I saw worry in his eyes too. Then I realized that this Townshend Act was affecting everyone. But I knew that somehow, in someway we would get through it. I knew it wouldn't be the easiest thing in the world, but we would.

Soldiers

Today is Tuesday June 11, 1767. About a week ago I heard a knock on my front door. I watched from the top of the loft to see who it was. My father opened the door. Then I saw three British soldiers standing there. There was a judge with them. My father invited them in, and they all sat at the table. I could only hear mumbling though I strained to listen. After about an hour, they left. My father called me and my mother downstairs. We sat at the table discussing what the soldiers had said to him.

He said, "The soldiers requested to live here. And that they would throw me in prison if I didn't agree." I looked at my mother. I saw worry and anger in her eyes. My father continued. I listened.

He went on saying, "If they live here we would have to treat them like our own." I felt afraid, angry, and betrayed. After my father had finished talking I said how I felt. My father said, "As long as we treat them as they please there will be no need to worry."

That threw me over the edge. I was furious. But was afraid to show it. I ran upstairs, stomping with every step. Later on that night I lay there in my bed, thinking, wondering what was to happen. I heard my parents talking downstairs. I listened. My mother was crying. I heard her mention the soldiers. And I heard my father ask, "What choice do we have?"

The next day I woke up to the sound of a knock on the door. It was the soldiers again. But this time they had bags. They moved in and after a while I met them. And after a few days, we became friends.

Fear

Today is Friday June 15, 1770. This morning I was heading to Jane's house. She invited me over for tea and I accepted. I arrived at the house and knocked on the door. Jane's father opened the door and invited me in. He said that Jane was upstairs in her bedroom preparing the tea. I went up. The door was closed. I knocked. I heard Jane's voice coming from inside.

She said, "Who is it?"

I answered, "It's me. Let me in."

The door opened a few moments later. There was a small table in the middle of the room and on it was a teapot, two teacups, and biscuits. I went in and sat down. Jane joined me. I tasted the tea and biscuits. They were delicious. We were talking about what we wanted to do when we were older.

"To tell you the truth," I said, "I hadn't really thought about it."

She looked at me with a surprised look. I didn't get why that was so shocking. Then I said, "Well, I would love to run the inn and restaurant someday."

And Jane said, "Well, there you go. I would love to run my father's store someday as well. I just don't know if I would be able to."

"Why not?" I asked.

"Well, women generally are forbidden to run a business. Some people think that a women's job is to cook, clean, and take good care of the kids," she said.

"Well, then that is what I will do," I said. "From now on my new expectations for myself are to have a family and raise them right. It might be hard but I've been through worse. A lot worse."

The Day I Made a Candle

Today is Friday November 15, 1770. Today I got to see my friend Annabelle making candles. Annabelle owns the candle shop down the lane. She wanted me to try to learn how to make candles. So I watched, and learned. It is very interesting. You need a dowel rod and a piece of string. You wrap the string around the rod a couple of times. Then you dip it in the melted wax. You leave it in the wax for five seconds. Then you take it out and let the wax drip for three seconds. Eventually the wax builds up and forms two candles. Or you can twist the strings together to make one. But then you have to dip it a few more times.

After that she let me try it. I messed up a few times but that's ok. She didn't think I was ready for dying the candles. Though I begged her to let me try it she still refused. After I had lost the argument, I set my candle on the table to dry. The next day I came back to get it and take it home. It was still there, it had dried beautifully. I picked it up to make sure it was all dry. Then I took it home to show my mother. She was surprised that I had already learned how to make a candle. I put the candle on the table then lit it. I was amazed. It looked beautiful. I realized then that it looked fine without the dye.

Tea Act

Today is Monday October 15, 1773. This morning I woke up to the sound of, what seemed like screaming, coming from town. I got out of bed and dressed quickly. I checked my parent's room. They weren't there. I went downstairs quietly. Just in case they had fallen asleep downstairs. They weren't there ether. Then I figured that the screaming I had heard was probably a town meeting. I wondered why my parents hadn't waked me up. I threw my coat on and went outside heading towards town.

As I got closer to town, the screaming grew louder. I walked on. In the distance I could see a large group of people gathered around in a circle. I walked closer. I saw a man standing atop of a crate yelling out something about a new

Tea Act. After I heard him say that I thought that this couldn't be god news. I wandered the crowd, searching for my parents. With no luck, I listened. I listened and figured out that it was more good news rather than bad. The only bad thing was that there was that the existing import taxes will remain in effect. I returned home to find my mother and father sitting at the table discussing the new act. I sat down. They asked me where I had been. I told them that I was in town looking for them. They looked at me with a surprised look. And I looked surprised back. They quit staring at me and let me in the conversation. After a while I got bored and went upstairs to bed.

Intolerable Acts

Today is Thursday June 22, 1774. This morning I went to my friend Tom's house. It is about a mile down the lane from where I live and is about a fifteen minute walk. I went up to the door and knocked. With no reply I knocked again. This time Tom's father answered. He invited me in and apologized for keeping me waiting. He said that they were discussing an important matter. Tom was standing behind him, and motioned that we should go outside and talk. We went outside and sat under a shady tree. I asked Tom what they were discussing before I arrived.

"My father was reading the newspaper this earlier and said that it said something about the intolerable acts," he answered.

"Acts?" I asked surprised that there was more than one.

"There are four of them, the Quartering Act, the Massachusetts Government Act, the Boston Port Act, and the Administration of Justice Act," Tom answered.

"Four! My, this can't be getting any better can it?" I said. But I was worried. "Can I see the paper?" I asked.

"Sure, be right back!" He went inside and a few moments later came back with the paper. I read it.

The Quartering Act stated that if any of the King's officers and/or soldiers remained without quarters for the space of twenty-four hours that the commanding officers, by law, is to take control of any homes, barns, and any other buildings to house his troops. The Massachusetts Government Act makes it so that the citizens of Massachusetts can no longer elect their own government officials. The Boston Port Act makes it so that the port of Boston is now closed to all vessels. I was speechless.

I said bye and ran home to tell my parents, but they already knew. I hugged my mother and she started crying. I was worried too, but I could only hope that we would get through this as well.

War

Today is Thursday June 25, 1775. Yesterday morning I was on my way into town, when Jane stopped me to tell me some bad news. "What is it?" I asked.

"A full war has broken out between the colonists and the British. And they choose George Washington to be the leader of the continental army." She said with much worry in her voice.

"What!" I exclaimed in worry. "No, that can't be. What caused it?"

"We don't know. All we know is that odds are it won't end well for us," she said, now starting to weep. I hugged her and asked her to walk home with me to inform my parents.

We walked about half a mile to my house. I opened the door and there was no sign of my parents at all. Jane came inside with me and she searched the back of the house and downstairs, while I looked upstairs. I didn't find them either. I called Jane up the stairs to see if she had found them and she hadn't had much luck either.

We left the house and headed into town to see if there was another town meeting or something. There was. When we got into town there was a large group of people in the middle of town, by the courthouse. There a man was standing atop of the stairs, announcing the war. Jane and I searched for my parents and with no luck headed home. This time they where there. They were sitting at the table discussing the war.

I hugged my mother and asked, "We have been through a lot, but do you think that we will get through this?"

"I hope so." She said. Then all of us group hugged, Jane, Mother, and Father, and I. Then we prayed that we would be able to get through this as well.

Connecticut

CHAPTER 19:

ZIVA AUSTIN; A SHOPKEEPER'S DAUGHTER

By: Courtney Minardi

About Ziva Austin, A Shopkeeper's Daughter

Dear Journal,

I'm currently in my room writing to you. I finally got asked to learn about leading the Corde Austin Irish shop. We have everything here rock candy, food, rum, and a bunch of other stuff that I need to know about. I hope I get the spot. Oh guess what? It's my birthday tomorrow. I got to go my mother is calling me for class. Did I forget to tell you I'm schooled at home?

Dear Journal,

It's the beginning of a new year and my birthday. At 13, I miss Ireland, we moved here when I was five and then we moved here because my great-great-grandfather owned a store in New Haven, Connecticut so when he died my father moved here to run that shop did you know the capital changes every year from Hartford to New Haven that cool. We thought it was a small shop until we got there and it was a two-story shop with a lot of stuff and I mean a lot. I got selling lessons at noon and dinner at dawn we got a lot to talk about. My dad found some blue dyestuff so now my hair is blue. This potion stuff is from Australia so I don't know the ingredients.

I hang out with the Indian children a lot but the adult ones hate us because we take their land. We don't have any slaves my dad said he was going to get me one for my birthday but I said I didn't want one. What if that was my brother or me what if we were punished because we were Irish. So now I'm trying to convince him that there not bad people you don't judge a book by its cover why judge an African or an Indian. My friends call me a drummer because I like drums and my name is Ziva. They elected a Governor named Jonathon Trumbell. I met him once or not at all. A lot of people are Puritans it's scary. Lots of Native Americans or Algonquian live here, there are different types called the Pequot, Podunk and the Moheganl. They do not enjoy British troops invading there land.

Dear Journal,

What I learned today is that we sell corn, pumpkin and beans but I have to pick blueberries, strawberries and nuts. We also own this export center where we export dried meat, flour, iron, rum, fish and seafood. Oh, I have a friend whose dad is a mineral finder and finds iron, copper, lead, and silver.

British Soldiers

Dear Journal,

We got a letter in the mail stating that my family is being forced to have British soldiers to live with us. If we won't let them my papa will be sent to prison and we will have to pay a huge debt. How bad is that? It's not that there we are poor it's that they are Disgusting British soldier. We even have to feed Have beds for them and even treat them well. There is only one nice soldier his names is Charlie. All that he does is help clean and be polite. He sometimes tries to show off to the other guards but he gets blank looks back. One of these days we are going to fight for are Independence and win or freedom. If I could fight I would but all that I can do is sit back, and watch them try to beat fire with water. It does no use they have guns armor shields we have pick forks hay and dirt. Besides I'm a girl so I don't need to even worry about those things I got a test coming up about shop keeping. We should have stayed in Ireland wee owned numerous thing there too. I have to go see write you later…………

Ziva

Scared

Dear Journal,

Standing here with my hand on my chin thinking about how long I have to work here. 30 years, 40 years or even forever. The British came already saying the will take possession of this store, what if they do. We'll have to move back to Ireland. Why bother there already taking peoples homes, food and dignity away.

They just want there money. I wish we could one day have are own government. We will survive without the British. We can have are own tea.

Ziva

A Friend From a Time Ago

Dear Journal,

Walking to Grace's tepee thinking how they survive. I guess they hunt and carve stuff. You see Grace is my friend that I met during the Indian war. She had to live with us because the tribe leader didn't know where else to put her. My family has been close to the tribe leader for a long time. Walking into grace's tepee they took rocks and chipped them so they look like arrow heads. Asking them lead me to whittling a knife out of wood. It was actually pretty fun. It turned out to be not what I expect.

Ziva Austin

Tea Act

Dear Journal,

Have you heard of the new Tea Act? They had axes on the tea but they took some off. I think it's a trick to get us to buy more English goods. Majesty wants it shipped directly to him. I heard there just trying to save the British India Company's from Bankruptcy.

There's all kind of rumors floating around about how people are planning to cause another fight. Some import specialist actually had the guts to call John Hancock a smuggler. They got tar and feathers poured on them. That has to hurt boiling hot tar poured all over his body. It even can cause deaths. I have no hope that they will survive such a brutal punishment.

They haven't even taken of the taxes on anything. They believe we deserve this well not all of us do. I'm going to show them....we as a nation will show them that we can run our own government and not be rats in a cage. They came here to stop the problems well look were it got us. We are still hurting about the Boston Massacre. Five people dead

2 people died at the scene 3 died a couple days after the riot. We will be fine without them, but they had a part in life

Sincerely,

Ziva Austin

Declaration of Independence

Dear Journal,

Signing the Declaration of Independence. Thinking how this could affect everyone. Our freedom is one of the most important things to begin a government. We barely get to speak without the British hearing. I hope we get to choose whom our leader one day. The way it looks is that we will never have freedom anytime soon.

I've met one of the console men. He is my pa's friend, and his name is George Washington. He is a really tall man who towers over many men. Think about, the average mans height is 5'8 but he is 6'4. That's really tall. He was the one who was elected to be the leader of the army he said they created. Many already are affected by the small pox. They thought if you give the pox to someone early and small they would create antibodies to fight off the infection. I don't get them because I already have the antibody but for most they can't afford the so called cure.

Sincerely,

Ziva

Taxes

Dear Journal,

I was looking in the newsletter of June 29, 1767 sitting on a stool waiting for the bell to ring. Suddenly a guy walked up to me asking for a newsletter. As I hand him I noticed a tattoo on his wrist. It's a chopped up snake saying, "Join or die." As I stare at the tattoo he tells me they even put forth the effort to make our fellow colonials even more inpatient with our freedom. Who? I thought for a bit BRITIAN!!! He told me about the article he was reading and what the British were doing to poor citizens.

On the next page they have a picture of the British coming into Boston causing everyone to argue with each other. If they are here to help us control ourselves then why are they causing all the fuss? The nephew of a man who owns an import center was accused of smuggling. His name was John Hancock. He was the one who caused a guy to get feathered and tarred in front of a lot of people. He was put on a pole and walked around like an Indian meal. He had a slim chance to live. I've got to run the old shop.

Sincerely,

Ziva Austin

2nd Continental Congress

Dear Journal,

Guess what just happened. We are no in a war against the British for our freedom. On April 1775 was when the war began In Lexington and Concord. Will win our freedom and once again be an Independent nation. I don't care who they think we are but I don't like there attitude toward us.

I heard about the French and Indian War. The hero is George Washington of Virginia. He is now the general of the "Continental Congress". They protect the citizens of New England. I heard the Indians don't play fair. They don't line up in a row like any other battle….No…They drop spears and there weapons form the tree's. They soon find hundreds of arrow coming there way. They will do what ever it takes for them to win.

I hope we ever get acknowledged as a people's country not the British country. We need to focus on creating our own government and learn to have our own ruler not a King. My friends family's and mine are now having their men over 18 fight in the war in Concord. I hope they win our Independence.

Intolerable Act

Dear Journal,

British soldiers I do not understand. They think they can control us. Just watch, they will regret what they think of us. We will one day understand that with the skills we have, we will control them and scare them. They don't let our people be part of the government; they want the majesty's government people to be our government. Many people have lost their jobs and now are forced to go through such a terrible crisis.

They've closed the vessels until Boston has paid the find from the Boston Tea Party Act. I don't want to be the one to break the law; they will force you to trial in a vice admiralty court instead of our usual colonial court.

If a British soldier commits a crime, they don't even get sent to court, and they do, it has to be one from England. They have to travel all the way to sew if it's an important reason for them to. So if they shoot someone for hitting a soldier, the soldier would just get yelled at or sent home. They shouldn't have hit the soldier or else this wouldn't have happened.

They even want use to share a house with a soldier. They can't do this. They're taking their power for granted and now are the enemies of many citizens of my home town of Connecticut. I won't stand for such nonsense. If we don't, they will take our homes, stores, and everything else that keeps us alive. I'm going to be bankrupt soon. I am 25 and have no family alls that I have is a slave and a dog my family moved to Ireland and haven't wrote back yet.

Sincerely,

Ziva

CHAPTER 20

A PRIVILEGED DAUGHTER IN COLONIAL TIMES

By Kimi Wood

About Olivia- Privileged Daughter

Well, I was born on August 23, 1756. So that means that my birthday is in a couple of weeks. YEAH. My dad, Paul, he works a lot, so he can support us and my Mom, Liliane, is a stay at home mom because she has to take care of my little brother Stanley, and make sure the house is all clean so when dad gets home so he will be happy. The reason why he is at work all the time is because he is a doctor, and they always need him. The only day I get to see him is on Sundays because nobody works that day because it is the day to go to church and hang with your family. Mom always makes some kind of lunch for us, and after lunch I help with the dishes.

Me, well I'm normally at school. I go six days a week. I want to be a teacher when I grow up because I love little kids. My best friend is Abigail and she is in eighth grade with me so we see each other everyday. My teacher laughs at me a lot because she says that I'm really funny, bubbly and not shy. Sometimes when we don't have school, I help my mom with Stanley and pull weeds.

British Soldiers

We were on our way to go and get the three British soldiers so they could live with us. If we didn't come and get them then our father would've had to go to prison and then we would have to pay a fine. If we didn't go and pick up the British soldiers, then we would be in plot of trouble because my father is the one who makes the money an if he isn't here then my mom would need to find a job and I would have to drop out of school.

At first I was a little scared because I wasn't sure if the soldiers were going to be mean, nice, or just rude. I didn't talk to them because I'm not sure how they would react to whatever I was saying. I did not show my emotions so they didn't know if I liked them or not.

Paul, one of the soldiers, came into my room and was all like, "I need to use one of your blankets!" I didn't want to say no but I also didn't want to say yes. So I just walked out.

Then another soldier came up to me and he was like, "Do you ever speak?" So I went to my mother and what I did was start to cry. She was holding me, not saying a word because she new how I was feeling and she didn't have to say anything. Sometimes I wish that things were back to the way they used to be when it was just my dad, my mom, my brother, and me. I ask myself everyday why did the soldiers have to come here, why not somebody else?

Fun in School

Yesterday in school we had to make some candles and then we had to weave. The candle making was kind of fun, but really messy. We got to make our own design and how big we wanted it. My candle wasn't that very big but it's ok because I didn't want to burn it. When I did the weaving, it really wasn't that fun. I had two colors and they were pink and green. I didn't make a pot holder like everybody else; I just made a plain old weaving. While we were weaving we got to have tea. I don't really like hot tea, but I was nice and I drank it. My teacher even made a weaving and a candle and they both looked pretty.

First Day of Work

Well today is the first day of work for me. I am excited, nervous, and scared. I honestly do not know what to think. I see my father working all the time and he makes it seem so easy but to be truthful I am sure its not. I am going to go in there with a good attitude and do the best work I can possibly do. If I mess up I mean it is not like it is the end of the world. Since it is my first time following my father's footsteps instead of my mother it will be challenging but I will get through it. I would rather stay at home like my mother and take care of Stanley and clean. I like being like a "Stay at home Mom", or if that is what you call it?

But I will go and try it like I have already said. Actually my father said if I go to work with him for one week, and if I do not like it then he said that could pick a different hobby. So now if I do not choose to be a doctor then Stanley will just keep it in the family.

Notice

Ok, so my family just found out about the new Sugar Act. We are all very shocked. We do not know how to react! We cannot export molasses or lumber anymore other than to Britain. But, the seven year war is FINALLY over! A sad thing is that the Molasses Act is being expired. I think that this is going to impact us not financially, because my dad is a doctor, and that is how we make our money.

Now our friends, it might impact them, because some of them are not very wealthy and they make there money by importing things. This might impact us socially because now our friends and family are going to have to do extra things and that will take up a lot of their time. So now that means that we will not have very many gatherings with each other. I do not think this will help anything because it is just taking things away from us that we need. I mean, we can deal with it but still it would be a lot easier if we could take things back to the way they used to be.

Taxes

Well there is one thing I sure like, and that is that we get our tea sent right to us. And there are no TAXES! Now all captains have to have detailed manifest of their cargo. I personally think it is stupid. I think this will impact us and England, because they are kind of helping us with money situations, and we get our tea right away. I think that relations will improve, just because it just happened, but maybe in the near future there may be a few disagreements, just because everybody cannot get what they want!

Intolerable Acts

Well we just got the notices about the "Intolerable Acts" and wow. There are so many different things that my mind is going crazy right now. I do not know what to think. This will affect my colony in a lot of ways, like now some stuff got brushed off our shoulders that we do not have to worry about, but now more stuff got piled up and we have those things to worry about. I do not agree with the name Intolerable Acts just because they are tolerable and we can handle it. We always get through things. I am not sure if the people in my colony are with England just because I do not get out much. My brother normally does all the work outside of the house while my brother and I do the work on the inside, like cooking, cleaning etc.

Continental Congress

I just heard that the Continental Congress is going to meet a second time. I am excited and nervous at the same time. I do not like people arguing and disagreeing because I think everybody should get along without fighting. I do agree with all of this, I like having the meetings where the men can talk about different things. Then after the meetings the men finally come home to there families and tell them their stories while they were gone for so long.

Declaration of Independence

Ok. We just heard about the signing of the Declaration of Independence. I am so excited. My father just sent us a letter and told us that he had just signed it, and that we would be getting a copy of it in a couple of days. My father, when he came home brought a couple of the signers over for dinner that night. I felt very pleased to be sitting with such important influential people. Now that they have signed it my life has changed like now we have so much more rights to do things that we want to do. My life used to be all sheltered and I could only do certain stuff. Now since the signing happened my life is so much happier and better living for me.

CHAPTER 21:

PATIENCE

By: Cassidy Boyd

About Patience

Today was a good day. I helped clean the house, helped make food, and washed clothes. At school today I learned new things about math. I learned how when you multiply it's the opposite of dividing. I also learned about integers. I learned that an integer is a whole number. The number can also be a negative number or a regular number.

My father and I worked in the general store. We didn't sell very much merchandise. My mother is making me go to bed early because we have to go to church tomorrow morning. Our religion is Christianity . My family goes to church every Sunday.

I know many people. I know everyone in town such as the blacksmith, the doctor, carpenter, and other people. My mother doesn't have a very difficult job. She cooks, cleans, and takes care of house. I also do the same things and I help at the store. My father works at the store.

I think I'm a very funny, kind, sensitive, and a smart person. I always help out and do what I'm told. I'm glad my dad owns the general store because when I get older I'll get to own the store. I like when I get asked to work at the store. I like helping get money by selling things.

I love living in Connecticut especially since I live in Hartford. Connecticut is famous for the growth of tobacco and for the three most important ports such as New Haven, Hartford, and New London. The govern of Connecticut is Jonathan Trumbull. He is in charge of the state. He makes all the decisions.

My Creation

I carved a face. I made my face by whittling with wood using a carving knife. The face I made was a face of me. The face didn't exactly look like me because it's made out of wood and because I didn't smooth out the edges of the wood. When you make something out of wood,(whittling) you have to position the carving knife correctly. Otherwise it will be harder to carve something out of the wood. In a way making the wood look like me is a self portrait. Carving with a carving knife you have to take deep, slow shavings in the wood. As I created my product I cut all the dark parts of wood so the piece of wood would be smooth. Then I started created my product. That's how I made my product out of wood.

The Soldiers

Today my family got some news from the government that now has agreed that my family and other families have to let soldiers stay at our house and care for them. If my family doesn't cooperate, my father will be sent to prison and my family will have to pay a fine.

Today the three British soldiers arrived at my home. One soldier was short, fat, and rude. The other soldier was tall, kind, and smug looking. The last soldier was a medium sized, loud, and respectful.

I personally like Jon and Clyde. The tall one and the medium one. I don't like Adam. The rude one. I like Jon and Clyde because they're nice and they make funny jokes. Adam. He doesn't say " please or thank you", chews his food with his mouth open, and he puts his dirty old war boots on the dinner table. He's a slob.

I think having the soldiers living with my family is a giving me as well as my mother and father a good experience.

My life is kind of different now from what it was because I feel like a slave. I have to do everything for myself and for the soldiers. I know the soldiers are guest, but do I have to do everything? They can do some things by themselves. They can pour a cup of water. They can do many things. Why do I have to do it? Sometimes I wish they never came to my home and wish they would go back to where they came from.

My Fears

Today my mother said that I'm becoming a woman and that I will have many challenges and expectations. When she told me that I was kind of scared. Then as the day progressed, I started thinking about it and I decided that it would be fun to be and act like an adult.

Since my mother had told me about being an adult, I started to act like an adult. I figured it wouldn't be long until I was grown up so why not start now. All day long I was so mature. I did all my chores, plus more.

My mom asked me, "What have you done with my daughter"?

I said, "It's still me, I just want to act more mature." Ever since I've been so adult I've been getting rewards such as extra time before bed and other things I love being more mature. It's so fun!

The Sugar Act

Today a notice was sent out about a sugar act. A sugar act is a law that is enacted to increase tax revenues to Britain. The sugar act was placed in place of the molasses and lumber act because the molasses and lumber acts were expired. The sugar act affects my fathers business because he has to pay the makers of the sugar; money so my father can sell the sugar in the general store. I think materials and food will be scarce now prices will be higher. People will have to work harder to provide for their families.

Ridiculous Taxes

I've just heard about the new taxes on materials such as glass, lead, paint, tea, and paper. I find the doing of putting taxes on the simple materials as ridiculous. I think the actions of the British and the colonials are not fair. People shouldn't have to pay taxes for certain materials.

I feel that since John Hancock decided to smuggle materials that the government should stop taxing people for so many materials before more people start smuggling.

I think if the government stops so many rules people would want to cooperate instead of rebelling against them.

Things haven't changed for a long time and there has been acts and fights. If people have a town meeting then people will have peace and come together.

The Stamp Act

I just heard about the notice regarding of the stamp act. Right now the colonies are experiencing economic depression where there is time of high unemployment, low income, and reduced trade. When I heard about this notice my reaction was very surprised because I didn't think something regarding the stamp act would cause all this conflict. I feel the tax and fees charges are unreasonable because people in the colonies don't have a lot of money to be giving out to the government for a bunch of acts from the parliament and the government. The impact I anticipate it making on my me, my family, and friends financially and socially because money will get tight and people will become more angrier because there giving money to the parliament. This will effect me and my fellow colonialists because there might be a riot because of these acts.

Multiple Notices

There have been multiple new notices sent out. The Quartering act, the Massachusetts Government act, the Administration of Justice act, and the Boston Port act. The papers are referring all these acts as the "Intolerable Acts".

I feel that there are too many notices being given out. These notices could lead to more taxes and more conflict from England and the colonies.

I think the name "Intolerable Acts" is a good name for all the acts put together because the four acts given out are intolerable.

I also feel people in my area are siding more with the men of Boston and New England because England and the mother country is making all the notices.

Boston Port Act

I just heard about the Boston Port Act. The act is about the people who dumped all of the king's tea and threw the tea over the Boston Port. These people who I don't know who did this action but they did this because they didn't want to drink the King's tea and wanted to drink tea from other places and areas. Because this happened Britain made a law that the colonists can't take tea out or into the colonies until the dept is paid. I don't think the colonists should've done this action and that they should've had a discussion with Britain.

CHAPTER 22:

JOHN CARTER

By: Devin Hubbard

About Me

This is my first entry. My name is John Carter, I'm twelve with a fourth grade education, I'm catholic, and I'm shy and nervous. I'm also smart. I like to do archery and I'm a blacksmith apprentice. Being a blacksmith is tricky because you can really burn yourself and everyone is relying on you. When you're a blacksmith I can't see my mom, dad, and sister till I'm a journeyman. My master can be mean at times. I like to do archery and a lot of horseback riding. I was born in December/2/1763 in Boston, Massachusetts. My two best friends are Jessie and Michelle. Well got to go.

The Soldiers

Today was a horrid day, the government forced my family to care and feed three lobsterbacks. If we don't care for them my dad will go to prison and we will have to pay a fine. I hate the soldiers their obnoxious arrogant pigs. They steal our food and our fresh water. They also killed our cows. I do not like the government for doing this to our innocent family. They keep asking for favors like they

They can't do anything for themselves. They beat my sister hard. This experience is terrible but it taught me a lesson, the government is corrupted by the Brits. Tomorrow they will be leaving thank goodness and everything will be back to normal except I hate the redcoats now so much I might join the rebels

The Future

I am worried that my future will be bad for me. I hope I will become a great blacksmith but I do not know what god has in store for me. I wonder if I will be married or I'll die alone. I wish I can see into the future. The world's future is a great big mystery. My father says, "If you can learn the past you can learn the future." I always wondered what other people future is. I'll just have to wait.

Hands On

Today I was accepted as an apprentice for a Blacksmith. His name is Mr. Jefferson and he will be my master till I learn the trade. It will be a long and hard time for years to come.

Today he taught me how to silversmith and I made a silver medallion. I had to make it many times to make a perfect medallion. I felt like I could not make it but I saw my master do it and he let me try. As I poured it felt like the heat was burning me but I just backed up and the pain stopped.

I made a new friend her name is Michelle. She is very nice and funny, her parents are Store owners. She said that she has another friend named john, I think I will visit him tomorrow. I have to go for now

The Stamp Act

The British king has enforced a new act called the Stamp Act. We have to pay extra money to pay for the British seal of approval when we are already in an economic depression. I myself have had fewer jobs to do for people because they do not have the money to pay for my services. I am barley scraping enough money to get by and feed my family.

My family will have to adjust for living with less money to spend on essentials. Normally I could buy something extra for my kids but I will not be able to do that now with less money. I will have to try and work two jobs to help support my family and my parents who live in Boston.

This will probably Change the opinion of some of my fellow countrymen. The Sons of Liberty will be upset and will probably plan a riot. I must see to my fellow countryman needs up front.

The Townshend Act

I have heard even more terrible news. The British have made a new proclamation called the Townshend Act; it taxes lead, glass, paint, paper, and tea again. Also it will even be harder for smugglers to smuggle goods.

The Sons of Liberty and I have been revolting against the British king. Most revolts have been non-violent but some are becoming more violent. This tax is affecting me because I need glass cups to drink from and I need lead to make certain items.

The British will probably make new laws to oppress to colonies. There might still be a peaceful way out of this but it is unlikely that it will happen. I have to go Bert Channolor is waiting.

The Tea Act

I have some good and bad news; The British have enforced a new act called the Tea Act, which lowers the cost of British tea. Although this lowers the cost of the tea I feel like they are tricking us by doing this so the will sell more tea but at a lower cost. This does not help many colonists because some colonists hate British tea and refuse to drink it.

This will hardly help me at all because I do not drink British tea I usually drink coffee. I believe more colonists should switch to alternatives to tea like coffee and water. I do not think the King realizes the struggles within our colonies because he does not give us much support.

A lot of colonists from Connecticut believe they are being tricked into paying more taxes. Some people still believe in the king and are backing him in his plans for America. I have to leave, Margaret is calling me to help carry timber to her house.

The Intolerable Acts

I cannot believe what the British have done. They have made multiple new notices and Boston Observer calls them the Intolerable Acts. They include four acts and they all are just made to oppress the Colonies and me. Most of these effect most of Boston, although they still effect me and my family in Connecticut. My uncle In Boston says there are lots of riots outside and there are more and more crimes against the king and the colonies.

It is already hard to support my family because of low money and not enough food. Bert the Cabin boy that is down the road says he barely has any money at all and has to beg for his money. The British army has occupied a farmhouse outside of Boston.

These Acts will affect my life because they make taxes on items I need to run a Blacksmiths shop. Businesses all over Connecticut are being slowed down and are losing money. I respect England and the king but I am slowly losing the respect because of the Acts and that we are losing rights as human beings. I must go my wife is sick and she is calling me to bring her water.

War

There have been battles between the British and the American Militia. The battle at Lexington and Concord was bloody but a great victory. The Congress has declared a boycott on England and is planning to meet again to discuss what to do next.

I believe they should declare independence from England and lets us be free from the King. There might still be a peaceful way out of this but I do not think it will happen anytime soon. The war has already begun and we need more leaders like General George Washington.

Whatever the Congress decides I will be at their side defending our rights. I have the feeling they will make the right move next and will resolve all hostilities. I must leave to attend the town meeting to discuss the Congresses' actions.

The Chance of a Lifetime

I have heard the greatest news from the butcher's wife, Margaret. She said the second continental congress has signed the Declaration of Independence proclaiming our freedom from the King of England. I am so happy I do not have to pay taxes anymore to the king and I can use the money to feed my family.

Today I met one of the signers from my beautiful state of Connecticut; His name is Samuel Huntington. He is a very kind and generous man. He said he believed this great nation needed to be free and to be able to make our own decisions that the people vote on.

Unfortunately I could not talk to him for long because he had to see his family, so I thanked him for his patriotism and his time, then he left. As I am writing this for the first time in the United States of America I can not help but to think of what the future holds for me. I must go my wife is calling me to help set the table.

CHAPTER 23:

DONE WITH TAXES

By: Devin White

Soldiers

I do not want to believe what Mr. Carter told me today about the Soldiers coming to town. I don't want these soldiers in my home because they are so greedy. The first thing they said, "Give me some food!"

But I did realize over a few days that the big tough dude is really sensitive, the short man was very mean most of the time, and the average soldier can and will get very angry if you yell at him.

Tea

I just got back from the townhall meeting and the new act surprised me, because the tax and fee charges are very unreasonable. Like earlier today I paid an extra three cents on tea and I was so mad at the Tea Merchant because he said, "These new acts make me richer everyday!" I just walked away and drunk my tea.

More Tea

My good friend Mr. Carter told me about the new notice, but I really wish he hadn't because now, I'm so angry at the New Tea Act but I love not having to pay all that extra money for English Tea because I LOVE the English tea it is so good I am not even messing around with you.

My friend said, "Although they lowered the price of the tea they still have not lowered the tax on the tea." And I told him that I do not understand what you're saying. He did not bother to explain it to me though.

Top of Form

Today at the Blacksmith my good friend John told me about the Second Continental Congress signing the Declaration. When he told me I grabbed the item I went to pick up, said goodbye, and ran home down the streets yelling, "We're Finally Free!" Half of the people asked me what I meant so I told them, "Our Independence has been Declared!" And most of the people ran home to tell their families!

A week later I traveled to Windsor, Connecticut to deliver a Sword for John because I owed him a favor. And while I was there I decided to go and see one of our four signers from Connecticut, Oliver Wolcott! I was very nervous when I knocked on his door when he answered I introduced myself to him and asked him when he actually did sign the Declaration but he did not remember what day all he said was a few days after the actual Signing had happened as he was very ill during the Signing.

New York

CHAPTER 24:

A LIFE OF TYRANNY AND VICTORY

By: Sid Carpenter-Wilson

The Sugar Scandal

April 7, 1764

I woke up feeling so hungry I could eat the cordage in our supplies cabinet. I got up off my chaff bed and got on my cricket so I could see out my window. I could see the sunrise from the east. I went outside to see that all the people in Albany have yet to get up. The only place in town that I know is up and runnin' is Pete's Inn. I look through the window to find nothing but tables in sight. Not even a tankard left out! Pete lost his job! I walked away disappointed in how people seem to have no rights these days.

When I got home my dad was reading the paper. My mom was holdin' her seedlip in the rockin' chair. My dad started yelling at me for some reason. He was pointing at the newspaper and he was talkin' like the ol' man down the street. I took the paper and found an article about the new Sugar Act. I found out that we wouldn't be able to run our inn! We couldn't buy molasses cause of the tax. No one would come cause of the taxin' either. We'd have to pay so much for the inn that we couldn't pay for the new flock beds we were goin' to get.

I was so upset I took the chaff out of my chaff bed and ran through town. I ran all the way to the spring. I stopped so suddenly I almost flew into the river. I was about throw my chaff into the river, til' the farmer stopped me. He asked me if I needed that chaff I was holdin'. He even told me about how his horses were goin' to starve. If his horses died he wouldn't be able to travel between towns. I felt sorry for the farmer so I gave him the chaff. He asked if there was any way to repay him. I told the farmer that I had an inn and we couldn't pay for the molasses. He kept talking about his animals. He mentioned he had quite a few pigs. I stopped him and said that some pigs would go perfect for some pork for our breakfast meals. I must be one of the most fortunate people in Albany. I know everyone. I just happen to know who's in charge of the slaughter house fairly well.

It didn't take long to almost have a supply of pork for about half a perch. That day we had so many customers! We couldn't go up to someone and have them say "Who are you?"

Everyone knows who we are now! We could be the most successful inn in New York! Before I went to bed that night I saw the farmer in his chaise outside of my window. He tipped his hat and disappeared into the shadows.

Christopher

Unwanted Guests

March 5, 1770

I cannot stand having British soldiers live with me. They will not let us go to the market without their supervision. If we try to get supplies for our inn (For an inn you need cleaning supplies, cooking supplies, and occasionally blacksmith supplies) they threaten us with our lives. We have to give them free meals. They eat too much of our food. We do not have hardly enough food for our inn. My dad has to get his musket out when they get drunk. They almost kill my dad last time they got drunk.

I got in a mob with the other villagers and protested against the British living in our houses. All of us started throwing whatever we had at the soldiers. The cowards ran away! Before they left they said we were not nice to them anyway. Not nice to them!? We cared to their every need! We pampered them like they were the king(s) of Great Britain! They even threatened us if we did something for ourselves!

The next day I read the newspaper that was very peculiar. In Boston a mob of people protested against the British just like we did. One of them threw a snowball at the soldiers. The soldiers fired at the mob and five people died. Maybe, they just meant to get their attention.

Christopher

"Birthday Presents"

March 16, 1770

Today is March Sixteenth. It's my birthday. Tomorrow is 1st time we do our soon to be well known St. Patrick's Day Dinner. We would have had a St. Patrick's Day dinner before sooner but the holiday is only about 15 years old. So it was unknown to most of the colonists until they started putting it in the newspaper. For some reason not many people have been able to get the newspaper. I think that might effect how many costumers come to the inn tomorrow.

Since I'm setting up most of the dinner I'm getting half the profit. If my parents were going to help they wouldn't be able to do much. My mom, Laura, is at the market most of the time so she can get food for the dinner. My dad, Aaron, is out in nearby towns looking for ideas and tips so we can run a better inn. He said he won't be back until mid day tomorrow. The only person I have to help me is my sister Marie since she's nine she's not tall enough or strong enough to do half the things I have to do for tomorrow. I sent her to get paper be cause we ran out. She said that she looked around town and she could not find any.

I went out side and found a newspaper out just laying on the ground. It was not by the door of our inn so I assume it was not delivered to us. I was surprised no one had picked it up do to the shortage of paper. There was an article in it about there being a fire burning down several trees and burning all of the handles for the blacksmith's and lumberjack's axes and hatchets. I went down to the forest where the trees were burnt. There were still trees there! I went to talk to a blacksmith and he said he could put the axe together in just a few minutes if he had the wooden handle. That gave me an idea! Since I help run an inn we have lots of cleaning supplies. I went back to the inn to get a broom to give to the blacksmith. When I gave him the broom I did not even have to say anything. He just cut of the handle from the broom and sealed the handle to the axe. Since haven't been able to get bark for the paper they already had the process materials to make the paper. It's always good to be prepared.

That night I was reading the paper and I found an inordinately article. A British soldier started the fire. It appears that a couple children were just having a snowball fight with the leftover snow on the ground. The soldier thought somehow they were threatening him. My sister, Marie, turned out to be one of the children in the snowball fight. I should have listened to her. She said a soldier had tried to attack her. The solder actually tried to throw a torch at Marie! It set the forest on fire. This just goes to show how the British treat us like we're nothing but animals! They should not even be living here in the colonies.

Christopher

Responsibilities

March 26, 1770

I am finally going to get my own inn. My Parents are leaving town to find ideas of new food to serve at our inn. They left me in charge so I would have an idea of what it's like running the inn. The different things I have to take care of. As of now that includes my little sister, Marie. She has not had much experience yet. So she struggles very often. So I am having her do what I know she can do. Sweep.

My Friend, John, from across town tries to come and help me but he's a cabin boy so he's out on the sea most of the time. He always has exciting stories. He's almost always there to help. He was even there for our first St. Patrick's day dinner.

The business is actually going fairly slow. Maybe now that we the British solders aren't eating all of our food (unlike they were earlier this month), everyone must have there own food.

Christopher

Intolerable Acts

August 9, 1774

My friend, John, got back from the Brits' ship about a fort night ago. John was almost never in the colonies. He was able to come back to Albany once a year, except last year. Last year he was in Boston. He participated in the Boston tea party! He was caught. Instead of arresting John, the Brits decided to keep him as a cabin boy for until they came back to the colonies. They made him do all the tasks. He said that he stole a waistcoat from the British. When the British come back to Albany he will get onto one of there ships and ambush it. I think he's the only person that would speak his thoughts that much. We slept in the forest that night. He knew how to make fire! I wonder where he learned how to make fire as a cabin boy, out in the sea all the time. We weren't able to stay awake for long.

The next morning I came back to my parent's inn to see how they were doing. My parents and my sister were standing outside the inn. My dad was yelling at the British solders about how they can't just take over their inn. I think I'm the only one that can understand my dad when he gets upset. My mom said they were taking our inn so they could get supplies and a place to stay for the solders. As soon as she said that I ran to my inn (when I turned seventeen I got married and open my own inn) and I also found British solders living in my inn. I went to argue that they couldn't stay in my inn but they said the quartering act makes it so they can (I'm so glad I'm living in Boston now). They also said if I wanted to trial them (which I did) that I would have to go to Britain. What's the reason to go to Britain since; the King won't arrest one of his own. The solders say the Administration of justice act is the cause for that. Then I decided to move to Boston early.

Now that I'm in Boston, I'm running a new inn. We don't have much in the house yet. I overheard some solders in town saying that they might take our inn for their solders! Since, the governor was in town today I went to go see him. I complained about how the British can do this. He showed me another act. The

Massachusetts government act. It said the British can do whatever they want to Massachusetts's government. How are there so many acts in affect right now? The governor said the colonists started called all these acts the intolerable acts (I can see why). He showed me one more act. The Boson port act. It says that no vessel can come into the Boston port and no vessel can leave the Boston port. That means John can't leave! I think I might not be able to buy supplies for the inn my wife, Olivia, and John. Not to mention that the British might take my inn for a place where the solders can stay.

Christopher

Ripped in Half
May 11, 1775

Why does every one have to be better than the other? I go outside today to see two men fighting. I could tell one was a Whig and one was a Tory by what they were saying. One was complaining about how the British were taxing us on everything and how they're just making it so they can't be hurt or imprisoned. The other man was saying that without them we wouldn't survive and that they have the strongest navy in the world. I tried to stop them from arguing and they both tried to get me to side with them. It's how religion takes over our lives. How we dislike each other because of what we believe in. There was Great Britain and there were the colonies. Once Britain started taking charge everything went down.

I am a Whig, but I don't argue with a Tory about what's right just because they're a Tory. Living in Boston helps me learn about the patriot and leaders of the war. There has been news about Sam Adams, John Hancock, and George Washington. It turns out Gorge Washington is leading the colonial army. He seems confident. I ran into John Hancock at the Boston port. He actually made what the British thought of him true. He was smuggling the English ships. He was dressed in an English waistcoat. I don't hear much about Sam Adams. I just hear his name from different people around town. He was mentioned in the newspaper too. I think it will be hard to find people who don't have conflict with others.

Christopher

Independence

July 30, 1776

Blasted British deserved what they got! Because of them I couldn't even fight in the war. Two years ago my inn in Boston was taken by the British. The quartering act said that any British solders could take over any house to house other British solders. Quickly after I got my inn and my house were taken by some British solders. I wasn't able to get back to my house and inn for a fortnight. When I got back I found that they had taken my gun and my journal. Why would they want my journal?

It's a lot easier to buy supplies for the inn. No more taxes! It's alot less exciting here though. I wanted to go to war. I wanted to fight against the British to show them how horribly they treated us Americans. I wanted my great grand kids to know who I am and think that I helped the nation to be free. I wanted my journal for my decedents too.

It turns out my journal was in the back of my clothes press.

For about two years I was stuck just working at my inn. There weren't a lot of customers during the war. A couple days ago I went outside to see Sam Adams, and John Hancock riding around Boston on two white horses. People all around town gathered around the two famous patriots. People were cheering. Everyone looked so happy and relieved.

This shall be my last time writing in this journal. This journal is historical to me. As I write about this I'm thinking about 200 years from now. One of my descendents could be reading this journal. I give my best wishes to them and hope they think fondly of me.

Christopher

CHAPTER 25:

MELONY JADE; LEARNING HOW TO GROW UP... THE RIGHT WAY

By: Audrey Traylor

About Melony Jade, a Doctor's Daughter

Dear Diary,

I've decided to start keeping a diary of my life so let's get started. My full name is Melony Felicity Jade, but I just go by Melony. I'm thirteen years old and I'm turning fourteen on December 24, Christmas Eve. I live in a large brick house with my mother, Mary, my father, Thomas, and his brother (my uncle), Vince, and my three annoying older brothers Christian, Clarence, and Caleb. Caleb is my twin but he brags that he's three minutes older, so you could say I'm the youngest. We are a Christian family and all go to the church down the street every Sunday morning.

I don't have very many friends but I do have one friend that's very close to my heart. His name is Jeremiah Smith. He calls me Melon, and we've been friends for many years because our fathers knew each other. We are the same age, but his birthday is on December 3. His dad is a blacksmith and lately Jeremiah has been busy learning how to follow in his father's footsteps and to take over the business. He only has one brother and sometimes I get jealous.

You can't tell any one but I kind of like him; it feels like true love but I'm not sure. I've never been in love but from what I hear it sure does feel like it. My heart starts beating rapidly and I get big fluttery butterflies in my stomach. There's no way I could ever tell him though because I don't think my father would approve. He says we come from two different worlds.

My favorite things to do are have competitions with my brothers and Jeremiah like walking on the stilts or running. Sometimes I just like to run around. I really like to play sports but my brothers say I can't because I'm a girl. I don't care if I'm a girl or not I should be able to play any time I want. I'm better than most of the boys I know, but Jeremiah is nice. He always agrees and says I should be able to play too, but it's not up to him. And it's not even up to me, it's up to my father. He completely controls my life. He tells me when to get up, what to eat, how to talk, and almost everything else that goes on in my life.

Something I didn't tell you is that my father is a doctor and is not rich but isn't poor either. We're somewhere in the middle. He does expect me to be a proper young lady though. I don't really want to be but he says it's required and now he says I have to take lessons. I have to learn how to walk, talk, dance, drink tea, dress, and ride a horse… the right way. Riding a horse is my favorite thing to do (I have a horse and his name is Blazer) but I don't know how to ride the way they want me to with both legs on one side with a big dress on. I don't even like dresses. Well, I have a lot more to say but I think Jeremiah is outside so I'll write more later.

Sincerely,

Melony Jade

A New Law

Dear Diary,

What? A tax on sugar! I can't believe it! How long can people take this? There should be people out there boycotting, striking, or an angry mob outside this window. We won't have any money left in our pockets; it's all going to be used on taxes!

Jeremiah just got done telling me about the new tax law. That's when I exploded. Our King has gone too far. They've put a tax on molasses and lumber. I'm going to go insane. Jeremiah and I love sugar; we can't live without it. My Mother is worried too, she can't cook without it. She just told me that we don't have enough left to make blueberry pie. I love Mama's homemade pie. I won't live!

Sincerely,

Melony Jade

A Stamp Act

Dear Diary,

A Stamp Act! The government put taxes on paper, stamps and anything written on paper. Now I can't buy the playing cards that I was going to get Jeremiah for his birthday. I am very blessed with my family and our wealth but my father's pay keeps going down because he is getting less patients every day; not because people aren't sick, its that people don't have money to pay to get better. That is why all these diseases are going around.

Speaking of diseases, mother is very worried about the case of small pox going around. She's so concerned that tomorrow when pa comes back to town, he's going to treat me, mother, my brothers, Jeremiah, and his family personally, even himself. I'm not too thrilled knowing that I have to be cut and have a sick patient's puss purposely put in my healthy body to make me sick for weeks; knowing that might not help but only give a sickness to me that could cause death. It's supposed to help fight off the sickness. I personally think that there is a better way to solve the problem.

Jeremiah's family is going through a rough time too. His father can't sell anything because no one has enough money. We have to take action!

Sincerely,

Melony Jade

Three of a Kind

Dear Diary,

I have some good news and some bad news. Late last night a government official came and knocked on our door. My father asked what they needed and they replied, "We need you to take in some soldiers for a month or two. If you don't, according to the law, you will be sent to jail and have to pay a large fine."

I was very surprised when my father then said, "We would love to have them stay with us! We have more than enough room! We have a guest room up in the attic."

They said the soldiers would be in bright and early tomorrow morning. Now that I think about it, it might be okay to have them stay with us maybe they can teach me some things about the military. The only bad thing is we have to feed them and take care of them. I just have to think positive!

There here, and they're not exactly what I expected. They knocked on the door and were very polite they said please and thank you and said yes ma'am and yes sir. Their names were Mason, Justin, and Austin. Mama made their beds up in the guest bedroom up in the attic. They weren't very exciting though. They ate and that was really the only time I saw them. I keep wondering what they're doing. One day I'll find out what it is. My brothers are suspicious too. Even Jeremiah is always asking what its like to have them living with us. Uncle Vince keeps telling me I should go spy on them and I've been thinking about it. Should I? I'll fill you in later.

Sincerely,

Melony Jade

Candles Again

Dear Diary,

Today I had to make candles again because winter is getting closer, and that means shorter days and longer nights. We have to use candles because it gets very dark. We don't use scented candles because that attracts bugs and we only use colored candles on holidays like Christmas.

The process of candle making is very easy. You must do this outside. Get a pot and put it over the fire for a while and put wax in the pot so it will melt. Then when the water is hot enough take it off the hook and put it on the ground, let it cool. While you're waiting for the water to cool take a small but strong twig and take some wick and wrap it around the stick then dip it, take it out and let it drip. You'll want to get a lot going. When you're letting the wax drip, hang the candle on a tree branch. When you're done make sure your candle can stand up itself. Then cut the wick and light your candle!

I will admit that they are amazing but sometimes I get bored. My mother always says they're beautiful even when they don't look like candles. Well have to go, my brothers and Jeremiah are playing baseball.

Sincerely,
Melony Jade

Expectations

Dear Diary,

Now that I'm getting older and taking etiquette classes I've been thinking more about my future and what I want in life, and what I expect of myself. One thing I expect for myself is to be a great wife and an even better mother (hopefully of four).

I'm hoping one day I can be married to Jeremiah but like I said before, my father would never approve of him just because he's not rich. I don't really like to be proper but if I'm going to do something I might as well be the best I can be. One day I'll be as great as my mother but I could never be better than her. She's wonderful. I have lots of expectations. I've got to go mother needs my help with the soldiers.

Sincerely,
Melony Jade

Defend Them?!

Dear Diary,

"There is absolutely no way that happened. I don't believe it, I refuse to believe it."

"But it did Miss Melony. It was goin' to happen sooner or later, everyone saw it coming." Jeremiah had just got done telling me about the mob that broke out in Boston. "My aunt lives in Boston, she witnessed it all. She wrote me and told me everthin'. She said it started out just the regular people and their usual yellin' at the soldiers, calling them lobster backs and bloody backs, then one of them threw a snowball right at their face! That's when they got angry and attacked, killed a bunch of people, even some innocent people. And even worse John Adams is gonna defended them good for nothin' bloody backs! Weather you believe it or not that it happened, Melony Jade, it might even happen again!"

"Defend them?! But they did nothing but hurt and kill our people. I just don't understand," I said back to him.

"What don't you understand Melony, it's clear as day right here," Jeremiah told me.

I guess that's what I don't get. All the proof I need is right here in front of me and I still don't believe it! It just seems so impossible, like it would never happen. I knew something like this was coming and it still surprised me! When will I ever learn?

Sincerely,

Melony Jade

Intolerable Acts

Dear Diary,

I am done! Jeremiah's father, Tod, can't even keep his shop going. My father sent me to Jeremiah's father's blacksmith shop to get some nails for the horse's shoes, but when I got there Jeremiah and his brother were cleaning out the place. I asked him what they did to the place, thinking it was their weekly pranks. But when I demanded them to put things back in order they just shrugged their shoulders and answered, "No can do, Miss," and kept on sweeping. I asked them why and they said, "Pa can't afford it no more with all these taxes, the

Intolerable Acts put us over the top. We've even been drinkin' coffee instead of tea. Pa's puttin' the shop up for sale at dawn tomorrow mornin'."

I begged them if there was anything else they could possibly do and they just sighed, shrugged and kept on cleaning.

We can't handle this: The Administration of Justice Act, the Boston Port Act, the Massachusetts Government Act, and the Quartering Act. Amazing! Why call them all those names? Everyone's calling them the Intolerable Acts which is a perfect name. I can not believe they can do this to us! We are still part of the Mother country, even if we don't want to be. Taxes are on everything we need. We're here, not there. We shouldn't have to listen to them! We came here to be free from Britain, but since I've been here it has been nothing but trouble. We can't just sit here and wait for something to happen. We have to take a stand! Become true Americans.

Sincerely,

Melony Jade

It's Still the Same

Dear Diary,

It's still the same. I thought things would be different by now. There is no excitement, not anywhere. Pa says it's because this is such a serious matter. Early morning I went to fetch eggs from the hens for breakfast and give the horses their feed and it was dead silent; no mobs, no cheering, just rain. I felt like the world was frozen in time and that the only thing moving was me and the pouring rain around me, dripping on my face and soaking through my cape.

At that moment the only thing I could think about was that we sent those representatives to make a decision for the better of our future in America, and that they didn't even make one! I'm wondering if we chose the right people to represent us because they didn't even vote! They bailed and disappointed us all! They are a disgrace to us all!

The bad part is that we, New York, will be the first or second to be attacked and we almost definitely will be killed soon. The British government has no mercy for us or any one else! Not even for innocent by-standing citizens; not for their wives, their children, friends, or family! The mother country is merciless!

Sincerely,

Melony Jade

Mr. George

Dear Diary,

What is going on here? I don't even know these people any more; they're not the same since all of this happened. I haven't been the same since the massacre in Boston happened, no one has. I just don't want to believe anything that's been going on here. I thought we came to America to get away from all of this but I think every thing is just worse here. The thing that makes me so furious is that the King has all the money he could ever need but apparently it's not enough because he just keeps taking and taking from those of us who do need it. It seems like he doing it because he can and that's the kind of person I don't want to hail to.

I think none of this is right. Although, I sure am glad we have Mr. George Washington. He is a good man, and will definitely keep our soldiers safe and well. I just hope everything goes over well. That's all mother and father talk about, George being in charge of the army. They say he's a wonderful man.

Sincerely,

Melony Jade

Parting Slowly

Dear Diary,

Now even Uncle Vince is talking about the British government. He never talks about them. He says they're traitors and a few other things that I can't say without mama washing out my mouth with soap for an hour. Now that's all he talks about, day and night.

Well that's not why I'm writing. I'm writing because the colonies had their second meeting the other day and they've decided that we're going to boycott against the mother country. We really are going to become independent; it just takes one step at a time. We will accept nothing from the British and will offer the British nothing.

It sure has been different though. This afternoon I road Blazer down to the shop to buy some fabric for my new clothes and all the shelves were almost empty! Every one's bought the supplies because we weren't going to get anymore until we made peace with Britain, which could be a very long time, if at all. Every thing is different in the shop. I guess we do really depend on Britain, but I'm sure we could all live on our own. Of course, there would be changes but that's to be expected. I just hope one day we will be able to live on our own.

I'm very sad to say that I have to stop writing. I have no more money to buy paper so, unfortunately, this will be my last page. Maybe I'll write again someday. Good bye.

Sincerely,

Melony Jade

CHAPTER 26

SAMUEL'S LIFE

By: Mark Hamner

Samuel Gates' Journal - My Feelings on My Life

November 29, 1772

Dear Journal,

I'd like to introduce myself to you. I'm Samuel Gates, and I'm goin' to be an apprentice to a carpenter. I'm fifteen, I signed my papers yesterday; and tomorrow is my first day at work. Usually apprentices start at age 12, but I had physical problems with my right arm the first year and a half; the other year and a half I spent some time recovering. I hope to get married and have four kids. I want a wife who will support me and will love me for who I am. I will work as hard as I can to support my family.

~Samuel Gates~

Samuel Gates - New York Carpenter

I'm Samuel Gates. I was born on September 25, 1757. My I'm an apprentice to a carpenter. I as part of my contract I live, sleep, and eat with my mentor's family. Also as part of my contract, I must serve as many years as my mentor would like me to; and when I've finished my years, I have the opportunity to marry his eldest daughter. I must also help with chores around the house as a payment for my stay. My mentor has a wonderful family of three children; the eldest daughter is Elizabeth Carver, fourteen, the next eldest is Johnathan Carver, thirteen, and the youngest is Matthew Carver, ten. I have a beautiful family of seven brothers, Samuel(me), Luke, Isiah, John, Exodus, Enous, Jakeob, Jared; and five sisters, Eliza, Esther, Eve, Mary, and Laura. I have a wonderful mother and father that love me. I know where certain types of trees grow, and how difficult they are to carve with. I know how long it takes to make something depending on the strength or density of the wood. Carpentry is exciting; I get to work with different tools to make things from tops and other toys to furniture, wagons, and houses. I sometimes get to work with blacksmiths.

My religion is very important to me in my life. I go to church, read the Bible and believe in God and his son Jesus Christ and his resurrection and the atonement. I'm very firm in my beliefs and stand up for what is right. I take part in both religious and political actions. I care very much about who the political government officials are in my colony. In my spare time I make and fix my clothes, dishes, candles, and soap. I sometimes have time to play games like Ninepins, Checkers, Chess Jacks, Cards, and Dominoes. When I start living by myself in a few years, I'm going to have to build my own house to live in.

~Samuel Gates~

Samuel Gates' Journal-Soldiers Living in My House

October 16, 1769

Today I was walking home from school, and found three soldiers standing on the doorstep of my house. I asked them what they were doing here, and they said that the king has given the colonists another act. This act does not include taxes, we the colonists have to invite in three British soldiers that are sent to our home, to feed and care for them; this act is called The Quartering act. If we do not obey this law, the British officer has the right to take over my property.

My reason for saying this is because my father is gone to Boston and while he is gone, I'm the oldest male in the house, I'm the man of the house; so I am in charge and own everything while he's gone. I have allowed the three British soldiers to stay with my family. The soldiers are kind, in some way they are making me nervous. I don't like the idea of them eating, and sleeping in my father's, my mother's and my bed. I do not know or understand why or how long they'll be here. Who knows what they'll do next. I wish they'd go away. I feel trapped. Just like a toad in a cardboard box.

~Samuel Gates~

The Signing of the Declaration of Independence

July 6, 1776

Earlier today I got the paper, it was sitting on my doorstep. When I looked down at the paper, I read the front page and it said that the Declaration of Independence was signed two days ago. I am so excited to think that now, after this war we, the United States of America, will be free from Great Britain. Just think, no more taxes, no more tyranny, and no more hardship. I talked about this to my folks last night at supper. My father got so angry, that he screamed his guts out and ran upstairs, slammed the door and did not come out 'til late in the morn.

Yesterday I was able to meet with Francis Lewis; one of the signers of the Declaration of Independence. I talked to him about what he and I felt was right, and what would happen to him and the others, if they got caught. I saw Mr. Lewis at the market, and asked them if I could speak with him tomorrow night. He replied, 'Yes, I will attend to that at eleven past six.' I then spoke to him.

This nation's government at one point was corrupt and crooked. I went through some tough times growing up. I truly think that this country will move forward, and progress, new things will be invented, people will grow, this nation will grow, and that our country will remain free until Christ comes again.

~Samuel Gates~

The Stamp Act

March 31, 1774

I am discussed that we have to pay taxes on contracts. This is probably the worst thing that has happened to me in my entire life.

Parliament has gone crazy, they don't listen to us, they won't listen to us, and we're being taxed like we have all the money, and we'll give it all to those dirty Brits. I'm a Whig; I hate those dirty Brits, I hate what they stand up for. I wish that those Brits would leave us alone. Besides, those Brits are nothing but raccoons that would run and hide inside a hogshead because of all these mobs.

~Samuel Gates~

We are at War

I think this resolution is great. Finally a war, and then if we win the war there will be no more taxes! I don't want a war though because I do not want young lives being lost. For all of the colonies, this war is great. For my colony this is great. My job might be a little worse because of the war, but besides that I will earn more money and be able to support my family better. If we lose this war, it will change my mind, and I will be miserable for the rest of my life; with all of these taxes. My friends, family, and others (not all others) feel exactly how I feel about the war, and us (the colonies) gaining our freedom. (If we win the war).

~Samuel Gates~

The Bloody Massacre Perpetrated in King Street

The Bloody Massacre Perpetrated in King Street?! That was a heck of a battle. So many died that it took a few weeks for us to find out if any of our family members were in the battle. When I found out who all died, I found that my uncle John died in that war; I told my folks, as soon as I could. My mother began crying, for my uncle John was her only brother; my father was so angry, he ran out the door, leaving behind his cap. Later I read in the paper that there was going to be a trial for all those soldiers. I was so happy to read the news about John Adams defending all of those soldiers. John Adams is a marvelous man. I would love to be as great as he is.

~Samuel Gates~

This is Mr. Revere's etching. I trimmed it from the Boston Observer.

The Tea Act

May 10, 1773

    I heard from my mentor that the King has now placed a new tax on tea. Now, this tax is small, but, this means that if the tax is small, colonists will buy more and more from Great Britain, which turns this small tax into a large tax. It's like a small tax is a large tax with a mask on. Parliament and the King are trying really hard to be slick and sneaky.

    I love tea. Why would Britain do this to us? I can't believe that those filthy Brits would tax us this much. Our relationship with Great Britain is falling apart; it's decreasing. You can tell that it is, you can see it happening, every day. We're breaking away from England, hooray! Hooray! This conflict will soon be over. There are some problems though, Great Britain's companies aren't being supported enough to run; So, if/when we break away from Great Britain we won't be paying taxes to "them" anymore, in which their companies lose money.

                     ~Samuel Gates~

The Intolerable Acts

June 29, 1774

    I was comin' home from work yesterday, when I turned the 'round the corner heard some kind of commotion goin' on. I couldn't see, so I asked some one standin' next to me, and he said he didn't really know either. From his understandin' and what he could see and hear what this mob was a shoutin', he told me that another one of those tax collectors was being tarred and feathered. When I could finally get a view, that poor tax collector was as colly as heck; and as feathered up as a chicken. I was a readin' the news paper two months later and some were in the middle, it said somethin' 'bout one of them tax collectors died from burnin' of tar and was later shot in a hospital with a fowling piece.

    Why does King George got do this to all us, we all got rights too. The Intolerable Acts are just too much. There have been too many acts comin' to us at once. You got the Boston Port Act on the 31st of March, the Administration of Justice Act and the Massachusetts Government Act on the 20th of May, and the Quartering Act a week ago from today. Boston Port and Massachusetts Bay is closed; which means we have less supplies. Soldiers will now only be tried by the Kings Bench and under English law, and no longer under our law or juries; instead, some of those trials will take place in the mother land. There's more; I am sad that King George doesn't know what's right. If he did we would have been taken' more care of. I love this country, I love America! And I will fight for my beliefs, and what I think is right.

~Samuel Gates~

Whittling With Wood

    Today all of the carpenters and cabin boys had a gathering. We whittled with wood, and carved what we wanted to into the wood that we whittled. The whittling and carving took some time. I made a stick with things carved into it for my Mom. We tied many different knots. My friend Levi and I taught everyone how to tie knots, because we studied them when we were younger and memorized how to tie them.

~Samuel Gates~

CHAPTER 27:

THE STORY OF A BLACKSMITH'S APPRENTICE

By: Billy VanMeter

Journal 1

Dear Journal,

February 1, 1774

Well the Sugar Act really does not hurt me. Today I was with Samuel Grates. He is trying to fight for the act to be removed. He did not like it at all because of the lumber tax. Since he is a carpenter, it makes his bills go up. Plus he is making a house for the doctor and his wife.

Journal 2

Dear Journal,

February 23, 1774

The Governor told the colonists that 3 solders will be living with us and that we have to feed and cloth them. My master told me all of that. Then about ten minutes later I started to worry that the solders were really coming and are coming to our house and our workshop. I am so scared that the solders will kill me if I don't work for them. I wonder if they will hurt my master or kill him. Do we have to make muskets balls?

Journal 3

Dear Journal,

August 8, 1775

I have fears that I will go home, and there is a war going on. I am scared of war because of the killing and I'm afraid Great Britain is stronger than the colonial army. Do I need a musket to be safe? I am scared to go to war because of the act. I wonder if the king sent the solders to kill all of the colonists.

CHAPTER 28:

MARY, A STRANGE GIRL IN NEW YORK

By: Melissa Lee

About Mary: A Cabin Girl Living In Colonial New York

Dear Journal,

Its September 10, 1751.The weather is hot and I'm starving. What I wouldn't do just for some fish. I could try begging but that wouldn't work. There could try stealing but, "I'd get in trouble for sure," I thought. I didn't listen, next thing I know I've stolen a peace of bread from the market. I ran for my life as the chase began. Running in and out of alleyways 'till I came to a dead end.

They said, "If you are going to steal like a boy you can work like one". That's how I ended up on this merchant ship as a cabin boy, I mean girl. Now I have jobs like mopping the deck and mending sails. I also have to clean dishes plus other jobs they don't want to do. Well it's better than living on the streets.

Love,

Mary

Some of My Fears

October 9, 1760

Dear Journal,

I was thinking if I'm a girl but I work on a ship, what am I suppose to do when I grow up? Will I be out living on the streets again? Probably not. Perhaps I might get a job? No, girls can't work like that. What if I get married? I'm so worried. What will I do? The only thing I know about sewing is to mend old clothes and sails. I have no idea how to do embroidery. I can clean though. That reminds me I have to go clean dishes.

Love,

Mary

Townshend Act

June 29, 1767

Dear Journal,

    I heard Captain Thomas talking about some riot. It was about a guy smuggling food or something. Our ship doesn't smuggle but I sure hope someone doesn't think so. This is the only home I've ever had. As for the soldiers, they better leave soon, even though they never bother me because I'm on the ship most of the time.

Love,

Mary

New Jersey

CHAPTER 29:

A BROTHER FOR A COUNTRY

The Story of Charity James

By: Lara Hoaglan

7 October, 1770 – About Me

Dear Journal,

I really do dislike the term diary. My name is Charity Isabelle James and I am now at the ripe old age of fourteen. If you do not understand enough to realize that I'm a girl than you have been informed. I was born on the 4th of January in 1756 in Cape May, New Jersey. My parents were thrilled.....at the time.

Having my eldest sister, Lydia, at ten and my only brother at merely three my parents decided to move farther away from the coast to a portion of land on the outskirts of Perth Amboy right after my birth. I really do wish my parents wouldn't have left Cape May for this, now small farming village, can be quite dull, especially after we lost Lydia.

Father is a wealthy doctor. He spends much time on his work and is known by many. He tries to be lenient and fair when someone is sick and has no money. His heart is in the right place.

I spend every waking moment mending Sarah, Hannah, Abigail, Rebecca, and Susan's clothing for they must be perfect. Because of this I have very little time to spend with Prudence or Joseph, my best friends. Or to see Mr. Swinoski, the general store owner. I am also often sent into town with Ben to get supplies or just for the fun. Our little village gets very little news at times.

Mother believes my other sisters will be proper young ladies......I on the other hand need work which I am often told and reminded in school and at home, even at church which we attend every Sunday. Mother reminds us also that it is why we our grandparents left Europe, to be Protestants. Father is the only one with an ounce of faith in me for not even I have faith in myself. No matter how often I am told I secretly do not wish to be a proper lady.

Recently mother decided I was quite smart enough to attend finishing school come next year but I do believe she thinks finishing school will force me to be a proper young woman. I will admit that I am quite intelligent. I hold on to things and can remember. I play piano better than any of my cousins and am quite fluent in French. But mother says it can cause more harm than good at times, especially in the case of my big mouth.

I am troubled at the thought of how little rights I have. Mother says it's not good to dwell on sinful thoughts, for a lady is what she is. My brother, Benjamin, can do little more than comfort me. Mother disagrees with me spending so much time with Ben. She thinks he is dragging me away from ladylike mannerisms.

Tomorrow shall be much the same, but who knows what a new day shall bring.

Until Again,
Charity James

26 October 1763: A Knock at the Door

Dear Journal,

I was alone at home this morning. I was fixing breakfast, which was normally Mary's job but it gives her time to practice reading, when there was a knock at the door. Naturally I opened it but to find a man and a couple of boys. I stood there for a moment before realizing who they were. I never expected a soldier to be so young.

The man must have been in his mid thirties, the elder boy looked to be about nineteen, and the youngest merely around fifteen. I invited them in and stood in awkward silence, for I had invited them to sit down, until Benjamin interrupted it. He called my name across the house, a habit we practice only when mother is not around, for he had entered through the back door.

He was asking what was for breakfast when he stopped mid sentence. He had seen the soldiers and with my favorite grin immediately shook hands with them and introduced himself and me. I learned the man was Adam, the eldest boy Noah, and the youngest Joshua. I dragged him by the arm sleeve into the other room, which happened to have been the kitchen, excusing myself and my brother in my haste.

"What is the meaning of British soldiers at our door?" I almost had whined.

Ben put his hand on my shoulder as though he were talking to someone dealing with a great loss, "Mother and Father didn't tell you but they are here to stay for some time Charity; we will be hospitable until the very time of their departure."

I was a bit afraid of the soldiers and hurriedly left the room to finish breakfast screaming "eggs," the reply to Ben's question. I thought long and hard while listening to the eggs sizzle, it really wasn't as bad as had taken it for. It wasn't like they had to stay in my room. They weren't really even staying in the house for they had chosen to stay in the barn.

Benjamin talked to the soldiers until I was finished cooking. They were obviously hungry for we ate breakfast in silence, they didn't have time to talk between bites. I showed them their quarters, the barn, and decided to go fishing with Ben in the creek before mother returned home to discover what my plans for the evening consisted of. For if it was up to mother I would have spent the rest of my day sewing.

We didn't catch much but Ben talked and I listened. He explained that he admired the soldiers for their courage but didn't think he would defend the British compared to the colonies, too many things had happened. He wanted peace but didn't believe British America was quite as mad about the price of tea as they seemed, things could always get better. I smiled and was thankful to be spending the afternoon with my favorite person in the world, though I could not say I thought things would just get better. I would find out the truth is that this was merely the quiet before the storm.

Until Again,
Charity James

9 November 1763: I Don't Want to Grow Up

Dear Journal,

Since the day of the arrival of the soldiers I have taken to cooking for myself and the soldiers as well, although like always, mother disagrees but it also comes as a help to Mary so she can practice reading, which I began teaching her only a few months after I began.

At first I was afraid but now I wish to know more of the soldiers. Adam does not talk for I do believe he does not wish to be here, the sneer on his face seems to tell me that much. Noah seems undecided but is respectful and thankful. Joshua is quite kind. He often talks to me although he's advised not to. He feels for America but England has provided. In two days Ben and I are traveling to town to get supplies and a new dress, I ripped mine fishing. I also had a request to pick up some sweets for my new friend which I am more than happy to do.

Lately I've been worried. I am fourteen and nearing fifteen every day. It shall not be long until husbands are being chosen. I am confused and scared because even though we do not have arranged marriages it is not common to marry someone out of your social class. Most men in my social class are snobs, wusses at that.

I was never nervous about what was expected of me until Lydia died, even though I disagreed with it. She and Ben were always there for me. Lydia more like a mother and Ben my best friend, and still is, but Lydia became very ill. We tried so hard to nurse her back to health but when it came to the day of her death I will never forget her words, "Death is not my fate for we all must face it, and death is my escape. In truth I am starting over not ending." I will never forget her memory.

This evening I went to Prudence's for tea and cakes and naturally includes sewing, which in turn generally pleases mother, one of the very few things that does. Prudence has much the same attitude as I but not the guts to show it. As we sewed we discussed finishing school next year and talked of the latest fashions which was more her than I for I care nothing for fashion.

To get home from Prudence's you must go through town. In doing so I passed the general store just as Joseph was leaving. He walked me home and spoke of how he too hungered for peace. He typically doesn't speak much but when he does it is worth listening to. He kissed my hand before departing leaving me at the fence that lined my house.

I often wonder why Joseph is my friend or, to be truthful, allowed to be my friend; he is not in the upper class. I do believe it a simple matter of fate for he had been my friend since I was just starting school. Father is great friends with his father, a farmer, and does not mind our friendship. I do not see him often but cherish every moment with him for he is much easier to talk to than Prudence, who makes a task out of it, and he is my age, unlike Ben, although I love my brother dearly.

Hopefully my anxiety will pass and God will answer my prayers and forgive me for my rebelliousness.

Until Again,

Charity James

17 November 1763: All That is Left is a Clump of Wax

Dear Journal,

Today we had to restock on candles. I really do enjoy it though my candles are merely great clumps of wax. I've been making candles since I was six when I was old enough to learn and not burn myself. It is a very simple process though it can be terribly time consuming.

You must first melt some wax in a pot. You then must wrap a string around a stick with three or more inches of string hanging off each side. When the wax is melted you hold the string portion under the wax for around 60 seconds. When the candle is thick enough you can begin to shape it and you then can cut the string to make a wick for each candle.

Candles are very sentimental to me for my grandfather enjoyed making them with me and Ben, although Ben thought of it as a waste of time and didn't attempt to go far in the art. Grandfather is the one that taught me how to make them, though he was much better at it than I. Now grandfather is gone and all I have left is his memory and the small bit of knowledge he was able to pass on to me.

Grandfather and I spent much time together. He was kind and generous. He loved adventures, crafts, and most of all exploring. He loved us grandchildren dearly but truly loved Lydia, Ben, and I for my younger sisters try to act as if grandfather's games are childish, even Susan whom was three at the time of his death. For I have no idea how such a gentle and kind old man raised a person like Mother. Grandfather was much like me; smart, rebellious at times, the only real difference is he would think before he spoke.

Until Again,

Charity James

10 April 1764: May Only be the Beginning

Dear Journal,

I do suppose this could turn out much, much worse in the end but we haven't come to that. We can deal with it when and if it comes. I will be a bit angry if the price of sweets has gone up though….they call it the Sugar Act.

Most aren't angry at the rise in taxes on sugar etc. They see that in doing this Britain claims more power than they deserve. As for me I won't judge until I have absolutely had too. My opinion isn't really that important anyway. I just hope we, the colonies, don't do anything rash. We *are* dealing with the mother country.

Father shows concern but not near as much as mother. He stays concentrated on his work, especially because of the time of year. I couldn't envision father doing anything other. He talks about the soldiers and the British but never once have I heard him complain of it all. I do pray for him and Ben.

Most lately things have gone by slow yet when I think about it, so very fast. I spend most days at Prudence's or working on the new dress mother had me start to keeping from spending so much time outside. She caught me riding a horse the other day. She was appalled. It was so hard to keep myself from busting out laughing at her expression.

We attended church on Sunday and while father talked to Joseph's father I talked to Joseph. I asked how he felt about the new act. He dislikes the British but expresses his feelings much different than most. He is just worried about how things are headed. He doesn't want a war.

At church I prayed for Britain, British America, and the so many of people out there doing so much worse than I am.

Until Again,
Charity James

30 May 1765: Out of Doors

Dear Journal,

I have had to take inventory of the paper to spare. It is slowly decreasing because of taxes. I realize how many things I do take for granted when I get most anything I need and in some cases just want. I slowly see the selfishness behind it all. I don't like to see myself as selfish but the truth must come out.

I use the most paper. Waste the most food, though Ben eats my leftovers. He is getting so big. I can only see his baby face behind his new set of muscles even though he's older than me. I struggle much with simply facing the small changes in life. The things I would have to deal with anywhere I lived, such as growing up or watching loved ones drift away from what you had always known them as. Another reason I am so very selfish, I complain about freedom of all things.

I am not free. I am pushed, dragged, spit upon by these acts. There are sure to be more of them. The Stamp Act. Trouble paying for paper, that's where I draw the line. Paper is my door to another world, my pen a key. You can not enter without a door. It is a world so very different from ours, a place to feel safe. Prudence's mother says as long as hope endures we shall endure. I will spend the rest of my day stitching up Abigail's petticoat,… and mother complains about me. Today I ask God for enduring hope.

Until Again,

Charity James

25 March 1766: Strangulation Can Be Found in Many Forms

Dear Journal,

Things don't sink in as easily with me as some. It seems they hit my cover and bounce off until I finally absorb it. This morning I awoke to a sunshine filled day. When I sat up and stretched I saw a note on my bed. It read:

Charity,

Once you're dressed come downstairs. We're going to town for a celebration with breakfast. The Stamp Act has been repealed! They have now issued the Declaratory Act!

Your favorite brother

As I said it didn't seem real. I dressed in my favorite yellow dress and ran down the stairs. Before I even saw it coming Ben had me lifted off the bottom step.

"Can you believe this Charity, it's been repealed. While we're in town I'm buying you 50 new sheets of paper."

We went to mother's favorite eatery and shop. I had the most delicious biscuits and bacon. Ben was true to his word to every last sheet. No more counting doors. I spent my evening playing games in the field near our house, even my sisters joined in. Things may make a turn for the better, and if not at least we have a moment to breath. Strangulation can be found in many forms. I am through with acts for now.

Father and Ben are thoroughly pleased. That makes me happier than anything. So I will enjoy my life while I can and enjoy my beautiful new sheets of paper. My prayers have been answered at last.

Until Again,

Charity James

25 June 1774: A Mess of a Mess

Dear Journal,

"You must make a decision sir-"

"Go! Go from this place! I must think."

"Sir, choices are becoming more urgent by the day."

I heard a deafening pound against father's desk as he reestablished that he had to think and for the man to leave the house.

My room is just above father's office but rarely do I ever hear that extreme a commotion, especially in the wee hours of the morning. For the outbreak had woken me. On very few occasions have I even heard father speak so abruptly.

Two questions entered my mind. What decision, and why was it so much more important than before?

After lying in bed for a few more hours I got dressed and I stepped lightly down the stairs as not to disturb. I saw my place set at the table where Mary had fixed my plate of breakfast. Mother was at the other end. I sat down at the table. I began to eat but noticed the silent atmosphere. I knew something was much more serious than I had estimated.

"What is wrong?" there was a moment of contemplation before she answered.

"You do understand some of the meaning behind these acts?" I shook my head.

"They have established the Intolerable acts," my puzzled look must have triggered her to go on, "Boston's ports are closed until the debt they owe is paid in full. All trials are to be held in the mother country, in doing this allowing no judicial fairness, though they aren't fair in the colonies either. The quartering act enables soldiers to take over a home if the barracks given to them aren't sufficient enough. They are also taking away our right of electing government officials."

I stared, as if in slow motion as my breakfast seemed to float to the floor. It seemed so unreal until I heard the awakening crack as the china hit the floor. A world put in chains overnight.

A few days later......

I pray so very often for Ben, father, Mother, and my sisters to somehow get us through this. Even though I'm angry I pray for Britain, the soldiers, and British America. I hope God can find a way to get us out without too much blood shed.

I don't bother going out much anymore. The news is so very monotonous. Anger, disbelief, those who believe we can make peace, those who think that there's no turning back. Our colony.... colonies are in desperate need of strength. Guidance wouldn't do much harm either. We must find some answer.

I want so much to be able to speak to Lydia. I need comfort, reassurance that we can make it through this type of crisis unscathed.

Ben is so frustrated there seems little I can do for him. He refuses to reason with me so I don't bother. I try to visit Prudence but it's so difficult to find a topic that's comfortable. It's on the top of everyone's mind.

Until Again,

Charity James

16 May 1775: Runaway Rock

Dear Journal,

I overheard them talking. I didn't mean to but once I started I was dragged in. I regret it so very much.

"Why can't I go? Things are awful in Boston."

"Things have been exaggerated. As word spreads things are changed."

"If it's not really that bad why can't I go?" I heard the penetrating silence. My heart began to run. "I will only be gone for a couple of months, if things aren't as bad as word may imply I will send word and be back in no time at all."

My heart absolutely stopped. The silence that filled the little sitting room below the stairs was deafening. Mother's silence meant she had had lost the fight. Ben would be leaving. The worst part about it was Boston *was* in trouble. What if something happened to him while he was there? Ben, my rock, my only sane security. I just couldn't lose him. On the other side Ben was being a good person. I'm so selfish; this certainly put the cherry on top of my selfishness and nosiness.

Now I have to live with myself. Everyday; thinking about it. Why didn't he talk to me about this? He didn't even give a hint of what his plans were. It seems every day Ben and I grow farther apart. Why has this happened? Day after day, prayer after prayer.

I went with father to Joseph's. Father enjoys speaking with Joseph's father. While they spoke Joseph and I sat out by the lake and the oak tree. I told him everything I'd heard. I trusted him more than anyone except Ben, but I just couldn't tell Ben.

"As long as God is there, he's watching over your brother. Don't fall apart, he's only going to Boston," we sat and listened to the rippling of the water until father came out and announced it was time to leave. They had given us some saved crops from last year. I will admit that I was still very nervous. I don't know when he'll leave but every second I grow closer to the moment.

Until Again,

Charity James

8 July 1776: The Beginning of the End

Dear Journal,

I couldn't believe it. To hear the words escape his mouth was so much more real. My mother began to argue but father stared her to silence. My sisters sat in silence sniffling, crying. I ran to my brother, as if holding him would keep him here with me.

He held me in his arms as the tears faded. I had known he was leaving though he didn't know I knew, but since my eavesdropping, things had changed. All of this was because of the Declaration of Independence. I don't want it now. I wanted freedom but to lose my brother isn't worth it. He would be gone for months or years as I sat in this house rotting away, waiting. My brother isn't a soldier, he's my brother.

He just couldn't leave. What if he didn't come back? I don't want to be what they now call and American, I don't want to be British either. I'm no one, I'm Charity. This isn't fair. I poured my heart out, pleading with God, don't take my brother.

NO! This isn't happening!

Until Again,

Charity James

12 September 1776: Maybe Forever

Dear Journal,

It's been months now. I couldn't tell you what happened. I sat, I sewed, and I ate only when forced to. Ben stopped in my room every day attempting to get me to talk. He spent most of his time in town or out doing something to get himself away from me. He didn't want to go back on his decision and spending anymore time than he must with me would have convinced him to do so.

We stood in the yard as I stared blankly at my family while they shared goodbyes with my only brother. When he got to me and my blank stare he stood. I didn't look up at his face; in fact my expression didn't change at all. He waited. Finally, I gave in and looked into his tear filled blue eyes as he stared down into mine.

"Take care of them for me," he reached down and gave me what might have been my last hug, "I love you, and if I shall die it is for you. Do not let me die in vain in your eyes."

A stifled sniffle escaped me. I didn't want to cry. I didn't want to remember things like this.

"I love you," the last words I may have said to him.

I stared blankly as he walked down the lane and out of site, maybe forever.

CHAPTER 30

LIFE OF A CABIN BOY

By: Austin Keith

About Me

I have stolen and sold a great deal of silver from the shop near by. My parents don't have the money to replace all of it. I heard them say they were going to sell me to pay for the silver carafes and other trinkets. Then a man with a cart full of vision was is front of the shack. They told me to go with him. I refused to go. They said it was for my own good even though they told me to steal all of it and they still have the money. Then I think my dad hit my in the head because I arose from my sleep to find myself tide up by the old meat.

Skills

The old man and I were traveling on a trail to port when he said, "My name is Vireos Timberlines and if you tell me your name and any skills you have I will untie you."

I replied, "Gorge Conner, and I can cook clean and steal".

"Hum," he said. "How'd you like to replace that last one with sowing?"

I said, "I'd like that."

"There's your new home."

When we got on the ship I was shown to my corner by a sealers cabin. Vireos said, "The captain will be by tomorrow to give you your orders. Get some sleep." Later after I was almost asleep Vareos came back to say, "These are some guards and they need to stay here. So suck it up for a week and do what you are told."

New Plans

I almost died cleaning the brig today by a crazed dog and it made me think of what I will became if I stay here. That's why I'm going to move back to New Jersey when I get done. I don't know what I'm going to do when I get there besides get a job and set fire to my parent's house. But I hope I can get a family that has a home with a dog without rabies.

Passing Time

I slept well last night and I thought the day to come was going to be better, but I ended up with nothing to do. Then along came one of the solders that lived on the ship from the week before. I thought he was going to harass me but instead he showed me a good way to pass time; it's called whittling. So I did that for a few hours until the captain told me to sweep the deck off and quit wasting time. After a few hours of that he had me scrub it until my fingers started to bleed. So I got to take a minuet break and I got back to work.

The Conflict

I'm pretty happy that the Stamp Act is over but the other townsmen are not because they say it means only one thing: another tax is coming. Besides, I have no house, or money, and I'm not the healthiest man alive, so not much more can bring me down.

I consider myself an American but I feel like a British colonist. I don't know why my family came here. They said we'd remain free like the other British men. But if you think getting taxed twenty times in your fifty to sixty year lifetime is freedom I'd hate to see what my aunt's personal servant feels like. I just wish I'd had stayed on the ship.

Someone come to me and asked me if the feud between Great Britain and the colonies will end. That's when I laughed and said we have always had issues and it will continue for hundreds of years to come.

Going Down the Drain

This notice is worst than the other one. It is even more unreasonable than not being able to take the pie they leave on the windowsill of other peoples' houses. King George is crazy if he expects us to pay for all this. I can barely pay for a fifth of some of those things.

We are all going to be poor if this continues I'm still paying my friend for the lumber I built my house with.

The End is Coming

I'm not a person that has a lot of stuff so I really don't care. But one thing I don't care much for is John Hancock having his ship confiscated. A lot of people got angry when they heard about it but the law is the law I guess and he broke it.

I wish I knew when the riots will end. That way I know it's safe to go outside without getting shot. And the resistance is almost as bad. Maybe if they'd be more delicate in there work? I wonder if there will ever be peace between Great Britain and the colonies. I doubt there will ever be peace in this world one day; everybody will kill each other.

A Little Get Together

Joy to the world or at lest me for today! I heard they are signing and announcing the Declaration of Independence by the Continental Congress. I still can't believe the declaration is complete.

I also got to meet Abraham Clark. He is one of the signers but he was not the liveliest of the men that signed it. I have a felling I'll sleep well tonight.

CHAPTER 31:

THE LOST JOURNALS OF SEAN W. HERON

By: Joe Coffey

About Sean Heron - NJ blacksmith

Hello, my name is Sean Heron. My hometown is Trenton, New Jersey. I am 24 years old. I was born on April 23, 1746. I am a very generous person; I am willing to forgive and forget almost anything. I was learned at my old master's house for 6 years. I am, according to my old master a very talented young man at a forge. I was raised as a Baptist. I have been married to my wife for 4 years, my mother and stepfather are still alive and so are my 2 brothers and my sister. The only other people I know are my old master and his family, and a few frequent customers.

Ornament

Today I made an ornament. The design was a mace and sword clashing together. To make this I had to etch out a design in the clay, melt the metal, and pour the metal into the mold. Then I let it cool. After that I took it out of the mold.

Sincerely,

Sean W. Heron

Whig

I think that these decisions will be good news and will definitely be for the best. I am a Whig. This is either a new beginning or the end. As for my colony I just hope that we make the right decision. I just hope it doesn't affect me. I am going to stand next to my colony through thick and thin. There is absolutely nothing that could be done to change my standpoint. The reason being, I am one hundred percent American! All of my friends and most of my family are all Whigs also.

Sincerely,

Sean W. Heron

Declaration of Independence

I am overjoyed at this excellent news. I mean, with the signing of the Declaration of Independence and all that. Now, what I found to be the best of all of this, was me getting to meet one of the signers himself, John Hart of New Jersey. He came to my shop after the 2nd Continental Congress asking me to make him a basin. He told me of all of the important events of the meeting, such as the signing of the document, which I was all in favor for at the time. But now that I look back on it all, I wonder, was all of this worth it? I mean, could we have become free for a lesser price, all of those precious lives lost, or did it have to be this way?

Sincerely,

Sean W. Heron

CHAPTER 32:

RICHARD WILLIAMS; A CARPENTER

By: Marcellus Edwards

About Me

I am Richard Williams. I was born in Philadelphia, Pennsylvania on November 19, 1755, my personality is what most people would call an average man's personality. A little fact you might want to know is that Pennsylvania is one of the most talked about colonies.

Like I said before my personality is what most would call an average man's personality, here's why. I sometimes show signs of bossiness especially to my boss because I love to work by myself. I'm very independent. I can be dependable at times but sometimes I can be forgetful. With this job I'm guessing you would think that I have strength. I get mad a lot at my boss because when he teaches me something new he likes to go step by step when I just want to try until I get it right. I guess you could say that's sort of a bad thing but its just who I am.

I would say I am not the most skilled person in the world, but I am good at the few skills I do have. One skill I have is that I'm good at math. Math is a major skill needed to be a successful carpenter, because you have to be able to measure the length and width and depth of the wood. Another skill I have is strength. I need strength to be able to lift wood and the creations once they are built. The final skill I have is creative thinking; I need this skill because when someone walks in and tells me to build something random I have to be able to think of something to build for that person.

I have a pretty large family. I have 2 brothers, 2 sisters, a mom and a dad. My brothers' names are Thomas & Jeffery. My sisters' names are Roneta & Jessica. My mom's name is Angie, and my dad's name is James. I also know the lumberjack, the market workers and keeper, and other carpenters.

Three soldiers

I think that the soldiers should not be forced upon us. Also they shouldn't say that we owe them I know they kept us from the Native Americans but they don't have to say we owe them like we are their slaves or something.

Also if our house isn't big enough to keep soldiers in our house and they take stuff away from us if we don't then that should make us not want them to protect us even if the Native Americans attack us

Hands On

The hands on activity was fun we got to carve wood. I didn't really make anything fancy I basically just carved away at the wood. I also cut myself on accident because the knife slipped off of the wood and my finger was supporting the wood where the knife slipped.

Fears

After a certain age I will own the carpenter shop. That scares me because I don't know if I am ready to take over a shop by myself. There's a lot of responsibility that comes with owning a store because when you have hired other staff you have to worry about how much to pay them and you have to remember to pay them every week. Another thing that scares me is cutting myself when I'm carving wood, I know it's apart of the job but it does not feel good at all. Another fear is knowing if there is enough wood to be able to make what people want. I won't need to worry about wood if I don't have a customer which is the scariest thing for any businessperson. So I need to be a good person to anyone who walks in here so they would want to come back.

Tea

I think that the British are serious this time when they lowered the tea prices. I know that other times they have done certain things to trick us into paying more taxes but this time I think they are trying to make amends.

Everyone knows the British have done a lot of things in the past that would lead people to not trusting them, and some people still don't trust them, in fact a lot of people hate them but I think they are tired of us destroying their property so I think they are going to be fair now about the acts they send out.

Intolerable Acts

I think the name "Intolerable Acts" is a very appropriate name for those particular acts. I think it is a very appropriate name because the acts really are "Intolerable" to some people. Like the "Boston Port Act" is just not fair because how are you going to ban any ships from leaving or coming in? If you do that then your losing money and its leaving us with less recourses so then we will have less money which will slow down your income because of taxes.

Rich Stockton

I met Rich Stockton. He's from New Jeersey. He came to the Second Continental Congress because he wanted to play a role in the Declaration of Independence. He was swayed to independence because he wanted to be able to live and not be ruled or be told what to do by another country. Back at home he is a carpenter too. He said it is not that hard of a job you just have to be able to measure and other mathematical abilities.

CHAPTER 33:

GEO'S JOURNAL OF LIFE

By: Kylee Standish

About Me

I'm a native girl. My expectations in life are to be a wife and a mother. To be a tribal wife, you stay home and cook, clean, and take care of the kids. Being a mom takes a lot of your time away from your work. You have to feed them, change them, burp them and more stuff than regular work. I think I only want one kid, a boy.

The wife part is a little scarier. I want to marry and have kids with him. I want to just be what I'm supposed to be. Well I'm just a teenager right now so I would just like to think about other stuff besides that. I will wait a few more years for that!

The Unexpected Guests

Dear Diary,

Today has gone great but two British soldiers showed up. They looked hungry and tired. I am afraid and scared that if we don't help them they might betray my family, and who knows, if we don't the government could do even worse to us. Well now that we know them better I kind of changed my mind but I still have a few bad thoughts about them.

Leather Making and the Story About My Piece

We made stuff out of leather! I made a headband and a bracelet. I used the colors brown and black for the bracelet. The bracelet has my grandma's name on it.

I got the headband from my friend's mother but I put the story about my friend on it. The story goes like this… Her grandma gave it to her mom and her mom gave it to her on her 13th birthday. Last year on the 19th of July she and I were walking to the market. There was a shooting. She was shot 3 times in her stomach. Her mom gave the headband to me to remember her. I will always remember her forever and ever!!!

Here is how you make your own bracelet or headband:

 step 1) you pick out a piece of leather

 step 2) then you start thinking of what you want to make and how to tell the story.

 step 3) then you decorate it with designs

 step 4) then you tell your story and you are finished

Tea Act

Dear Diary,

 Oh my, my. There is a new notice. It is the Tea Act. It is lowering taxes. Now we can get new clothes for school. And can eat lunch there too.

 When we went to the store I bought a used dress and an apple, so I can look nice at school, and eat. Maybe I can make some new friends. I'm so, so glad taxes went down and I got new things. Thank you for everything lord.

 Now I'm home from school. I made three new friends, and a boy blushed when I sat next to him. He was cute. I think he likes me. I'm glad I got new stuff. I can't wait until we go shopping again.

Geo

The Four Notices

 Oh my goodness! There are four new notices! Oh wow, I must go tell father. What will he say about all these new notices? I hope he is not mad.

 I ran up to him out of breath and said, "Father, Father!"

 "What?" he said.

 I said, "There are four new NOTICES."

 "Which ones are they?" he asked.

 I said, "There are the Boston Port Act, the Quartering Act, the Massachusetts Government Act, and lastly, the Administration of Justice Act."

 "Oh wow," he said when I finished telling him.

I asked my father what all of them mean. He said to me, "It is hard to explain but I'll give my best shot. They are different in very many ways but simpler at the same time. Tell me if you get confused. Well, we will go one at a time. We will start with the Quartering Act. His Majesty's troops need places to stay. This means people have to give up their house if there isn't any other place, or the soldiers will take it over until they leave.

The Boston Port Act is happening because of the Quartering Act. The people are done being told to give their house up and being treated like crude slaves. They are through. So that is what all the commotion in town is about. So that is what The Boston Port Act is.

Now The Massachusetts Government Act is problem the simplest one. It is where the British are electing a new government. I'm told that one was the easiest."

"But why would they want a new one?" I asked.

He said, "That one just didn't cut the job. So we are down to our last notice. The Administration of Justice Act. Well my child that is all of the Notices."

"THANK YOU father for telling me what the notices all mean. Now I know what all of them mean.......for this week!"

Resolution of Congress

Dear Diary,

Today I went to town and I overheard to men talking about the resolution of congress. I ran home and told mother what happened, and she said that she went up to the school house. I asked her what for and she said that she wanted to se how I was doing. She told me that the teacher gave her and I a letter saying that I need to write a paper on being a Tory or a Whig.

I think it is nice for us to say something like this and it is taken into consideration and not just getting thrown to the side. I like that we get to have an opinion now. We also have to pick a character who is a Whig or Tory. I pick Whig, because he is on our side.

The Second Continental Congress

Dear Diary,

The Second Continental Congress signed the Declaration of Independence.

Independence. Does that mean we're FREE??? That day I went home and asked my father how he felt about it and what he thought about it. He said he thought it was great and jumped up out of his seat. I suppose that covered what he thought.

My father asked what I thought about it. I said, "I don't quite know yet. What do I think about it? Well, I think I feel like I should talk to someone who was there and signed it."

"What about Gorge Ross?" said my father.

So I went to talk to George. He told me he did what was best for his family!!! We have different expectations in life as of now because we are FREE!!!

Geo

CHAPTER 34:

PATIENCE –
DAUGHTER OF A GENERAL STORE OWNER

By: Shelby Ellis

About Me-Patience

My Christian life started on June 15 1756! I live with my mother and father. I have a little sister. We live in New Jersey City. I go to school. I'm in 7th grade. I work at the town store. I sell all kinds of things, but my main items are apples and milk. I also do all the work by myself.

I grow and pick all the apples I milk all the goats. Today I made 20 cents, everyday this boy name Jake comes in he always gets one bucket of milk and 2 apples. I think he is so cute, but I'm too scared to talk to him. Because anything could happen like I could try to talk to him and nothing would come out, then I would fell dumb. He lives with just his dad. I don't really know what happened to his mom. Me and my best friend Jessie wonder if that's why he if that's why he won't talk to anyone.

But I bet if we talked he would be very sweet. I gotta stay up and sew my little sister's bear and shoes it takes forever. Then in the morning I have to make papa breakfast, then I gotta get ready for school and then I go from school to work.

Well that's all,

-Patience

Whittle

Today I got to whittle I didn't really know what I was doing but this Native American showed me a few tricks and trick. He showed me how to crave my stick into something. I wanted to crave a heart. He also told me that I have top push the knife away from me so I don't cut myself. If you take small chunks instead of bug chunk it's easier and it looks better.

The Native American name was Junwopa he was very kind and every thing. I said he had a store for it. He was very detailed.

Well that was my day.

-Patience

3 Soldiers

Today at dinner my parents informed me that we are having 3 British soldiers live with us. There 32 and two of them are 34. They are in the living room with my parents. I'm a little shy to talk to them or see them.

Today Jake sent me a letter. I was so happy to see that I got a letter from him. I was just thinking why would he write me? I opened it to find out he was moving, moving to Connecticut. I felt my eyes water up. I dropped the letter and ran out side to see if he was still there. I didn't know what I was going to do! When I saw him I ran as fast as I could. I found him waiting by my store. I said, "Jake can I help you?"

He said, "Oh no I was just getting one last look before I left."

I said ok and he grab my hand and said, "Patients I have always liked you." My heart was beating so fast but I could hear his dad yell for him.

I told him goodbye and before he let go of my hand, he gave me a kiss on my cheek. I walked home and my parents didn't even notice I was gone.

I walked into the living room and saw the three soldiers. One was tall with brown hair; he looked as if someone upset him. The other two looked like brothers short and plumed. I told them my name and shook their hands. I told them that dinner would be chicken and tomatoes, and with corn for dessert would be apple pie. After we got done eating I showed them where they would sleep. Mia and I have to sleep together. One of the soldiers slept on the couch and the other two slept in my room.

I have to open my shop early and try to make as much money as I can. Feeding three big soldiers is very hard. I have to make a buffet every night. Then I have to wash all the dishes I used, I don't go to bed until about 10 pm. Then I have to get up very early and open my shop. I have to help Mia with her math. Then ill start dinner. I'm really tired, I'm gone make me some milk then getting to bed.

- Patients

Fears

Today me and my husband talked and planned out our futures. We both said that two kids would be good. We would love a boy and a girl. They would be so much help.

I'm scared that we won't have enough money or food to feed and buy for our family as a 13 year old I worked at the town store until I was 22 then I tried to become a school teacher. I haven't got the job yet I hope I do.

I'm just scared that they wont listen to me or they won't want do their work. Or, I'm scared I will take it to easy on them so they think its ok to not do their homework or their work, I think they will think I'm to nice to yell or something. I don't know, I guess we will see what happens.

I hope we just have all the things we need to help our family. My kids will have the best education I can give them.

That's all I have today.

-Patience

Taxes

Today was not like most! We got a ton of notices. They were all different. I didn't like the one where you had to get the Majesty involved. I think Boston screwed up big time. How are they going to pay for all the stuff they broke or destroyed? I hope they think of something.

Smuggling

I don't think John Hancock should be able to smuggle. All he's going to do is start a riot. I'm scared and afraid of what might happen over there. I think people are going to do it because they agree with the law and some people are doing it because he is popular!

That's really all I have to say about John Hancock.

Declaration of Independence

The Declaration of Independence is a big thing. If I was a signer I would be very happy I'm doing something for my country. I think we should have it because I don't want take orders from someone else. I think we should have a free country.

If I was a signer I would have felt scared and thinking of how many people would be mad at me if I did the wrong thing they have a lot of courage!

Pennsylvania

CHAPTER 35:

OLIVIA'S LIFE

By: Taylor Vanover

Me and My Family

Dear journal,

Hello, my name is Olivia. My birthday is 6/17/50. My home town Philadelphia is. I am 17 and I am a female. My dream is to do a surgery and to become a doctor. I think my personality is inquisitive and I am a lot different from most girls. Thanks to my father, I have skills in doctoring, nursing, and minor surgery.

I am a Quaker. My mom is Sarah, my dad is Thomas, my sister is Destiny, my husband is Matthew, my son is Paul he is only a couple weeks old.

Just Another Day in Many

Dear journal,

My son and husband both need me now. I have to take care of them as well as myself. My son, Paul, is only two weeks old so he is a lot of responsibility. Also I am not back to normal yet from the pregnancy. I am so glad I have a son with my husband.

Matthew is now working for the government in Philadelphia. He is very happy with his job so am I. We are so happy we have a son and when he gets older we have a lot of expectations for him.

Although I am a mother and a wife I am also trying to become a doctor. But it is very hard because a woman doctor just doesn't happen. But, I am very happy with myself and so is my husband. It is so neat to be a mother and a wife. I love my son Paul and my husband Matthew.

Creativity at Work

Dear journal,

Today, I made candles. I had to take a clean piece of wick and turn it into a candle. It's really neat. You have to get a block of wax and melt it. Then you take the wick and dip it into the hot wax for about 3 seconds and then you hold it in a bucket of water for three seconds. You keep doing that till you get it the size you want it. Then you can take and turn it into a design. After all of that you let it dry for about 18 hours. Then you are done.

The Townshend Act

I think that the Townshend Act is really foolish. I think that the British are trying to make us mad. I think my husband's friend, John Hancock, will be extremely upset because that he ships paper, glass, lead, tea and paint from Britain so he will be taxed more. I think that if we can stop buying all of the items for a while and maybe it will get better. Some of the other colonies might do the same but I really don't know. But as for me and my family we are trying our best to make it through all of this.

The Tea Act

I believe that the Tea Act is really not as bad as people think that it is. I really believe that the tea act is really good for us as a whole but I do not trust the British very much at all now. I think that government is trying to trick us. A lot of people are so worried that this is going to hurt us as a whole.

I am really not as people think that I am. I am not the kind of person that can take a lot of stress at once. But in a way I am so glad that I was born in this time period and I get to experience all of this in my life. I look at this as if it is a good thing instead of a bad thing. A lot of people say that this is foolish but personally, I AM TIRED OF IT ALL. I am so excited that I am alive in this time as well as my son so he can see a very big part of history.

The Intolerable Acts

The Intolerable Acts somewhat refer to me because that I am somewhat close to Boston. But they are making me very upset because we have had four different notices given to us in a very short amount of time. I also agree with all of the acts being called the Intolerable Acts. To me, my colony and I are more with New England than its "mother country" as a whole. My son and husband are proud of me because that I can deal with all of this and be pregnant.

Surprise

Dear journal,

I am in so much pain right now, but I am putting that aside and I am just focused on having this baby. I am so excited and so are my husband and Paul. I am just overwhelmed. There are all kinds of emotions running through my head.

later

I have a new baby GIRL. I am so glad that I get to have a little girl to take care of. Our son is our little angel. But our daughter is our little bundle of joy. Her name is going to be Julia. My husband and I are so glad that we have another child. We do plan on having about two more. We are very excited.

Declaration of Independence

Dear journal,

I believe that the Declaration of Independence is so good for the colonies as a whole. I am so excited for my family and my friends. We are finally going to be free. I was actually at my friend's house and they were talking about it and I just started crying and couldn't stop. So I left and ran home as fast as I could and told my husband, he was so excited.

Later on that night we went to my parent's house to celebrate and have dinner. My husband is so glad as well because that the government can not hurt us with taxes anymore. My father is excited, probably as much as I am or even more. I am speechless. This is something that I will remember for the rest of my life. It will be a mark in my life that I will tell my children about.

The Signer of the Declaration of Independence and Member of the Second Continental Congress

I am also excited because that I actually get to meet one of the many signers of the Declaration of Independence. I want to ask him how he felt about the sighing of the Declaration of Independence. I want to ask will it be worth all that he and we will go through for this and also how his family feels about everything he is going to put them through.

CHAPTER 36

A NATIVE AMERICAN GIRL IN COLONIAL TIMES; THE STORY OF AKUE BONUE

By Samantha McDonald

About Akue Bonue

My name is Akue Bonue. I am 15 years old, my birthday is 8/6/1752. I live in a Native American Village. I have two brothers and five sisters plus me and there names are Tim, Robert, Bre'Aja, Amanda, Monue, Avue, and Ashley. My personality is that I am caring, loving, kind, nice, helpful to people who need the help.

I love when my parents teach me about how our tribe works and how to catch dear to skin them. I like to read and write. My most talented skills are braiding hair and drawing designs on people skin. My religious values are that my tribe believes in God spirits and regular spirits. We think spirits are all around us and they protect us.

The people I know that live near me are the people in the town. There is the blacksmith, the library man/woman and the school teachers. My friend Mya Napier lives in a tepee right next to me and we hang out a lot. We go fishing for food and we gather wood for the fire that we build in the circle. Mya and I do everything together; we are the closest friends ever. There is no way we will get split up. I love hanging out with her, it is so much fun. I love writing in my diary everyday.

From, Akue Bonue

British Soldiers

Dear Diary,

Today was a great day but there are three tired and injured British soldiers here and they want food and shelter. I do not know what to do because I feel like if we do not let them in and take care of them until they are better they might have the government hurt my family and might hurt me. The soldiers look like they were fighting to the death and they were not giving up. They had shaggy, ripped clothes and they were all bleeding.

They chose my family because we were the first teepee they went to. I told my family to let them in because I do not want anything to happen to my family or anyone else. We do not know when they are leaving but I hope they leave soon and get better. The reason I think that is because everyone is acting really weird because they are here in my teepee. I think it is really scary because no one knows what they are going to do after they get better. We all think they might hurt us after they feel better. Well I think they will leave soon.

From, Akue Bonue

My Fears

Dear Diary,

Today my mother wanted me to go to her work with her and help her wash the white people's clothes that were dirty. She was telling me to go get the hot water for her to wash their clothes. After I got the hot water we started to wash them the water hurt our hands because it was so hot. I thought I was going to cry because it hurt me.

My mom and I were talking about what I am going to do when I get older. She was telling me that I might have to work in the fields all day, but I do not think I can work in the fields all day long and every day of the week. That is my biggest fear ever; to work all the time for   my whole life. I hope I will not have to work only in the field. I hope I get to work in other places too.

I think I can change her mind about me working in the field. I plan to address them by doing other work and sit my mom down and tell her I do not want to work in the fields all day and every week of my life. I can find something else to do for the rest of my life. I think my mom wants to help me out when I get a little older and so I can have a job and help out my family out by getting the crops.

I do not think I can face my fear by working all the time. I want some time to myself so I can take care of my family. I hope I will face it and work not all the time but most of my time. That is my story for today I will write you later diary.

From, AKUE BONUE

My Product

Dear Dairy,

I made a headband today. The process I used to make my headband was that I grabbed some leather and I put some designs on it so it can make a story and so I can tell the story to everyone. I put a feather on it because I helped a hurt eagle. The story to my headband is that the dog that is on the headband represents the wolves that attacked the village. The sun is talking about how bright my village is and that it is also talking about what I work under every day of the week. The feather is really special to me because I took care of an eagle that was hurt and I took care of it until it felt better and it could fly.

From, Akue Bonue

What is Happening

Dear Diary,

Everything that is happening is so wrong because it is going to be hard for the people who do not have the money to buy the food or supplies they need to live. I think they should keep everything the same and do not change anything. I do not like how we, the Indians, have always trade because we cannot get a job to pay for anything, I want us to get jobs too. But I like that we get to trade and not buy because we get to make the stuff and trade it to the people and they love it. But if we cannot trade any more everyone would be sad. I do not want them to be sad because they will not get our beaded necklaces or our leather fur coats that we make for them so we can get supplies that we need.

By, Akue Bonue

The Townshend Act: John Hancock

Dear Diary,

I think that the action of the British and the colonials are kind of good and kind of bad because they show us what we do not do. The impact I think will be on the tea and paper because of the man named John Hancock. I see a lot of solutions that go on mostly around the town and sometimes in my village.

I think my family and friends want to help the Great Britain and my colony too. I think some of the town people wanted to help out because it would effect them a lot, so we should let them help out too because it effects them the most.

By, Akue Bonue

Raising the Taxes

Dear Diary,

Today we found out something bad. The something was that they raised taxes on everything because of the tea problem that happened. I think that they should lower them, not make them higher or keep the prices as they are so people can buy them. It is going to be really hard for the Indians to get anything they need because if they raise the food and other stuff we would not be able to get anything because we do not have money we trade for what we need. They might not let us trade because there are not getting a lot of money if they trade with us. That is my big reason why I do not want them to raise the prices. I also think that the people who dumped it should have to pay taxes not everyone because we, the Indians, did nothing to the townspeople.

By, Akue Bonue

The Boycott of Great Britain

Dear Dairy,

I think it is ridiculous that they are trying to make us do the stuff that we do not want to do. I am having a lot of trouble because of the boycott that is going on. I am standing way, way, way far away; well at lease trying to. My opinion is that it is wrong and ridiculous for them to do that. I think it well effect us a whole lot more because it involves Great Britain and a lot more. My tribe is particular in this because of everyone. I stand up for myself and others I help do stuff they can not do. There is only one way that I will change my mind it is that if they stop all the notices. It will help us a lot more. It compares to everyone that I know because they all think that to and they are mad and very worried.

Akue Bonue

Declaration of Independence

Dear Diary,

Today we just heard that the Declaration has been made. My tribe doesn't know anything about the Declaration of Independence. So when they heard that they were confused. So I had to explain it to them what it was and I got to meet a signer that got to sign it. I thought that was neat that I got to and no one else from my colony got to.

The circumstances of meeting him were outstanding because he talked about what they had to do. He talked about the speeches they had to give and they talked about the singing they did and how they did it. I thought it was neat that they got to sign for our colony.

I think our colony has changed lot and we all like it this way because we don't have to listen to the king or be rolled by the crown. We all think the people are acting themselves again. Yes, that is a good thing I think it is great.

Akue Bonue

Selling to the Town

Dear Diary,

This is what happened after the Declaration of Independence happened. Today was an okay day. We got to go to the town and we traded some of our beaded necklaces to the town people. I thought I was going to faint because a lot of people wanted our beaded necklaces, they thought they were so good looking. They wanted to give them to people they know so they would get a lot like 10 to 20. We were so happy and tired because they loved them so much. They traded us food and supplies for them so we had a big wagon filled with supplies for our tribe.

When we got back there with the supplies that we got from trading with the townspeople, they were so excited because we got a lot of stuff for them to use like blankets, string, food, cups and so much more. They all asked how we got it. We said we traded beaded necklaces for all of it we sold all most 100 of them to them. We told them that they said they wanted more, but different not the same like the ones they got now. They thought they were so pretty that they want more. So I told them we should get to work so we make them happy they all laughed and so did I; we have a lot of fun making them and telling jokes to each other.

Akue Bonue

What Went Bad!

Dear Diary.

I am so proud that my tribe is hanging in there because of what happened. There was something bad that happened after the Declaration of Independence signing. One of the people in our tribe passed away and he was very young; he was only 7 years old it was his birthday when he died November the 20th. Everyone is so sad even me because he was so young. He wasn't apart of my family but he was new to our tribe they just moved from their old tribe that said they do not belong.

Their mother is very, very, very, very upset about it. The dad really did not care. He told her that they will just have another one so it can replace him.

His name was Damon; he had an older brother named Marshell who cared about him a lot. After I heard what the father said I was even more sad than anyone because I was the only one who heard him say that to her. So I talked to Marshell to see if he was okay and he said yes, but he will miss him a lot. But after all that happened Marshell asked me out and I said yes I would like that a lot. He was very happy so he walked me to my teepee because I was by the fire my family built for the tribe. My parents love to do stuff for our tribe.

Akue Bonue

CHAPTER 37:

FROM THE JOURNAL OF SARA TAYLOR

By: Stephanie Taylor

About Me

Hi! My name is Sara Taylor. My hometown is Philadelphia. I am 13 years old. My birthday is June 30, 1775. I live with my mom, dad, brothers, and sisters. My dad's name is Jody, he works out in the fields at our house. I am a farmer's daughter. My mom's name is Julie. I have 2 brothers and 2 sisters. My brothers names are Zach, and Josh. My sisters' names are Alica, and Stephanie. They are nice, but sometimes my brothers, my sisters, and I don't always get along. My mom doesn't like that. My dad gets mad, but he only grounds us. He never whips us, because he is afraid that he will hurt us.

I am very educated. I go to school, only because we can afford it. We all go to School. My mom teaches us all the stuff she knows, so we can get better in school. I am in the 7th grade. I can sing, farm, and work very, very hard. When we are not in school we work very hard in the fields. I also help my mom out around the house.

I can also make friends very easily. I am very nice and sweet when I want to be. Just don't get on my bad side, and you will be fine. I am a very outgoing person, and I am a good person.

I am a Quaker and a Christian. I go to church and hangout with my friends when I have the time. I love going to church and worshiping, and giving praise to the lord God. Today I am going to help my mom out with the housework. I love helping out with the housework, and the fieldwork. It makes me feel so good inside when get to go outside and work and inside with the work. I know a lot of people at my school, my church, and the people in my family, the shopkeeper, the innkeeper, the doctor, and the doctor's daughter. I have to go now my family is waiting for me, and they want me now.

From the Journal of Sara Taylor

Strange Visitors

Today is the day where the secret visitors from the government are coming. Then they finally arrived here. We were dressed in our best. Are three of them. Their names are Blake, Joe, and Kevin. Blake is from Philadelphia, Pennsylvania. Joe is from Erie, Pennsylvania. Kevin is from Pittsburgh, Pennsylvania, but I am not going to fall in love with them.

The government said that they have to eat our food, and stay – sleep in the same house as us. If we don't do it, the government will put our father into prison for a very long time. My mother made everything nice and neat. My father, however, wasn't very happy. He was very upset. As soon as they arrived, my brothers, my sisters, and I were down stairs waiting for them to come in and become apart of our family. They were 18 year old soldiers. They are really cute.

We were not happy either. Joe was very positive, and happy that he was going to be staying with us. Blake was very proud, and negative about staying with us. Kevin was very mysterious. He had a weird sort of likeness to him. I told my mother that they should stay in the barn. She said that they would sleep in the living room. They said that they would be staying here for 3 years with us. I told them that they most be joking. They were not joking.

I was upset, but my sisters were not upset. They liked them very much. I was quite taken by Blake, but he was rude, selfish, and prejudiced. He might be good-looking, but he needed to be nicer. I told my mom that we don't have enough food for all of us, and them. She said that we do have enough food for all of us and them. She also said that we will just have to not have sell our food to other people until the government tells the soldiers to leave. My feelings are that I am very upset about them staying, eating our food, and taking over the whole house.

It has been 2 years and almost all the food is gone, and all the money is almost gone. The soldiers have been very kind to us, and so has the government.

Blake has been very nice to all of us, since he been here he has been very generous. My sisters, Kevin, and Joe are very happy because they date, and the soldiers now have something to fight for. Blake finally asked me out, and I said yes. Now he has something worth fighting for. My thoughts have changed a great deal. They are free to use our home and resources when ever they want to. The soldiers are leaving today. It has been 3 years, and I am glad that they came. I have to go now. Talk to you later.

From The Journal of Sara Taylor

A Scary Situation

Today after breakfast my parents told me they wanted me to stay in the living room to have a little talk. This was new they never asked me to stay and have a little talk before. I knew it was important because I could see it on their faces, they just have this look that you would know was important. They want me to marry someone. They said that the guy I was going to marry was coming over to the house after lunch. They told me the guy they wanted me to marry was my third cousin. My parents told me that they were rich, and was a very good match for me.

I was very nervous, a little angry, and I had a lot of fear. I was full of questions. Some of my questions are, dose he want kids? Did he have a farm? Would I even like him? Would I think that he was cute? Is he nice, mean, proud, or rude? My last question is would I even like his family, etc? I had so many thoughts in my head the whole morning. My fears are not being able to farm, would he make a good 1st impression, would I like him, having kids with a total stranger, leaving my home and family, and if I rejected him would my parents hate me.

Finally he arrived. He was really cute. He was very nice. He looked very nervous, which made me feel better. Then he started blushing at how pretty I was. It made me feel like maybe this would workout okay. He told me that they had a farm. He also told me that he was rich, and that I would be well cared for. He said that his family was very anxious to meet me, and that made me feel better too. His family wanted to meet me next week. They would also send a carriage for me. They also said that my sisters could come too. My soldier was very mad that I was going to marry my third cousin. He said that he didn't agree with arranged marriages. Then he asked me to marry him and I said, "Yes".

The Journal of Sara Taylor

Hands On

Hello again! It has been a while since I have talked to you. I made a bracelet today. The color is a really cool tan. It has my name on it, which is Sara Taylor. It some Indian designs on it. It has a sun, water, a statue, and some others that I can't remember right now. I am in the living room, and it is in my room right now. I am going to show you in steps. There are 3 steps.

Step 1: I put my name on it. I used a hammer, a silver tool, and letters to put my name on it.

Step 2: I made some holes in it to put string in it, and put beads on the string.

Step 3: Then I added some Indian symbols on it. Then you are done.

I was walking through the woods one day. Then I found this weird looking bracelet. It had my name on it. It also had some string through it with some beads on the string, and some creepy symbols on it. I finally found the Indian tribe that made it. I told them thank - you for making it for me. They told me you're welcome. I told them that I had to go. They told me that I was welcome back any time I wanted to come back.

From The Journal of Sara Taylor

Intolerable Acts

The Intolerable acts are the Boston Port Act, the Massachusetts Government Act, the Administration of Justice Act, and the Quartering Act. My reaction to the new acts was that I felt sorry for everyone who has to pay those taxes. Like so many of the other notices I just couldn't stop crying for some of the stuff that we have to pay for. It will affect us greatly; we have so much to pay in so little time to pay it. We have more taxes to pay and we are not going to be able to elect our government officials.

I do agree that the taxes are not very reasonable, because we already have enough taxes to pay. I think people are siding with Boston and New England, because they are really upset with all of the bad news and all of the new taxes. They are also not very happy with the crown and the government right now, because they're really being unfair and unkind. They really need to be fair and kind, because we need money to feed our families. If they don't answer to our wishes they will have a full uprising on their hands.

From The Journal of Sara Taylor

Townsbend Act

I view the actions of both the British and my fellow colonials very badly. I am very disappointed in both sides they know what they did was wrong and yet they did it any way. I am very disappointed in the Massachusetts colony for tarring and feathering that poor inspector. He was only doing his job. They should be ashamed of themselves. The King will probably punish them for that.

I believe that the impact from resistance to British authority by men like John Hancock will be great. I find that very disappointing. John Hancock had no right to stop a man from doing his job. I see no solutions to the conflict now or in the future. No, my solutions have not changed from the prompt. I think fellow colonials like me who don't agree with what our fellow colonials and colonies are doing. I think that we can stop the argument, because we can talk to them and try to change their minds about what they are doing is wrong.

I just don't want my fellow colonials and colonies to be punished or put to death. Maybe they will finally listen to us. If they don't listen to us then we will stay out of it. They will get what is coming to them. Then they will learn to listen to us next time that we are right.

From The Journal of Sara Taylor

Boston Massacre

We have just heard about the killings in Boston last night. We heard it in class today. It happened on March 5, 1770. It also happened at night. I was asleep when it happened. It was really strange I had a dream about it when it was happening. Good thing nobody in my family was there when it happened. I live in Pittsburgh, Pennsylvania. Pennsylvania is not far from Massachusetts.

My reaction to the news was not good at all. I started crying for the people who were killed and for their families. They started it and they knew that they were going to die or be injured. I also feel sorry for the soldiers who were injured and all of the soldiers that are in jail. I don't think that captain Preston told the soldiers to fire. I hope that all of the soldiers are not guilty of murder.

My family and friends agree with me even though they are mad too. I don't think that this will have any affect on my life. I do think that it will affect me emotionally for everyone.

I think that men like John Adams that are willing to defend the British actions are very hard working, kind, and willing to be yelled at and other things is really life giving. He is very brave and smart. I also have a lot of respect for men like that, because they can make a very big difference in the world. They can do anything. I also heard that he won his argument and saved the soldiers.

From The Journal of Sara Taylor

2nd Continental Congress

I love my job. I also love my boss. My boss is very nice and is concerned about what is going to happen. I love my school. I also love my teacher. My teacher is very nice and concerned about what is going to happen. She is very kind. My teacher has just given us some letters that the continental congress has written to the king and his men. I am finally done reading all these letters that people are sending to his majesty. When all of us were done we all talked about it.

On the way home my friends and I talked about what happened. We all agreed about what they were talking about. They were kind of nice in the way that they wrote their letters. One man said dear sir in his letter. They wrote to the crown because they wanted the intolerable acts to be repealed. The crown never responded back to their letters. So they started getting angry with the crown so they had a second meeting in my home town of Philadelphia.

I don't like the war that is going on right now. They are acting like little kids. I think that the resolution needs to stop and put an end to all of this death and sorrow. It is going to tear the colonies apart.

As a farmer's daughter I think that it will affect my family and our pay will go down on our cash crop. So, I stand with George Washington and his men. There is nothing that can be done to change my mind about the issues, because I am an American, because I have really transformed from when I was working for the king. I will never work for the King again. The King has treated my people badly. So, I will stand with George Washington and his men as long as I am still breathing. My friends, family, and neighbors agree with me, because they are true Americans too.

From The Journal of Sara Taylor

Independence

My day was okay. We have just heard about the announcement and the signing of the declaration of independence at work today. I am scared and excited about Independence. I am scared, because the signers and their families could get hurt. King George will not be too happy about the idea about independence from his country. He will probably send his British soldiers to do his nasty business and it won't be too pretty. I am happy that we finally get Independence from the mother country.

They have treated us very poorly and badly and they deserve it. I think that I have met some of the signers once or twice. The meeting was really, really good. We discussed everything that is about to happen.

My life has changed tremendously from when I was 13. I am now 25. I remember all of the notices and all of the fights that have gone on between my colony and the British soldiers. My colony and I have now changed ever since we have heard of the announcement and signing of the Declaration of Independence. My colony and my expectations for the future are not having anymore fights between us and England. We will fight our own fights and wars as a new country.

From The Journal of Sara Taylor

Delaware

CHAPTER 38:

EMILY MERRIWEATHER –
A GIRL CAUGHT IN THE MIDDLE

By: Emily Kirchenbauer

Emily, A Doctor's Privileged Daughter Growing Up In Delaware

24 August, 1763

Dear Journal,

Today is my fifteenth birthday and it was a very uneventful day. I woke up and to my surprise there was no one down stairs when I went into the kitchen. I was expecting my family to be down there preparing for my birthday celebration. The only person I managed to find was my brother Sam. He was waiting for me outside with a gift in his hands. He gave me a kiss on my cheek and said, "Happy Birthday Em!" I opened it up and was surprised to find a journal under the wrapping. He told me he thought I needed something to get my feelings out when he was no longer there. I gave him a hug and thanked him for his gift.

We then went out to the stables for my usual riding lessons. This time he let me ride his horse. We galloped along the banks of the river and talked about why everyone was gone this morning. Apparently Mother and Father completely forgot about my birthday and had to go out to prepare for this evening. After the lesson I decided to have a little down time and write my first entry in here. But when I walked in my room and settled on my bed I began to remember that Sam was leaving us next year. (Sam is going to England to work for a man my father knows.) He will only be allowed to visit on holidays. I began to realize how much was going to change. Who will I talk to after he leaves? Who will ride with me along the banks? I don't want Sam to leave but I know that I'm just going to have to accept it.

I can't believe I'm fifteen! Just two more years and I will be leaving the house too. I have already been declared by my mother that I'm a proper young lady. I'm so happy to have completed my lessons with Miss White. I'm very thankful for what she has taught me. Now I must learn all I can about household duties from my mother, Anna. I think I have already learned all I am going to from Sam. Horseback riding, painting, violin, and reading are all that he has taught me.

My father seems to be doing well with his job at a local clinic. Thankfully he has not caught any contagions from his patients.

New Castle is such an exciting place! There is so much commotion about what church to attend here. Most of us are Quakers but there is only one church, an Anglican church. My parents do not agree with going there so for now we are continuing our relationship with God by ourselves. We hope to one day start our own church to meet in but I don't believe that will happen in the near future.

Until Later,

Emily

Early Morning Frustrations

27 August, 1763

Dear Journal,

It has been only a week since my birthday and so many things have changed. The government in Delaware has made it mandatory for all families to take in at least three soldiers. My family's soldiers arrived three days ago. At first I was very uneasy about having three young men in our house but now I don't see them as frightening but just aggravating. Yesterday I was woken with the sound of my mother's door being pounded upon.

"Open up we're starvin'!" the soldiers screamed in their thick accents.

It was before dawn and the soldiers were complaining about being hungry, demanding to be fed. I felt sorry for my mother so I quickly threw on my garments and hurried down stairs. They were already seated at the table and began pounding their utensils on the table. Mother had by now started boiling the water for their tea and began warming some porridge left over from the morning before. By the time they had gotten their meal mother was exhausted and I was beginning to think I was never going to be able to go back to bed. They began eating and what a sight that was. They didn't care that they were in the presence of two ladies and began eating like horses out of a trough.

"What are you lookin' at girl?!" the eldest soldier growled at me. I did not even realize that the noticed me staring at them with disgust.

After the meal they stood up threw their bowls on the table and walked out, leaving my mother and me to clean up their mess. I can't believe they expect us to be their slaves while they stay with us.

My brother does not like them either. Every chance he gets he tricks them into making fools of themselves. After the first day Sam decided to get back at them. He decided to "polish" the stairs to help mother but I knew exactly what he was planning.

"Sam!" I yelled in a whispered tone, "Do you want them to take a switch to you?"

"It is just a harmless joke Em, they won't get hurt." He said to me with his smiling face. Sam and I walked away from the stairs and hid behind one of the large chairs. They slipped and slided all the way down. Sam and I have never laughed so hard!

Sam and I have started to have more riding lessons to get away from the soldiers. I love riding with Sam and I want to cherish all the time I have left with him. He is now teaching me to jump over obstacles with the horses now. I never thought I would be able to do that in my lifetime. Well I must go help my mother wash the soldier's clothes and mend them as well. Lord knows they are not going to do it themselves!

Until Later,
Emily Merriweather

Fear of the Future
24 June, 1764
Dear Journal,

Today has been very stressful. With the weight of growing up on me I feel like I'm never going to stop changing. Right now my mother wants me to focus on my needlepoint and I can't seem to get anything right.

"Mother my thread is tangled again!" I said out of frustration.

"Come here I shall untangle like I have the last three times." She said "I did not succeed my first time at needlepoint when I was your age either. Give it time, you will learn."

Another task I seem to have trouble with is preserving food. I can't seem to get seal just right on each jar.

"Do not worry Em, you will improve in time." She said in an encouraging tone.

When I was younger I never had to worry about things such as these. Why do I have to learn these tedious tasks? I never had to worry about all of this when I was a child.

I also have to deal with the fact that Sam is leaving in another year. I hate to see him go but I know that being apprenticed to a shopkeeper is what Sam wants. A few months after that I will become betrothed and what an event that will be. I do not want to get married and have to worry about children and a husband. I am just now learning how to take care of myself. I just hope I can be the kind of mother my mother has been.

Until Later,

Emily Merriweather

The Task At Hand

5 July, 1764

Dear Journal,

Today was a very exciting day. My mother finally taught me how to make candles. It was hard at first but I eventually caught on to the idea.

"Put the string onto the dowel with the strings ends being two or three inches apart," Mother said in a gentle tone. After the wax melted, I continually dipped the ends of the string into the wax and then into cool water so it could harden in between the dips into the wax. This went on for a while and I had to shape the candles every once in a while to ensure that they would retain their shape. The candles after a while of dipping looked good enough and I was finished.

"See all it takes is a little patience," Mother said smiling.

My candles were not exactly perfect but they were just going to be melted down anyway.

The next thing she taught me was how to weave, that was a difficult task to say the least. The process was even harder than the candle making. I had to string up the loom first with different pieces of fabric which were tattered and worthless. Then I had to weave over and under for what seemed like forever. After a long and grueling hour of weaving I was finished with that part of the task.

"Mother, what shall I do now?" I said anxiously.

"You must now take the ends and knot them together," She said hoping that this would be the last time I asked for help.

I had a little trouble with the last step. "Mother, I…"

"I know now watch me," she said smiling like only a mother can. I still did not catch onto the idea and she, in the end, had to finish what was on my loom. I know that learning these things are important but for some reason it doesn't help me forget the boredom. I know that I will need to know these things for when I am married but I don't see the significance yet.

Until Later,

Emily Merriweather

Hushed Tones and Harsh Words

30 March, 1765

Dear Journal,

Today when I got home from walking Toodles, my dog to my surprise I found my mother and father talking in a hushed tone in father's study. I desperately wanted to know what was going on, so I quietly went up to the door, stepped closer to the opening and carefully listened to their conversation.

"Do they think this is right? Taxing the colonies so unfairly?" Father ranted.

"James, the King is only doing this for our own good I'm sure. It's not going to last forever," mother said in her gentle tone.

"We are not the ones having financial troubles Anna! England needs to solve its problems without taking us down with them!"

After father had finished ranting about the king, mother was in tears and father had just seen me through the crack in the door. He motioned for me to come in and sit down. I directly went to Mother's side to comfort her but I knew it was no use.

"Emily," father began, "did you hear every word your mother and I have just exchanged?"

I nodded my head but did not look at him in fear that he would give me a look of disappointment. But, when I finally made eye contact, he had a smile on his face.

"Emily, you're old enough now to be a part of this conversation. Do you think it is fair that we should have to help pay for England's debt?"

"Father, even if I knew I would not tell you."

"And why is that?" he asked sternly.

"Father, speaking out against the King is treason. We are still Englishmen even when we are this far away from England. I agree with mother, the King must be doing this for our own good."

I did not even give Father a chance to respond. I abruptly stormed out of the room, running straight towards my room, not even realizing how disrespectful I was to my father.

When I got up to my room I immediately threw myself down on my bed and began to cry not really knowing what was wrong. Then I realized I did not really believe what I had told my father. Being only seventeen, I was still unsure of my personal beliefs. Why had I said such hateful things to my own Father? Why was I acting so childish by storming out of the room?

After I had cried all my tears, Father gave a knock on my door. I said nothing, too ashamed to answer him. He walked over to my bed and sat on the edge.

"Emily," he began, "I'm not angry with you. You have a right to your own opinion, but I have just one question to ask of you. Do you agree with the king because you truly think what he is doing is right or are you afraid of the consequences that come along with being against the king? I know you're only seventeen, but you need to start making opinions for yourself."

I knew what he had said was right, but for some reason it did not make the anger drain out of me any faster. Lord knows we all are going to have to choose a side before this is over.

Until Later,
Emily Merriweather

All This For Tea?

30 June, 1773

Dear Journal,

Today began with a sleepless morning. For some reason, something did not feel right. I had an unsettling feeling when I arose from bed at dawn. Somehow I knew something was wrong I was not sure what it was. I got up, of course, to begin my normal morning responsibilities. I crept down the stairs hoping that I would be able to sneak past everyone to take an early morning walk. Unfortunately, my mother knew my trick and caught me.

"Thought you could fool your old mother, eh?" she said with a smile.

"Just wanted some fresh air before being in that stuffy kitchen for a while," I said innocently.

"Maybe later, but right now we must prepare for Sam's arrival from England."

Sam was coming home from England for a visit and we were to have a great celebration, which meant lots of preparation. I knew I would be in the kitchen for a good portion of the day, but I knew my suffering would not be in vain.

By the midday meal, Mother and I were finished. Knowing that the both of us could use a break from being in that stuffy kitchen all morning, Mother suggested that we take a walk down to the general store and buy some tea to relax with later this evening.

We walked into the store and almost immediately I could immediately smell all of the store's items. I could smell the sweetness of the candy, the metallic smell of the gun powder, and the musky smell of the wooden furniture. The flood of so many different aromas was overwhelming. Mother handed me some money and told me to ask the shopkeeper for five pounds of tea and a cone of sugar. Expecting tea to be expensive I went to the counter to find that it had been lowered.

"Why had it been lowered?" I thought to myself. But I was too worried about making it home in time to be there when Sam arrived, so I did not give a second thought.

I walked in, father had just gotten home from the clinic and he seemed to be in a good mood.

"Where have you ladies been this afternoon? Have we been doing some shopping?" he said with a grin.

"Just a few things we needed dear. Tea and a cone of sugar," Mother replied.

"Tea? How much did you dole out for five pounds this time?" Father asked pointedly.

"Less than usual," she said knowing again that he would have something to say.

"What's this now? The King thinking he can trick his colonies into buying more tea? The nerve of…"

"James!" Mother lashed out. "Do you really think this appropriate talk for a girl of Emily's age?" Mother said, looking at me.

"Emily leave us, your Mother would rather you not hear my ranting," My father said quickly.

I walked slowly up the stairs and into my room. From the moment I shut the door I could hear Mother and Father discussing this new "trick" the king was using to make the colonies pay more for tea. For once I was beginning to feel like Father was right. I asked the same question that came to mind while in the store. Why had the price of tea been lowered? Was it really to make the colonies pay more? Or was it just the price being inconsistent? I pondered this in my head for a while until Mother came up to tell me she needed help with preparations for dinner. But I knew this would not be the last time that I would be questioning myself about what I truly believed. No, I would have to do this many more times in my life.

Until Later,

Emily Merriweather

Intolerable, Unthinkable

25 June, 1774

Dear Journal,

Today I am again angered by the acts set forth by the mother country, England. They have just put out more acts for the colonies known as the Intolerable Acts. Intolerable Acts? That doesn't even begin to describe how ridiculous England is being.

Why must they set more and more acts out each and every week? I wish that Britain would just leave the colonies alone. Why can't we have our own system of government? Why can't we have democracy? Why do we have to continue fighting like children? I feel like we are fighting a battle that we will ever win. Sometimes it seems like the conflict will never be over.

The people in my colony are very upset about what is going on between the colonies and the mother country. I wish I had seen how wrong England was before now because I used to think they were always right. I feel so stupid right now for never questioning the crowns laws. I'm beginning to see that the patriots have been right this whole time.

Until Later,

Emily Merriweather

Dinner Discussions

12 May, 1775

Dear Journal,

"Finally!" Father said with great emphasis. We were sitting at the dinner table and we were discussing the resolution made Continental Congress.

"Do you mean that we will be separated from England now Father?" I inquired.

"No, not yet dear," Father answered back.

"It's about time!" Mother spouted. I have never heard my mother talk like that. Much less raise her voice. Father just stared, unblinking until he could think of a response to Mother's comment.

"What did you say Anna?" Father said in a confused tone. Wondering why Mother, a loyalist was speaking out against her King.

"I can longer deny the truth James," she began. "I realized long ago that you, Emily and most of our friends have been right. I was just not willing to admit my poor judgment."

Father could not help but smile at me. He knew I was just as happy as he was that Mother was finally on the same side. We finally got to discuss something as a family, united as one. I have never enjoyed a discussion about the relationship between the King and the colonies.

After we had finished dinner I, of course, went up to my room too. I couldn't help but ponder all that was going on in the colonies. Would we really start a war with our own King? I knew that this question would be answered soon, but worried about the consequences we might have to face for our freedom.

Until Later,

Emily Merriweather

A Meeting of Great Importance

15 July, 1776

Dear Journal,

Being twenty-eight I have seen this country change so much. I have experienced many things but what happened today has topped them all. Sam and I decided to go out to run errands for mother when we happened to come across Caeser Rodney, one of the signers of the Declaration of Independence. Sam of course was eager to meet him and immediately introduced us both.

"Good day to you Mr. Rodney and may I thank you for representing Delaware in the Continental Congress?" Sam said with a large smile on his face. Sam, Mr. Rodney and I talked for a while about the actual discussion and the signing of the Declaration. It is amazing how much bickering took place during the discussion of independence itself. I am surprised to find that one colony withdrew from the actual vote of writing the document of independence. I am so glad that I had the opportunity to meet one of the actual signers. I know that this event will be carved into my memory for the rest of my life. Our country will one day forget the bitter fight and will only remember the glory of our country's victory.

Until Later,

Emily Merriweather

CHAPTER 39:

THE DIARY OF FELICITY BENNETT

By: Vanessa Nakai Mashushire

About Me

August 29, 1763

Dear Diary,

My name is Felicity Bennett and I am 14 years old. I live in New Castle, Delaware with my mother, father, brother, and sister. I was born on August 23, 1749. Of course I am a girl. My parents own a general store. I got you as a gift from Eva {employee at the general store} so that I can rite down my thoughts in you.

In my opinion, I think I have a great personality. I am very caring, out going, down to earth. Most would say that I am dependable and honest. And I always love to meet new people and friends, and to try new things. I am in the 8th grade and I am home schooled from 8 am to 2pm, the rest of the time I am either at the general store or at home doing other things. In my spare time I love to draw, paint, sew, and knit sweaters and such.

My skills include working with people who come to the store; momma started teaching me about makin' clothes when I was about 7 years old. So I make clothes for myself, my family, and to sell at the store. I make dresses, aprons, and men's overalls. I also mend clothes (part of our service at the store), cook, clean, draw, I am also really good at math; there is nothing that I cannot figure out! And I have one of the top literature and fluency teachers in the colonies. She is actually British but she is really nice she is not like the other Brits. She is much friendlier.

My family is Quaker and so am I. In my family, there is my mother, Addie, my father, James, my brother, Benjamin, and my sister Annie. And of course myself, Felicity.

Other people I know are my grandmother who lives three miles away, just strait down the old dirt road, my best friend Malia, Eva and her two children, Eli and Jerusha, Eva is the only employee we have, only because she couldn't find a job and she is 18 and lost both of her parents. And she needs money to support herself and the youngins. She is an exception; pa has to set aside a certain percentage for Eva every week. She is a very sweet young woman. She is very outgoing and fun to be around, the only thing is that she has a lot of stress on her hands sometimes she has to bring the children with her to the store because she hasn't enough money to send them to school everyday. Let alone enough to pay for her to go to school. So she works at the store during the whole day and has a friend take care of Eli and Jerusha while she works. And sometimes I go to the store after I get done with my work and I go and get the children and take them to our house and keep them occupied. So that's Eva, oh yeah and her name is pronounced like Ava but is spelled Eva.   Well I will try to tell you more later. I have to go to bed! Nice to meet you diary, I look forward to writing all my deepest, darkest thoughts! Good night!

Sugar Act

April 10, 1764

Dear Diary,

We have just been passed a new law that says that we have a new tax on lumber and molasses. We can no longer trade or export to any one outside of our area or other than Britain. If we break this law we would be tried vice admiralty courts. This really affects both us and the general store because of the economic depression we are very low on money! I guess I can say I'm an not used to this at all because I'm usually able to get anything I ask for but now all I get is " Felicity if you can get the money for that I would be more than happy to get that for you."

This is very frustrating to me now I see how the poor people feel! Gosh why am I spending all this time complaining? But after all of this is over now I know some of what the poor go through. I will never know all of what they go through though. But every law so far that is passed is affecting everything that has to do with our store! I don't know when or how this will end but I know that things will get better if people will just stand up for what they believe in and do something really dramatic, and when I say dramatic, I mean dramatic. At least something that will get colonial attention! I think it will happen with just a few brave people willing to take anything just to gain our independence! We do not deserve to go through this ANYMORE!!

British Soldiers, Coming to My Home? Day 1- Finding out.

Dear Diary,

A tall good lookin man knocked on our door, bein that he was so good lookin, I would thank he would have some good lookin news! But he didn't.

Momma went to the door, I saw the man through the window, so I followed. Momma opened the door, and the tall man in a nice suite, well polished shoes, stood shoulder-up as if lookin to have some kind of pride in knowing how divine he looked.

And he said, "Hello Mrs. may I have a moment with you and your family? This will only take a matter of minutes."

Momma stuttered, "Why yes, I suppose, come in."

Momma went and called Pa', Benjamin, and Annie. They all came and we all took a seat. John scooted forward and went on, "Thank you for this opportunity to speak with you all, but we don't have much time. What I am about to tell you is a GOVERNMENT ORDER, therefore refusal to follow this lawful order will result in serious consequences to all members of the household! You all have to host three British Soldiers, in your case these soldiers will be two adult men and one juvenile soldier. They will be staying in your home, in which ever room they desire. If you have to sleep on the floor, so be it!

"But these soldiers will be granted what ever they ask for; they will be living with you for two weeks. Make sure you have enough to eat around here, and one more thing, one of you, mother or father, have to stay back from all your daily activities, so that you can attend to the Soldiers and grant their every wish! You all are so well mannered, and are wonderful listening children, I am terribly sorry that you have to go through this but it is an ORDER from Great Britain. I am sorry."

We sat in unison, what are we going to do? There goes our life for two weeks! I mean it that is literally our whole life. And even you know, I have told you time after time how busy my folks are, they cannot afford to be one person short. Oh no and What about Eva? What is she going to do? She is on her own, her two children! I am so worried for them. And my room, I won't get to sleep or go in my room for two weeks?! I can't do this! Maybe Eva and her children can come and stay with us for the time being so that she will not be on her own. She lives in a smaller four- roomed house/ cottage, to be more precise.

I find it unreasonable that they would come on our premises, take over our home, kick us out of our rooms, band us form all our daily activity? This is awful! I don't know what I am going to do! Will I be able to do my school work? Will my teacher's home be broken into? Or is she an exception because she is British? I don't know, all these thoughts racing through my head!

After a long time of being quiet, momma broke the silence and said, "but up at the store, we need all the help we can get, and with everyone else being banned from going out, won't service be kind of slow?"

John came in, "Yes misses, and I am terribly sorry, you all look like a great family! But unfortunately, there is nothing we can do, even I and my wife have to host uptown, and this will as well make a pretty big impact on our life, I am very uncomfortable with my wife having to stay at home with three men I don't even know! It will be tough, but I know that all things are possible and we can do it!"

Well, I guess John was right, maybe it will be tough, but it is only two weeks. We can do it!

Soldiers are Coming Tomorrow
Dear Diary,

The soldiers are coming in the mornin, and we have so much to do! We decided that Eva, Jerusha, and Eli are coming tonight as if they live with us and Eva is locking up her little house to come and stay with us in the hopes of her staying so that momma can go to work with Pa'. We will see if they will allow that to happen.

I am still trying to absorb the fact that we will be bossed around in our own home and will be kicked out of certain rooms in our own house. I think it won't be as bad as it sounds but we will just have to see how it goes. momma says that she doesn't know exactly what time the soldiers will be arriving, so she said that she will not sleep tonight, because she doesn't know if they will come in the wee hours of the morning or mid day. So she will be up the whole night.

As I sit on my bed, several thoughts race within my head, how will these men behave? Are they going to be rude and bossy? Will they be polite? Will they yell at us or push us around? What will the next two weeks hold for us? It is indeed a good thing that Eva will be coming over to stay with us, and I know that that will make it much easier on our part. I will be having school just as normal (only because my teacher doesn't have to host any soldiers, the only soldier she will host is her son! which is kind of coincidental.) Others will not be going to school because other teachers have to host also.

I do not know what to expect, but I do know that we will have some hard times (other than this two weeks) ahead. I believe that we are vulnerable enough for an economic depression. Being under the rule of Great Britain, we don't know what to expect next! We will see what our future holds, but I can tell you already the colonies are up for some tough times, but we are strong people!

Soldiers Have Arrived: First Impressions (Not So Good)

Dear Diary,

Sure enough the soldiers arrived at the early, early hours of the morning. They knocked on the door when I was asleep in the sitting room. While I was still asleep next to Jerusha and Eli (Eva's children), I feel someone shaking me roughly to wake up, I looked up to see a big fat man with an oversized belly, that had an awful odor standing next to me and he yelled, "Get up right now! This is where we are sleeping!" I knew immediately that this was one of the soldiers.

Why was he being so rude? And he is in our house! I don't understand this! This is indeed going to be a terrible two weeks, I CAN SEE IT COMING!

So I awoke, and introduced my self just to be friendly, and the soldier turned around and said to me, "My name is Bart. We will NOT be speaking to you during our stay here. You will do what we say and that is it! We were ordered to not have any conversation with you what so ever, you got that? So just stay out of our way and keep your mouth closed!"

But why? I was just being nice! I don't understand. Like John had said when he told us about the order, we are a nice family, we like to do nothing but help others who are in need. Why us? Why anybody?

Why should we be forced to sleep in a different place in our own home? This is not right. Why is this happening?

Two Weeks with the Soldiers

Dear Diary,

These past two weeks went by quiet fast and wasn't as bad as I thought it would be when the soldiers first arrived.

Yes, they were very rude when we "crossed paths". You notice I said crossed paths, meaning that most of the time they kept to them selves. I haven't been able to sleep very much because they would be up all night laughing and playing cards, a lot of times they woke up both momma and Eva through out the night when they needed something. They didn't even come out of the room very often, I wonder if they even bathed......

They didn't even talk to Annie or Benjamin; they didn't even talk to Pa'. I thought from the first day they came they were going to be very mean, and push us around but there was none of that, even though they were very rude when they did talk to us, I actually like that better than being bossed around, a lot of our neighbors said the same thing, there were some families that said they had to sleep outside, because of being kicked out of their house by some of the men, but a lot of us were happy that they didn't do much, they were rude but they were no work at all. And I thank god that this two weeks is over with!

My Day Whittling!

July 5, 1764

Dear Diary,

I know I haven't told you at all about my best friend Malia, the reason for that is because she moved to South Carolina and I don't like to talk to much about her only because it makes me really sad to talk about it, because it makes me think of all the times we spent together when she used to live just strait up the dirt road from us, on the other side of the ridge and our other neighborhoods. I miss when we used to run through the fields together and her parents owned the blacksmith shop (her father was a black smith here in Delaware). It is also hard to talk about her because she lives so far away and every letter I send to her returns back because I send it to her grandmother's house but I guess the address changed. So now there is no way I can get a hold of her. That's why I do not talk about her much because there is nothing to say about her only because I don't see her.

Malia's cousin, Adam still lives in north Delaware so we bumped heads at the Delaware talents festival, and he was in a booth, his booth had to do with whittling, so of course he was one of Malia's many family members that I know very well, however, Adam doesn't know their address either, therefore I still cannot write to her. But anyway, Adam is very talented at whittling.

So when I got to Adam's booth I asked him what he was making and he said he was whittling a bowl. It was so neat I never knew that someone could be so talented, that they could make there own dishes! That is an idea, matter fact, I think we should consider something like this at the store; it will bring more of an income in.

So as we watched Adam, he looked up at me and asked me, "If you think it looks so fun, would you like to come back here and make yourself something very special?"

I said, "Of course I do but I would never be as good at whittling as you!"

Adam looked at me in unison, "It is no matter of how good you are at something, all that matters is that you have made nothing into something."

So of course I went behind to see how I can create a piece of firewood into something you can actually use. So I decided to make a wooden spoon. He gave me a knife and started it out for me, and I smoothed out the surface so that you could tell it was a spoon, he carved the dipping part. And soon, I made a piece of wood into a spoon.

When we were finished, he said, "I see you at the general store all the time and I know that your parents own it, I was wondering if you were looking for something else to sell at your store."

Wow! How'd he know? "Why yes, we always try to find people to vend for, or we buy their merchandise and sell it and also give them an amount every week."

Adam had that look that people usually get when they have an idea, "Well I do that for folks all the time! I do it for a living. I make so many items and make deliveries everyday, me and my roommate. So talk to your folks about it! We would love to do business with y'all!"

As I walked I said, "Okay, take care!"

I think my hands-on day was a great experience. I thought it was amazing how you can turn not much into something special. Almost like with Adam, he makes money by making items from wood and making items that are not only for decoration but you can actually use them everyday. That is something everyone can learn from!

The Tea Act

May 10, 1773

Dear Diary,

A whole other notice has been given out; this notice was of course another attempt for taxin' us and the folks around us! This notice is for a tax bein' placed on tea, the Tea Act. As you know, tea is a very important resource of our day, most have it during breakfast, and others in the evenin', either way, and tea is basically a routine that cannot be left out.

We heard about this notice from the twice weekly paper. twice a week, every week, {Mondays and Fridays} we get a news paper delivery and every Monday and Friday morning, people come to the store right when Pa' opens the door, to see folks dashin' in to get the weekly news. now that the economy has gone bad, people rarely buy the paper but they do come in and read it in the store and leave to spread the news that is why Pa' started keeping them behind the counter desk, so that when folks need the paper, they ask for it. Pa' says that we cannot afford to loose a dime especially on papers. A lot of folks {our faithful customers} buy them for history so that they can be shown to future generations. The ones that have been saved from previous acts {from}

Not only does the new tax affect us in our home, but it also affects the shippin' of tea to the store. We are not supported by the government in any way. We run it all by our selves, so that does mean we have to pay extra for the shipping of tea because it's coming to us and then we sell it to the folks around. Which it's hard for us but we gotta tax them too in order for us to be able to get a new shipment. Yes, folks complain to momma and pa' but we plead with them that there is nothin' we can do; it's the British. We are under their law, so we cannot refuse to tax them.

Every notice that there is, is hurting us step by step, because wee still gotta set aside the money for our home and to support our life, and the money to support Eva's house.

Momma and Pa' talk about how havin' Eva at the store helps out with some stuff they doesn't have to worry about, but now with the economic depression, it is hard keepin' the money to pay her because we need every pent we can get durin' this time. But we also know that Eva depends on the store with her life! So she can't afford to be without work.

So as you can see that as a general store owner, farm owner, and any kind of person, the tea act is a very tough tax to deal with, maybe it might not be that much in a day, but it sure does add up!

Being an Emerging Adult - Expectations for me!

There are many expectations that my parents have for my life. As you know, I love to paint and make clothes and things like that right? Well I don't know what to do because being the oldest; this is their expectation list for me;

- Ø   Pass through school
- Ø   Get good marks
- Ø   Go to finishing school
- Ø   Take on the shop
- Ø   Be the owner until my oldest child turns 21 and is able to own the shop.

Well I do not want to do that!!! I have and agenda of what I want to do after I finish with my schooling:

- Ø   Design a different style of clothing that will finally bring style to these parts
- Ø   Open up clothing and accessories shop
- Ø   And be well known all throughout Delaware

It is very hard on me being that I wanna do what makes momma and pa' happy. and there is nothing that I wouldn't do for them, it's just that I have a vision, and I want to fulfill my dream but at the same time here my folks are plannin' out ma life and I have a different vision of my life.

I don't know what I will do. I don't know if I should do both. But what about all the stress? Just seein' momma and pa every day scramblin' to make everything okay down at the store. Heck' they spend more time workin' on store business then they do personal business.

I do not want to disappoint my family. It was passed down to pa, so then why does it have to be passed to me why can't it be given to Benjamin? He is the second to oldest! This is a tough decision! There has got to be a compromise to the store situation. But I have a totally different idea of what I want to do.

Momma puts it in the context of, "Okay, THIS IS WHAT YOU ARE GOING TO DO!" almost like I have to do it or else! There has gotta be a better way to do this!

Intolerable Acts

June 26, 1774

Dear Diary,

We have just been passed a new law that says that we have a new tax on lumber and molasses. We can no longer trade or export to any one outside of our area or other than Britain. If we break this law we would be tried vice admiralty courts. This really affects both us and the general store because of the economic depression we are very low on money! I guess I can say I'm an not used to this at all because I'm usually able to get anything I ask for but now all I get is " Felicity if you can get the money for that I would be more than happy to get that for you." This is very frustrating to me now I see how the poor people feel! Gosh why am I spending all this time complaining? But after all of this is over now I know some of what the poor go through. I will never know all of what they go through though. But every law so far that is passed is affecting everything that has to do with our store! I don't know when or how this will end but I know that if I just persevere!

Free At Last!

Dear Diary,

Today, I am so excited. As you know the Declaration of Independence was signed. We didn't hear about this until yesterday evenin'. Cause you know how sometimes new takes a little while to spread. But when it got to us, a town meeting was called up in downtown New Castle.

A young news boy runnin' through out the old dirt roads yellin', "Town meetin'! Town meetin'! Head down to town, soon as possible!! Town meetin'!" With all the notices and taxin' we been through a town meetin' is the last thing we need! So we went with expectation to be getting' bad, bad news {as always}!

When we got downtown, we saw everybody in New Castle, the whole town is down here! This can't be good! We all got there it was very loud because everybody did not know what to expect! some thought that we were gonna get booted out of town, some thought a war was gonna hit our city, so many thought raced through a lot of folks' minds. I thought that they were gonna make us move out of our home just to let those stupid ol' lobsterbacks take over our land! I wished that that would not be the case.

So I looked around as the anger of the people swept through the crowd.

"ATTENTION PLEASE!" The loudness died down, "WE HAVE GREAT NEWS!" I listened as I heard the sigh of relief scattered in the crowd. "THE DECLARATION FOR OUR INDEPENDENCE HAS BEEN GRANTED!! WE ARE NO LONGER UNDER THE RULE OF BRITAIN! WE ARE NOW DECLARED THE UNITED STATES OF AMERICA! WE ARE ONE PEOPLE!! WE HAVE GAINED OUR INDEPENDENC!"

When I heard those words and the sounds of the happiness of the crowd!! I knew that there would be HOPE for tomorrow! I can't explain this feeling! It just makes me so happy to know that there were people bold enough to stand up for our independence! WE HAVE MADE HISTORY! I know that future generations will still be looking back on this day! And recognize those who lost their lives for OUR independence! And know that on that day we were declared the United States of America!

Twelve Years Since the First Act

Dear Diary,

I am now 26 years old and am going to collage to study to be a teacher. After the declaration of Independence, I was inspired so much by the leaders that were bold enough to sign that little, but POWERFUL piece of paper, so all of that inspired me to go for something bigger than just making clothing or doing paintings for families. I want to teach future generations about those bold men. They deserve to know because this document went down in history. I want to teach them stand up for what they believe is right, and even though women aren't allowed to do very much, well, let me just be the first then! It has been twelve years since all of the hardships with Great Britain, the hosting of the soldiers, the Acts and notices, all of the sicknesses (Benjamin getting the small pocks). And thank God for the Declaration of Independence!

Things have gotten much better since the Declaration of independence, things are slowly starting' to get back to normal and the store is starting' to gain its' regular income. And we we're finally able to bring Eva back. She can now get back to supporting herself and her two kinds. It hasn't yet gotten back to the point where I can say that I get everything I want again because momma and daddy are still trying to get our "financial status" back to normal. We're planning' to have some kind of celebration when things get completely back to normal!

When I first found out about the Declaration of Independence, something just jumped inside of me! Knowing that our leaders are bold enough to DECLARE our independence. That example that people like George Read (who was my favorite leader, being' that he is from New Castle, Delaware!) set inspires me to never be afraid to stand up and voice what you believe is right! And to never be too intimidated by others because we know that we are all equally powerful. And as Momma always said, "never hide the power that God gave us all equally". Those words will always stay with me even when I go to collage. I have also learned to say nay to any one who tries to make me feel less powerful than I am! Thank God for the Declaration of independence!

I really want to be able to tell my children and children's children that I was able to see that day, and that as a teenager, I witnessed the times that we were colonized by Great Britain.

My advice to the future generations is to never let anyone make you feel less than you are, like I said we are all powerful, as I said we are equally powerful! And when you are not free to do what you think is right, never be afraid to let your voice be heard, we all deserve to be free in the United States of America. Trust me, when you let your voice be heard, you will not regret it!

CHAPTER 40:

THE STORY OF ABIGALE

By: Victoria Hernandez

About Me

Hello, my name is Abigale Kensington. I am 13 years of age. I help my father run his inn. Sometimes it's fun but the other times, well it's not so fun. I help people carry their belongings. But the job I like to do most is hostess. People ask me all the time, "Aren't you just a little too young to be working at an inn?"

I never have time to just go outside and play some jump rope or hopscotch with my friends. My days are mostly the same. I go to school, go and help at my father's inn, come home eat dinner, work on my homework, and go to bed. On weekends I get a little more free time. On Saturday mornings I wake up at 6am and do my chores. I have to straighten my room up, sweep the whole house, do my laundry, and then wash the dishes from breakfast. Why can't my days be a little different?

I am a very caring person. I try to help people every chance I get. I am a very smart child. Father gives me 2 pence for every good mark I get! So that gives me energy to do the best I can.

I absolutely love to be outside. Whether it's working outside in the yard, or just sitting under a big shady tree and reading a nice book.

I am ~~very,~~ no extremely excited to help with the inn. Cause' it will be our busiest week of the year! Well, it's about time to be getting off to bed and I think I hear father calling me to come and help!

Until later,

Abigale

The Sugar Act

I was shocked when I heard out about the sugar act. I absolutely hate, hate, hate the idea about taxes. What's the point of them? It is going to cost us a lot of money that we all can't afford to spend! I hear people talking about it everywhere I go! I first heard about it when I was at the market place. I didn't know what they were talking about. So I forgot about it for a couple of days.

Then when I was out taking a nice little stroll, that's when I heard people talking about it again! So that's when I started wondering about it. I questioned it. We had to pay taxes? I was absolutely shocked!

Now that pretty much everyone in our town has found out about it, they have not been the same. I think that a lot of people are taking this very seriously. They are very angry! Now this is serious. Me? I think that whoever is making us pay these stupid "taxes" is not a good person. Not a good person at all!! That's what I think about all of this! I am so mad at all of this that I could just scream! It will especially hard for families like mine, that don't have a lot of money. I don't think that we will be able to afford it. If we can afford it we won't have any extra money to spend on anything.

We can't afford them! I am just very disappointed. Not only that but I am furious too! Why don't the people who are making it a law have to pay any taxes ehh? That is one of the many questions I have about these "taxes" we have here. Well, I shall get back to reading my book.

Until later,

Abigale

Soldiers

We have to have soldiers come and live at my house. I really do not like the idea but I guess I have to deal with it because I don't want my father to go to jail. It might be a good experience to have soldiers live in my house. It might teach us some discipline. But it will be kind of weird to have them living in my house. But I have to get through it.

Mother does not like the idea of them coming to live with us at all. But she said she could not live without my father being in the house to help raise me. She said she could not afford to pay that big amount of money.

Now that the soldiers are here at the house it's been very clean! They pick up after there selves all of the time. Mother does not like them there at all still. She thinks that they are very disrespectful. They clean up after themselves. What more could she want? She said they don't have very good manners. Father likes them here. He likes having other guys in the house. It's not as bad as I thought it would be.

Until next time,
Abigale

Expectations

When I grow older my parents expectations for me are to get married, have children, and take over the family business. My expectations for myself are to buy a house, get married and have children. I have some fears of buying a house because I'm afraid of not paying the bills on time and not being able to afford to buy things for my children. My husband and I hopefully can make a good income and afford to buy our children nice things like toys and games.

But I'm still young and I still have years to go until I have to worry about these things. As long as I find the right guy and raise my children the way my parents raised me I think that I will be good. I really do not want to take over the family business. But I'm afraid that if I don't my parents will be disappointed in me.

When they die, if I don't take over the inn, then who will? These are things that I have to think very hard about this over the years. They have talked to me about taking over the inn and they told me to think very hard on it while I am still young. By the time I'm seventeen they want me to have an answer. I'm thirteen right now so I have four years to make a decision.

Until next time,
Abigale

New Notices

I just read about multiple new notices that are tied to the Boston area. I live in Delaware. My reaction to all of these new notices is... Hmmm, I'm not really even sure how they are going to affect the life of me or other people who live by me in my colony. After all I still am only 13 years of age. Yes, I guess I agree with the name "Intolerable Acts". It's not that bad of a name. I think it kind of fits in with them. Ummm, I'm not even sure who people in my colony are siding with. But if I were them I would side with the men of Boston in New England. But, that's just me and my family.

Until next time,

Abigale

The Continental Congress

I just heard about the resolution made by the Continental Congress which includes the boycott of Great Britain. I absolutely do have an opinion on it! This resolution is a fantastic one! I really really, really, really like it! I know I don't have much say on it since I'm still kind of young. But I think that it's very good. My family and I are Torys. ~~My entire family agrees with me.~~ No, wait I actually agree with them, considering that they have a whole lot more say then I do. I think it will be absolutely wonderful for the colony of Delaware. I also think that it will be wonderful for other colonies too!

Hmmm, I'm not very sure at all what will happen to us as a whole group of colonies. But I think it will be very good for my colony, Delaware. I think it will be good for me! There is absolutely nothing that will change my mind about this. I think that because it's best for everyone. Not just me, but everyone. I'm not sure at all how it will compare to my family, friends, and neighbors. Other people like the idea also! Like my school teacher, she loves the idea! Well, I've got to get back downstairs for dinner.

Until next time,

Short on Workers

Today was a very difficult day. We were very short on workers! It was only, father, me, and Benjamin. We usually have five people working. It took us a while to get people checked in. My father was getting very stressed. It was a rainy day so people couldn't go outside and wait to be checked in. It was crowded inside, and for some odd reason people kept asking silly questions for absolutely no reason at all! The worst part was is that they kept on asking ME these questions.

Father started to feel quite better when he heard that I was doing the things that people asked me to do on my own. He was ~~very,~~ no EXTREMELY proud of me. I was proud of myself also! Yes, even know that it is a mess in the Inn I did enjoy helping my father!

Until next time,

Abigale

The Second Continental Congress!

I, Abigale Kensington have just heard about the Second Continental Congress signing and the Declaration of Independence. Now that the Declaration of Independence has been made I feel kind of scared. I have no idea what's going to happened now. Is my life going to change? Is it going to be for the better if it does? These are some of the questions I wonder. Something that makes me feel better about the signing is that I actually met one of the signers himself. I met George Reed. He seems like a great man. He knows that he wants to sign it and there's no turning back now.

We had a meeting the other day about it. This signing is most DEFENETLY going to change my colony. I don't know how but I know it will. I'm kind of scared about the whole Declaration of Independence thing. But for what I know it will make an impact in our life. My colony is going through a lot of changes right now. People have changed and it's kind of strange. I hope good things will happen in the future for my colony Delaware. I know this will go down in history.

Until next time,

Abigale

CHAPTER 41:

A GIRL FROM THE LANAPE TRIBE

By: Morgan Smotherman

About Me

Hello my name is Pocahontas and I am a Native American. I am 12 years old; my birthday is Aug. 23, 1757. I live in Delaware, the tribe of Lenape. I am a nice and polite girl, but very talkative. I am also a kind of person that likes to take responsibility as in taking care of my tribe; I also take care of my younger siblings when there not distracted by something else. I love to learn new stuff, but I don't have a lot of education but the education I do have is enough to live in my tribe. I also love to cook, sew, and craft they are also some of my favorite skills. In my family I have two brothers and grateful parents. In the morning my two brothers go hunting with dad or stay and help me in and mother that stay home and help our tribe. As you can tell my life is pretty easy. My tribe believes in spirits and that they are all around us. Lenape tribe is known for our kindness and with in our tribe is my two best friends Rozene and Hinto they are my life if I lost them it would be the end of the world. And that is about me and my tribe.

The Sugar Act

This morning I woke up to screaming. I hurried outside to a soldier with a thunder cracker or as they call it a "musket". The young soldier had a piece of paper with big letters on the front saying "The Sugar Act." I ran back inside and waited for the soldier to leave. When my mom sounded me outside I saw the paper again. I read it; it was a tax for the ending of the 7 year war. My mom was ok about it, but I was furious. Us Lenape already don't have enough money to pay anything else so why would this involve us? Well I have a lot of thinking about this new act so I better go.

Pocahontas

The Stamp Act

Last night I could not sleep, this morning I could not eat because another act they added called the stamp act. The tax is on paper, skin, ink and etc.

That hurts my tribe very much because it hurts our trading here in Delaware. I feel sick right now, I think Rozene gave me the sickness she had. I think I will go now.

Pocahontas

The Tea Act

I was just over at Rozena's house and when I got there she was talking about an act and told me about it. Yes finally an act we don't have to pay for, but I'm rather sad even though it lowers tea tax. But most of us Lenape's don't drink tea and it's rather hard to trade for tea since the Boston folk like there tea but lets move on. It doesn't really help us at all I'm just glad they didn't add another tax. I don't think mother would be very happy about it!

Pocahontas

Townshend Act

MMM…the smell of breakfast this morning was wonderful, but do you know what isn't wonderful the ridiculous Townshend Act. Me and my tribe are peaceful and don't appreciate the riots and the military responses. I just despise all the acts no matter what there about or what it is. I have to go and help my tribe now but I will be back.

Pocahontas

The Intolerable Acts

This morning I ran strait toward Rozene's house because she told me she had to tell me something in the morning. She told me we had another act. She is usually the first person in our tribe to know, but we didn't have just one, but four. I just can't believe that they had enough time to name it something like the intolerable acts. We Indians spend our time on important stuff like figuring out what we will do about the trading problem. I guess they didn't even come at the same time but almost at different months! My tribe is furious that we didn't hear about acts at the time they were addressed.

Pocahontas

My Bracelet

Today we had a celebration for the chief's birthday. As a gift to our tribe he let us make special things for ourselves instead of making it to help the whole tribe. I made a beautiful leather bracelet that had my name on it in big letters. (Pocahontas) each letter means something:

P=patient
O=occupied
C=caring
A=accomplished
H=heavenly
O=official
N=neat
T=trust worthy
A=appealing
S=surprising

My Fears

For a whole month I have been waking up to the great smell of breakfast , but when I'm awaken I worry about what my new job will be when I become grown enough.

1 hour later:

This afternoon I was watching the little siblings and my mother approached me and said I wouldn't have to do the hard labor work until next year. I was so reviled. Until next time.

Wonderful Morning!

When I woke up this morning I felt different I just don't know what is making feel so weird. Maybe looking around the room might help me, I was looking around the room and I couldn't believe it my mother was actually smiling! It's been a long time since the last time I saw my mother's smile. The last time I saw her smile was a couple days before the acts started. She looked over at me and said "Why are you looking at me?"

I told her that I felt weird because I hadn't seen her smile in a while. She told me that there where men that came to the tribe early this morning. I had no idea why men would make my mother smile ever since father died. Then she finished, that the to men came to tell are chief that some men from every colony were going to sign something called the Declaration Of Independence's chief hired two Boston boys to come to him and tell him important information so we wouldn't be surprised by important information like we were when we heard about the sugar act.

So I asked my mother what is that? She told me that it was a document that these men were going to sign and if approved it could help our tribe very much. She didn't explain very much because the chief didn't tell her very much, but I'm excided about it if it will help our tribe.

Pocahontas

Maryland

CHAPTER 42:

A MARYLAND INDIAN; IVY SQUIRREL

By: Kat Davidson

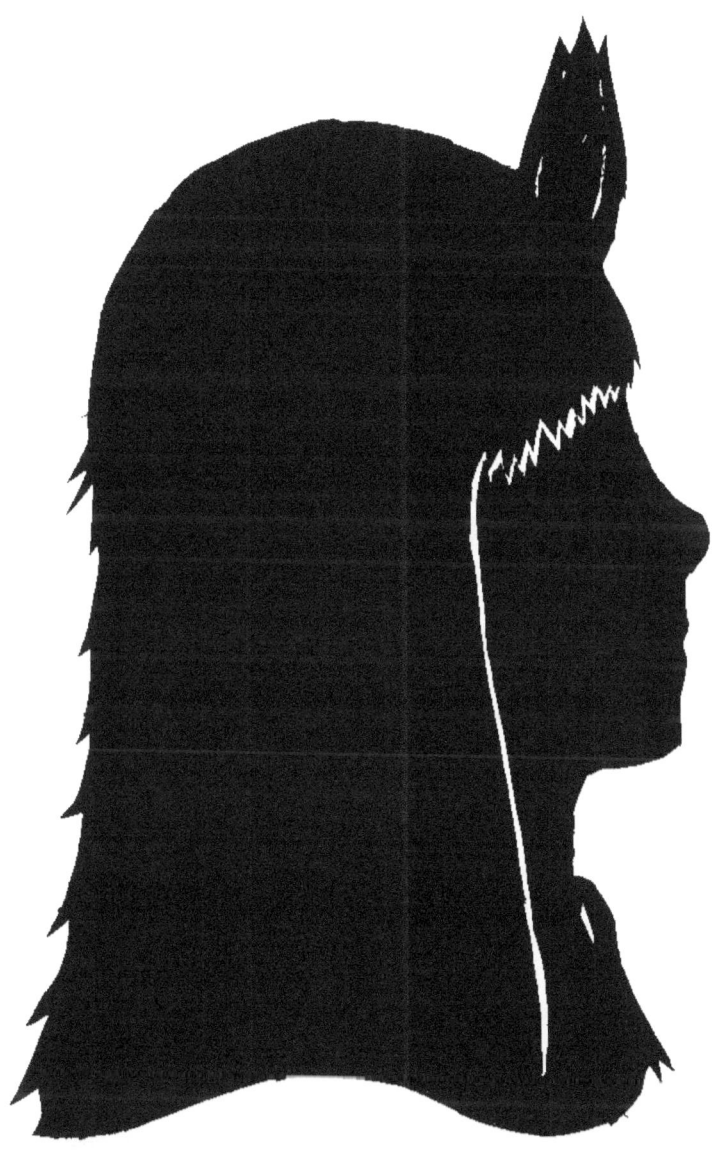

Introductions

Dear Diary,

I'm Ivy Squirrel. I become an adult in just a few more moons. I can't wait until I get my adult name!

My father, Chief Dove Tail, is going to hold a huge ceremony celebrating my coming into womanhood. If my grandmother hadn't died, she would have performed a bunch of rituals for it. I guess I'm going to have to do them myself. Good thing she taught me how before she died.

The other day my friend, Gea, from a sister tribe, asked me to tell her a story. I decided to tell her some stories that my grandmother told me.

Besides storytelling, I also like to hunt. I am one of the few women that know how to hunt. My favorite form is archery, but I also know how to use a spear and a tomahawk.

Well, I have to go now. Bye!

Three Soldiers

This morning I was in the woods hunting, and I saw three soldiers. I guess they saw me too, because they started coming towards me. I turned around and ran strait back to my camp.

About half an hour later, the soldiers appeared. My father asked them their names and what it was that they wanted. They said their names were Charlie, William, and Smith. They asked if they could have food and shelter.

My father of course, being the nice person he is, let them stay as long as they were under watch. I thought he was being a little too generous, but as long as they are good, I guess its okay.

The Sugar Act

I was walking through town carrying a few skins, looking for someone to trade with. I noticed most of the people I saw looked somewhat mad, especially the people who live in the real big houses. It made me a little depressed, so I decided to trade for some of that sugary sweet stuff that always makes me happy, molasses.

I found someone I could get molasses from and traded one of my furs for as much as it was worth. It wasn't as much as I had gotten before, but it was enough to last a while.

As I continued walking around the town, I spotted a paper sweeping across the ground with the wind. It was a NOTICE stating that there was a new tax on molasses and lumber. It claims this is because of the end of the war, so does that mean it's partially our fault? Ah-well, one little tax won't hurt that much, will it? I wouldn't think so.

The Tea Act

All of the town's people have been really angry since the Tea Act came from Parliament. I think it's mostly because they only lowered it so their company didn't go bankrupt, or because it's just a dirty trick. Do they really think their own people are stupid enough to fall for something like this? That's a little cruel.

I found out about all this when I was once again walking through town looking to trade. This time though, I was trading extra meat. Since it was the start of summer, my tribe didn't need the extra meat. There had been a lot of it too; I guess we had gone a little overboard on the new summer game the day before.

In the store where I was getting my father's whiskey, there had been a group of men talking, and I couldn't help but eavesdrop while the man got the bottle. They were talking bad about Parliament and about the Tea Act. I guess they think they're stupid too.

About what I said before, I was wrong. One tax can start a fight, five can start a war. I sure don't want to see what would happen if they gave us more.

Intolerable Acts

In a little less than three months, four acts were passed, the Boston Port Act, the Massachusetts Government Act, the Administration of Justice Act, and the Quartering Act. The town's people nicknamed them the Intolerable Acts. The name fits well.

The Boston Port Act and the Massachusetts Government Act don't affect us much, but the other two do. Because of the Quartering Act, if the officers want their soldiers to live with us, we have to let them, and if we don't they'll take all our land. Also, if anyone in my tribe gets in trouble with a soldier, we have to go all the way to Britain because of the Administration of Justice Act.

Everyone is angry with them, except for the soldiers on every corner, of course. They're probably cheering in their heads. All the towns people know the war has started, and whether they're for it or against it, it's going to continue to happen.

CHAPTER 43

THE SECRET LIFE OF EMMA LYNN KAY

By: Hunter Michelle Kay

September Tenth, Seventeen Sixty-Five

Dear Diary,

Hello, I'm Emma Lynn Kay. I am a 10-year-old girl living in Annapolis, Maryland. I was born on September 9, 1756. My father, Jonathon, owns a shop where my entire family works. I also help my mother, Sybil, with dinner and at the homestead. I also have one cat. I got him on my 5th birthday. His name is Luke. He doesn't get along with the chickens very well though. Sometimes, I must say, it gets pretty hilarious when they peck at his rear. Well, I am an only child. I enjoy living in a small home. That way I can be with my family more and there isn't as much to clean.

I love my family and friends. I have one amazing friend but her father made her and her entire family move to Massachusetts. Her name is Eliza May. Her father didn't approve of her being friends with me. Only because my family and I are not rich like they are. Even though her father doesn't like me, Eliza May is still my best friend. I would do anything for her as she would for me.

Well, mother is calling me to help gather the eggs. I must go. I hope I get to tell you more about my life soon.

-Emma Lynn

September Fifteenth, Seventeen Sixty-Five

Dear Diary,

You would never guess what I overheard mother and father talking about. It shocked me when I heard what they were saying. With all the taxes on lumber and sugar, father is starting to lose business in the shop. So mother and I are going to have to start pulling our weight around here. I also have to start helping out at the shop after school everyday.

I also heard father say that if people can't pay the taxes and help to keep the shop we must get rid of it. All the taxes are getting ridiculous! I really don't want to lose the shop. I want to own it when I get older. Well, when father passes away. I will depend on the shop to make a living and help feed my family, when I have one someday.

Well I have to help mother fix dinner for when father gets home. Hopefully he had some business today.

Emma

September Twenty-Second, Seventeen Sixty-Five

Dear Diary,

Guess what... I just heard more terrible news! The Crown put higher taxes on skin, parchment, paper documents including but not limited to: legal documents, permits, commercial contracts, newspapers, wills, pamphlets, dice, and playing cards. I think this is absolutely ridiculous. I mean if it doesn't have the King's stamp on it is illegal! That is nonsense. This is just horrible. Now we are really going to start losing business at father's shop. I haven't a clue what we would do without the shop. Hopefully, we can make a living off selling chicken eggs.

Also, if we can't earn enough money, we will have to sell the house. This is just all very terrible. I think the town is going to go on a rampage. I would be surprised if they didn't. Well father is home. I must help him take his boots off.

-Emma Lynn

October Nineteenth, Seventeen Sixty-Six

Dear Diary,

My father just told me that we would be having three British soldiers staying at our house for a while. They are coming next week. I am terribly upset. I don't want three rude, ignorant men staying in my home. They will destroy everything. But they must stay, or else father will be put into jail! This is just unplanned for. Well, more about them.

The first one is named Cameron. He is 20. He's been a soldier for 3 years. That means he's been a soldier since he was 17 years old. He is staying with us until his ship comes to take him home to his family.

The next man is Mathew. He's 19 years old. He has been a soldier since he was 18. That means he has been in the war for only one year. He has to stay with us until he finds out when he is getting shipped back over seas, or until he has been discharged. I hope he finds out soon.

Last but not least, there is Ben. He's 22. He's been in the colonies for 4 years. So that means he joined the army when he was only 18 years old. He is staying with us for one week.

They will be helping us with the shop. They will stock shelves and be getting items for our costumers. So that's pretty much it.

-Emma

December Thirtieth, Seventeen Seventy

Dear Diary,

I just want to tell you a little more about me. So at this moment I will start telling you about my fears. I am completely terrified of spiders. I absolutely hate their furry legs and all of their beady little eyes when they look at you. I definitely dislike when they crawl on you. I am terrified just writing about them.

I also hate snakes. One reason I hate them is because some are poisonous and I hate when they slither around you. I especially hate it when they just pop their heads up and stare at you.

I would definitely have to say that my biggest fear of all is that I won't find a descent husband. Then I won't be able to have a family. If I don't get married and have a family I will stand out from all the other women. Also, father would be terribly disappointed. I would hate to disappoint my father. He is a wonderful man and I just wouldn't have the guts to do it.

Mother is calling for me to get ready. I am helping father out at the shop today. I am so excited.

-Emma Lynn

January Thirteenth, Seventeen Seventy-One

Dear Diary,

Today my father, Jonathon, helped me whittle a block of wood. It was so very exciting and very tiring. Father says whittling is an art. Father also says we may sell our final masterpiece if we like. I'm not that good at whittling though, so I don't think I will sell mine. The block I whittled just has a smiling face carved into it.

My father also started to teach me about rope tying. We didn't get terribly far in the lesson because it was almost time for father to get back to the shop. But I did learn to tie a basic knot and also that rope tying is a survival essential. That is why Father must sell it at his shop.

Oh! Dear Lord! I didn't even realize the time. I must set the table before father gets home.

Until next time,
Emma Lynn

February Twenty-Eighth, Seventeen Seventy-Two

Dear Diary,

Today father, mother, and I discussed what I am to do with my life. Father has so many expectations for me, I am not sure I can or even want to do some of the things we discussed.

First, I must learn the family business. I have already started to do most of the work only to show father I can handle the shop.

Then, I absolutely must marry. Although father insists I marry a man with money. Although it may not happen, he is doing this for his own greed to save the shop.

I hope that after about a year we try for children. But before we have children, we need to find a nice strong house that we can live in. Also the house must be suitable for children to grow up in.

The entire time we talked I wanted to shout out, "FATHER! What if I don't want to marry a man with money? And what if I can't physically have children?" But I never would have shouted this out; I would have been in deep trouble. Father might even have slapped me on the wrist! Now you see how much trouble I would have been in.

It is just that the truth is… I think I have already found the one I will marry. I met a young man at a park. His name is Jakob. I would tell mother and father about him but, he doesn't have much money. Father would be disappointed.

Jakob and I meet up all the time and talk. He is always complimenting me. He is too sweet but I enjoy it. He said that I will be the one he marries. I blushed when he said this.

Well, more about Jakob. He is 15, and has shaggy brunette hair. He is tall and strong. He is also a blacksmith apprentice for William Vanderford. His mother is Mary Alexander and his father is George Alexander.

The truth is… I think I love him. And I do plan to marry him. I am just waiting for the right moment to tell mother and father.

Father is calling for me to get ready to go to the shop and set up for opening.

Emma Lynn Kay

July Twelfth, Seventeen Seventy-Two

Dear Diary,

I am now 17 years old and am now ready to tell my mother and father that I am in love. I am absolutely in love with Jakob M. Alexander! We want to tell my parents tonight that we plan to get married and buy a home together. I am afraid of how they will react when I tell them. Father, I know, will be terribly disappointed in me, and tell me that I should have found a man with money. It's just that I don't care what father says. I am in love!

As you know, I met Jakob one year ago. We do almost everything together. That's why I am almost never home. I also can't tell mother and father where I am. The truth is that I am usually at the park walking and talking with Jakob.

Hold on one moment please!

I am terribly sorry; somebody was knocking on the door. It was Jakob. Well, I think father is about home so I am going to greet him at the door. Wish me luck!

> Time to tell mother and father,
> Emma Lynn Alexander (Kay)

May Tenth, Seventeen Seventy-Three

Dear Diary,

I overheard my father talking about the new tea taxes. All of these taxes may, again, make Father have to close the shop. I really don't want him to have to sell the shop. I love it. I was pretty much raised there.

Father is losing so much business. I mean the King added a three pence tax. Isn't that ridiculous? The people of Annapolis are upset and angry. They are saying this is the last straw!

I must go now. I hope I get to write to you soon.

> Emma Lynn

November Fourth, Seventeen Seventy-Four

Dear Diary,

My class just read a ton of new notices sent over by England. These notices are called the the Intolerable Acts by all of the papers. All of this is getting completely out of hand.

Let's see, now we have the Administration of Justice Act, the Boston Port Act, the Massachusetts Government Act, and the Quartering Act.

There are so many new notices that were sent over. I'm not going to tell you what each one is about. All I'm going to say is that, His Majesty is getting way out of hand.

Well, I must finish the potatoes and rest of dinner before Jakob gets home. Talk to you again soon, I hope.

-Emma

August Second, Seventeen Seventy-Five

Dear Diary,

You would never guess what's happening. People everywhere are having secretive meetings! I over heard a young woman talking about it during tea. Then Jakob came in and told me that men are asking him to join these meetings. I told him absolutely not! I couldn't take the risk of him getting caught and me losing him.

I don't know what the meetings are about yet, but if the Crown finds out they are in deep trouble. Well, I do know one thing about the meetings... I know that the men of the colonies are talking about war to get these ridiculous taxes to stop. They are also talking about getting us to become our own independent country. I am terribly frightened for the men. I agree with what they are doing, but they need to stop before King George finds out about them.

Jakob says they are organizing a Continental Congress. I was startled when my darling husband told me this. I just about dropped my tea cup!

Although I must say I do agree once again. I want to have independence, but I don't think it is worth the risks our men are taking.

I wish I could write longer but it is almost time for Jakob to get home. I want to be downstairs when he gets here.

Until next time,
Emma Lynn

August Fourth, Seventeen Seventy-Six

Dear Diary,

Today I will tell you all about <u>The Declaration of Independence</u>. It was written and declared that we are FREE! We no longer are under the rule of the Crown and King George himself. I understand this will mean war. I am sort of frightened, but I will get through it because it will be worth it once it is over. Now hopefully things will change and there will be <u>independence!</u> Father and Mother are terribly happy. Jakob is happy too.

Oh! You will never guess but I met three of the fine men that signed the Declaration of Independence! I met William Paca, Thomas Stone, and Samuel Chase. I was absolutely nervous when I met them, but I'm happy I did. They helped me, my family, friends, and everyone around the colony declare our independence.

Well, Jakob just found another notice on the front porch about the Declaration of Independence. I want to go read it.

Must go read,
Emma Lynn

CHAPTER 44:

ISABELLA; A GIRL IN MARYLAND

By: Kelsea Kello

About Me

Hello, my name is Isabella. I am 15 years old and I live in Baltimore, Maryland. I was born June 7th 17, 1755. I am a shy girl. But I'm still nice, really nice. I love to weave, make candles for the house and really love to read. My dad taught me how; I'm so proud. I go to a private school, well not private I'm schooled at home. My teacher's name is Mr. Wesslen. He is a great teacher. He has raised me while my parents work. He has been with me since I was a little girl. He takes me to my church. I am a Christian and I love God. I also love church.

Sincerely,

Isabella

Soldiers

January 15, 1775

Dear Journal,

One Monday morning I was in my house and men from the government came to my doorstep. They told us that we had to take three soldiers from the courthouse or they would put my dad in prison. So we went with them to the courtyard and they had three solders in front of us so we took them home. We showed them around the house but they seemed to not like it at all. They didn't cat the food we offered, they ate food that they had been given when they were in the army. We give them a place to sleep then we asked their names. They replied, "Mosses, Peter and Charles." They are nice people and they are very clean. It's been a while since they were first in the house so we had a very big dinner. That was the end of them.

My Fear

I am going to take the next step in life soon and I fear it. I'm afraid that I won't have enough money for life. I want to have kids, but I'm afraid that there won't be food on the table at breakfast, lunch, and dinner. I want to have a husband and kids... I want to have a job but I will have kids soon and can't work... I will have to do cleaning around the house and be a stay home. My husband will have a job to help provide things for my family.

My father said that when I move on with my life he will be there... My father is wealthy enough to help me and him at the same time. I will school my children but if they want to they can go to a regular school. I will support my children with the things I have. That is why I'm scared to take the next step in life. My husband will hopefully follow in my father's job of being a doctor. We will make enough money to do things in life. I am kind of looking forward of getting out of the house in my own life...

Candle dipping

One morning my mother introduced me to candle dipping. It is really fun at times but you have to dip about 100 at a time then you hang them up. It's tiring but I got used to it. I make plenty of candles for my family every day. I also weave; I weave clothes, blankets, and cloths.

Boston Port Act

1774

Today I was walking down the street and saw angry people and a mob gathered around a paper. I walked over there and I asked a man what was going on. He said that there was a Boston Port Act passed. He explained that when we dumped the tea in the harbor the government said we hade to pay it off. Now we cannot ship things or get what should be sent over until it's paid. He spoke his mind about it and then I said that I did not think that we should have to pay for it and that we cannot make money if we do not have any thing to sell. How are we going to pay it off any ways if we have the money? I do not know.

CHAPTER 45:

LIFE ON A MARYLAND FARM

By: Maranda Sosa

All About Me

April 28

Dear Journal,

Hi my name is Elizabeth Laynes and I'm a 14-year-old girl living in Maryland. Today was a very difficult day! I had a whole bunch of chores and schoolwork to do!

I'm in the ninth grade and am living on a farm with my mom and dad and brother. We harvest all kinds of veggies like corn, carrots, cabbage, etc..... We also sell milk meat and eggs and tobacco, to the other local farmers, and to the general store.

Well got to go chores are waiting,

Elizabeth Laynes

My Fears

When I grow up I want to be just like my mom! I want to have three children and have a good husband to live with. I do not think I will ever want to change my life! It might be even better when I grow up!

When I grow up I want to have some family reunions on my new big farm! Also I want to have an "a b c " building for kids to stay at when they have nothing to do on Saturdays so they can hang out with their friends and have fun!

I want to do all of these things, but I also have a few fears for the near future! Some of them are just like what other young women are worrying about these days, family and home. I hope that I have a really good future ahead of me.

I'm really afraid of my future ahead of me.

Elizabeth Laynes

The Three Soldiers

Dear Journal,

It was yesterday that we had three soldiers come to our home and they were the ages of twenty, thirty, and eighteen. They had brown hair and were very tall. But amazingly they respected us. It was a very scary experience and I'm afraid it'll happen again. My thoughts and feelings change every day but the most common thoughts are, "Would they steal something?" and my feelings that were most common was that I was scared!

But having to share a home with them is even scarier. My other two sisters and I were crammed up in one room. And when dinner time came around the eighteen year old soldier named Adam helped us with the cooking, and he offered to help with the cleaning!

Ill never forget the time I had to take care of three soldiers last Christmas.

I will always have a story to tell now!

Elizabeth Laynes

Townshend Act

Dear Journal,

Today I have just heard 'bout the new Townshend Act and I don't really like it. I was walking from school to the store to buy my mother some tea and there was a tax put on it! And it ain't a very reasonable tax! But its not only on the tea, it's on the glass, paints, lead, AND paper! It's ridiculous!!!!

And to stop smugglin' all ships' captains have to have their detailed manifests of their cargo and their papers will be checked before anything can be unloaded from the ship. Alex Laines said that his uncle can't import illegal goods anymore. That ought to teach him a lesson.

So I bought my mother her tea and I bought me some new needles to help mother make some yarn dolls for my best friend's birthday. Well I have to help mother around the farm now.

Elizabeth Laynes

Tea Act

May 10, 1773

Dear Journal,

Today when my best friend and I were walking home from tea, we read a notice about the new Tea Act. It explains how from now on tea shall be shipped directly to his majesty's colonies, and nowhere else. Many people were really happy about this part: tea shall be sold with no new taxes placed upon it and shall be immune to previous English exportation. But that was just the beginning of my horrible day!! But then a lot of people started thinking that there was a hidden tax in the still high cost. The cost has lowered but by just maybe six cents!

Yesterday I went over to my friend Diana's house and we talked about her children. But then I had to go because Diana's Grandfather had been killed in a riot. I feel deeply sorry for her and hope she feels better in the service tomorrow. And to make matters even worse it is only two days until her birthday. When people die I want to ask God why he had to take a loved ones life away from family and children.

I never really thought of how I want to perish. If it was in place of my family or my friend, I'd want to go peacefully.

In memory of: Franklin Hughes

Birth: December 16, 1696

Death: May 8, 1773

Elizabeth Laynes

Notices

July 28, 1775

Dear Journal,

Today I have heard of the new resolution made by the Continental Congress today while visiting with my mother. It started at about sun fall, mother and I were cooking some dinner, and then father came in with the news. He told us about how the Second Continental Congress called for a second meeting. And he explained what had happened when he was at work on a business trip. He explained about the war in New England and what had happened there. I cannot believe that George Washington is our war hero and has also been appointed General of what has been dubbed the "Continental Army" to help protect the citizens of New England in this conflict. Even though I'm somewhere in between a Whig and a Tory, I think this resolution will mean that change will happen!

Even though many people will think this is destroying Maryland, I think it will fix some problems. What am I saying? What if my soon-to-be husband read this and got mad? He should not! This is my life and not his! He hates the whole Whig and Tory thing and I just cannot decide which to choose. Just like me, my brother and mother have their own beliefs. My father will not yell, he will just ignore us and pretend that we do not exist. But my husband will most likely pretend he never saw it and just try to ignore it. He's an ex- British soldier and does not want people to fight over the little things and possibly die for some other person's wrong doing!

We're due to get married next week but if all of the problems keep happening, we might post-pone it until next month!

Sincerely,

Elizabeth Laynes

Future Mrs. Elizabeth Warren

CHAPTER 46:

COLONIAL GIRL

By: Sarah Crouch

The Three Soldiers

My mom just told me that three soldiers are going to be staying with us for a couple of months. I asked her, "Can they stay somewhere else?"

She said, "No, because the government told everyone that they had to have three soldiers stay at their house and that includes us." Well who cares? I will be gone most of the time because I will be farming and going to help the little kids do there work from school.

When I was still there they came to the door the next day they have the stupidest ascent ever. Their accent is British. I told my mom that I never want to hear them speak to me as long as they are here.

The next day I was in the back yard farming and they came out and asked if they could help. I said, "If you want." So, they started farming and we got done way faster. Then I went in the house because I had house work to do. They are not that annoying. I guess they don't have that stupid voice that gets on my nerves.

A couple months have passed and they have to leave in one day. I will miss them. They were actually very nice.

The next day it was very quite because they were very nice. Then everybody was back to normal, kind of.

CHAPTER 47:

A COLONIAL GIRL; MYA NAPIER

By: Amanda Holtsclaw

About Me

My name is Mya Napier. I'm 14 years of age and my birthday is October 4. I can get kind of shy, but helpful and outgoing. My education is based on my mother. When you want me to listen I'll give you full attention. I am a Christian.

I enjoy making clothing out of fathers, and hunting down animals. I also like to dance and paint. I have three sisters and two brothers. My best friends are Abigail, Eliza, Akue. I love to enjoy myself in my spare time by helping my mother and myself.

The Stamp Act

Today I went to town so that a friend and I could trade. I was giving her feathers and my friend was giving me candles so I could put them in my home with my family. Once I was down there I heard everyone talking about this stamp; it was a seal. In order to get the stamp you have to pay more taxes based on what you decide to get.

Three British Soldiers

There are three injured and tried British soldiers. I want to help them because I don't want them to hurt my family. I want to feed and shelter them until they recover, because I don't want the government to take my family. I'm here to help out the soldiers until they recover and feed them and bathe them, and treat them with lots of respect. My concern is not having them harm or disrespect my family. Yes, I would really help them just so they can get better. Then I could have my family decide if they can stay here for a little until they can recover.

The soldiers' have hurt legs and shot wounds on them. Harmful things have happened to them. They also have cuts and all different kinds of injuries on their bodies. I'm a little nervous because I haven't had soldiers in my household before. I don't want them to turn against us. So as soon as they heal we want them to go back to doing what they did before they came with my family. But, we will let them have food and make them feel very welcome and comfortable here.

Working with Leather

I experienced using leather and it isn't as easy as it seems. It's hard to work with all the hammering and materials needed for this experience. It's very hard because you have to pay very close attention so you don't pinch your finger trying to nail it down or what not. My friends and I were all working with leather getting what should be done but lots of us got injured. Besides this, it's really fun but if you don't keep an eye out you could get cut or lose pieces of material.

We made all kinds of things out of leather; key chains, bracelets and head bands. They were all pretty neat looking. Everyone did their own thing that they wanted to get done and it was easy for them to get materials for what they decided to work with. A lot of work can get done within 2 or 3 days or sooner, depending on what you're working with.

Next Step in Life

I am taking the next step in my life. I fear that I won't have enough money to live and support my family. Because I want a big family I do have a husband we want kids later on. I have to make sure to have money to put food on the table at breakfast, lunch and dinner. For my household I need to clean and cook for my family, but once I have kids I'll have to help them and teach them how to work. When my kids get to a certain age they will get sent off to do their own apprentice work and provide for themselves. My family has to have support to live and be able to work and clean, and love each other all the same way.

What I'm not to afraid of is knowing that I will have my husband by my side. I can work all that I can before having my kids and becoming a mother. I'll need all the help and support of my family so we can eat and survive. My husband does not expect much from me; just to have dinner on the table. He will be just fine by the way we live. I am afraid for later on in years that I will not be able to survive with all these problems and still make time for the children and at the end to earn money to make food by the garden and crops to afford the gardening work.

Boston Massacre

I am eighteen now and we just discovered the Boston Massacre has happened. We are scared about what may happen now. But me and my family and friends aren't too worried because we know it can be worked out somehow and that the colonies will get through it. We know we will find out all that we needed to and that we will do what is told.

CHAPTER 48:

A BLACKSMITH'S APPRENTICE IN COLONIAL MARYLAND

By Dustin Newt

About Me

August 8, 1770

Hello my name is Rodney Jackson. I am a blacksmith's apprentice. I live in Maryland and our mayor is Charles Jackson. Our capitol is our biggest city called Paulsville. My everyday life consists of going to church on Sundays.

I'm usually found welding things, but I do have other stuff I do like hunting, fishing, and other things. I'm also Christian. I do not live with my family so I don't remember their names very well. I live with my master Ricardo Sevilla. I am a very talented person in all kinds of ways, like for instance I am very smart and fast so you can see why I was chosen to be an apprentice.

I am learning to read and to write in school right now so I can be pretty busy all the time. I also am learning how to blacksmith more advanced things. I also sometimes watch my colony's livestock for extra money which is chicken, cow, sheep, duck, steer, and horse. I also go to the local Indian camps at night to make weapons for the local Indian tribes, the Nanticoke and the Chesapeake. My master doesn't know that I'm helping them to get back their land so it's best not to tell anyone.

My colony originally came from England and that's where our mayor used to be a blacksmith. Our colony is mostly Christian. Our colony also has a lot of gold, quartz, and crystals. We also have a lot of imports and exports that we handle at our docks and harbors.

My friends are also usually busy too, but we hang out in our free time. Their names are Johnny, William, and Maurice. They always say I have a better personality than them. I don't know why though.

I sometimes even travel with them to our five biggest cities and towns which are Paulsville, St. Mere Eglise, Elkville, Charleston, and Wheatland. I also transport imports and exports with them to our docks which are called The Sebastian Port, Eastland Docks, and the Portland Harbor. Some of our imports and exports include tobacco, wheat, rice, and indigo. They are usually sent to England.

So as you can see life for me and my colony is always busy and we are hard workers so keep on trying.

The Black Hearted Soldiers

Dear journal,

The strangest thing happened today as I came home. As I came home I saw some soldiers in my house. At first I was worried so I then I went inside of my home and asked my ma why there were soldiers in my house. At first I didn't mind, but then what ma told me next was a little nerve wracking. Even though the soldiers had to stay with us I had to show my manners still. I was actually kind of happy that the soldiers were here because there has been a lot of trouble lately. It wasn't all bad either. Besides, British soldiers are like friends to me.

As they stayed in our home the soldiers played games with us and I enjoyed it , but later that night the soldiers hearts that I thought were in the right place turned out to be as black as night. I had left that evenin' to go get some food at Mr. Diem's store. When I entered I was in shock. There standing over Mr. Diem were the three soldiers. I didn't say a word as I stood there. Then slowly I headed towards the rifle in the back. I was still very nervous as I heard Mr. Diem beg for his life as the soldiers beat him senseless. Then in one quick stroke I jerked the gun from its perch and shot one soldier in the arm.

They ran out the store. In the distance I could see them running and yelling to other soldiers on the way. I helped Mr. Diem get up and when he was on his feet he thanked me very much. I asked what were the soldiers doing here and he said, "Defying the law around this here town."

I asked if he was alright. He said he was and the he told me, "Run home as fast as you can Johnny and don't say nothin' about what you saw." Then he said, "When you hear gunfire don't look back, and whatever you do don't tell the soldiers where you were tonight. Understood?"

I shook my head yes and ran. A couple of minutes later "Bang!" I heard Mr. Diem scream in pain and a few seconds later "Bang!" another gunshot had fired and I only heard the silence of night.

The next day the soldiers were pulled out of my home. I was relieved after what happened last night. I did what Mr. Diem told me to and I never ever told a soul about what happened that night. As the soldiers left I was also very relieved they didn't see me shoot the gun otherwise I would've been hanged. After the soldiers left my pa had arrived home. As he walked in he asked if anything interesting had happened at all. Ma had told him about the soldiers and what would happen to him if they didn't get to stay with us, but I just said, "Nothing interesting happened at all for me pa." Then as my parents left I said to myself, "I did what you asked Mr. Diem."

My Fears

Dear journal,

The fears I am going to talk about are ones that I have had gotten over the years. They are mostly ones that I got from blacksmithing. My first fear is being killed by a British soldier. As you may know I got it from when I saw that those soldiers killed Mr. Diem. My second fear is not passing my apprenticeship for blacksmithing. I could lose that fear by concentrating on my work and study more. These are only a couple of my fears.

My next fear is getting a family and not being able to support them. Of course I will know what to do when I get older. My next fear is a little odd to most people, but to me it's not funny. This fear is the fear of opera. Go on ahead and laugh it up. You are not the first person to laugh.

Finally I will tell you what my deepest darkest fear is. I have a fear of heights. I got this fear when I was 9. It was a sunny day and the streets were bustling. Me and my friend Thomas and his family went to church since my mom and dad were away at Boston. While we were in the church I looked up to see how many floors there were and of course we had the biggest church in Maryland and it had 8 floors. We went to the top floor and as we sat down on the chairs a fire had started behind us and we were trapped, but we got down by sliding down the drapes. So there you have it. Some of these fears I have may never go away, but in due time I will lose these fears.

Hands On

May 10, 1767

Dear journal,

Today my master taught me something so amazing and so interesting that I felt like I was in heaven. He taught me how to silversmith. At first I didn't know what it was, but when I learned I was eager to do. My master told me the basics of silversmithing and he also told me where it actually originated from. He also said it was how people make money. After he told me the basics I told him I was ready to work over the hot, blistering furnace when I finish my coin.

After I told my master I was ready to make a coin he handed me a piece of parchment to draw my design. So I thought to myself what my own design would be and I chose the classic skull and crossbones for my amazing design. Then I showed my master my hand drawn design. He asked if I really wanted this design and told him yes. Next he handed me two pieces of clay to carve my design in. When he gave it to me he said that this may be the only chance I'll ever get. So when he gave me the clay I headed to my home to work on my design.

When I got home the cold darkness had taken over the light and I knew it would be hard for me to see to carve my design into the clay that my master gave to me. At first it took me a while to get started because I forgot that I was supposed to make a base and in frustration I carved my base and recarved my design. Soon after I carved my base I had finished my design and went to bed to get some rest for tomorrow. As I went to sleep I thought of how good this coin would look once it was finished and then I fell into a deep sleep for the night.

The next day I woke up and realized that today was the day to get my coin created. As I stepped outside I noticed that the air had turned blazing hot. So I went inside to get a drink of water first. Then I grabbed my clay and ran out into the wilderness to get to my master's workshop. After I got out of the wilderness I could see my master waiting for me outside his workshop. I quickly ran up the musty dirt road and I had finally reached my master's workshop.

When I got to my master's workshop he greeted me and told me to get ready. Soon after I got ready I went back outside and went into his workshop. I then gave him the clay and he then went to the furnace and I followed. When we got to the char covered furnace my master began starting it up. He then showed me the process of melting the metal and he showed me the part where you get your coin. As the metal finished melting he began to pour the hot liquid metal into the clay and then he got my coin out of the clay. He gave me the coin to hold and then he said I can take it home. As I left he told me that I did well on the coin and he complimented me. I told him, "Thank you".

As I headed home I thought to myself about what I did and the experience I had. I looked back at my coin and then I said to myself what a good job I did. When I got home my thoughts were broken as my ma told me to come and eat dinner. As I sat down with my ma and pa I told them what I did and I showed them the coin I made. They told me they were proud of how well I did when I showed them the coin. After dinner I went to bed and I thought to my self yet again. I went to sleep a few moments later.

The New Tea Act

Dear journal,

Today as I was heading into town there was a big ruckus. I went to see what was goin' on and you wouldn't believe it. King George the Third has sent another act. I didn't know it at first until I went into my workshop and saw a notice on my door about the Tea Act. I read it and as I read it I thought that this is another scheme that King George has made to get more money. I crumpled the notice and tossed it away as I finished reading it.

As I went to start today's order for a sword I heard screaming and crying. I took a peak and some of the people who disagreed with each other on the act start shooting at each other. I ran to the back and grabbed my rifle to end the fighting. I shot a warning shot. The men turned to me as I told them to put down their weapons. They did and the people in the crowd cheered at what I did. I thought to my self. King George has done it this time.

As I went back into my workshop I said, "Even though this new act isn't as bad as the others I will still never accept Britain." I definitely didn't like this act.

That evening I went to my home to discuss the new act with my wife. I told her that this new act will tear us away from Britain's trust even more and this will not help our relationship with them. She agreed. I then told her that if this continues there may be more senseless fighting with Britain. Eventually our trust and relation with Britain will be no more.

I hope that Britain will stop soon as I kept discussing with my wife. She agreed and gave her opinion that we might as well just ignore Britain. They are just bad news. One things for sure though that Britain will just do more things like this. I said to my wife that if Britain doesn't stop we may land in war or some kind of revolt. I also said that if Britain thinks I will help the East India Trading company then they are wrong. After the discussion I went to sleep and didn't think about what happened today.

A Big Mistake

Dear journal,

The British have gone way to beyond the call of duty! The actions the British have done are unforgivable and foolish! I mean, I understand what my fellow colonists are doing and that they have a reason for it, but the British have definitely gone too far. On the other hand the British are doing this because of men like John Hancock. I think if men like John Hancock keep doing this it will land us in a huge war.

Right now the only solution is to rebel against Britain otherwise were done for. Hopefully this solution works. There may be other solutions, but I doubt it. Besides I already know negotiation won't work. My solutions definitely changed since last time. Right now I fear no one can help us.

The Despicable Intolerable Acts

Dear journal,

"Morning already," I said to myself as I drug myself out of bed. I headed to the kitchen hopin to get somethin to eat, but as I went into the kitchen there was no breakfast. I noticed my wife had left and then I realized that my wife had to go get some food for the week so I left to go to my workshop out in town. As I entered the town as usual somethin was goin on in this town, but this was nothin ordinary. A riot had begun so I ran into my workshop for safety. When I entered my workshop and locked the door behind me I noticed another act on the table, but these were nothin compared to the ordinary acts. There were four acts. When I read the notice I went into blind rage and ripped up the paper and I yelled, "What is wrong with Britain?"

This time I knew that this may very well destroy my life and my fellow colonists' life. I then grabbed my gun and ran outside to find some British soldiers. As I was outside I could see a squad of British soldiers killing my fellow colonists. I then began firing my gun at them. They fired back. As the gunfire went on and on more people died in the crossfire, but eventually I had killed the British soldiers. The moment the shooting stopped I really felt that these new acts really should be the Intolerable Acts. I agreed about the name about the name for the new acts.

I went to town hall after the riot had ended to go to the public discussion. People were yelling and screaming at the mayor. One person said, "What will we do about the damages caused in the riot?"

Another said, "We need do to something about Britain's behavior". People seemed really upset as I did. One thing is for sure people are with the men of Boston and New England as am I. It is time for something to change around here now.

Viva Revolution

Dear journal,

Today is one of the worst days of New England. War has begun with England and an outbreak of fighting and riots have begun in the colonies. I only hope we will not lose the war though. I have also heard that the 2nd Continental Congress has announced a resolution has been made to break away from Britain possibly. I think the resolution made by the Congress is a good idea as well. I agree with it because of King George and Britain making us pay for everything and ruining our lifestyle. I know it's not discussed a lot though. People are not sure that they want to break away from Britain though because that's were we get our resources from, but staying with Britain may not be a good idea anymore.

If we do break away from Britain life may be harder for a while, but we will eventually learn to survive on our own. I mean who is dumb enough to stick with Britain though. All they do is make our lives harder for us to control while they sit in piles of money. To break away from Britain for our colony would mean a happier lifestyle for us since we are having a hard time with Britain. Hopefully a decision would be made soon enough before New England falls to Britain.

One thing is for sure, breaking away from Britain for me would mean absolute happiness. I would get more money people would buy more of my stuff from my workshop. On the other hand resources may be harder to get and production would be low. So far I stand with my fellow colonists and what they think. As I said before it would mean more peace and happiness. Besides who would want to be with Britain? I have heard that they plunder towns and villages now. So I stand with my fellow colonists.

I know another thing too. Nothing in the entire world would make me change my mind at all. Not even gold would change that. I will tell you why I won't change my mind. It is because of what King George has done. This compares to the entire New England because people are mad at what is happening to us. So there is my point. I only hope this resolution will have great success.

The Declaration

Dear journal,

Today I have learned about the Declaration of Independence and that it was read aloud. I have to say that now America has broken from Britain I have to say I'm pretty relieved that this tyranny from King George has ended. I also finally got my job and my home back so things seem to be turning back to normal. Everyone was still celebrating after July fourth. I have to say when I heard the news I was overjoyed and I still am.

Another thing is that I met one of the signers of the Declaration. His name was Thomas Stone. He was the one who helped me with some problems. I was definitely honored to meet him too. He is also a nice man too. I hope I will see him again.

Looking back on what happened in the past, a lot of stuff has happened like those acts. Things I also said back then that there were things that were right and wrong at the same time. One thing is for sure is that things have changed a lot. I definitely mean it to. My wife agrees as well.

Another thing is that our new country will have a rough start, but that will change all in due time. I expect is that things will quiet down. People will also be relieved to return to their normal lives. Another expectation is that we will one day make bonds with other countries. Our country will also prosper.

So as you can see we made a difference. That difference made a change and that change formed a country. Were finally free from tyranny and can relax for once. We will never have to worry about Britain again. Above all we can do whatever we want to now.

CHAPTER 49:

A GIRL IN MARYLAND

By: Brooke Thayer

British Soldiers

Oh dear this week has been very harsh. We had three bloody, hurt soldiers all British come to our inn. One was very hurt, his name was James Peers, he was 17, and wasn't wanting to talk to me. He had a wound in his side and arm. Second was Robert Tilly, he was the youngest of the three, he was 15 and very clingy. He had a shot in his arm. Third was Thomas Duff, he was the oldest at the age of 19 he was really tall and had a broken arm.

I let them in and they asked if I had a bed for James I said yes and helped James to the bed while the other boys sat at the table and started eating the food I sat out for them. While helping him to his bed he said something that I did not hear, so I asked what he said and he said it was nothing. After awhile we got to the bed and I laid him down and was about to leave when he asked me not to go, I stopped and asked why. He said he had something for me and asked me to come here so I came. He grabbed my hand and as I was about to pull it away he put something in my hand, something cold. I took my hand away and left the room, closed the door, and opened my hand to find a little silver heart all rusted and dirty.

Going upstairs the boys were done eating and looking at our stuff. I asked them if I could show them their rooms and to follow me. They followed down the stairs to show Robert the smallest and Thomas the biggest rooms, James had the second biggest. A few more hours went on and it was dinner. I served Robert and Thomas a slab of beef, beans, and cornbread while they played a card game. I took James' plate to his room, but as I entered the room I saw him quickly hiding something I would ask but I decided not to. He got up and took the plate, grabbed my arm, and sat me down on the bed. He closed the door, sat next to me, and took my hand in his.

I was about to ask what he was doing but he shushed me and whispered, "I have something else for you." He then kissed me on the cheek. I was shocked and my face turned red. He let go of my hand and started eating.

I got up and walked out the door Robert and Thomas was done with their game and was done eating. I grabbed their plates and before I could get them off the table Thomas grabbed my arm, stood up, and asked "Did he kiss you yet?" I turned bright red then he smiled and let go.

I went upstairs and put the plates in the wash bowl. The door opened letting the warm summer breeze in right along with my dad, sister, and brother. When dad saw me in the rocker and he started yelling about me not being at work at the inn. Then James came up the stairs with his plate and I went over to get it.

Jocelyn, 17, my sister, asked who that was and Kyne, 18, my brother, said, "Are you her man?"

I said no and told my dad that the three soldiers are here. The rest of the week was weird and romantic with me and James. We both got together and made my dad emotional.

My Fears

Hi, it been really long since I wrote but I know something that will never take long, my fears. Well I don't really have any fears anymore but when I was little my parents told me there was a monster under their bed, so as a little girl I used to think that there was a monster under my parents' bed. But then a few months later I found out that it was just my mothers dress and a pair of my dads trousers, I asked them why they told me that and they said it was to keep me out of their room.

Candle Dipping

This day can not get any better, I'm going with my mom to my very first candle dipping lesson. The candles mom brings home, those magnificent candles are so beautiful. Well I'm going to make candles as beautiful as moms'. I have to go eat breakfast then get going. Got to go BYE!!! …………………………………………………….. Well it turns out that you can only make beautiful, 'colored' candles in the higher classes, turns out mom has been there for 6 years but I still made my very first candle. Still I'm going to light it in my window tonight.

First Act

Wow an act, we got an act. I wonder what's going to happen next. Financially I can't afford taxes on molasses and my brother just can't get the right size lumber if taxes go up on it. If these taxes go any higher it might be difficult for my auntie to come and visit.

Running Dry

Ugh, we have no customers It's almost like everybody is dead or something. Ever since the act got pasted there is less and less money, jobs, and trades. I really think the Stamp Act is just a waste of time getting stamps on paper, that's ridiculous. Still I can't afford any of these taxes not ONE. With stamping every piece of paper they can find socializing is going to be hard. Everybody is going to be mad, why does the king have to tax us on a mere piece of paper.

Smugglers

Well first how would John like to be tarred and feathered? That tar is scorching hot after seeing one of our residents that is staying here. And why tar the poor man John is clearly a smuggler you can even check his ship to prove that that man is innocent. People who buy these products from the people who smuggle them might or will get put in jail. Right now I see no solutions that come up in my head for these people.

Trick or Treat

I too, think it is a trick, but some of me is so happy that they aren't raising any taxes with this new act. I sense very little trust between us kids and our mother. Any more taxes they will degrade but lower taxes it might increase. Yes, I see some problems with supporting them why can't they get any money form the king, who I may remind you is running us dry.

Intolerable Acts

I told you there were more acts. There might be only one act that is concerning us and it is the Quartering Act but that don't mean there isn't more coming our way. I don't know exactly which side they are choosing but if you ask me I couldn't give you a strait answer because, I have no side.

Whigs and Tories

Well I don't like to choose sides but for this to it would be for the Whigs, the ones who want us to be a colony, the one who wants us to stay together and not give up on hope. No, there is nothing there could be done to change my mind even if they had some poisonous snakes ready to kill me I still won't change; I'll still be for the Whigs. I don't know about comparing but affecting my friends and family is ok their not that excited about it . . . if they're even supposed to be happy?

Declaration of Independence

Ahhhhh this is so great I'm so happy they are finally doing something about these acts and other nonsense. Also I met 3 of the signers of the Declaration. I got to met John Hancock, Thomas Jefferson, and John Adams.

How I know these people is that my dad is friends with John Hancock after bumping into him some where my dad wouldn't tell me though then inviting him over to the inn for dinner. I know John Adams from that court thing with the solders. I mean the towns' people were really mad when they won.

And I met Jefferson at the Boston harbor. That bump in was quite weird. The meeting was quite weird. There was yelling and debating I thought that we wasn't going to get independence then Mr. Adams said something. Man that turned everything around we started to 'win' then on the election of the declaration and everyone said yes.

Virginia

CHAPTER 50:

THE HARD LIFE OF A COLONIST

By: Benjamin Barlow

About Me

My name is Levi, and I am 14 years of age. I live with my mentor and his family. My mentor is about 38 years of age. His name is… well I don't know his name. I always refer to him as "sir".

I have 2 sisters and 1 brother and of course a Ma and a Pa. My brother's name is John, and my sisters' names are Constance and Juliet. My father's name is Robert, and my mothers name is Ramona. My mother is Spanish.

I am sorry to say I have a poor education. I can do simple mathematics, such as 2+2=4, but I can't do Algebra, like some of the rich kids.

People make fun of me for being a Christian. I go to church on Sunday, so people can not say I am not religious.

I have many skills, such as cooking. On Sunday I help my mentor's wife, cook supper. It is one of my favorite things to do.

When I do have free time I like to talk long walks in the woods, and go fishing. It helps me clear my mind, so I'm not confused with the world.

The Quartering Act - 1765

I walked through town to get my Ma and Pa's house, because my master let me have to do no chores. As I walked my nose deceived me. I smelled my Ma's fresh baked apple pie. Warm and juicy, the best pie in the colonies. I tried to hurry in fear of not getting a slice of the pie. As I continued on my way, I found a multitude of people, surrounding the notice board. Naturally my curiosity received the better of me, and I worked my way through the crowd.

When I reached the notice board, I found a new notice from King George the third. According to the name on the notice, it is called the Quartering Act. It declares that all colonials must house three British soldiers. If the colonials do, not do as this notice says, their family will be fined, and the man of the house will be thrown in prison.

With this new news, I headed off for my parents home.

When I arrived at my parent's house and I knocked, I was surprised to see three burly soldiers standing inside of my parent's home. And then the stories started. How the soldiers came to this house, and others. I tried to stay away from the Brits, so I would not get hurt. As I was doing so, I was surprised to see my younger brother John, hiding up in his room. After I asked why he was hiding, he explained that he was scared of the soldiers, and I was surprised again. The reason that I was surprised is that he is one of the bravest little boys I know. It shows you that no matter how hard you try, you will always be scared.

I wonder what will become of these thirteen colonies.

Levi

Levi's Thoughts

I was walking through the forest, because my mentor gave me the day off, and that is what I like to do. After walking for a distance I came to my favorite place to sit. The place is on a tree stump that is soft wood, so it feels better than most seats. I pulled out my knife and I started to whittle on a piece of wood. As I whittled I thought about my future and my fears.

My future is going to be a carpenter, and there is nothing I can do about it right now. I hope that I will become a legendary carpenter, and that people from all lands and all places will come to have me make them a chair, or a cabinet or maybe something else altogether. I would like to get married and raise a family. To be able to provide for them. To have some form of shelter. To have freedom, or have a righteous king.

My fears are that when I finally become a carpenter, that there will be no need for them. That I will not marry and that I will not have any children. That I will not be able to have a home. That I will either live in fear of the king, or that I will be executed, before this country is free of this wretched king.

I hope that my future will be bright. And that I will have no need to be afraid.

Levi

Whittle Workshop

Today, when I went to town with my master (because there was a meeting for all the carpenters in town) I was told to wait outside. While I was out there they had a workshop for all of the apprentices. The workshop I participated in was a whittling workshop. As I started to whittle a canoe all of the other apprentices said it looked like a banana. I hope that I will finally finish the canoe at home. What I am trying to do is get it whittled down so it is perfect and then I will give it to my master's children as a Christmas present.

Hopefully I can keep it as a secret from my master's children and I hope they will enjoy it. If it works as I want it to, it will be really, really cool.

Levi

The Townshend Act - 1767

I was whittling on a piece of wood, when a man, on a horse, came onto my mentor's property. He saw me and called out in a croaky voice, to help him off of his horse, and after he did so he started to sway in his seat. As I ran up to catch him, the mistress came out to see what all of the noise was about. When she saw the man, she yelled into the house to get some towels and some hot water. Her oldest daughter Elizabeth came running out with the items. Then the mistress told me to take him inside of the house, and to put him on a bed. We took care of him and after a short period of time, he woke up, told us who he was.

When he woke up his brow furrowed in concentration, trying to remember where he was. Than he saw his horse outside and he remembered his trip. He told us that he was a messenger for the king even though he did not support him. He was told that if he did not represent the king his land and family would be taken away. He was to post the new notice in every town in all thirteen colonies in thirteen days, or he would fail and be punished. He then gave the mistress a slip of parchment.

After she read it, she explained what it meant in a form of words that made it easier to understand. She said that it was the Townshend act. That it taxed paint, tea, parchment, lead, and glass. The taxes where small but they are on everything. And so when you pay the taxes you pay a lot of your hard earned money.

This is what was going on in my head, after she told us that. This is stupid! The Townshend act!? When will Britain realize that we colonists are people too? If Great Britain is not careful, this will go down all around them. Great Britain or as the traitorous Brits say the "Mother country" needs to hang. They are so incompetent I wish that the king would rid himself of these fools that he calls advisors. If he did that I know he would be a better King, but until that he will be known as the treacherous king.

But she was not done. She said that John Hancock has had his ship confiscated, because he had a false list of the manifest, for the things on his ship.

On a completely different note, I had a dream last night. I saw These 13 colonies free from Britain, and all united. There was a man to run the country, but if he became corrupt we could over though him, and it was not against the law. That the colonists were free and that the British were not mad at us, that they were at peace with us!

This would be wondrous if the world were as to my dream.

Levi

The New Tea Act - 1773

I was walking to the shopkeeper's shop to buy some peaches for the mistress. When I went inside I realized two things. First that it was noisy, and second that it was full of people. You could imagine my surprise. I had expected two or three people, because this is not the most popular shop. When it was my turn to order what I wanted to buy, I asked why there were so many people there, and he said that because he was no friend of the British, he was secretly selling the tea at its normal price. He was disobeying a British law. I was scared and I thought that the soldiers would barge in at any moment.

After I got out of the shop I noticed the piece of parchment that was on the notice board. It is called the new tea act. It makes the tea price small, and ends all taxes on the tea except the Townshend act.

As I walked home after reading that, these were the thoughts that were going through my head. I can not believe the British think that we are that stupid! They make it so you can only buy British tea. Their tea is not the best and I know that some people would like a change in tea some time. Everyone in town knows this is a trick. At least the East India Company is allowed to bring the tea strait here. It was that they had to take it to Great Britain, and then to the colonies.

I wonder what will become of the colonies, and Britain.

Levi

The "Intolerable" Acts - 1773-1774

All these acts at once, it makes my blood boil! People around town are calling these the intolerable acts. The Brits deserve to die for this. Do the British want the colonists to revolt!? If they are really that stupid then these 13 colonies deserve to break free.

The "Intolerable" Acts are the Massachusetts's Government Act, the Administration of Justice Act, the Quartering Act, the Boston Port Act, and the Quebec Act.

The Massachusetts's Government Act means in simpler words, that Massachusetts can not choose their own leaders. It is a cruel act that fellow colonists can not choose who they want to lead them.

The Administration of Justice Act means that if a soldier has wronged you in any way they have to go to the mother country. If a soldier kills your cow, they go to Great Britain to receive their punishment. They will receive an unfair punishment in their favor.

The Quartering Act means that if there is not enough room in the barracks, you must give them a place to sleep. If you do not do this the person in charge of the soldiers is allowed to take your home by force. A lot of people deem this as unfair, but no one is brave enough to stand up for themselves.

The Boston Port Act means that the port is closed. No vessel of any size is allowed to get in or get out. This is part of their retaliation for the Boston tea party. Seeing as how that is where we get all of our resources, this is a very bad thing.

As I said before it makes my blood boil.

Levi

Continental Congress - 1775

I have just heard of the first and Second Continental Congress meetings. I have heard that we will probably go to war with England. On the up side of things, I hear George Washington has been dubbed commander of the Continental army. He was a war hero in the French Indian war, so every one in town is very happy, and they all want to meet him. And they will get their chance because he lives hear in Virginia.

If all of this goes to plan, this should go very easily. Let's hope this does go to plan.

Levi

We Are Free – July 6, 1776

I was outside trying to carve a design, into a cabinet, when a multitude of people ran up the street. They were yelling, and they were running. As they were doing so the thing they were yelling was "freedom, freedom!" As they ran past, one of the colonists stopped and explained what was going on, and why they were celebrating. He explained that the piece of parchment that would make Great Britain lose their hold on us has been signed. After he told me that, I ran inside to share the good news. I told my mistress, and my ears were almost blown off. She yelled and said that, that was what she has been wanting for a long time. After she went to tell my mentor. The oldest girl Elizabeth came around the corner and she embraced me in her arms.

When I went to bed, I could still smell her hair, feel the embrace, and the joy that I felt when she did so. I realized then that I enjoyed her company, and I had feelings for her.

I woke up in the morning, to a large multitude of people. I looked out the window, and I saw one of the men that signed that piece of parchment, that meant so much to these colonies. Thomas Jefferson. I ran downstairs and asked him a few questions. He told me that he was just another person, and that it was us the people that made him great.

The states are free. They will continue to be free; I will make sure of that.

Levi

CHAPTER 51:

EMILY EAKER'S TRAGIC LIFE

By: Makaela Rader

About Emily Eaker, a Doctors Daughter

Dear Journal,

Hello my name is Emily Eaker, and I am the doctor's daughter. I am 13 years old, and my hometown is Jamestown, Virginia. My birthday is August 8, 1757. Since my father has enough money, he is able to pay for school for me, so I have a very great education. I was never home schooled. I have a few different skills, I am very organized and I love to read, sew, and cook. The reasons I love to do these things are because, these are the things that I will have to do later in life when I have a family, so why not enjoy it?

I am a very proper young lady. The reason I am that way is because, I have grown up being taught that way. I think it is important to be brought up that way. My dad is the doctor of Jamestown, my mother cooks at home, and I have two sisters, their names are Hope and Faith. My family and I know a lot of people from our colony. We really know the carpenter because if my father thinks that one of his patients is not going to make it much longer, he asks the carpenter to make a casket. My family and I are Christians as well as most of the town. We go to church every Sunday and I read my Bible every day and night. I guess you can say that I have a very religious family. Those are the main facts of my life.

Sincerely,

Emily Eaker

The New Guests

Dear Journal,

One night my family and I were eating dinner and all of a sudden someone was knocking on our door. My father opened the door and it was the local government. My father asked if there was anything he could do for them. The government said that we need to let a few British soldiers stay at our home. My father said that we don't have enough room. Then they said that if we do not allow them to stay that my father will have to go to jail and my family will have to pay a huge fine.

So the next night the soldiers were at our home. My mother was washing the dishes and the soldiers walked in. They were all dirty and they had sweat dripping down their faces. Their names were Ben, Nate, and John. My father said the beds are this way and you are welcome to bathe yourselves. They seem very different. They seem too not to have any manors. My mother had already made them pallets on the floor in the attic. Now knowing that there are going to be guests in the house, there is going to be more work to be done, so I offered to help my mother.

My sisters Hope and Faith are shaken up about it also. The home is very crowded, knowing that there are eight people living here. The next morning I woke up extra early to help start on chores and help cook breakfast. After we all ate breakfast the soldiers left and more chores were to be done. At least they won't be here all day everyday for long. Those are my thoughts for now, and I will write again soon.

Sincerely,

Emily Eaker

My New Items

Dear Journal,

Today my mother and I had just recently made a wax candle and a colorful pot holder. The reasons I made these things are because, I can use them in our household. The process I used to make it is simple. For the candle what I did was I took a stick and wrapped a string around it. Then I boiled some hot water and took a container and put wax in it. Next I put the container in the hot water. After the wax has heated up and melted, I gently dipped the strings in the wax. The first dip I held it in the wax for sixty seconds, then held it out for three. Then I held it in for three seconds and took it out for three. Next I held it in some cold water, and let it dry. I just continued repeating the process until I had it the shape and size I wanted it.

Then I weaved a pot holder to keep my family and me from burning ourselves on hot objects. The process I used to make it is very easy. At first I got a loom and some scrap material. I picked a pattern to use and I just weaved in and out. Well we are vey busy right now and I will soon write again.

Sincerely,

Emily Eaker

The Boston Massacre

Dear Journal,

My friend Rebekah had just arrived at our home today. She told me about something very horrible. It was called the Boston Massacre. She told me everything about what happened. It was so horrible, I wanted to cry. This is very shocking to me. I heard there was an angry mob throwing ice and snowballs at the British Soldiers, then the Soldiers started firing their muskets. People claim they heard the word "fire" come out of the Captain Preston's mouth but Captain Preston swears that he did not say "fire". It came from the alley behind his soldiers.

Only God knows the truth. I just hope that whoever said it gets punished for it. It has shaken up the whole town. It has affected my life in many ways. John Adams must have a lot of guts to stand up for the British Soldiers. Hopefully the right thing will happen and there will not be a fracas about it. It is very confusing and very sorrow. Those are my thoughts for now and I will soon write again.

Sincerely,

Emily Eaker

The Two New Notices From My Fellow Colonists

Dear Journal,

I was on my way to the breakfast table and my ma and pa were silent. I asked them what was wrong. They handed me the two new notices. They are about how His Majesty will not respond to our letters of complaints. Now a conflict has erupted between the soldiers and us. I think it is a great idea for George Washington to finally step up. We need someone to help us who knows what they are doing. I hope the conflicts will eventually ease up. This is great because, George Washington is from my colony, Virginia. I think this is great, the only way I would change my mind is if he betrayed us. Most of my fellow colonials agree with me. That is it for now and I will soon write again.

Sincerely,

Emily Eaker

The Declaratory Act

Dear Journal,

Today a fellow colonial had handed me a piece of paper. I was thinking to myself wondering if it was a new notice. They need to make up their minds on what they are going to do with our thirteen colonies. I am just tired of all of the arguing and fighting. Sure enough it was a new act, it was the Declaratory Act. This notice advised Prime Minister Rockingham's replacement for Prime Minister of Grenville and repeal of the Stamp Act. I think my fellow colonials may feel over powered. I know I do. I believe of myself to be a free American. I think the issues will just continue. I do think we need laws, but not when we are under complete control. Those are my thoughts for now and I will soon write again.

Sincerely,

Emily Eaker

New Changes

Dear Journal,

Things have been very stressful lately. I woke up this morning and I just sat on my bed and thought to myself and I was thinking of all the responsibilities I have. I yawned and was telling myself to get up and face the facts. My ma and pa are pushing me close to the edge. There is just so much I have to do today alone. I guess it is because, I am an emerging adult. Probably what I am going to do with the rest of my life is get married and be a stay at home mother. I am a little upset because, that is what I am expected to do.

I want to do more than that. I want to be outside with my friends and own my own shop. I have the fear of being a mother and a wife. I feel like I am a grown woman in a teenager's body. I do like being mature but, sometimes I need a little break. I plan to meet my soul mate, know him for a few years and get married. Later I can have children. It is just so very nerve wrecking. Well I have a lot still ahead of me today, so these are my thoughts for now and I will soon write again.

Sincerely,

Emily Eaker

Four New Notices

Dear Journal,

This morning I was walking through town and I could smell a loaf of bread coming straight out of the stove. I received four new notices from the baker. My fellow colonials are calling them the Intolerable Acts. They all revolve around the Boston area. There has been the Boston Port Act, The Administration of Justice Act, The Massachusetts Government Act and the Quartering Act. My friend Rebeckah and I think that is a huge amount of acts.

Even though I live in Virginia and this is taking place in Boston, it is still a huge deal to me. It is shocking in some ways. I don't think the East India

Company should get paid back because, if they want to tax us higher just to get richer, they should go bankrupt. The way that could happen is the Sons of Liberty should pour the tea into the ocean.

It just won't help Boston out by pouring the tea into the ocean, it will help us. I don't know about my fellow colonists but I support Boston. Everything is just going crazy right now and my head is spinning. People are worried and nervous all at the same time. Those are my thoughts for now, and I will soon write again.

Sincerely,

Emily Eaker

My Mistake

Dear Journal,

I woke up this morning and realized that I wanted to have an occupation and own my own store. So I cleaned up my loft and got dressed quickly. I went to the local store and asked Mr. Green if he was thinking about leaving the store any time soon. He said not any time soon. I asked him if there was any help needed around the store. He said no. He seemed very upset. I was just thinking about my family and I. I guess I made a huge mistake by asking, and I should just stay with what I am doing. Those are my thoughts for now and I will soon write again.

Sincerely,

Emily Eaker

The Declaration of Independence

Dear Journal,

My friend Rebekah just told me about the 2nd Continental Congress. It has officially been signed and I am so happy. I feel a huge amount of joy inside of me. This is a great impact for our thirteen colonies and our future to come. I get to have the experiences my grandmother did not get to experience. In a couple weeks I get to meet Carter Braxton and Thomas Jefferson. They are two of the signers from my colony, Virginia. I have had so many great experiences in my life. We will no longer be ruled by Great Britain. We have gone through a lot in my colony and the other colonies. Now we are free and we have our own Independence. Hopefully things will run more smoothly. My days of being a young little girl are long over.

Sincerely,

Emily Eaker

CHAPTER 52

A BLACKSMITH IN COLONIAL TIMES

By: Lamarcus McClain

About Me

My name is William H Smith. I am a blacksmith. Growing up I watched my father work as a blacksmith and I wanted to be a blacksmith too. It is very hard work.

My father trained me to be a hard working blacksmith. My mother was taking care of my two brothers and sisters. I am only 13 years old. That is how old you have to be to become an official blacksmith. I am a Christian which means that I believe in God. I have no friends because father always said that friends are bad. Well that is all I have for you now.

The Soldiers

I have just gotten a letter saying that I have to take care of three British soldiers. I do not like that at all. Then if we don't take care of them we either get fined or jailed. I also heard that some of them have houses already. Why can't they go to their place? If they have family I am sure that they would want to see them. I don't really have that much food and I have to support my family. Besides what have the British ever done for me? Well I guess I have to deal with it. I know that I don't want to go jail. But that is how I feel.

When I am Older

I know that I am emerging as an adult and that there are expectations. The first thing that I am going to do is get my shop into order. I will have enough money to support myself and my family if I decide to have one. I also realize that this can be a really scary thing to do and to look forward to. I am going to have to face my fears.

I might have a few fears to face like living on my own. Especially with the British people doing what they are doing. I am expected to be at my shop every morning. I am expected to support the British soldiers. Last but not least I am expected to follow the rules no matter how much I don't like them. Well that is my thought on that.

Actually Blacksmithing

My first hands-on experience was very intriguing. I really enjoyed it. First we heated up the stove with fire which was good. Then we put the bowl that you had to use to burn metal. Then we put the metal in the hot bowl. Then we watched the metal burn into a liquid. When you put the metal into the hot bowl and it melts into a liquid it looks like lava that does not have any red in it. Then we put the liquid into this carved sculpted frame. The liquid instantly froze. Some sculptures did not work. I know mine didn't. But it was really fun.

The Tea Trick

I am okay with the fact that they took off one tax. They still are not in charge. I am in charge of myself no one else controls me. My fellow colonial friends and neighbors will probably get mad. They don't just want one tax off they want all of the taxes off. I believe my self to be an American. That is my country.

I don't think that the British will stop. They think that they own each of us. They are going to try to control us. In my opinion we need to go to war. We have to show them that they cannot just do anything. In this case a war would be the perfect thing to do. We need to stop being scared.

The reason I want the taxes is to end all of this madness. I sort of don't want the war to happen because a lot of houses could get destroyed. They have gone mad with power. That is what I think about this act.

Intolerable Acts

Dear Journal,

That is it! I am so tired of these acts. This time they have gone way too far. All of these acts do not make any since. I am so fed up with the British people I could go hang one right now. When the town crier announced those act I wanted to hurt the British people that did this. I mean everyone accept the children. That is how mad I am right at this moment.

They said that they want us to pay off all the money that we owe. This is the money from the tea that they dumped into the harbor in Boston. This is not fair, not one little bit. I am not paying any money and there's nary a thing that they can do about it. This is their entire fault. If they had never taxed the tea in the first place they wouldn't have dumped it.

Then they said that the citizens of Massachusetts may no longer elect their own government officials. This stuff has really taken another turn. Someone needs to stop this.

We need justice, liberty, respect, and freedom.

Continental Congress

Dear journal,

The 2nd Continental Congress has been made to stop all of the bad things from happening. The people who will write and sign a Declaration of Independence are making a statement. They are saying that they don't want to live like this anymore. That they want to be free and not to be like slaves. They want to be treated like everyone else including the British. I believe it says that man shall be treated as one individual. Also a war has continued to break out between the British and the English colonies.

Declaration of Independence

I like the idea of the independence. I am here at the 2nd Continental Congress in Philadelphia to witness the signing of the Declaration of Independence. I have hopes of meeting John Hancock or John Adams. This will be the moment of truth. We will see who will sign the form and who won't. We will see who is for it and who is against it.

I like this idea because I want to end all of this. That is why the people who are signing this will go down in history as the people who sign the Declaration of Independence. This is telling the King that we disagree with the things that he has done. This is not just about making a statement this is about making a change, making a difference. This is to stand together as one whole and not separate parts. That way we can stand together as a unity.

That is what I think.

CHAPTER 53:

THE EXPERIENCE OF A LIFETIME

By: Haley Napier

Three Soldiers

Dear Journal,

I was sitting at my house prepared to eat supper when, all of a sudden, three soldiers banged on our door. We all took cover. "LET US IN!" screamed one soldier. When Christopher opened the door they barged into our home and they introduced themselves.

The first soldier said, "Hello my name is Jonathan."

The second soldier said, "Hello my name is Jeffery Kenyan."

The third soldier said, "Hola, I am José Sanchez and I am studying Spanish. I am a great traveler and I joined the army to help build up my strength. If I die I would die for my men. I was very grateful the very first day that I came into the army, and every one greeted me with a big hello!"

Everybody in our family said hello, except me. I was scared of the three big men that gave me a fright as soon as they walked through the door. But mother told me to say hello to the nice gentlemen. I kind of shrugged and quietly said, "Hello, my name is Illiana, I hope you enjoy your stay at my home."

Jeffery Kenyan, the second soldier said, "How did you know that we were going to ask to stay here? We just got here and we haven't even said a word about our staying."

I looked up at him with a smile, "Oh, how did I know? The only reason I know is because Mama and Christopher were talking about it in the kitchen, and I also found a notice on the ground and I read it. It said that a few soldiers were going to be coming to a few houses and be staying for a while at some of the houses on Conch Street. We are on Conch Street."

* 1 week later *

The three soldiers have been very nice and polite to us all throughout the week that they have stayed at our home; all except one soldier, Mr. Jonathan. He has completely taken advantage of us ever since he got here. He is also very rude. He talks like he is in a barn with horses and cows around, making the sounds that they make. It does not make any sense to me the other two soldiers were very nice and calm and quiet and he was such a disgrace! He trashed our home and does NOT clean up after himself. I will report back later, mama is calling.

Until then,

Illiana Johnson

Fears

Fears? Hmmm ...... The most fear that I have ever had is running the general store and not doing very good. I think that when I become old enough to run the store that I will burn the place down or maybe I will make friends with the wrong person and they will tear the shop to shreds! This is the most fear that haveabout when I become an adult. When I am not working, I fear that the Indians will soon decide to take over our land and claim what is rightfully theirs' Those are my worst fears about becoming an adult;   I sure do hope that none of them will come true.

When I Grow Up

Dear journal,

In the near future I think that I will do a very good job of working at the shop with my two brothers. Mostly I would like to work at the shop for Father. He was such a kind gentleman, but he was so strong and playful! * sigh * I do miss him oh so much, he was so nice, and things were a lot easier when he was around. I think that father would be very happy for me to take pride in something that he once loved. I shall think of him every time I sell something. Mother is calling.

Until then,

Illiana Johnson

Whittling

Yesterday I watched people whittle. It looked very fun, but hard. Some people struggled to get it right and some people cut themselves. If you do not know what whittling is, then I shall tell you! Whittling is when you take a knife and cut wood to shape it into anything of your choice. It can be a chair or anything that you can think of, as long as it is able to be made of wood. And as long as you have a big enough piece of wood, you can do anything! When you whittle you have to be very careful, or else you can cut yourself.

The first thing that you do when you whittle is take the knife and get all off the bark of the wood. When you get all of the bark off and it is nice and smooth, you can start to shape it. If you are thinking that you will never know when you are done, the answer to that is yes you will know. How you will know is it will start to take the shape of whatever you are making. Don't worry about a thing if you are going to learn how to whittle. The only thing that you have to worry about is cutting yourself, just be very careful if you are going to whittle and always have adult supervision!

The British Trick

Dear journal,

I agree with everything; it is probably a trick so they can get to us and pretend that they are the good peoples. We won't fall for this little act that they are putting on for us, it is a show. The impact will be very bad because most people think, or know that it is a trick. I think that the relations will degrade. No, I do not see any problems at all they are just very bad liars.

Sincerely,

Illiana

Peace

Even though I hate the British, I think that the British are innocent. They did that for no absolute reason. The King has nothing to say about the colonist. I think that this will have a bad impact and we should no longer trust him. John Hancock could be a better person and step up and say something if he knows that it is not right. They have changed but not very much. The Indian group would help with the peace thing a lot.

The New Notices

Dear journal,

I do not like any of these notices; I think I will rebel against them. It doesn't affect the people in my colony very much. They are pretty much the careless type. I guess I do agree with naming them the Intolerable Acts; it really fits. I side with nobody because I do not pick sides and do not trust anybody.

Always yours,

Illiana Johnson

The Boston Port Act

There is a question that wandered through my mind as I read about it and it was, "Did they close the port without telling whoever is in charge?" I think the answer to that is yes they did, because people were very unhappy about what they were doing.

The Resolution

Dear journal,

I am not sure what this resolution will mean to the colonies, but it might be very bad and I don't think any one likes what they are hearing. Yes, mostly for my colony. Yes, I hate what people are doing they are destroying mankind. I think I stand right in the middle, I do not trust very many people. The mother country is not on any body's side but her own. There is nothing that could be done to change my mind on how I think about those people. It is not the same as my family, friends or neighbors; they are not like me. They CAN trust whoever and whatever they say; I don't trust anyone but my mother.

Hopefully yours,

Illiana Johnson

North Carolina

CHAPTER 54:

ALEXANDRA MICHELLE FLYNN JOHNSON

By: Elizabeth Cronnon

About Alexandra-privileged daughter

Dear diary,

I have never had a diary unlike all my other friends so if I mess up then I am sorry. I should inter duce myself because it's rude not to and if I were you then I would want to know who was writing in me.

My name is Alexandra Michelle Flynn Johnson. All my friends call me Alex or Michelle. My father's name is Timothy Allan Johnson and everyone calls him Dr. Johnson because he is the town's doctor. My mother's name was Elizabeth Michelle Flynn Johnson, I was named after her. My mother died four days after giving birth to me. Father says that I look and act just like her, even though I have heard some stories about him when he was fifteen. They sound like things that I would have done if I would have thought of them first, I do not repeat others actions if I can help it, I think that if your going to do something it might as well be original.

I should tell you about my friends. The only guy friend I have is James. He has light blue eyes, spiky black hair and really pale skin. When we first met we were in first grade, he did not get along with very many of the guys in our school class and most of the girls picked on him. I felt really bad for him so I became his friend. At first he thought it was a trick so everyone could get a laugh out of it if he said yes, for some reason he changed his mind and we have been friends ever since.

Another one of my friends is Molly Allen. Molly is sixteen. She has dark brown long curly hair that is to her waist, light green eyes, and a lot of freckles. Molly and I have known each other ever since I was born. Molly and I are like sisters because her mom helped my dad nurse me when I was a baby, and ever since then no one has been able to separate us. Molly's mom, Iona Allen is one of the house servants that live with us. When I was six I convinced dad to let me and Molly share a room, so literally they could not separate us and they still can not.

I have one more friend. Her name is Catherin Rose Marten. Catherin is fourteen. We usually call her Rose. She has long black hair which is half way down her back, brown eyes, and is very tan. Rose just moved from Boston, Massachusetts. She was adopted by Mr. Daniels and Mrs. Daniels. All I know about Rose's parents is that her mom was an Indian and her father was a British lawyer, they both were killed in a fire when she was ten and lived with her uncle until Mr. Daniels and Mrs. Daniels adopted her. She does not talk much like me and molly but she writes the most beautiful poems I have ever heard.

Oh, I am sorry! I did not tell you what I look like. I have very long curly dark red hair which is to my hip, a lot of freckles everywhere, and really bright blue eyes. I do not know how to end this dairy entrée for today so I will end it like I would for a letter and I will ask Molly tomorrow morning how to end the dairy entries.

Sincerely Yours,

Alexandra Michelle Flynn Johnson

Townshend act

Dear diary,

I am very sickened about the news we got last night at supper. There is a new tax called the Townshend Act. This one puts a tax on glass, lead, paint, tea, and paper. I mean I am not sickened about the taxes, father makes enough to support the house, I am sickened about what Billy said.

Billy is a merchant that rides on the ship that goes back and forth from the mother country and Boston; well he was on Mr. Hancock's ship this time. When they got into harbor that morning a ship inspector wanted to get on and look around but Mr. Hancock got really protective and would not let him on. Mr. Hancock roused the crowd into doing the unthinkable. The poor man, he was tarred and feathered for doing his job! Mr. Hancock deserves the punishment that he gets for what he did to that man. Next they will be hanging people for fun! The nerve of that chamber pot!

If I were the British soldiers I would not even give him a chance in a trial, I would have him the same sentence he gave that man! Let me tar and feather him for something he deserves! I can't believe people look up to this, this, this disgraceful, unintelligent, heartless man!

What do they see in him? Why would the people like him, because his 'mob' stands for freedom? He causes more problems then he solves! I understand what he is trying to do, but it is not any of his concern, we can't just break away from the mother country so easily. To break off from them would cause a war! We do not have an army, we do not have anyone to lead us, and if we did succeed then the whole world would be against us. I know what the mother country has been doing to us is not right, but what the Sons of Liberty are doing is making it worse on us.

Love,

Alexandra Flynn

Private:

Dear diary,

2 nights ago I woke up and molly was not in her bed. From the warmth of my bed I looked out the window to see if she was in the garden, because when she can not sleep nor has an ill dream she may go out there, but she was not there. I looked around the room to see if maybe I did not see her and sure enough she was sitting at the desk writing something. I was going to go back to sleep but I was curious.

Sugar act

April 5, 1764

Dear diary,

We did not have school today, the teacher Mrs. Wilfong, is sick. The only reason I know this is because father went over to her house last night to see what was wrong with her. She has the cold so we won't have school for awhile!

I went with father to a couple of his patients houses even when I got bored I did not ask to leave. I know that sounds odd but even though it was boring it was fascinating at the same time. I think it's because father is a doctor and grandfather is to so it is in my blood.

After awhile father and I got thirsty so we stopped at Mrs. Daniels sweet tea and crumpet store for a cup of tea and a sweet snack. When we got there the store was almost deserted as it looked. Which is odd because the store is usually packed. I got Mrs. Daniels world famous rose petal tea with one spoon of molasses in it and two crumpets, father got the same. Mrs. Daniels told us that we might want to go to town hall because the king has made a new tax on molasses and lumber.

At the time I did not understand why the store was, as it looked, deserted except for me, father, and Mrs. Daniels until we read the notice on one of town halls big white pillars. It said that taxes on molasses and lumber were going up because the mother country needs more money to pay off the enormous dept from the seven year war and to replace the Molasses Act that expired. The reason that no one was at the store was because no one wanted to spend so much money on sweets. Speaking of sweets, I am going to go to bed early my stomach hurts from eating too many sweets.

Love,

Alexandra Flynn

Fears of the future

Dear dairy,

I did not sleep well last night. I kept having the same ill mannered dream about what will happen to me when I grow up. Not all of the dream was ill mannered though, I fell in love with a handsome man named Alexander then the dream went all wrong! Father did not approve of him and I was not aloud to see him. Then Alexander came for me and we ran away together. Two years later I started to miss my family so we went back to my house and no one was there. I asked around and James said that my parents died of the smallpox looking for me last year. Then when I thought nothing else could go wrong, Alexander leaves me for another woman! I was glad I woke up before something else happened. This would be the worst future ever!

I asked father at breakfast what I would do when I grow up and he said go to collage, fall in love, get a good job, get married, and have kids. I liked all those steps in life except for the last one. I love kids but my mother died because she gave birth to me. That would make anyone afraid of giving birth. So even if father wants to be a grandfather I will not have kids! Collage does sound a little scary too but as long as my friends are at my side then anything can happen.

Oh I just remembered! Molly said I can end a dairy entrée however I wanted to so there is not a wrong way! So I will end it with love!

Love,

Alexandra Flynn

The soldiers come to live with us
Dear diary,

I had an ill dream last night, I can not remember what it was about but I woke up screaming. I asked my father what he thought about this because I have not had an ill dream in so long. I think the last time I had an ill dream was when I was dreaming of what I thought it was like at the Boston massacre after the news came to us. My father said that I might be stressed about school and my best friend, James, has not wrote me back in three weeks. I truly do not know what the dream was about, but I thought that a walk in the market would help clear my head.

Well the walk was peaceful until I saw a crowd at town hall and completely forgot about my dream predicament and went to investigate. I was a little annoyed that no one would let me through but after falling two times, elbowed thirteen times, and getting one bruise on my cheek I finally got to the front. There were fliers and angry people shouting things to each other everywhere I looked. I stood still for a moment to listen to everyone around me for a clue of what might be the problem, but it was too loud. Everyone was screaming ill proper things for a man or woman to think god forbid to even say, so I will not repeat them.

One of the fliers came loose on the pillar from someone yanking on it to the right of me and landed by the gentleman's foot in front of me. I picked it up thinking that this peace of paper might give me the answers I needed. The paper was a new notice called the Quartering Act. It said that if we were asked to shelter and feed British soldiers, then we had to by the next day. If that soldier or soldiers still did not have a place to stay then they could take away your house and your land. Now I see why everyone is so mad at the king. Some people can not even afford to support there own family let alone three or more soldiers. From the faces I saw and the words I heard, I do not think that the colonist will take many more of these most outrageous acts

From what I saw on the faces of the people at town hall it reminded me of a part in the toast James made at dinner the night before he left for Boston.

When we first got these notices people were mad but we withstood it time and time again. With every notice people started to think with the brains and hearts that our holy father gave us and realized that the treatment the mother country gives us is worst then you would treat your chamber pots! The rights we should have as British colonists were taken away the instant we stepped on the boat to take us here. Some realized it before others and stand for what we never had, freedom! People thought that these were a bunch of kids running around saying treasonous things and causing trouble in public to aggravate the soldiers, but for those of us that believe that a change for the better is coming, for those who love this country more then anything we own, and for those of us that can see how we have been treated by them know those 'kids' as the Sons of Liberty and will always fight against the enslavement the British keep trying to do to us, we will always fight for FREEDOM!!

Love,

Alexandra Flynn

CHAPTER 54:

STANLY THE BLACKSMITH

By: Reed Jaynes

The Flashback

"Well, here I am!" I thought to myself as I was getting home from my first day as a blacksmith, "A blacksmith, finally!"

I went into the kitchen to eat dinner that my wife had made for me every evening. "Finally you're home, Stanly. I thought you'd never show up!" she said laughing.

"Well I was working over; you know how much we need the money," I said.

Then after dinner I brushed my teeth. I then headed for bed and stopped in my tracks. "I almost forgot to write in my journal!" I rushed down stairs to get my journal, I searched everywhere for the blasted thing!

Then I finally found it in my desk. I sat down and opened it to the first page, "Mm, what a long way I've come to become a blacksmith," I said. I sat down and began to read my Journal entries before I wrote my last one...........

The Shop

09/08/1763

Dear Journal,

Today was my first day as a blacksmith's apprentice. I met my master, his name is Josh. He's really nice! Except he works me like a dog! I think he forgot I'm only 14 and not his age. He had me cut down wood, carry the wood to the shop, melt metal, and make a mold all in the first day! I guess if I want to become a blacksmith I'll have to do this kind of work... After today's work I went down to the shop to pick up some things for Pa, and there she was, the prettiest girl I had ever seen! She had a vary cute face, blue eyes, black wavy hair that went down to about her shoulders, she had a blue dress on and shinny black shoes . I tried to say hi but I was to shy and she walked out of the shop before I knew it! I wish I had said something...

After that, my best friend, Adam, walked in to buy a pack of cards with his money he got with his allowance, He's a farmer boy and gets up to works in the fields really early and gets done about the same time I get off from training, his dad pays him weekly for his hard work. I met Adam when we were in school for about 5 years and we have been friends for a long time now. I just never took the time to write that in my other journal.

Anyway, he walked in and said, "Hi Stan! How was your first day as an apprentice?"

I said, "Good, did you see that girl that just walked out?"

Then Adam said, "Yes, her name is Samantha. Why? Do you like her?" I blushed and didn't answer his question. "Don't worry Stan I won't tell anyone about your girlfriend," he taunted and tried not to laugh…it didn't work too well.

"Okay, well I have to get these things back to dad before dinner, bye Adam," I said and then I walked home.

Then when I got home dad told me something bout' a couple of British solders staying with us for a week or two and dad said if I were nice to them while they stayed he'd give me a nickel! I don't know what I would do with the money but it's always nice to have some money in your pockets!

Stanly Allen Lain

Church
09/11/1763
Dear Journal,

Today wasn't so hard at work as the other day when I wrote in my journal, in-fact today was really good! All I had to do today was watch Josh melt metal and watch him pour it in the mold, I noticed that he poured it in vary carefully so he didn't burn himself. After work I had to go to church because it was Sunday night.

I don't like going to church that much however because every time I go the preacher asks, "What are you doing here?"

I could never tell if he's joking or really doesn't know why I'm there, I guess I shouldn't have wiped my hands on the preacher's robe after working with oil at work but today was different because Samantha was there!!

Well, I sat down next to Adam in church as usual even though my ma' doesn't want me to because she says Adam is a bad influence. Then again I think she just says that because Adam's mom and my ma' don't get along too well....

Anyway, I sat next to Adam and he couldn't wait to make jokes about me having a crush on Samantha, "So when you merry Samantha, can I be your best man?" Adam said as he laughed hysterically.

"SHHH!! She's sitting right over there," I said.

"Well if you won't tell her you like her I will!" he said. "HEY SA-" I quickly covered his mouth with my hand, she turned around and looked at us, I was covering Adam's mouth and waving at her smiling while Adam was yelling and trying to get my hand off his mouth.

She giggled at use and turned around then I took my hand off Adam's mouth, "What was that for?" Adam said.

Then shortly after that the service began. I had to go home to those solders bickering about who sleeps in what buck on the bunk bed. Remember when I told you about the solders staying with us for a week or two do to some dumb old act? Ya, it stinks. Those solders never shut up! But I have been nice to them for dad, I'm sure its worse for him than me, he's a writer and stays home all day, oh well, not long now.... I hope.

Stanly Allen Lain

The Bicycle

09/19/1763

Dear Journal,

Today was actually kinda fun at work. I got to make a coin today on my own! Here I'll tell you how I did it.... First I made a mold out of clay, I made sure my design on my mold had the mirror effect, in other words I carved it on there backwards, then I went and chopped down some fire wood and brought it back to the shop, I then melted the metal and poured it in the mold, I had to pour it a few times to get it just right, then I was done!

Afterwards, I walked over Adam's house to see if he was done with farm work, but he wasn't so I waited outside the fields for him to finish and after about a half hour of waiting I saw Samantha riding here bike down the dirt road I was on!

She looked so beautiful with her hair flowing in the wind, but then a rock got caught in her bike tire and she fell to the ground. I quickly rushed over to her and helped her up, "Ouch ouch ouch! Oh, thanks...," Samantha said as she struggled to her feet. "Hey wait, you're the boy in church aren't you?" she said.

"Err, yes, yes I am," I said. "So you must be Samantha."

"Yes, how'd you-," she said.

"Oh, Adam, the kid in the field over there, told me your name," I said.

"Oh, that's my next door neighbor. See, I live over there," she said pointing to the house next to Adam's.

"Well I'm Stan nice to meet you" I said.

"Nice to meet you Stan, and you can just call me Sam." she said.

"Well, I need to get home for dinner, bye!" then she hopped on her bicycle and rode home.

Shortly after Adam came out and we played some cards and I went home. The solders left yesterday so it was peaceful once again at our house too! Like I said before today was fun!

Stanly Allen Lain

The Stamp Act

04/05/1764

Dear Journal,

Wow, it's been almost a year since I've written in this Journal. Well I guess today's a good day to do so. I got the day off today because Josh couldn't get enough firewood to start a fire since they started taxing it and he can't find his axe. Did I mention that they passed an act yesterday on molasses and firewood? Yes, people have been raising Cain outside of the shopkeeper's store because of it. I wasn't too worried though because I barley use wood or molasses unless I'm pouring molasses in my tea.

So today for my day off I went over to Adam house and see what he was doing and he was picking the corn for dinner he stopped for a minute to talk to me, "My pa's pretty mad about them passing the stamp act," he said.

"Well, there's nothing we can really do about it," I said.

"Ya, I guess," he said then he went back to his work.

On the way home I saw Sam out in her front yard drawing flowers, I stopped by and talked for a bit. "Hi Stan what are ya' doing?" she said.

"Walkin' home, you?" I said.

"Drawing," she said, and I grinned and walked home....

Stanley Allen Lain

The Shortage

04/22/1765

Dear Journal,

Today I had to go back to work because Josh finally found his axe, so all day to make up for my days off; I had to chop down wood. After work, I found Adam pouting outside of the neighborhood store. I walked up and asked, "What is the matter?" and I regret ever doing that.

"I CAN'T BELEIVE IT!!! They raised the price on cards and dice! I already had some cards but they got ruined when my dad had a bad idea to play cards in the bath tub and I was just on my way over here to get some dice!" he said.

"Oh, well that's some bad luck," I said.

Then Samantha came running up cursing under her breath "HOW AM I SUPPOSED TO DRAW NOW!!! They raised the price on paper just when I had enough money to buy some more!" she said.

"Well, Adam, maybe if you say you're sorry for breaking that china last week the store keeper will maybe give you a discount," I said. Adam shot me an ugly look.

"Well, I got paid yesterday. You two could maybe borrow a couple pounds if you want," I said.

"Sure!" they both said. So Sam bought her paper and Adam bought his dice and cards. Then Sam kissed me on the cheek! I blushed and Adam cracked another joke.

"Ha! He's turning red!" he said. After that I went home and ate dinner…

Stanley Allen Lain

The Conclusion

"Huh, there was a lot I did before becoming a blacksmith…," I said. My wife came and sat down next to me as I dipped my quail pen in some ink. "I love you Samantha Lain," I said.

"I love you too Stanly Allen Lain," she said. I smiled and began to write this last entry before I put it up for my kids….

08/11/1776

Dear Journal,

Last week, I proposed to Samantha and she said yes! Adam was my best man (just like he had asked). It was the happiest day of my life. After the wedding Josh came up to me and offered me a Job as a full-blown Blacksmith. I was honored to take the job and went to work today and when I got home I said to Samantha, "You still owe me those pounds you know" and she and I both smiled.

It has been a long time since my last entry because I have had to live through all the acts which made North Carolina angry at Britain. I participated in the Boston Massacre and survived. I also have participated in the Boston Tea Party. After that I came home (which was last week) and proposed to Samantha, I proposed in the shop were I had first seen her, we are going to live a perfect life, I just know it....

Stanly Allen Lain

CHAPTER 56

A NATIVE AMERICAN GIRL LIVING IN COLONIAL NORTH CAROLINA

By Katie McKinney

About Me

September 9th 1770

Hello new diary, my name is Upe Algonquian and today is my 15th birthday. So far I have gotten 2 presents; a new diary, and pink ink made from raspberries for my quill pen and it's still morning. I currently live in Wingina, North Carolina in a Native American village, just south of the capitol, New Bern, with my mother, father and one brother.

I enjoy crocheting, cooking, writing poetry, and taking long walks in the woods at night, even though it is kind of dangerous. My mother and grandmother taught me everything I need to know and now that my grandmother has passed on, I would like to keep her tradition alive by finishing the colorful blanket she started before she died.

Even though my grandmother and I were very close our personalities are completely opposite. I would describe myself as a calm, shy, caring quiet person, but my grandmother was a fun, loud, crazy person.

Life as a Native American is hard but sometimes fun too, like for example, sometimes my brother and I make a list of objects and see who can find them first. Dinkal usually wins but only because he's only more athletic than me.

My Responsibilities

As a Native American adult I am responsible for a lot of things. As a woman I am responsible for raising a family, cooking the meals. Since I am the youngest female in the house I am also responsible for cleaning our teepee, changing the sheets every week... Okay, you get the picture. I am scared for my and my family's future because our village is almost constantly under attack and that is not an environment I want to raise my family in, so I will probably move into another village so I can have a family there.

Upe

Leather Working

I love leather working even though it is meant for guys I do it anyway. Today I just finished making my leather bag so I can put my food items in it. I have made all sorts of things like, a headband for me, an arrowhead cover for my dad, and a book cover for my mom.

Upe

The Strangers in My Village (Soldiers)

The weirdest thing happened today in my village, three injured soldiers showed up asking for help at least until their better. So I offered to help them but then my brother stopped me and said that I shouldn't help them because they might tell other troops that we helped them, and then they will ask for help too. For once I listened and I'm glad I did because afterwards I asked my mother what would happen if I would have helped them and she said they probably would have had the government harm me or my family. I don't want that to happen to them because I love them very much. Yesterday I worked on the blanket my grandmother started, and I enjoyed it a lot.

Bye for now,

Upe

New Acts

The past three acts of Parliament affect me even as a Native American. One way this effects me is if no one can come through the port then we can't get the meat and all of the food we need and neither can anyone else. Then they will come onto our land and hunt all of our wildlife and our animals to try to survive but that leaves us with nothing so we will eventually die.

Upe

Tea & Sugar Acts

The Tea and Sugar Acts affect me greatly because we have to buy certain supplies and use them to feed my family because we Native Americans don't grow everything. I know it is not custom to our history but we have to be somewhat normal too. There is no point in letting a perfectly good market go to waste because in the winter we can't grow anything anyway, the ground is too frozen and cold. But the tax is a little harsh. It is hard for the people who don't make that much money but I guess Ill just have to save a little more money week to week because winter is coming soon and I don't want my family to starve.

Upe

2nd Continental Congress

After hearing about this "Declaration of Independence" thing I have mixed emotions. I am happy for all of the people this affects but at the same time I am frustrated at the fact that this is a BIG argument and it does not affect me at all.

Upe

A War; No Way

Today when I was at the market I heard some city people talking about a war, that made me sad I don't want to have a war because I'm afraid they will send my brother and my father and we need them to keep the family "In Check" because the women aren't allowed to have any authority in my village. It is believed that men are in charge and I don't see any change in that anytime soon. I got so angry about this that I got mad and broke one of dad's spears because I threw it at the ground and it snapped. Hmmm… hope he doesn't notice…

(Sad) Upe

South Carolina

CHAPTER 57:

THE AUTOBIOGRAPHY OF MADELINE RENEE HARPER

By: Jenna Drinkard

About Me

Dear Diary,

Today, Ma woke me up early. We had to go to the activity planned for today. She said, "We're making autobiographies!"

I was so excited, I jumped out of bed, and I put on some decent clothes. I searched for the perfect dress. I finally found it; my yellow and white dress. That was the dress that I put on when I was very happy. Ma called me downstairs. I did as I was told, and we left. As soon as we got to the activity center, which was at Ma's friend's house, we sat right down, opened the empty, dirty book, and started to write. I was so into writing, that I had lost track of time. I named my book: The Autobiography of Madeline Renee Harper. Inside my book, it said word for word:

My name is Madeline Renee Harper. I am 13 years old and I was born on April 16, 1757. Sometimes, I am very shy. Other times I am very talkative and outgoing. I love meeting new people. I am an ordinary kid that loves to explore the world, and learn new and exciting things everyday. I don't like to do my chores around the house, but that is what earns me all my stuff, and I need to help my mom out since I have a new baby brother on the way. I also like shopping, selling, and running. I love sports. I am in 8th grade.

I have many friends, but my best friends are: Faith, Judith, Dalani, Larry, and Kevin. My parent's names are David and Velma and I love them more than anything in the world. They own the town's General Store, which one day I will own. I am an only child, at the moment, and I love it. Sometimes, I get lonely, but, my baby brother is due on December 25th, Christmas!

I was born and raised in South Carolina. The town I live in is Charleston. Here in Charleston, we grow wheat, corn, indigo, and tobacco. I love South Carolina and I never want to leave! Here in South Carolina, there are a lot of shops, but my parent's shop is one of the busiest. My parents have been running the shop for quite some time now, but the shop has been passed down for generations. My parents sell a lot of stuff at the shop. I work at the shop when they can't, or they are ill. The shop has a lot of Indian things in it because I am Scottish Irish.

I have blonde hair, and green eyes. My mother has red and brown hair, and green eyes. My father has brown hair, and blue eyes. When I grow up, I want to be a teacher. I love teaching, it is really fun. Another thing I would love to be when I grow up is a designer. I can make clothes, and I could sell them in the store. But the most important thing of all, if I have to give up the shop to pursue my dreams, I won't do it. I have to keep the shop in business. That is most important in my life. The End.

I showed Ma my story when I was finished. I could tell by the twinkle in her eyes, that she loved it. After she finished reading, she put down her small, brown beaded bag, gave me a big hug, and said, "I'm proud of you."

Today was a good day, but after all that writing, I need some sleep.

-Madeline Renee Harper

When the 3 British Soldiers Came....

Dear Diary,

Early this morning, Ma and Pa explained to me how the government told them that we have to have three British soldiers live with us and we have to feed them. The government said that if we don't follow these instructions, the government would take Pa to prison, and we would have to pay a large fine. The soldiers are to arrive here at noon. I looked at the clock, it was 11:59. I jumped out of bed, and scurried to my closet. I searched for a decent outfit. To the far left, I found a pink, knee length dress with ruffles on the bottom. After I got dressed, I put on my white shoes.

Then there was a quiet knock at the door. There were three soldiers standing tall and in uniform. My father greeted them in, and introduced us all. One soldier was Kane. He has really decent blonde hair and blue eyes, and he is about 5'9". The second soldier was Adam. He has thin, black hair that goes to his ears. He also has blue eyes that are bright and he is about 6 feet tall. The last soldier was Devon. He has light brown hair and blue eyes. He is very young; he looks too young to be a soldier. He was telling me a story about how he was shot, and had a lot of injuries. I'm sure that he has seen better days.

After we all conversed, Pa asked me to show the soldiers to their room. All of these soldiers live in the guest room of my house. The guest room is right across the hall from mine. It is really big and there are three beds. The soldiers thanked me and I told them that they had to be down for lunch in 30 minutes.

At lunch, they came down and thanked us for everything and told us that they enjoy their room. The next morning, the three soldiers had to leave. Living with these soldiers for one day has been and honor. I wonder what plans Ma has next.

-Madeline

Fears

Dear Diary,

Last night, Ma and I sat down and discussed the fact that I am growing up. She said that soon, I will be moving out, and I will have to start a life of my own. I am glad that I am growing up and soon will be moving out. But, I am kind of scared. I am scared that I am going to be alone for long periods of time. Even if I get married, my husband would be busy working a lot, and he would be away from home most of the time. I don't like being alone because it's very quiet and lonely. Another thing Ma warned me about is the fact that I will own the shop one day. I am afraid that I won't get as much business as we do now. I think that all I have to do is run the shop exactly how Ma and Pa are at this exact moment.

Another fear I have is bugs. One thing about South Carolina and living in a house in the woods is bugs. They are everywhere and they seem to find a way in the house. I don't like any bugs except lightning bugs because they light up the night. But all I have to do is buy bug nets that my parents sell at the shop.

Ma and Pa also talked to me about losing the shop. They told me that one day in the future they will not be here, and that no matter what, I have to fight for my right to keep the shop. There are a lot of reasons why Ma and Pa want me to keep the shop. One reason is because it has been running in the family for generations, and they would hate to see it go. Another reason is because I can keep it in their memory.

When they explained that to me, I was worried. Although I am old enough to know, yet too young to worry, I still was afraid. My heart was beating very fast, and I could feel my temperature rise. Just the thought of losing my parents, and the shop, kept me speechless.

-Madeline

Carving Wood

Dear Diary,

Today, I was so happy to get to school. I put on my old blue and red dress which had a couple stains on it. I know that that dress was clearly not decent enough, but I didn't want to get another dress all dirty. I wanted to wear an old dress because my class and I were carving things out of bark and branches from trees.

My teacher handed me a piece that was about the size of my hand. Next she passed out carving knives. It was silver, heavy, and had a little bit of wood on the sides. It was sort of easy to carve, but on some parts of my branch, it was difficult.

My friend Abi next to me accidently cut her hand. I gasped for air. I was disgusted watching blood drip from her hands. After the teacher cleaned it up, I was still frightened that she did that. "Use your loaf next time!" I said in a worried voice. Abi just laughed. I wasn't kidding though; I hate when my friends get hurt.

I had to wash my hands because they were dirty. When I got back, my carving was gone. I got scared. Abi started to chuckle. "Did you snatch my carving?" I said laughing. Abi is always taking my stuff. I don't mind though; she always gives it back.

I finally finished my carving. I carved a face in mine. I carved two eyes, a mouth, and a necklace. Then I colored mine. The eyes are just two small dents that curve, and the mouth is one big dent that is somewhat curvy.

This activity was very fun, and I would love to do it again someday. I ran home to show Ma and Pa. I showed them my work. They had a big smile on their faces. They loved it. They were so happy with what I did. After all that carving my hands hurt. I ate supper very fast, then I went up to my room, cleaned up, then went to bed.

-Madeline

A Tiring, Tea Act Day

Dear Diary,

Well, see, what had happened was, my family and I were in our kitchen, drinking some tea, when all of a sudden we got a knock at the door. It was the town crier. He seemed very upset. He said: "England is trying to trick us into buying their tea, and they lowered their prices!" Grandpa kept asking what the Town crier was saying.

No one spoke up so I said interrupting, "Could you please speak up? Grandpa's a bit mutton."

The short, town crier with raggedy hair repeated everything again. The town crier was still goin' on for ages. So I went up to my room. A while later, I went downstairs; it was almost time for bed. I couldnt believe what I saw. The town crier was still talking! I got tired of it, and I could tell that Ma and Pa were tired. I spoke up, "Are you going to rabbit all night, or are you going to go to bed?"

Ma and Pa looked at the sky. They saw that bright white full moon, with a dash of clouds covering it. The told the town crier that he didn't have to give specific details why this was happening, and that he needed to go home to his family. Ma and Pa pointed towards my room. I wanted to speak, but I could tell Ma and Pa were not in the mood to hear from me. I went up to my room, changed into my long, white, night dress with pink ruffles on it. Then I lay in my bed for a while.

I was thinking to myself; maybe something is in the tea, and England is trying to kill us all. And maybe they are trying to half-inch us all. I thought and thought about that. Then I slowly closed my eyes, and fell asleep. The next morning the notice paper from the following night was on the table. I read it silently. It read that the price of English tea was lowered, but the taxes remain the same. This is another trick of theirs, and it's kind of awkward. Pa sat down and talked to Ma and me.

He said that he doesn't want anyone in my family buying tea anymore, until the conflict is over. Ma said that England thinks we aren't smart enough to know this, but everyone does. We all think that the relationship between, not only South Carolina, but all the colonies and England will further degrade, because they sure aren't getting any closer.

A town meeting has been called at 11:00. It was ten till. I went upstairs and I put on the first thing I saw in my closet; My lovely blue dress. I put it on, and then brushed my hair, and then I put on my white shoes, the ones with the pretty blue flower on them. Ma, Pa, and I hurried out the door, and went to where the meeting was being held. We were there for a long time; it wasn't interesting to me at all. So I fell asleep, and missed the whole thing.

We got home later that evening, as the sun was going down where you could barely see the top of it over that hill in our backyard. I was too tired to eat supper, so I went right to my room and fell asleep in the clothes that I had been wearing all day.

-Madeline

Voicing My Opinion about the Declaratory Act

Dear Diary,

This morning, very early, Ma and Pa woke me from my nights sleep to tell me about the Declaratory Act. Ma and Pa handed me a slip of paper that read: "As a result of: Prime Minister Grenville, Benjamin Franklin's speech to Parliament explaining the taxes on international colonial transactions, and also, the official repeal of The Stamp Act." After I read that sheet of paper, I couldn't think of anything to say. Ma and Pa just frowned and went to their room. I couldn't believe that this was happening. Why was it happening?

Later that day, I went to school, my fellow classmates and I discussed this situation. Everyone had to go up to the head of the class and speak our thoughts. I was first. I stepped up. I was very self conscience because I didn't want to get punished by the teacher if I didn't have a good opinion. With everyone looking at me, I nervously said, "I consider myself an American Colonial. But, I do think that these problems will be resolved, just not anytime soon. I think that these problems can be resolved by everyone doing what they are supposed to be doing and what they have to be doing." Then I sat back down. I don't think I should've said that.

-Madeline

The Intolerable Acts

Dear Diary,

This evening, Ma and Pa gave me another slip of paper. Another notice already? This notice says that if we break the new law, then our cargo will be seized and held by the majesty's government. Ma and Pa don't like the changes. And me? Well, I don't like them either. But I'm old enough to know better, yet too young to worry about this stuff. I walked around my town for a while to think to myself. Looking around I noticed that people in my area are siding with England more than with the men of Boston. I even talked to my friends, but they agree with the men of Boston, so at least someone gets me. I just think that the South Carolina government had to do what is right. It's not their fault. I'm off to school; I will have to think about all of this.

-Madeline

The Day We Got Our Freedom

Dear Diary,

Today, I was in such a bad mood because I had a hard day at school. I got punished for talking during class. So when I came home, I was so frustrated that it made me tired. So I took a long nap. During my nap, Ma and Pa woke me. They rushed into my room very loudly and in a rude manner. They sat down calmly on my bed side. I was so tired that my eyes were shutting slowly, and I kept falling asleep. Ma kept snapping at me when I shut my eyes.

Pa started talking. He told me that now the United States of America was a free country! I was so tired, but that made my eyes bulge out of my head. I was so surprised and excited. My temperature rose inside of me. I jumped up, and searched through my closet for my red and pink rain boots. I found them, slid them on fast, grabbed an umbrella, and ran outside in the rain. I needed fresh air to go through my brain. Hearing those words made my day! I was outside for about 30 seconds, and by time I came back inside, I was soaked. About 4 pounds of water dripped from my clothes and my hair. But my parents were so busy talking to all of my family members that they were too busy to notice.

Today was a big celebration day. I met John Adams, one of the men who signed the Declaration of Independence. He was really nice, and just as excited as I was. I am so proud that now, for the rest of my life, I can live in freedom, and be worry free. July 4, 1776, was the day that changed my life forever.

CHAPTER 58:

A BLACKSMITH'S APPRENTICE

By: Kevin Simison

About Me

Hi, I'm Bob my nick name is Robert. I'm a thirteen-year-old blacksmith's apprentice. I will live in his workshop until I'm about seventeen then I will take a full-time job. I go to church every Sunday, and read the bible because I'm a Christian.

6-17-70

I have helped make one-thousand nails so far, but the filer broke right in half. Now, one-third of the order is on hold. Mr. James (the customer and town carpenter) isn't very happy with only two-thirds of a house.

6-18-70

Today didn't go well. Master couldn't find his gloves, so while he was making a new filer, the hammer slipped. The hammer hit me on my left shoulder. The pain goes away once you put FIVE POUNDS OF ICE ON IT. (Ouch) maybe I should become right-handed.

6-19-70

Well we found the gloves by the thousand nails we made the other day. And I helped finish the order, sadly no tip. (Mr. James is mean!)

Expectations

6-25-70

The master doesn't expect much of me; just to know all the tools, how to make nails, oh and how to not burn my hands off. But he also said that over time his expectations will get bigger. He told me not to worry though because he said that his expectations will never be as high as for a female.

Coin Making

7-1-70

I think the most fun thing in being a blacksmith is getting promoted to silversmith. Silversmiths get to make coins. I made a coin yesterday. I put my own design on it and learned how to make one. My friend is a silversmith; he's got his own shop and all! Master let me go see him yesterday. He lives on the other side of town. He doesn't want an apprentice yet (sadly). I'd love to be a silversmith some day; they work less, but make more money!

Three Soldiers

7-13-70

There was a voice in my head telling me to run. I wondered why until someone knocked on the door and sharp British voice spoke the words "Let us in."

We didn't even budge until he said, "or pay the fine." Master leaped towards the door and opened it faster than I could put my fork down. Once again the sharp British voice spoke, "Thanks we will need to stay here for three days."

At first I thought, "Awww, what a drag!" but then I thought, "Time for revenge". When I got done eating, I quickly filled their pillows up with hard stuff.

7-14-70

Today was great! Thanks to what I did (which when I told master what I did he burst out laughing) they left early.

Sugar Act

7-22-70

This "Sugar Act" has got Mr. James seeing stars. I thought it wouldn't affect us, but it does a lot. No wood means no nails! I don't see why the British have to charge us. Maybe they're so selfish they're trying to steal our money. Wait a minute! There not trying, they're succeeding! I can't believe this! I say we have war with the British! Stealing from their own kind, and not only that their own country!

Tea Act

7-30-73

Ouch, was all I could think for about twenty minutes and it's all because master thought I was awake when he came to the workshop. When he came in he said, "Lets get to work" and tossed a hammer at me while I was lying down ASLEEP! He said, "Don't worry about its not as bad as the Tea Act'.' Then he went on and on about it. "Well, it does lower tea prices. But, there are more taxes that are stabbing us in the back. I think it's a trick, maybe its worse tasting, or poisoned. Wait a minute, if they kill us how will they get our money!? I think that this will hurt our relationship with England. In fact it feels like a war is about to begin. Everywhere you look there is a British guard; at the docks, by the store, in people's houses."

What I don't get is WHO'S AWAKE AT SUNUP!?

Intolerable Acts

8-5-74

I think that the "Intolerable Acts" are just the British getting mad at us. I hope that we become our own country soon. All of these stupid acts are pointless. Just thinking about them makes me mad. I'm starting to think that this George the III is more like George the Trash! Were getting our rights taken away one by one, all because of these stupid acts! I wish we would be our own country!

The End

8-17-76

Woo Hoo! I am as happy as can be! I heard about the Declaration of Independence! I get to meet John Hancock! I can't believe master is taking me with him to meet him. Come to think of it, in the six years I worked for master the thirteen colonies have really changed. Not to mention the change in name!

CHAPTER 59:

DALANI'S STORY

By: Heather Skaggs

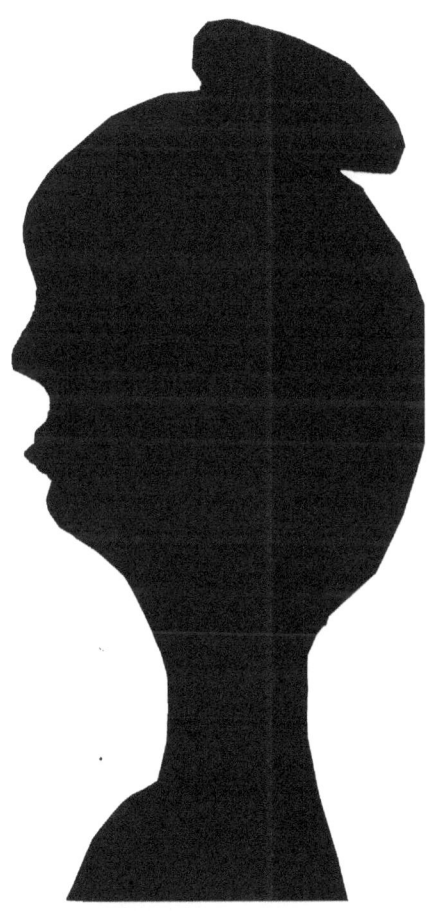

About Me

Diary,

My mom yelled, "Dalani, hurry up and get ready so we can do your hair." I was sitting there as my mother was braiding my hair complaining about how I should have her hair not red curly hair. My father jumped in and told me that I shouldn't have her hair because my hair matches my green eyes. I sat down at the table with my mother father Anthony my older brother and James my little brother.

After I had washed the dishes and fed the animals. I set out for a hole three hours of school. I enjoy 8th grade it is more advanced. After school my best friend Tomas and I headed home. We always stop at the general store to grab a piece of maple sugar. After that we head home.

Tomas and I have been friends for a really long time we live right next door to each other he is 15 and makes fun of me because I'm only 14. I love going home cause after me and Tomas get our chores done, we go riding. We race each other a lot and I promise I'm in love with this kid. He is the only guy I feel comfortable around. I love him so much be he won't ever know that cause he is my best friend and its just not going to happen. Anyway other than Tomas I know a lot of people like most of the general store owners because we are the leading producer of fruits and vegetables and the in keepers. All because I am a daughter of a farmer.

The Day I Met a Little Indian Girl

So today I was walking to town and I was stop by an Indian. She asked me if I had little food and I told her I did and that it was for my lunch. She looked at me with hungry eyes and it made me so sad. She looked and me and told me to wait so she could get something out of her bag. So I did just that, she came back with a really pretty leather bracelet. She said that there was a story behind it and that she would tell me the story and give me the bracelet, if I gave her my bread. I never really eat my bread.

So I agreed to it and we sat down and she started to tell me how she was swimming in a lake and a bird came up to her and started talking to her and just went on and on and on about this bird that talked to her. I was interested in hearing it all but I couldn't stay so I told her I had to go and got up and left.

I walked in to ton running in to my best friend Tomas Baker. He asked if I need any help and I told him yes. On our way back I didn't see that little Indian girl at all. I told Tomas all about it but asked him not to tell my parents because they might get mad. He promised and helped me up to the house. After that I never saw the little Indian girl again neither did Tomas.

The Stamp Act
Dear Diary,

So today I was in the barn cleaning out the stalls. When my Brother Anthony comes stomping threw the doors. So I asked him what on earth the matter was. So he starts going on and on and on about this thing called the stamp act. So after he tells me this I became very upset. The things the Crown is doing is very unfair. We are already going through a depression. We don't need taxes on paper, stamps and books. That was the only thing we had left that want tax. Now how will I write to my grandparents who live in Boston? Is the question I asked myself. The way the Crown is treating use is so unfair. They claim us as part of them, yet they treat us like we are nothing but a bunch of children. I highly disagree with the choices that they have made on how they mush treat us. We should be free and independent country. If this is how they are going to treat us.

The Fears of Growing Up
Dear Diary,

Today when Tomas and I were walking down the trail, Tomas asked me if I was afraid to grow up and start a new family, a family of my own. I simply looked at him while we were walking down the trail and smiled. He stopped walking and looked me so I stopped walking. He told me he was being serious so I turned around and stared walking again. He ran to catch up and told me that he understood that I was scared to tell him. I looked at him and said that I wasn't scared to tell him.

He stated laughing and said, "Tell me," so I did. I told him it isn't that I'm afraid to start a family it's that I'm afraid I can't do it. I am afraid that I won't be able to support them and I won't be able to make enough clothing. Even though my mom new nothing when she became a farms wife because she was an innkeeper's daughter she still managed to do a very good job. Even though my father told me that she complained here and there when they first got married, about how bad the farm smelled. I hope I become a farmer's wife because if I become anything else I don't think I am going to be able to do anything.

After I told him all of this he just looked at me in amazement. I asked him, "What are you looking at?"

Tomas looked away blushing then looked back and said, "Dalani I am in love with you I want to be the guy you marry. I'm going to talk to your dad about it since he likes me anyway!"

I looked at him surprised and said nothing I just keep walking. He stopped and said my name, I turned and looked at him and smiled. He looked kind of surprised and I ran and gave him a huge hug knocking him down. I got up and started running home. He tackled me and gave me a kiss on the check. Helped me up and told me he had to go home and do chores and that he will be back over later to talk to my dad. I told him I loved him. We separated and headed home. When I got home I had a big smile on my face and my eyes had a look no one had ever seen anything. I had never been happier in my life.

The Soldiers

Dear Diary,

So couple of days ago the government told us that we had six hours to get ready for three British soldiers to live with us. If we didn't my dad would go to jail and we would have to pay a huge fine. So to prepare for the soldiers my mom started to cook, I was cleaning the house barn and tending the animals, my dad was harvesting corn, my little brother James was picking fruits and veggies, and my oldest brother Anthony was out gathering things that we needed. That day happened to be a long, long day for most of us.

So come to find out that they are not as bad as we thought. They are easy to talk to and they even help out around the farm, well at least two of the three help out around the house and farm. That's probably because they eat more than our entire family put together. It drives my mother insane cooking and cleaning all the time. I have actually missed a day of school because mama was so tiered she wouldn't get out of bed. Other than that having them here isn't all that bad. Actual me and one of the soldiers get along really well, not like the other ones.

One day I was headed to the barn to get Jasper as I was heading out. Jack who is an 18 year old asked me if I was going some where. I reply yes lm off to the trails and if you would like to join me you can. So he goes and grabs his horse. As we are half way on the trail I was singing in a low voice that I thought only I could here. Then out of no were he was singing along in a very low voice. Ever since then we hang everyday at the same time and he helps me with my chores so we can go sooner.

Now the other two lm not to sure they are anywhere near the same. Jeremy is 21 and him and Anthony have become really good friends. They hang out and Jeremy helps him with his chores. Then there is Joshua he is 26 but he acts so much younger. There are times that I just want to hit him in his face. My dad doesn't even like him. He is so selfish and he eats sleeps. He is the only one who doesn't help around the farm. He rides our horses and when he puts them back he leaves them dirty with the saddle on them. He is far past annoying, he is just obnoxious. Some times I want to lock him in the barn and leave him there. Other than that everything has been great and not to difficult.

Boston Massacre

Dear Diary,

I was in class today when my teacher came in and started passing back and forth. I asked her what the matter was. She told me that there had been men Killed slaughtered murdered in Boston. She told me everything I just couldn't help but think. How can you be so cold hearted and kill murder people because someone tells you to fire? I knew something like this would happen, but never in my wildest dream did I ever think it would happen now! Everything is slowly falling apart its crazy.

Then later on that week we heard that John Adams was defending the soldiers. I was far from surprised! I then realized they must have not murdered them out of call, because John Adams is a man of honor a man of freedom am man of justice! He fights only for what he believes is right. Whether that's going against the crown, or going against his own people. So I believe this must have not been a war against us just a fight for there safety. Call it what you want I do believe the soldiers should be sent home not hung in the gallows.

Boston Port Act

Dear Diary,

I was sitting in the library and my librarian came up to me and started talking about John Hancock and the tea. I was simply amazed what had happened. I believe people like John Hancock have a lot of courage. I also believe there should be more people like him in South Carolina. I believe that Boston is going to gain more soldiers to protect the imports. I believe that the Crown is over reacting a lot and have no right to be here. This is America not

Britain we are free. I also believe they need to stop trying to control America; Even though we had no right to dump the tea in the ocean. Then again they don't need to be here. I am tiered of hearing about the Brits did this and the Brits did that.

Intolerable Acts
Dear Diary,

I was helping my dad sale produce. When we saw my neighbor Mr. Baker, he was talking to us about how he hates have the soldiers living in his house; and how if it was not for the stupid intolerable acts he wouldn't have them living there! We just nodded our heads until he left and I spoke up. "He must have some terrible soldiers in his house. We only have that on guy that has learned by now he wont get to do anything until he learns how to clean up after himself. I don't understand why everyone has a problem with the intolerable acts other than the fact that the tea hasn't gone down at all, it just has gone up.

When my mom told me we wouldn't be having tea from England because John Hancock and some other gentlemen threw the tea over in to the ocean. I understand the Boston import act as it called. Even though they have no right to be upset with us. Only because the Crown has raised the taxes on them. It is ridiculous. I just don't care anymore and I am tiered of hearing about this act and that act I just don't care any more.

The Continental Congress
Dear Diary,

I was walking with my friend Tomas Baker who is the son of our neighbor Mr. Baker. When we ran into Sean Tanker the man who lives in town and always knows about what is happening with The Continental Congress. I asked him what was going on with them and he said, "Its a long story so come sit and enjoy the maple sugar."

So as Tomas and I took a seat he began to tell us everything including the Boycott of Great Britain. Also how they were calling for a 2nd meeting. I asked if this had to do with the open hostilities and outright war.

He answered shaking his head in doubt and sadly said, "Yes." I was so surprised of this. I wondered all day if we would ever be free. Once we left and Tomas and I went back to my house. I heard my father talking about it and how his best friend Thomas Lynch Jr. sent him a letter saying that they were talking about Independence and that had never been discussed among a group so bug and powerful. I want to know so much more than just this little information. I can't sleep at night with the thought of being free excites me.

The Singing of the Declaration of Independence

I was walking down the rode on my way to get some water. When my neighbor who is also my best friend Tomas Baker came running down his drive way waving his arms and shouting my name. So I stop of course to see what on earth he wanted. As I was sitting my pail down he ran up to me giving me this huge hug almost knocking me over. After he finally let me go he started dancing and singing hallelujah. It was so fun I started laughing.

After everything stopped and he calmed down, I asked him, "What on earth are you so happy about?"

He looked at me with a surprised look and asked me calmly, "You haven't heard?"

I was so confused so I asked, "Heard what?"

He got the biggest smile I have ever seen and said, "Dalani we are a free country, we are our own people!"

I got so excited I gave him a huge hug that made both of us fall. I picked my pail up and started skipping down the trail to the creek. Tomas of course fallowed because we are best friends. He offered to carry the pail home so I let him.

When I got home I was surprised to see my dad's best friend Thomas Lynch Jr. looking very sad. I asked why he was dressed in mourning. He got down on a knee and asked me if I remembered his father. I of course replied with a yes. Mr. Thomas Lynch Sr. was like the grandfather I never had. He was there for me and talked to me when I was down. Well that was the day I found out that he had died. We mourned for 3 whole weeks. It was a sad time for our family, Mr. Thomas Lynch Jr. and his family. After they buried Mr. Lynch, Mr. Thomas Lynch Jr. and his family left on ship and we have yet to hear from them!

CHAPTER 60:

A CABIN BOY; A FUTURE CAPTAIN

By: Jon Stumpf

About Me

This morning I was looking over the side of the boat. In the distance I saw a storm coming our way. It looked bad, so I went to tell the captain. On my way one of the crewmembers pushed me. So, I pushed him back, and seeing how he was bigger than me it didn't affect him much. They all started laughing at me. One of them fell on the floor laughing. I knew I couldn't say anything or they would just laugh some more. So I walked off and as I was they were calling me names.

When I got to the captains quarters I saw Captain George sitting at his desk. I walked over and told the captain there was a storm coming our way. He turned towards me and said to tell the crew to be ready. So, I went back to the crew's rooms and started banging on the walls and shouted to get on deck. When I got on deck, we were in the storm. The crew was everywhere. I ran over to a broken railing with a hammer and nails in my hands and fixed it. I'm the best builder and repair man on the boat. There was more to fix. I fixed holes, railing, and sails. We were finally out of the storm. The crew thanked me and said the only reason we didn't sink was because of the holes.

The Three Soldiers

Today, three people along with a cabin boy joined the crew. I have to share chores with the cabin boy. I already don't like him. The captain sees more of what he's doing more than what I do. The three new people, I don't mind them very much. They don't tease me like the other crew mates do. In fact, one of them I think is getting ready to be friends with me. His name is William the two others are Tom and Jobe. I thought Jobe, what kind of name is that. I'm still thinking of what I'm going to do about the new cabin boy. I don't like him and I don't even know his name. I am wondering if I should just throw him over board and be done with it.

Fears and Expectations

Today I was sitting in the Captain's quarters and I asked the captain if he started out as a cabin boy before was a captain. He said he started as a cabin boy. I asked him if he had any thing he expected from me. He said he expects me to be hard working and to someday be a captain myself. He said sometimes I act like a captain already and that I'm already hard working. He said I fix things like an expert, and I clean his quarters the way he wants it. I thought about that and felt proud of myself.

I remembered what my father told me before he left me at the ship. He said my mother and him want me to work hard and come home a man. I thought about that too. I knew that I was becoming a man day by day with the help and discipline of Captain George. I am afraid I might let him down or fail at the last minute. But for the most part I am proud of the way I am turning out.

Hands on Experiences

I, as a cabin boy, have had much experience with whittling. I have had many days where the captain hasn't given me a job to do. He just tells me what to do instead of giving me a chore list. So I have had a lot of time to sit down and start witling. It's rare for me to cut myself now. Rope tying is as easy. One of the Captain's chores is tying of ropes for different things.

Smi the Cabin Boy

This morning I was looking over the side of the boat. In the distance I saw a storm heading in the ships direction. I went to tell the captain, and on my way there one of the crew members pushed me. So, I pushed him back, and seeing how he was bigger than me it didn't affect him much. They all started laughing at me. One of them fell on the floor laughing. I knew I couldn't say anything or they would probably beat me up.

I walked away to the Captain's quarters. When I got to the Captain's quarters I saw Captain George sitting at his desk. I walked over and told him there was a storm coming our way. He turned towards me and told me to tell the crew to be ready. So, I went back to where the crew was and yelled get on deck. When I got on deck, we were in the storm. The crew was all over the ship taking orders from the captain. I ran over to where some railing fell over and fixed it as quick a I could. I patched some holes in the sails too. When we got out of the storm the captain patted me on the back.

The Intolerable Acts

I have been hearing about three new acts. People are calling them the intolerable acts. I have heard that officials and soldiers can not be tried by colonial jury or law. And another act allows a commanding officer make someone shelter any soldier. And I have heard that people can lose their home. I heard about the third act closed the port of Boston has been closed. I don't think people are very happy. At least that's what I have heard. I probably wouldn't be happy either if this effected me more.

The Stamp Act

I have been hearing about the Stamp Act and that it put taxes on skin, parchment, velum, and paper documents. And, that the national debt has increased to eight hundred million pounds. Because of the taxes, I've also been hearing that people are getting low income. People can't afford to keep going on like this. I think England just wants more money. When will all of these taxes end, because I don't want to lose my job. It seems like that's what it's coming to. People are starting to get angry from what I am hearing.

The Townshend Act

I have heard about a new act. I think it is called the Townshend act. I have also heard it put taxes on glass, lead, paint, tea, and paper. It's hard on me because the captain is being paid less. It's not very easy to get the ship repaired and get food on board with that much money. In fact one of the Fredrick, someone in the crew quit because he wasn't getting paid enough. I have a new chore too. That is going and writing down what's on board of the ship. This is very irritating.

The Resolution

I've been hearing about a resolution made by the continental congress. I've also heard there is a war in New England. This guy George Washington is general of the continental army. I knew some thing would happen, but I don't think I expected this. I don't know how this will effect South Carolina or any of the other colonies. I don't think it will have any effect on me because I'm just a cabin boy. I like the idea of war against the British soldiers though. The captain hasn't really talked about this with me or anybody I know of. I don't know that what he thinks.

The Declaration of Independence

I was listening to a conversation three crew members were having. As I was listening one of them said that the Second Continental Congress signed a Declaration of Independence. When I heard that, I ran up on deck and saw a man talking to the captain. I asked the captain who it was. He told me that it was Arthur Middleton, one of the signers of the Declaration of Independence. I walked up, shook his hand, and we talked. One of the things that we talked about was how it felt to sign the declaration of Independence. After he left I started to think about how much has changed. It was all peaceful at first, and then one of the acts came in. Now people are dying in wars.

CHAPTER 61:

FAITH MARIE JONAS

By: Bre'aja Bureau

Faith Marie Jonas

Dear Diary,

My name is Faith Marie Jonas! I love to swim, clean, and cook. I have a great personality! I'm funny, cute, and nice. I have a very good education. I'm Christian and I'm not a tomboy, I'm a girly girl. My dad is a doctor and my mom is a stay at home mom. I have two brothers. I also have 5 best friends, and they all live in my colony! We all live in Charlestown, South Carolina. As being a doctor's daughter I have to act very responsible and very obtain because almost everybody knows my dad. So this is about me!

Faith Jonas

My Fears

Dear Diary

I would do any thing the soldiers tell me to do. Because I don't want my dad to go to prison because people need him! Ill feel so safe that solider are in my house! But in way I do not feel safe because people will treat you different and the soldiers will treat like you they slave and where not! But ill have to deal with it so my family won't have to pay because of me!! Because I'm not that kind of person.

It well be kinda hard to listen to them because they would have me do a lot of things that I don't wanna do! I don't expect them to be mean or nice so I don't know how they should act when they yell me what to do ill will have to do it so my family won't have to pay!

See you later,
Faith Jonas

My Names
F=Funny
A=Angle
I=intelligent

T=tall

H=happy

These are all about me

The Stamp Act

I think the British colonial has no right to tell us what to do. We are a separate colony. We should have our own rules and laws. It's good that the British took the stamp act away that means no more taxes. But for the British to take away the stamp act and say there in charge is pure wrong! I just want to kill king gorge I'm through with him if I don't put my hands on him somebody will!

Faith Jonas

Boston Port Act

The Boston port act is when the British shuts down the Boston port! Now they can ship any tea or any thing anymore across the ocean!! Now as a privilege daughter I won't have to worry about anything because my dad is rich. But for other people that is bad .especially for the store keepers a lot of there stuff that they use to get from other places across the ocean the store keepers are messed up.

They can't get what they need so the little what they have the prices will go up!! And some people will be with out a lot of things because most of the items the store keeper ect get some time came from out of the country. But some people didn't do anything to deserve this!! This is madness we shouldn't have to pay the price!! South Carolina has not a thing to do with Boston we shouldn't have to pay!!

Faith Jonas

Our Independence

The British! I can't wait to we get our own independence and the British can't tell us what to do when to do it and we will be done with taxes! Hopefully this meeting will bring us to our on independence!!! We don't deserve this South Carolina has nothing to do with this we didn't do anything! We have nothing to do with the people who started all of this madness!! We have nothing to do with the Boston people more known as the colonists.

When we will be done with taxes? Hopefully this meeting will bring us to our on independence!!! We don't deserve this South Carolina has nothing to do with this we didn't do anything! We have nothing to do with the people who started all of this madness!! We have nothing to do whit the Boston it people more known as the colonist.

Faith Jonas

2nd Congress

When I was at home one of my servants came to me than said that they are having 2ND continental congress!! The only thing I could think is about is that the people from my colony South Carolina are there! I only no that Thomas Hayward!! He is a great re presenter he is a lawyer so he can stand up for a fight or an argument! He always has great ideas, he also signed the Declaration of Independence!

He is a great influence to the state of South Carolina! My dad Andre is his doctor so one day after Thomas Hayward's doctor appointment he can for dinner and my mama had made dinner! So I got to meet him all through dinner he talked about how the British and the colonial need to get it together. He also talk about how King George mean, and cruel, selfish, and rude. He said that he is more sorry for the British than us. That they have a disgracefully king to tell them what to do! He was also telling us how when he signed the declaration of independent changed his whole life! Ill never for get what he told me that day!!

The whole 12 years of this democracy of this whole adventure was crazy my life changed a lot! Most of the stuff has went up we went into war with the British! At one point the British said that they own us! That's not true we own our self! We are independent it's about time we came together against them to gain our independence back!! Now I fell free this all started when I was 12 now I'm 24 and I still remember the acts like it was yesterday.

See you later,
Faith Jonas

Soldiers

Dear diary,

I would do any thing the soldiers tell me to do. Because I don't want my dad to go to prison because people need him! Ill feel so safe that solider are in my house! But in way I do not feel safe because people will treat you different and the soldiers will treat like you they slave and where not! But ill have to deal with it so my family won't have to pay because of me!! Because imp not that kind of person.

It will be kinda hard to listen to them because they would have me do a lot of things that I don't wanna do! I don't expect them to be mean or nice so I don't know how they should act when they yell me what to do ill will have to do it so my family won't have to pay!

See you later,
Faith Jonas

Need to Get Together

I think that the British colonial and the American colonial need to get it together. They both need to worry about themselves. That would make it easier for everyone. They need to split everything in half so we wont have any problems just need to figure it all out or just need to leave each other alone! And the British needs to take back all there acts and leave us alone I know what the Indians did was wrong put cant the just pay all of the tea back that was damaged. Why did we have to go through all of this why did we have to suffer now cause of what they did!! That's no right!!!

Faith Jonas

Georgia

CHAPTER 62:

RAJANIGANDHA

By: Rebekah Loss

About me-Rajanigandha

May 3, 1763

Dear journal,

The last thing I remember saying to my father was "I really wish I would die!" No one else knows that though. I feel so terrible. He just died so fast....I didn't have time to say anything else. Now he's gone and I can't change anything. What am I doing!

I feel stupid talking to paper, but mother says it will make me feel better. To bad she doesn't know what he last heard me say. You see father just died trying to kill a bear that just attacked our camp. A total of three warriors died, including my father. Many others were badly harmed in the kill. Mother says it will take time but I'll get over it. She says writing it all down will help.

So that's what I'm doing. Trying to get over the fact that I can't take back what I said. Enough of the sob story. I think it'll help to tell you about me. First things first, you are NOT going to be called diary or journal. From now on you will be known as Paraphilyntenea. I don't know where I got it, I'm just a random person. I'll admit, I can be mean and a bit outspoken, but believe it or not I have the potential to be nice.

I'm not the best person to fool around with and I do not take a joke very well. But if you are my companion I will protect you with my life. I love to be active whenever I can. When I was little I could dress up as a boy and the tribe actually thought I was one. Now I can't do though, I'm to mature. I miss those days. I still hunt when I can and, even if it's from a distance, I still attend all the ceremonies.

I love to add danger where ever I can. My favorite feminine thing to do though is picking berries. I just love to be with nature! The things you can do with flowers, berries, and animal skins is amazing! I can make cloths from animal skin and dies from flowers and berry juice. I can also make pretty decent moccasins.

But above all that I love to garden. My best crops are carrots and tomatoes. My mom likes my carrots and my brother likes my tomatoes. My...my dad always loved my corn. I don't know why. That always turns out to be my worst crop. Well that's all I have to say for now.

Until next time Paraphilyntenea,

Rajanigandha

Three British soldiers

July 23. 1763

Dear Paraphilyntenea,

When I first woke up this morning I knew it was going to be a day full of irony. I planed to go out and pick berries or apples, you know something ordinary. Well as I set out to pick theses items I saw what seemed like a hundred of soldiers. Actually it was three and their chief. I think they called him sergeant.

Today three British soldiers just arrived at our camp looking for food to eat and a place to stay. I don't want to anger them by telling mom I don't want them with us, for fear of them hurting us. Oh Paraphilyntenea, I can't lose mom or my brother, Gray wolf. The soldiers look mean and strong. Well two of them do but the third one looks nice.

He looks young and has brown hair and eyes. He's built very nicely and has the cutest British accent ever. I'm more open to him being here but I still fear for our lives. I don't know what to do. I only pray that the spirits will guide us and keep us safe if we do keep them here.

Until next time Paraphilyntenea,

Rajanigandha

My birthday

October 17, 1763

Dear Paraphilyntenea,

In two weeks it'll be my 15 birthday. I'm afraid because I haven't quite grown out of my boyish habits. The only reason this is a problem is because when girls turn 15 they are looked upon as women, not girls. Now could you please tell me how I'm supposed to become a woman if I don't even want to be a girl! The only upside to it is that I get to "become a woman" in font of Daniel, that's the cute one of the British soldiers.

I can't believe we let them stay. I'm glad we did though. All thee of them ended up being pretty nice. Christian, Logan and I all became close friends. They gave me a white woman's necklace for my birthday. It's gold with a colorful butterfly on it. Although I got nice gifts from the soldiers I still have to have a wedding ceremony.

Apparently I have to choose who I'm going to marry. Well, my mother is supposed to choose since father died, but she's going to let me decide. Oh, Paraphilyntenea, I don't know who to choose. I don't even want to get married. How am I going to get through this!?

Until next time Paraphilyntenea,

Rajanigandha

Bookmark

July 10, 1764

Dear Paraphilyntenea,

Today I made a bookmark out of my dad's old headband. It means a lot to me because the fact it was my dads. Now I know he's always there. I took his headband and put a braided piece of leather at the end where the bear had ripped off his tie. I put three blue beads and three brown beads to represent his age.

The three blue beads each represent 10 years and each brown bead represents one year. My dad lived a total of 33 years. I then put three scratches on the leather to represent the other warriors who were killed. The feather represents how my dad is now with the spirits. His soul is flying free with the eagles and other birds.

I use my bookmark all the time. Whether I just hang it up or keep my place in a book the white men give us. It's always with me. I love my bookmark and now it'll be easier to let go of him.

Until next time Paraphilyntenea,

Rajanigandha

Stamp Act

March 30, 1765

Dear Paraphilyntenea,

I was walking through the forest behind my house today as I was trying to clear my head. Today was just one of those days when you just can't get things off your mind, you know. I kept thinking of the last conversation I had with my father. I still can't get over how I can never take back what I said. Anyway as I was walking through the forest I heard some of the men in the tribe talking about a new act.

It taxes all legal documents, permits, wills, and playing cards. I believe it is called the Stamp Act. Anyway as I bent down next to a Cherokee rose bush I tried to listen closely to what they were saying. It was hard to pay attention being right next to those roses. They have the most fragrant smell ever. They are oh so fragrant, with pure white petals and yellow stamens, and red, bristly hips. All I really heard was them going on and on about having to pay more for the cards they wanted. See a lot of us like to play cards. Now that they cost more it is harder to get cards. At least for the price they used to be. That is all for now.

Until next time Paraphilyntenea,

Rajanigandha

Townshend Act

June 29, 1767

Dear Paraphilyntenea,

Today yet another act was passed. It was called the Townshend Act. It taxes the colonists on glass, lead, paint, tea, and paper. It's like they're being taxed on EVERYTHING! Pretty soon they're going to be taxed for their taxes!

The thing I hate about it is that when they get taxed we pay the price! For example, when they got taxed for tea we had to trade two furs instead of the normal one. As if it isn't hard enough to get furs! Because they cut down our woods we can't catch as many animals. When we can't catch the animals we can't give them the furs they want and then we have nothing to trade with! Well, I guess that isn't entirely true. After all we have beads and Indian cloths but nothing that most white men want.

Until next time Paraphilyntenea,

Rajanigandha

Intolerable Acts

August 4, 1774

Dear Paraphilyntenea,

Today I found out that four more acts were passed, in a time period of just two months! First was the Boston Port Act, then the Administration of Justice Act, after that the Massachusetts Government Act, and finally the Quartering Act. I really do feel sorry for the colonist in Boston. Some acts seem so unfair! Like the Quartering Act. This act states that anyone who is told to let a soldier stay in their house has to give them a room and bed to sleep in.

Life is hard enough without the soldiers and now we have to let them stay in our house! Ugh. It is so unfair. I just lost my dad and the man I was supposed to marry just died of small pox. It has become quite popular and a lot of my camp is dying from it. It scares me Paraphilyntenea. Sometimes I feel as if I am actually lying on my death bed waiting to die.

Now any soldier who comes along and is told or wants to stay in the Cherokee camp, we have to let them. I guess that is not all that bad….I am just stressed. After all, that is how I met Logan and Christian. The only thing is that not a lot of the soldiers like the Indians due to the Seven Year War that ended in 1763. Most of the soldiers are here to "keep peace" between the colonists and the Indians.

Honestly, I think they are just here to take up more money than <u>anyone</u> has. I mean, we never wanted them here. The French won fairly and we all understand that. Just because some of us are not willing to accept that does not mean we're going to hurt anyone! I wish Brittan and the colonists would understand that!

I personally think it is stupid to have the soldiers here because they are the ones who started it. *They* wanted to take *our* land to extend *their* territory! I am sorry Paraphilyntenea. It just makes me angry that they still have to watch us. Anyway, there is this other act called the Administration of Justice.

I am not really sure what the colonists in Boston do to get all these acts. I think it might have to do with the Boston Massacre thing that happened on the fifth of March. I guess some of the soldiers got caught up in the killing of people. I hope Logan and Christian stayed out of it. I heard five people died.

It seems as if all the soldiers do is cause trouble. Do not get me wrong, I like Christian and Logan very much so, but it seems as if the soldiers ALWAYS start stuff. Now maybe I just get things from the wrong source. Now that I think about it, it seems as if I always get my information from my brother Greywolf. He HATES the soldiers because they killed his closest friend Navajo in the Seven Year War. I am guessing his words are not going to be the best ones to judge by.

Even if his words aren't the best to go by I still do not like the majority of the soldiers. They really are always in the middle of everything! The Boston

Massacre they were the ones shootin' people. Then they tried to say it was self-defense. Yea right!

The one I can actually understand infuriates me the most. It's called the Boston Port Act. The king has shut down the ports! Therefore the colonists can not import anything. I do not know how we are going to get the things we need if the colonists can not get them. I have to admit though, the colonists deserve this one. After all they are the ones who threw all the tea into the harbor.

They called it the Boston Tea Party. That is kind of ironic if you ask me. It really makes me mad that they would do this but then again the only reason they did it was to prove the point that the taxes are to high. Well now everyone has to work to pay off the loss of property and opportunity before the ports are open again. Until then no ships will be allowed in the ports of Boston.

Until next time Paraphilyntenea,

Rajanigandha

Whig or Tory

Can you believe it?! Freedom is almost here! It's like I can taste the sweetness of victory and the bitterness of defeat all at once. The colonists will be free yet we will still have to live by their hand. Sure they will be free to make their own choices and their own government, but I hear they didn't put anything about women folk, children, or Indians in this Declaration of Independence.

Not only that but it has caused such a mess between the British soldiers and the colonists. The colonists don't want the soldiers here and the soldiers are only doing their job. I imagine King George is probably pretty upset. I believe if I heard the colonies I ruled over were going to try to over throw me I would be upset. That is just me though.

I'm not quite sure where I stand on all these matters yet. A lot of my tribe wants to stay loyal to the king, and I do not blame them for that at all. Though there are few who want to over throw the king and be American's they have great power. They are like wolves in a flock of sheep, slowly devouring one sheep at a time.

Both sides come out strong at times. Loyalists are convinced living under the king's authority is better and safer. They say that if we separate from Great Brittan we will become slaves in our own nation. I believe this could be true but look on the other hand. What if the colonists are nice and they let us be our own people? Just think, they could let us be part of the United States. Being a free American doesn't sound bad does it?

Until next time Paraphilyntenea,

Rajanigandha

Declaration of Independence

July, 1776

Dear Paraphilyntenea,

It was signed! It was actually signed and passed! I'm so excited to see what happens next. Will we be free or just the colonists? Will we be able to take part in forming the United States? Will we be left out or made slaves? There are so many questions worth asking and no one really has the answers. Wow…put all your happiest memories combine them all together and I guarantee this feeling is ten times better.

Oh Paraphilyntenea, I really need to calm down. After all it is only the first step to our nation. I don't even know if we'll be able to help. I got a chance to meet a few of the signers of the Declaration of Independence. Their names were George Walton, Button Gwinnett, and Lyman Hal. Some of the tribe members got to talk to them.

They were mostly here to get people to join in the war against Brittan. They did talk about the Declaration and what it was for but they didn't go into great detail. That is all I have for now Paraphilyntenea. If I find out more I promise you will be the first to know. For now I am going to talk to my friends and find out their outlook on it.

Until next time Paraphilyntenea,

Rajanigandha

CHAPTER 63:

THE LONG ROAD FOR DESTINY

By: Katelyn Ann Parton

About Me

Dear diary,

Hi, my name is Destiny. I was born in Philadelphia. When I was about 12, I went to the town store. I accidentally bumped into a boy who was about 13. We went out walking for about one year. One night I went over to his house and found him with a ring. His house was all decorate with roses and he was dressed in a much tailored suit. It took an out three months to plan the wedding. I was dressed in a white dress and Mathew was dressed in the same suite he proposed in. The wedding was right in front of the new house we bought. About out three months after we got married there was a poor lady that asked if we would take her son because she had no money to pay for food, his name was Edward. About a week after that someone in that same condition asked the same thing. Of course I said yes. She told us that we could name him what ever we wanted to. It took us about two days but we finally decided to call him Emmett. When I told my friends what my children's names were they looked at us strangely because the names were not normal, but we were ok with it. At first Mathew was not ok with it but after time he got used to it. At this time I am thirteen years old, married, and have two adopted sons. Well that is all the time I have left got to go and change Edward and Emmett's diapers.

Love,

Density

My Day

Dear diary,

I think I mad about seven candles today. Emelly, Roseleta, and I got together and made some candles. While making candles we had some tea. It was a nice day and I got to talk to my friends and catch up with how their lives are going. Emelly now has two children one boy and one girl. Roseleta has a baby boy and is about to have another baby. I was surprised when we got all done and it was at the same time the kids woke up so we were able to get dinner done in just enough time for us to rest for about ten minutes before my husband got home.

Talk to you soon,

Destiny

The Townshend Act

June 29, 1767

Dear diary,

This morning was the best. My husband and I woke up to the smell of eggs, bacon and tea. Last night we got a servant girl to help me out with the kids. So as a thank you she made the kids and us breakfast. I told my husband we made the right choice when we saw all of the food on the table.

When the kids saw her they asked her a million questions like, "How old are you?" "Why are you here?" "What are you doing?" "How long will you be here?" and many more. After she answered them all without a hint of frustration, which surprised me, I explained to the Edward and Emmett that she was here to help me with them and the house. The first thing they asked her to do was take them down to the docks because they love the smell of the sea in the morning. Of course I said yes and off they went.

When they came back Edward told me that she told them a story and her name. After he said something about her name I remembered that I never asked her what her name was. I went looking for her. She was in her room when she saw me she said she was just make sure everything was in the right place then she started going on about how she was sorry she came up her to relax for a little bit. As soon as I could get a word in I told her it was okay, I understood it was her fist day and it might have been a little frustrating.

I told her I was wondering what her name was. When I asked her that her eyes lit up and said, "Whatever you want it to be." I could tell she was joking, but after a little bit she said her name was Isabella. For some reason she acted like it was a bad name. Then I told her I loved that name.

We sat and talked for about a half an hour about what her life was before she came here, but then I heard my husband yelling for me so I walked to his study. When I got there he had asked me why I didn't buy any paper I told him, "The price of it had gone up ten pence."

The next thing I know he was walking out of the house yelling, "I am going to yell at who ever raised the prices on paper!" I waited for about an hour than I went looking for him. I got down by the store and there he was with about twenty to thirty people at all the other stores. When I got there I pulled him off to the side and asked him what was going on he showed me the new sign about the new Townshend Acts on the door. The second I read the sign I felt like doing the exact same thing that they were doing.

When we got home I followed my husband up to his study. He started talking and it was the first time I had ever heard my husband say, "I am going to have to raise the prices for my bills so I can still by things because of this new tax."

We argued for about an half an hour and he finally agreed with me with me saying that just because times are getting hard doesn't mean he has to raise price. Besides no matter how cheep the bill is everyone always asks him to double it and if he doesn't they will. Well I got to show Isabella where everything in the house is.

Love,

Destiny

I Am Mad

7-17-1769

Dear diary,

Those stupid soldiers I have been trying to keep my cool, but they have just pushed me too far. They tried to hurt my baby boys because they wouldn't move. Well how do they know what you are saying? They are just kids so they don't understand what you are saying. So when they wanted to sit down and talk the kids were in the way so they yelled at them to move. Of course they didn't know what they were saying. When I walk in there the kids were crying and looking down the barrels of their guns. Oh great! Here they go again. Got to go and save them again. I swear they are going to push me too far.

Love,

Destiny

I Am Scared

Dear diary,

I am very scared. All these expectations are piling on top of me and I do not know what to do. My expectations are that I have to take care of my family, make sure I do not upset the British soldiers, and always be nice to others. Now I have all ready taken care of the first on because my husband is a doctor.

Now the second one is a little tougher because they are just fat mean people. I mean show us some respect! You are practically the same person as the rest of us. The third one will depend on how people treat me; if they are nice then I am nice, if they are mean, then I am mean.

That is all for now got to go fix dinner.

Destiny

The Tea Act

May 10, 1773

Dear diary,

Well I am down to my last spot of tea. I have to go down to the store later to buy some more. Where is my husband going? There must be another fire or people are ringing the bell because of a new tax. There is a new tax. I know because there just went the kid that posts the new acts at everyone's house.

Oh no. I will have to hurry up and get some tea before the new tax comes in. This can't be good. I bet you that with this new tax on tea there will be more women in fights with the British soldiers than there has ever been since we came here. I guess I have to get some tea or it will be too expensive when I get there.

Love,
Destiny

The Boston Port Act
March 31, 1774
Dear diary,

Well there goes about half of our shipped in goods. This is going to be hard to get over. Good Lord this all because they dumped some tea into the harbor! Well maybe the soldiers that were there when they did this should have done something about it, but instead they sit there and act like complete ninnies. This is something so small that the King had to make into something so big. I wonder if it would be better to go back to Britain than stay here. You know, I will go and ask if it would be better.

Love,
Destiny

The Quartering Act
June 22, 1774
Dear diary,

There goes another house! If this continues my family and I will be on the street trying to find a place to stay. With this new act the "Captains" can take over people's houses without any problems so that all the soldiers can have a place to stay. I guess it does not affect me since they just announced that all the soldiers have a place to stay.

I have heard from all the wives and they all said that my husband and family have done too much for them and that they can't ask us to take care of them too. I tried to convince them that it was alright, but they said that only if no one else would let them live with them. I guess it is okay, but I felt bad. It wouldn't bother us at all if they had to live with us their kids would probably ply with ours all day; but no one will even ask us. I think it is because they think that they would have to pay us. They don't know that they would only have to pay us if they wanted to and even then, I would not take it and neither would my family. Well I guess this act doesn't really affect us so I have nothing to worry about. That is so good not to have to worry about an act.

Love,

Destiny

The Administration of Justice Act

May 20, 1774

Dear diary,

Finally everyone is calmed down. Why did they have to ring the fire bell? There was no fire in the first place so why did they ring it? I bet you it is those young boys that think it is funny to ring the bell and get everyone worried. I made a good breakfast for my husband too. I bought some bacon, and bread down at the store and went to the barn and got a couple of eggs. My husband just sat down to eat when the bells went off. Now his breakfast is all over the floor. I think my husband has gone looking for the people that rung the bell. I guess I might as well go and see who is at the door.

WHAT? THEY RUNG THE BELL JUST BECAUSE THERE IS A NEW ACT.! They are so immature; it had to be boys. They had to ruin my husband's breakfast for this. No one here is trying to throw off the "authority" of the Parliament of Britain. He is just putting things in peoples' heads. Now he thinks we are crazy. We had a right to charge those stupid soldiers with murder. They killed three people and one was just a young boy. Now if we want to charge any of the soldiers with murder we have to go all the way to Great Britain. And even if the judge agrees they are guilty he won't say so. I mean, if they want to keep their jobs they won't. Well I have to find my husband before he kills someone.

Love,

Destiny

The Result

October, 26 1774

Dear diary,

I wish everyone would stop yelling. Oh great heavens! That crash scared me! I think it was a window? Wait, I think it was a window here in the house. Oh my Lord! It was a window. It will take us months to fix it and put a new one in. Why is everyone all of a sudden gone crazy? I mean about a half an hour ago you would have thought that only kids lived here. It was so quite then all of a sudden you heard someone yell. Than everyone got all mad and started braking things. I believe if it wasn't for my husband telling me to stay in the house I would probably be outside trying to calm people down or trying to figure out why everyone is upset.

Here come my boys. Oh now I know why ever one is yelling. So now the king is telling us that we need to straighten up. WELL IT IS TOO LATE FOR THAT. He should have thought about that before he put all these acts into place. Now it will take forever for my husband and his friends to calm these people down. I do not get why my husband tries to stop them when they fell the exact same way. Men they make no sense to me, like my friend said, "Men can't live with them, but you can't live without them."

Wait this is a good thing. At the bottom of the page someone wrote that people are getting together to try to either fix this or try to get independence. Why are they so mad? They aren't mad; it's the British soldiers who are throwing the rocks.

Where is my husband? Actually I bet he is celebrating with his buddies. Times will get a whole lot harder with what this act says. I've got to get to the store and stock up on tea.

Wait, there's my husband. Oh, that was so nice of him. He went to the store and bought tons of tea for me. Now I know why I married him. I hope he gets elected to be in the Second Continental Congress.

Well, I have to go and help my husband store all the tea.

Love,
Destiny

Today

Dear diary,

Today was a terrible day my husband had what felt like a million calls. I fell like everyone is getting sick. I am so surprised he is not sick yet. I am in so much pain. I am having another child. I hope it is a girl. My husband is really scared that the baby will not make it because everyone is getting sick. I keep on telling him that God will take care of our baby and I pray every night that the baby makes it.

The kids are helping me out a lot around the house. I think it is just because they are excited about having a new sibling. My husband has asked if a couple people that are not sick would help him build a room onto the house for the baby. I think that he has only three people helping him, but I believe they will get it done in time. The kids are asking if they can help decorate the room for the baby. I am so excited that the children are taking so much time to help me and their father out with this baby.

My husband has just come up with the first pieces to the new room he is going to build. He said that the ship would come today, but he did not know what time it would come in.

The children want to go and buy more things for the baby, but I said they had to eat breakfast first. They won't eat though; they are too excited to eat. I guess I've got to go take the kids out shopping so they will eat when we get back.

Love,

Destiny

A Talk with Lymon Hall

Dear diary,

I had a good day. Actually I think today was the best day ever. I got to meat Lymon Hall. He is one of the singers of the Declaration of Independence. Lymon is a really nice guy. I think I asked him a wrong question. I really didn't plan to ask if they had anything on there that said that women could vote or do things and not ask their husbands, but it slipped. Of course he didn't answer that question. He acted like he didn't even hear me ask that. I asked him if we didn't have to listen to what Britain told us anymore, and that made up for the bad question I asked. When I asked that question he said, "Maybe we'll have to win the war, but with George Washington at the lead of our army I am confident that we will win."

Then we sat there talking about how much better life would be if we didn't have to listen to Britain and able to trade with the Indians again and even learn how they did it so we wouldn't have to ask for so much. Then I put in that maybe we should give them back some of their land and I was extremely surprised when he said that he agreed with me.

About that time my kids Edward and Emmett walk in talking to Elisabeth. At first I was surprised that they were back so soon then he smiled and said that that he talked to my husband and was wondering when he was going to be able to meet them. Mostly Edward thought that they were in trouble because of the way I was looking at them, but when I told them that they surprised me he was okay.

After I introduced them, the kids ended up staying in the room with us listening to what we were talking about. It surprised me that they listened to everything we said. By the time Lymon left they knew about three times more then they did before he came to talk to me.

About an hour after he left, my husband walked and I had to tell him that about half way through my talk with Lymon Hall the kids walked in and listened to every thing else that we were talking about. He told the kids that they didn't have to help me clean up after dinner he would help me. Well time for me to go to bed.

Love,

Destiny

P.S. I am about to have my new baby I hope it is a girl.

CHAPTER 64:

THE DISASSEMBLY

By: Johnathan Miers

About Me – May 5, 1760

Hi, I'm Michael Libel and I'm 12. My dad is an inn owner in Savannah, Georgia. I'm next in line to take over the family business. Although the tavern helps out some.

I was working Monday. A lady came down and said she had to go to the store and she couldn't take her baby. So she asked me if I could take him while she goes to the store. I said, "Yes ma'am".

Then a customer came down to pay and I said, "Hello and welcome to the Family Fortune Inn." I took the money. Then I put it in the safe and locked it. After that I told the customer to have a nice day. Then I took the baby and checked the halls.

I saw fire in the hallway of floor three. A fire is kind of what was in my head I was left alone with no one to help me watch the inn and a fire just had to happen! I knocked on everyone's door and told them there was a fire. When everyone finally got out the inn was burned down to the ground.

We built a new inn and named it The Family Fortune Legacy. We did a grand opening and invited everyone we knew (most of the people in town).

Weaving and Candles

On Wednesday we made candles. First to make candles you have to dip your string in the hot wax water and hold it in there for 60 seconds. Then you take it out and hold it out for 10 minutes. Then you dip it in for 3 seconds. Then you take it out for 10 minutes. So on and so fourth until it looks how you want it to look. You have to let it dry for 20 hours.

The other activity that we did was weaving. First you put one piece of yarn on the loom until one side is full of yarn. When you start the next row you put the piece of yarn on the end piece then you put it over the first piece of yarn then you put it under the second piece and so on. On the second piece you put it under the first piece then you put it over the second piece and so on. You keep doing that until the weaving is done.

It was really, really difficult. It took a very, very long time. But when it's finished it looks very good. Both the candles and the weaving have meaning because you did them yourself not someone else and they were very difficult and you accomplished them.

Expectations

Dear Journal,

I was outside playing on Wednesday. My ma yelled for me so I went in the inn. When I went in there was a line of people. The line went all the way to the door. All of the sudden I smelt something. Then I saw two candles on the floor where the carpet was. My ma was yelling, "Put it out put it out!" But I am afraid that I will mess up and everyone will be disappointed in me. I will make sure that I watch everything that I do. An expectation for myself is to not to let my father think he made a mistake letting me take over the inn. I'm afraid that I'll make a mistake and let my father down. I'll have to do everything right.

Bye,

Michael Libel

Another Royal (King George) Act – March 22, 1765

I was walking down the street when suddenly I saw people with torches. They yelled no taxes on internal transactions! I could feel the anger building up inside them. It was like they were bears getting hunted and were about to shred the hunter. They were yelling that the sentry should do something about King George and that he should call a meeting with the Parliament. But the sentry was saying he didn't have the power to do that. He said that they should take the problem to someone higher than him.

I was watching the check in desk when all of the sudden, BOOM! British soldiers kicked in the door. They told me I had to give them rooms. The sentry heard the door get kicked in and he came down with the musket. But before the British soldiers knew it the sentry put a hole in their knees. When the sentry was done putting holes in their knees he turned around. One of the soldiers pulled out their weapon and before they could shoot I took the musket from the sentry and shot the soldier. The sentry put the other two soldiers into ropes and took them away. But he left the dead soldier for us to clean up. My ma and pa picked the soldier up and put him on the horse. My pa took him to the creek and threw him in it.

I hate King George III because all he cares about is Britain. Another reason I hate him is because he approves the worst acts.

The issues between Great Britain and the colonies will continue because King George III holds grudges.

The Sentries' Plan -- November 8, 1769

Dear journal,

My father just got word that we have to let three British Soldiers live with us. He doesn't like it but he doesn't want to go to jail. We have to pick them up in two hours by the war port. The towns' people are happy that soldiers are coming here because the crime has been really bad. They think that the soldiers will help us.

All of our rooms are filled except one because that's where the soldiers will stay. My dad just went to go get the soldiers. While he's doing that my mom's getting their room ready. Then she had to get dinner ready. By that time he was already back with the soldiers.

I was the first one to see the soldiers. The first soldier had blonde hair and was wearing a green shirt and black pants. The second soldier had black hair, a blue shirt, and brown pants. The last soldier had brown hair, a red shirt, and blue pants. They all had long green bags over their shoulders.

I asked them what their names were. The black haired soldier said Luke. The blonde haired soldier said Jeremy. The brown haired soldier said James. My mom asked them if they like Tofu. All three of them said yes. So we all sat down and ate dinner. I asked James if he had ever been wounded and he said yes. He said it hurt really bad.

After dinner all the soldiers went to bed. When they went upstairs my dad said that he liked them but he had a bad feeling. Then we went to bed.

The next morning the soldiers were up before we got up. They told my mom that they liked their room. My father had to talk to the soldiers to see if they would help the sentry with the crime. They said yes so they took their bags and went to the sentries' station. Today is their last day to stay here. The sentry told my dad they were a big help. When they got back we all played games and ate. They said that the sentry sent a telegram asking if he could have help with the crime and that's why they sent them. The soldiers went to bed after that.

The next morning my dad took the soldiers to the port. I felt happy having them here. I was sad when they left.

The Intolerable Acts – June 23. 1774

On Friday I went to South Carolina for my cousin's wedding. When I was getting off the ship in South Carolina I met a girl named Faith Jones. She's a privileged daughter. My father went to my cousin's inn while I stayed at the port. I was walking on the port when all of the sudden I heard yelling by a ship on the right side of the port. So I went over to look.

When I saw what was happening, I was outraged. I saw three British soldiers throwing one of the colonials down. I yelled for Faith to come over and look. When she saw her mouth just dropped. I told her she should tell her dad to do something about the soldiers. So she went and told her dad about the soldiers and her dad went to get the sentry. The sentry told the British soldiers to get away from the colonial. The sentry asked what the problem was. The colonial was the first to talk. The colonial said the British soldiers were trying to capture him for smuggling but he wasn't smuggling. The sentry asked if he could search the colonial's ship and the colonial said yes.

I was walking to the store when I saw my sister. I asked her if she wanted to come with me and she said yes. When we got to the store we saw that the door was lying on the ground. We went in and a bottle of milk almost hit me. We saw two British soldiers and the store keeper throwing things at each other. They hit my sister with the milk bottle. That was the last straw. I took the musket that was on the wall and pointed it at the soldiers. I told them not to throw anything else. Then I told the store keeper to go and get the sentry and the doctor. British soldiers came with the sentry and the doctor. I quickly put down the musket. The sentry took the British soldiers out and said you're going back to England to be on trial. Everyone cheered. I don't think that His Majesty's governor should appoint all positions of government and authority. I think we should get to elect at least two of those positions.

I was sleeping on Tuesday night when all of the sudden I heard yelling. I went outside to look. I saw a house getting taken over by British soldiers. The soldiers threw the colonials in the dirt. The dirt flew up everywhere to where no one could see anything past the dirt. I was just hoping that the colonials were ok. My ma and pa ran and got the colonials. They told them they could stay for nothing. Also we won't get new food because the ports are closed. I do agree with the name that has been given to the acts. I agree with the name because I can't stand the acts.

Taken Over – April 24, 1775

On Saturday I was watching the inn. I heard musket shots, I heard screaming, I heard bangs, then it happened I heard glass break and the sound was really close. I went up the stairs and I saw my sister. I asked her what was going on and she said there were people shooting and they were getting really close to the inn. Then they saw us through the window. We ran and woke up ma and pa. We went to the window but no one was there.

BOOM! The door dropped pa went and got the musket. While pa was getting the musket I went down the stairs a little bit and I saw three men. The first man had a huge mole it took half of his face. The second man looked like a colonial and I thought I saw him before. The third man I thought was a woman with a man's voice. My father went down the stairs with the musket and pointed it at the men but he was outnumbered.

BANG! My pa's musket hit the ground and so did my pa. I looked like a bull when it got mad. I took the musket and started shooting. By the time I was done shooting the men were on the ground not moving. I rushed over to my pa. I never saw anything like it. Blood was all over the floor. I told my sister to go get the doctor. He came and helped my father. We never found out who the men were.

Sincerely,

Michael Libel

Second Continental Congress – May 21, 1775

As I heard about the Second Continental Congress I smiled bigger than a plump boy when he saw a plate of crumpets and milk. Faith Jonas looked at me and said are you ok and I said yes. I met Button Gwinnet on Tuesday. My mom, my dad, and I went to the big tree in the middle of town with Button. We talked about how Button felt and then Faith came in. She and Button talked forever before we could start talking to him again. We were happy to hear that Button got to be Mayor after he left.

CHAPTER 65:

JESSYE'S STORY

By: Gabby Bennett

About Me

May 21

      Hello my name is Jessye. I'm from Macon, Georgia. I just turned 13 on May 18. I'm Catholic, and I'm a really good seller. I would describe my personality as an outgoing person who is always does what is asked of me. Well, I stopped school at the age 11 because, I'm going to own my fathers general store. I have a mother named Margaret and a father named James.

      My life is okay I guess. I really like this boy named Chance he comes to my father's store every single day to get some milk and candy. He never talks to me. He lives right down the road from me with his sister. Her name is Millie she's only eight. Wow I really don't like her. She is so annoying. Chance also lives with his father Billy. Billy and my father are really good friends. I'm glad because that means I get to see Chance more. Well maybe tomorrow Chance will try and talk to me.

      Oh yeah, I've got a best friend, her name is Morgan. She is so funny. But I don't get to see her as much as I would like because she lives kind of far from me. Also, I don't have a lot of time to see her. Well this is the real me.

-Jessye

The Soldiers

May 23

      Hello, today the government told my father we have to have three British soldiers live with us. If we don't, my father will have to go to prison and mama and I will have to pay a fine. So that means I'm sleeping with mama and papa, and my father said we will have to save a little more money. So, we have to open up earlier and close later. Today Chance came to the store to get a stamp for a letter for his butterflies and I smiled really big. I probably looked dumb.

      I might write to Morgan today if my father buys me a stamp. I really miss Morgan. I can't wait to tell her about Chance.

Well I'm about to eat lunch with mama. I told her about Chance. And she said that tomorrow Chance is going to his grandpa's for one whole week. I ran back to the store with tears running down my face then Chance said, "Jessye?" I was so embarrassed. He said, "What's wrong?"

I said, "I can't tell you."

He said, "Okay. Can I tell you something?"

I said, "Yeah."

"I have liked you for as long as I can remember."

I said, "Really?"

He said, "Yes, I swear." Then he said, "I have to go, okay?"

I ran home after closing the store. When I got home the three soldiers were there. The first soldier was about 35 and was tall and fat with brown hair. The next soldier was short and skinny with blonde hair and looked as if he was about 30. The last soldier was tall and skinny with red hair and was 38.

Then we all had dinner, it was smaller then normal. We had green beans, corn, and chicken. Mama and I split a piece of chicken so there was enough for the soldiers to eat. After dinner we went to bed. One of the soldiers took my bed. And the other took the chair in the living room and the other took the floor with a cover. Later on that night there was a sound at the door. I went to see what it was. It was Chance. I was happy to see him.

I said, "Why are you here so late?"

He said, "Because I'm leaving tonight. So I will see you in one week, okay?" I said goodbye he said it back. He asked if he could have a hug and I gave him one. Then he kissed me on my cheek.

"Well, bye," he said. Then I ran back inside and went to bed. I had a big day a head of me.

- Jessye

Sugar Act

Hello, I just got another letter in the mail. It's about something call the Sugar Act. I hate this thing. They make me so mad but they do help our economy some. I think this will impact our family because we sometimes have to ask for some lumber or molasses. It might be sold to our colonials. Well it might not effect me because my family taught me to be nice and sweet to everyone even if I didn't like them because it could cause a lot of fights and other stuff. Well, talk to you later.

- Jessye

My Fears

May 30

When I grow older my parents expectations for me are to get married have children, and take over the family business. My expectations for myself are to buy a house, get married and have children. I have some fears of buying a house because I'm afraid of not paying the bills on time and not being able to afford to buy things. I'm also afraid that my children might not listen to me and I will have to give them away. I'm afraid that my husband might not be able to get a job. I'm afraid that my husband and I might get a divorce and I won't be able to afford anything. But I think my life will be just fine if I find the right guy and I raise my children as my parents raised me. Well I have to go I got to get back to work.

- Jessye

Carving

Hello. I had some free time and I was hanging with one of the carpenters, Chance, before work hours and I told him his job was easy and he said I probably couldn't do it. Chance showed me how to do it and it didn't really work out. We carved wood and it was hard. I got cut a few times. IT REALLY HURT. Wow, he is so cute. I missed him so much, he just got back from his trip. He and I are going to hangout soon he told me.

Well I carved all kinds of stuff with Chance like bugs, dogs, cups, plates. It was so fun. I really want to do it again. I can't wait until I see Chance too. I'm so happy. And mama told me she loved what I carved. She said it was, "Amazing," and like nothing she had ever seen before. I think she was lying just to make me happy. But if she was I wouldn't really care because Chance made me happy today. Well, after all it was pretty good day. Well I have to go, so talk to you later.

- Jessye

Townsend Act

I just heard about the Townsend act at the market when I was getting food for our family supper. I don't really have any reactions on this because what happens just happens. I think John Hancock is a very nice guy but he has his days just like we have ours. I think we are going to get in a big fight with the Brits. I think we should stop all this right now. Yes, I think there will be lots of changes.

- Jessye

Intolerable Acts

Today I was out to get some milk for breakfast and I hadn't checked the mail in a couple of days, so I thought to and I did. I saw another act. Why do we always get these? They make me so mad. I also got a letter from Morgan. My friend Morgan, she lives in New York. She was telling me about the tar and feather thing. She said they poor really hot tar on them and then put feathers all over them. Morgan said most people die from the burns and blisters from it. That is really sad. Well I do agree with the name [Intolerable Acts] but my parents and I are more with England, the mother country.

- Jessye

CHAPTER 66:

THE LIFE OF A FREEDMAN

By: Natalie Dugger

About Me

Dear Diary,

Of course you know my name, Na'Tlyi Lee Coleman! I live in Georgia. I've been living in Georgia since I was born. I'm 16years old. Was born August 3.

I've never been to school before not even daycare. But I love to learn anything! Although I have never been to school, I still got good skills. Like cooking, growing food, cleaning, watching kids, and most of all making shoes.

My friends all say I'm funny, truthful, caring, and beautiful. They always got a good explanation.

Now about the people I love. Well first off we are all Anglican. That is our religion. I love my family to death. My Mami is my hero. Then my to little brothers, they are my world. I have never met my father.

My family and I are Freedmen. We do lots of different things. We also work for a lot of different people. Right now I am an apprentice, soon to be a cobbler!

I hope to get my own shoe shop going soon.

Boston Massacre

Well since the Boston Massacre had arrived I had to be ready for anything. Some people always are asking we were my family and friends. My family was really scared. My friends they knew we could make it!

Intolerable Acts

The name of "Intolerable Acts" is an okay name. But I would like to know why our colony is not that good? Why can we only be friends with British people?

I don't really agree with the things we do. Right now I'm just gonna keep to myself because we can only talk to some people.

MY LIFE

When I was 16, my life was very hard but it still hasn't changed and im 24 now. When I was 16 most people would say they talked about me because I am Black. I never got why everybody was SO rude and would call me names, and make fun of my color. I never got to go to school, and that was one of my biggest dreams. I always wanted to make something of myself, life. But I never go the chance to do that. I am still a very intelligent person. So I never complained! I take care of my family. I wash everybody clothes, make everybody's food. But besides that I have my own job. I'm a cobbler I use to be a freedman. But now I got my own shoe shop! Sometimes I miss being a freedman. Then I look back and think to myself look how far I am now. So even though everyday of my life is a struggle cause the people around me. I still just look forward to my family and my shop.

Part II:
Letters Between Friends and Foes

CHAPTER 67:

LETTERS FROM A SOMEONE

By: Lara Hoagland and Rebekah Loss

Dear Rajanigandha,

How have these notices affected the Cherokee tribe besides not getting imported items? You did live without them before we arrived. The notices sure have affected me, especially financially but yet emotionally too. Do the acts even apply to you tribe? Do you think they will in the future? Life is rough for us but how is it for you? I'm expected to be a proper lady even in this time of crisis. I'm also worried that my brother is too eager to smash a British head.

How do you and your family feel about the problems with the British and the new Americans? Who do you side with on things like the Boston Massacre? I already know how you feel about the Boston tea party but explain more the justice in the port act for I see none. How are Christian and Logan? I haven't heard much of the soldiers except for the fact that they are everywhere. Do you fear we as people will be attacked? Please write me back.

Until Again,

Your friend Charity

Dear Charity,

The thing you don't see is that we've become more dependent on you colonists. No matter how much I HATE to say it, we have. We count on you for some of the food we get, the cloths you give us, and some of the jewelry you give us. We count on you for much of our trading too. We don't want all the skins we have so we trade them with you guys because you like it.

Sure we lived without them before, at least some of my ancestors did. You don't realize that I was born in 1755. I don't personally remember becoming a part of the colony. Yes I'm sure my mom does, but most of us younger Indians weren't alive in 1733. Actually my mom was only 8 at the time. They did live with a lot of the things we have now but as for me, I can't imagine a world without all the things I have now.

Whether or not they affect my tribe directly, I still get hurt by the acts. Look at it this way. If you didn't give a cow grass you couldn't get milk. You don't need to eat the grass to get the cows milk so it doesn't affect you directly, but because not eating grass keeps the cow from producing milk you are still affected. Because the colonists can't import certain things or they have to pay more we also can't get what they can't and they make us trade more for what they do have.

Our life is pretty much the same other than the fact we have to trade more. It's not as easy as some of you think. You see us and think 'Oh, they're Indians, they grow their own food, make their own cloths...' and all this other stuff. What you don't realize is that we do depend on you colonists? We count on you for the fabric we need to make our cloths, and we count on you for the dishes we have to cook and eat with.

You probably think we could just go back to learning to make our cloths from skins and different things. The thing is a lot of us are also in our mid ages 13-19 and we are rebellious, just as much as you. Now that we have what we have we don't want to go back to where we have to make stuff. We want to live just like you colonists.

As for who I side on I'm not really sure. I like some of the soldiers, like Logan and Christian, but I don't like a lot of them. I guess it's all how you look at it. I don't know for sure what happened at the Boston Massacre so I can't say the colonists were right and I can't say the soldiers were right. From what I hear both sides were at fault.

I see justice in it [the Boston Port Act] simply because you colonists are the ones who destroyed the property in the first place. How can they be sure you won't do it again? I feel they closed the ports so they could show you what merchants would eventually do if you kept destroying property. Eventually no one would be able to trust the colonists so they would stop coming. Then you wouldn't have anything and it would've been your own doing. I personally think the King saved you from yourselves.

Christian and Logan are fine thank you for asking. I actually got a letter from them yesterday. They told me they weren't even in Boston. I was happy but you can probably imagine how stupid I felt after they told me they never leave Georgia. Anyway, they are coming to visit tomorrow.

Until we speak again,
-Rajanigandha-

Rajanigandha,

Thanks for the extremely long letter but you have been lacking on letters lately. I see what you mean on your dependence on us and the British too. Hopefully things will get better. There is much tension through us (British and Americans) there seems to be much more than harsh words between us nowadays. So would you ever have thoughts of marrying a white man (Christian or Logan) or is your relationship with them not like that?

Until Again,
Your friend Charity

CHAPTER 68:

LETTERS BETWEEN COLONIAL GIRLS

By: Dara Turner and Hunter Kay

Dear Eliza May,

I absolutely love your name! And you have the best life a young woman could ask for. Tell your father thank you for getting my father proven innocent. I can't believe someone tried to say he over charged them. It is absolutely ridiculous these days don't you think?

Until next time darling,

-Emma Lynn

Salutations Miss Emma!

I do much appreciate your glowing compliments. But my life is not at all easy. I am constantly reminded on how soon I must grow up, or how rudely I acted at Miss Millers Tea party. Although it does seem to be a lavish life I lead, I only wish others knew.

But I don't want to rant on about my life. I do remember papa hen talking about that trail. But my memory of it is a bit fuzzy. Can you help refresh my understanding of that trial? I will tell him that you and your family put a good word in, and thank you kindly. One last word? Would you be interested in attending tea sometime? I would absolutely love to have you over.

Until Later,

Miss Eliza May

Dear Eliza Darling,

I absolutely adored the letter you sent me in the mail. I haven't heard from you in a while. I would love to visit and have tea sometime. But, darling, wouldn't your father be angry if you sent for me to visit? You know he doesn't approve of my family. Only because father couldn't pay him upfront from the court hearing. Don't you just find our hidden friendship tragic? Well, mother is calling for me to set up the dinning table.

Until next time Darling,

-Emma Lynn

Dear Eliza May,

Hello Darling. How are you doing? I'm doing absolutely great! I was wondering what you think about the Declaration of Independence being signed. I am just absolutely over thrilled! Now we are free from the Crown!

-Emma Lynn

Miss Emma,

I am also overjoyed! But these things do sometimes come with harsh consequences. I must say that we have got be careful. And did you hear that the King is looking for the men that signed the Declaration? They will be prosecuted and hanged for treason if caught! I only hope for peace. And I've no other thought on how to go about it. We've tried any possible ideas without being violent, and otherwise. This was a good move, but it's not over yet.

Until Later,

Miss Eliza May

CHAPTER 69:

THE DEBATE ABOUT THE TEA

By: Johnathan Miers, Anna Scott, and Mark Hamner

'On Friday I went to South Carolina for my cousin's wedding. When I was getting off the ship in South Carolina I met a girl named Faith Jones. She's a privileged daughter. My father went to my cousin's inn while I stayed at the port. I was walking on the port when all of the sudden I heard yelling by a ship on the right side of the port. So I went over to look. When I saw, I was outraged. I saw three British soldiers throwing one of the colonials down. I yelled for Faith to come over and look. When she saw her mouth just dropped. I told her she should tell her dad to do something about the soldiers. So she went and told her dad about the soldiers and her dad went to get the sentry. The sentry told the British soldiers to get away from the colonial. The sentry asked what the problem was. The colonial was the first to talk. The colonial said the British soldiers were trying to capture him for smuggling but he wasn't smuggling. The sentry asked if he could search the colonial's ship and the colonial said yes.

I was walking to the store when I saw my sister. I asked her if she wanted to come with me and she said yes. When we got to the store we saw that the door was laying on the ground. We went in and a bottle of milk almost hit me. We saw two British soldiers and the store keeper throwing things at each other. They hit my sister with the milk bottle. That was the last straw. I took the musket that was on the wall and pointed it at the soldiers. I told them not to throw anything else. Then I told the store keeper to go and get the sentry and the doctor. British soldiers came with the sentry and the doctor. I quickly put down the musket. The sentry took the British soldiers out and said you're going back to England to be on trial. Everyone cheered. I don't think that His Majesty's governor should appoint all positions of government and authority. I think we should get to elect at least two of those positions.

I was sleeping on Tuesday night when all of the sudden I heard yelling. I went outside to look. I saw a house getting taken over by British soldiers. The soldiers threw the colonials in the dirt. The dirt flew up everywhere to where no one could see *anything past the dirt. I was just hoping that the colonials were ok. My ma and pa ran and got the colonials. They told the colonials they could stay for nothing. Also we won't get new food because the ports are closed. I do agree with the name that has been given to the acts. I agree with the name because I can't stand the acts."*

Dear Michael,

I don't think that the ports should be open just to non-smuggling ships. The port should be open to everyone and the ships shouldn't have to smuggle in the first place. Parliament and Britain are just being greedy. Remember that they eliminated all of the export taxes on tea in Britain. Is that fair?

And also, legally the colonists in Massachusetts shouldn't have to pay for the tea they dumped. The ship rightfully belonged to Britain. Britain should have to pay for the tea. How does it look if Parliament breaks their own laws? Right now you look like you're on both sides of the argument. You're going to have to pick a side sooner or later.

-Magaskawee

Magaskawee,

I do think that the ports should be closed on one condition. But they do smuggle so King George III is taking action. They aren't just being greedy. That's not fair but life isn't fair that's what my mom always tells me. They are enforcing King George's orders.

They shouldn't have to pay for the tea they dumped. But the law is the law. The ship did belong to Britain. I agree that Britain should pay for the tea. It looks bad if Parliament breaks their own laws. I'm in the middle of the argument. No I'm not going to pick a side because I agree with both of them.

- Michael

Dear Michael,

      I also think that the ports should be closed and not open to everyone like Magaskawee said they should be; and that the colonists are smuggling so King George III will take action rather than sitting in his throng all day long and listening to Parliament. I don't think this is fair, but I have to deal with it as a colonist.

      And you're both right, Great Britain should pay for the dumped tea because it was theirs and not the colonists anymore. But Michael, Magaskawee is right, you should and need to choose one side even if you agree with the other. I support you opinion though because there are some things that I do agree about with Great Britain and some things I don't. But do what you think is right; if your family disagrees with you and leave you, don't worry because I'll be there to support you, either way. So do what you think is right, go for what you believe in, and I'll be there all the way.

~Samuel~

CHAPTER 70:

LETTERS OF TREASON

By: Calin Johnson, Benjamin Barlow, and Mark Hamner

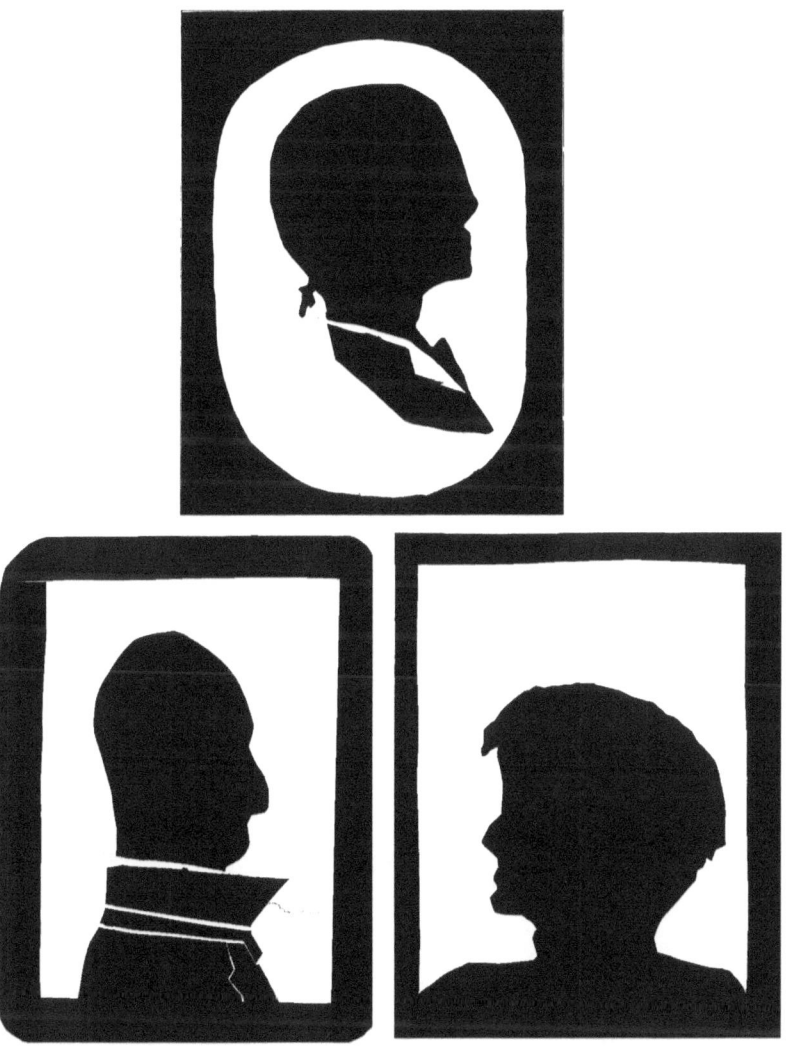

Dear Samuel,

BOY are you one lucky fellow. You only have to follow one of the three acts. I have to follow all stinkin' three of them. And, as long as them dirty tax collectors are from the same country as them bloody, red backs then I don't really care what happens. I mean I know that being tarred and feathered is bad but so is all them bloody tax collectors. And, you're right about all the mobs, too. Its like every corner you turn there's another mob. The problem is all they do is sit around. We need some action!!!!! We need to take them blimey, bloody red backs out for good!!!!!!!! If you agree with me please send me a letter telling me so, but if you don't still send me a letter. If you say no then be a lazy good for nothing! Just don't get in the way if we do get serious.

Sincerely,

James Johnson

(P.S. Please don't tell anyone about that whole blimey, bloody red back parts. Thanks)

Hello Samuel.

My name is Levi and I too believe these acts are wrong. Just to let you know the next couple sentences are very treasonous, and if the British find out about this letter you will be put into great danger. Whit that said the Brits are no good dirty rotten pig stealing, great, great grandmothers. Oh how I want all of these things to end. If this continues much longer I know colonists from all around will go to the mother land, because you and I are in the same predicament.

Levi

Levi,

Thanks Levi for the heads up, but I know what I'm doing. Not to be rude though; I'm saying that because I'm one of the Sons of Liberty. I go to meetings and discuss these things first, before I even take action. But then again, you're right because this is MY personal letter/journal, if I get found out about, I will be in GREAT danger; like you said. The Brits ARE no good dirty rotten pig stealing, great, great grandmothers.

~Samuel~

CHAPTER 71:

DIFFERENCES

By: Anna Scott, Benjamin Barlow, Lindsey Kurucz, and Stephanie Taylor

It has been eight days since my dear mother died. My father and brother continue to show no sadness for our loss, while Ayashe and I cry ourselves to sleep every night. Metacomet thinks that our tribe is in peril. Three men have arrived from the pale village. My brother thinks that they were sent here to drive us out and claim the land for their leader. My father has become familiar with one of the men, and they say that they are lost and have been mildly injured on their journey. They cannot find their way home to their town in "Rhode Island", as they call this land. While Metacomet does not trust them, I think we should let them remain in our camp. If they are hurt, then they will be powerless to harm us. My friends, Kachina and Anpaytoo disagree. They have listened to Metacomet and think that we will be forced to be slaves for the pale ones. They have ceased speaking to me until I have joined my brother's way of thinking. If the white men do not take our land, then their presence shall surely tear our people apart.

Magaskawee

Magaskawee,

I reminded that some of you Indians are very kind, but no offense; there are some of you that are kind of mean. But we could be nicer too.

Levi

Levi,

I have to admit that my brother Metacomet can be a little ruthless, and I agree, our attitudes vary throughout the camp. But I don't think the villagers are all that bad.

Magaskawee

Magaskawee and Levi,

I like to see you agreeing, I agree with both of you actually, you know some people just have those days where they hate everything, and to mix it up even more, everyone is different!

-Delilah Hrica
Rhode Island's Farmer

Delilah,

Disagreeing is not a bad thing. Think about a world where everyone gets along, but never show their true feelings. Nobody would get what they want, now would they? Life would be so boring if everyone were the same. It's good to be different.

-Magaskawee

Magaskawee and Delilah,

I also think you both are right. I like what you said about it's a good thing to be different.

-Sara Taylor

CHAPTER 72:

THE RIDICULOUSNESS OF THE
INTOLERABLE ACTS

By: Emily Kirchenbauer and Karlee Nielsen-Baker

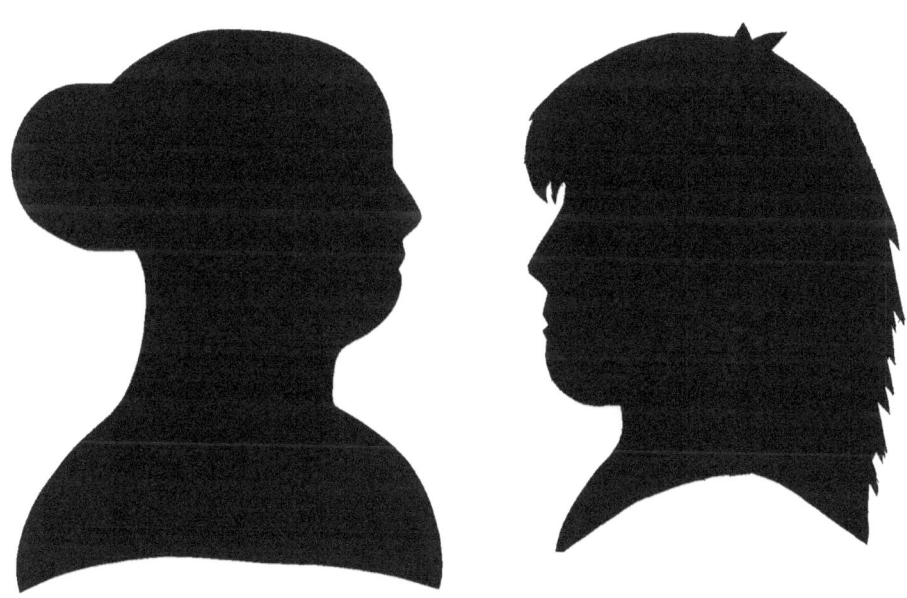

Dear Emily Merriweather,

It is unfair, the prices being charged by the crown, it is sad. And it is sad that people are losing jobs, I do hope your pa don't loose his job. If you don't like how England is treating us then rebel just like the patriots; don't let someone else fight for you.

Sincerely,

Alice McDoogle

Alice,

I'm glad I'm not the only one with these feelings. I hope that your pa doesn't lose his job either. I know that right now it's hard finding a job and keeping it is harder still. I'm beginning to think about taking action towards England but I don't think my parents are going to support my decision to do that. Like you said I shouldn't let someone else fight my battles for me.

So what are your thoughts about the Intolerable Acts? I know that many of the townspeople in my colony are becoming disgruntled with each passing day. I fear that all of this will end in war. I hope that it does not come to that though.

Sincerely,

Emily Merriweather

Dear Emily Merriweather,

I believe the Intolerable Acts are ridiculous except the ones about Boston, they have put that on themselves. If they didn't want to drink or buy the tea then they didn't have to, they shouldn't have dumped it. It's what they get. Your right, this might end in war, and then what is going to happen? I am honestly wishing that none of this would have happened and we were still under England's rule, it was so much easier then.

Until later,

Alice McDoogle

CHAPTER 73:

A PATRIOT IN A LOYALIST FAMILY

By: Tyler Hoffman and Lindsey Kurucz

I can't believe the war has actually started between GB and the colonies. Rhode Island is a mostly loyalist colony which stinks for me. Also, I'm not 18 yet so I can't join the army, but I will be able to be a spy or a messenger. On the bad side, I will need to be extra careful because most people in RI are against me, and they could always rat me out.

The thing I can't bare is that my families are mostly loyalists. So I am going to explain why I am doing these acts of rebellion; if it doesn't work I'll have to leave RI. The worst thing that could happen is I join the army and get moved to RI, so I might have to turn in friends and family or even worse, kill my loved ones. I won't think about that unless my family won't believe me. But until then I must try not to get caught in these acts of freedom.

Nathan

Nathan,

That sounds awful. Not everyone is against you though, remember that! It does not help that your family is mostly made up of loyalists, but they love you and they will most likely understand. You may not be 18 but you have the right to choose your path, and don't let anyone tell you differently! It seems as if you are doing a great job of following what you believe in, keep it up! I too understand how the pressure may impact your opinions and choices, but you have to fight against those pressure points and stand steady! This may sound odd from someone who doesn't really know you, but in a way, I do know you, because we share, one-our opinion, and two-Rhode Island. Yes, I can see this will seem very odd coming from a mere farmer, and you may choose to take no heed to my words, but a little encouragement never hurt me! I believe in you and all of those other AMERICANS out there have faith in you too.

May you fare well,
-Delilah Hrica
Rhode Island's Famer

Part III:
Scenes of Colonial Life in Silhouette

Anna Scott

Audrey Traylor

Austin Keith

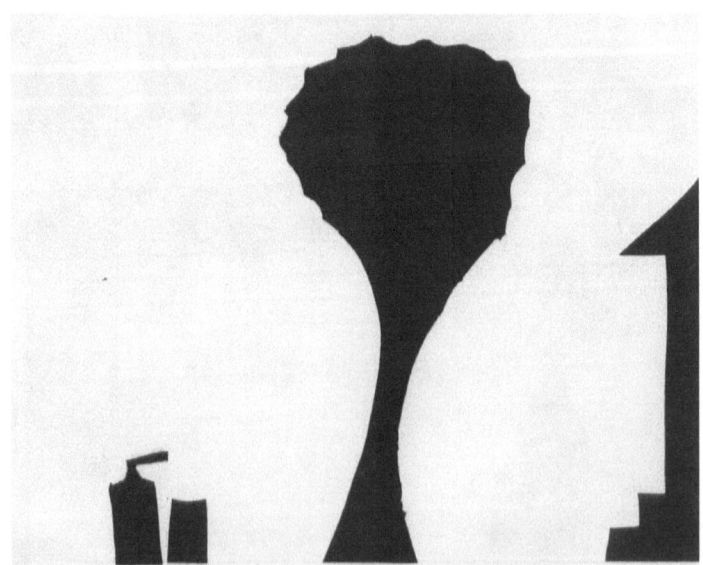

Austin Williams

Benjamin Barlow

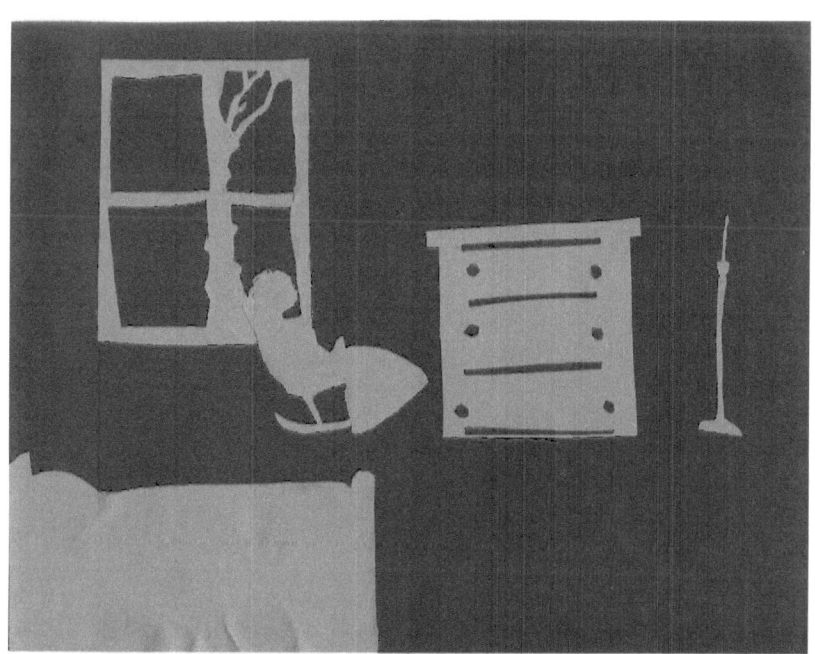

Elizabeth Cronnon

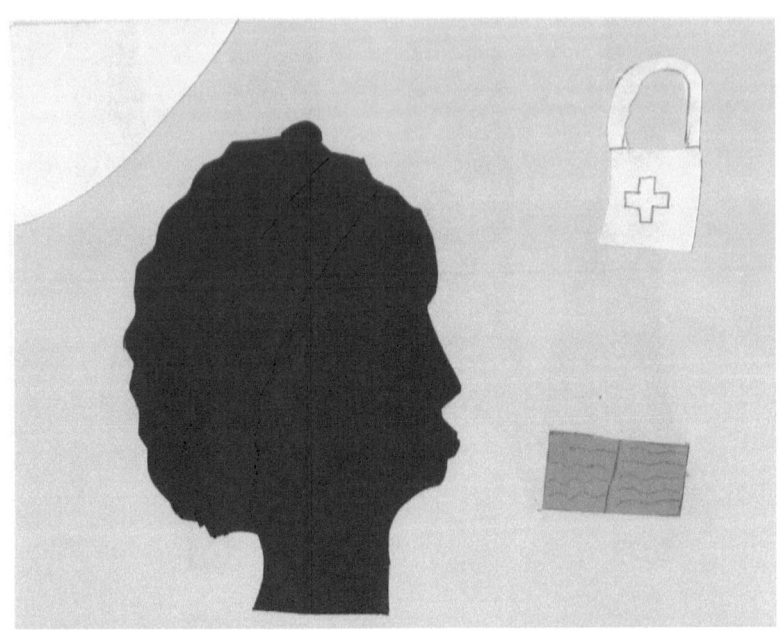

Bre'aja Bureau

Calin Johnson

Corey Dodson

Courtney Minardi

Devin Hubbard

Dustin Newt

Dara Turner

Emily Kirchenbauer

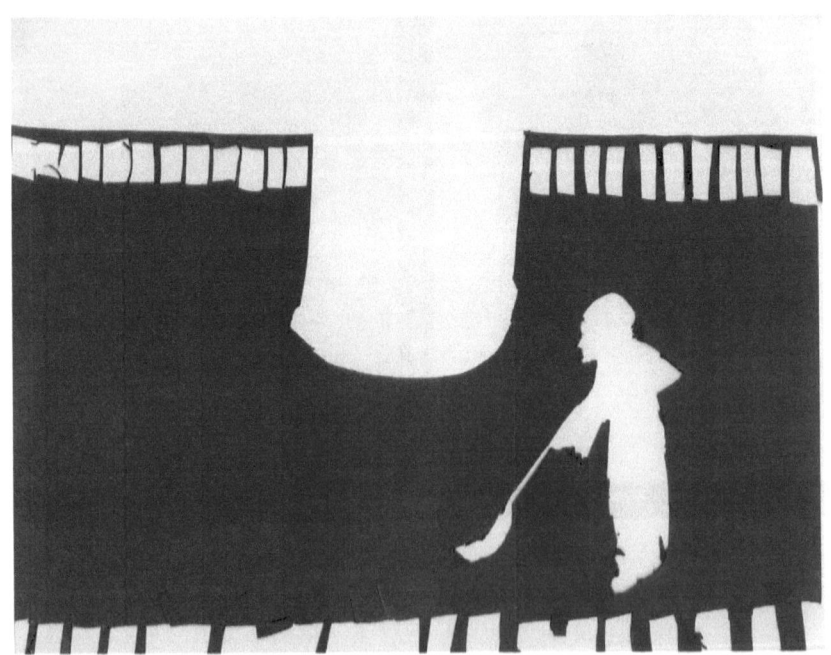

Eric Turner

Gabby Bennett

Heather Skaggs

Hunter Kay

Hunter Thompson

Jenna Drinkard

Johnathan Miers

Jon Stumpf

Karlee Nielsen-Baker

Katie McKinney

Kevin Simison

Kylee Standish

Lara Hoaglan

Lindsey Kurucz

Mark Hamner

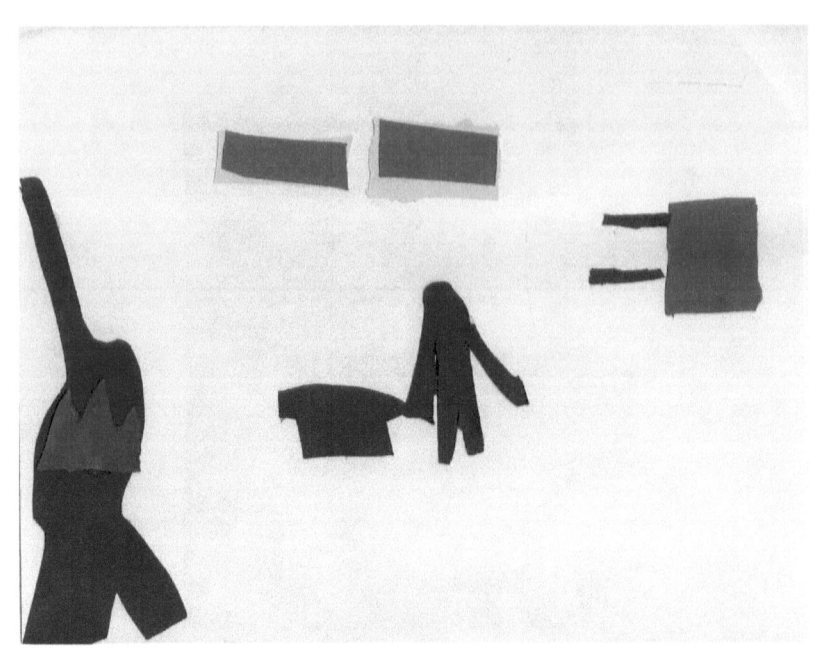

Maurice Jones

Makaela Rader

Samantha McDonald

Sid Carpenter-Wilson

Shelby Ellis

Victoria Hernandez

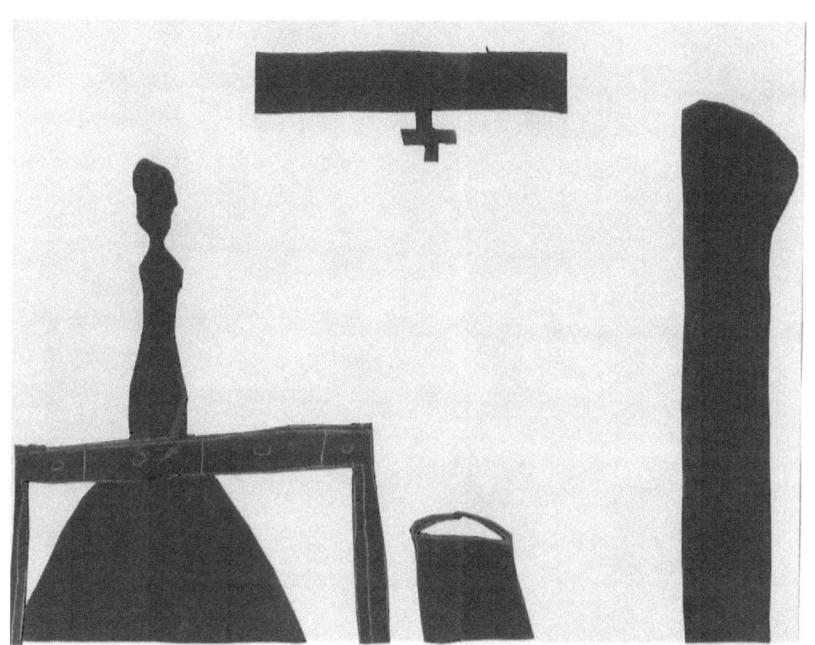

Taylor Vanover

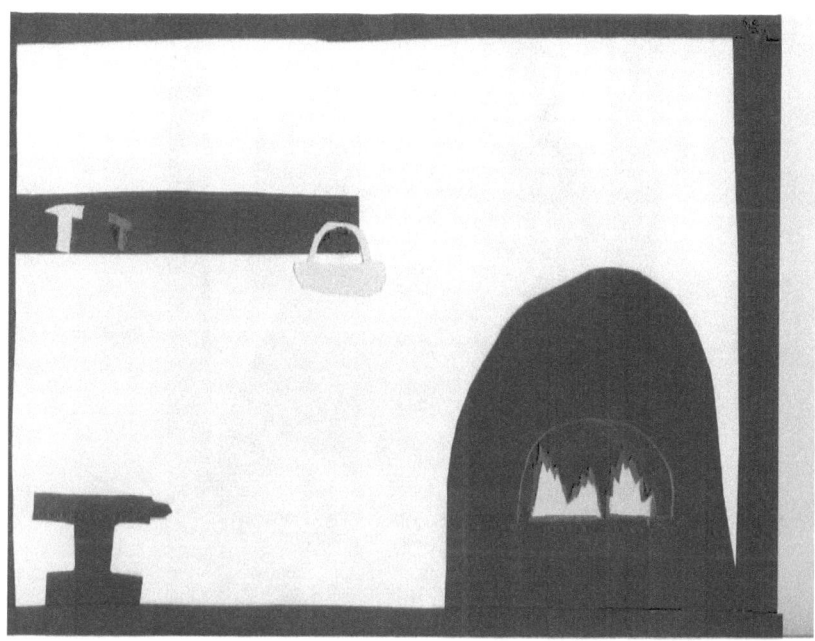

Tyler Hoffman

Vanessa Mashushire

Eric Turner

Stephanie Taylor

Cassidy Boyd

Part IV:
Student
Acknowledgements
and
Dedications

Benjamin Barlow

My portion of the book is dedicated to my family and teachers.

Gabby Bennett

I dedicate this book to everyone who has ever helped me. To all my friends, family, and teachers that have taught me what I know. Thank you!

Cassidy Boyd

I dedicate my portion of the blogs to all the people who believed in my work with the blogs including Mr. Schutte, Ms. Wilfong, Ms. Weimer and my parents. To you all I say, "Thank you!"

Demi Taylor Brown

I dedicate this book to all of my best friends, Gabby Shelby, and Kelsea who helped me and gave me ideas! Thank you so much!

Breaja Bureau

I want to give thanks first to my mom and dad for allowing me to attend this school!! I also want to thank Mr. Leineweber for paying us to publish our work in a book!! I know that has cost a lot of money from our school!! My last thank you is to Ms. Weimer!! She was there for me this whole way. I was stuck in times but she helped me through the whole thing!! Thank you!!

Sid Carpenter-Wilson

I would like to dedicate my blogs to Mr. Schutte, Ms. Weimer, and Ms. Wilfong for the chance to be an author in this book. I'd like to thank my parents for not letting me just ignore my homework, for answering me when I had questions (that's to my Facilitators also). And finally, also for my friends at DDA who helped me make my blogs when we went to work at Concentra and the Indianapolis Central Library.

Joe Coffey

I have dedicated this story to all who wish to read it and all of the brave men who helped found this country and those who still serve it today.

Elizabeth Cronnon

I would like to dedicate this book to my awesome teachers for never giving up on me and for all their hard work. To my boyfriend Alexander for all his help, and to all my friends for putting up with me while I was trying to write these blogs!!!

Marcellus Edwards

I dedicate this book to my mom. I dedicate this to my mom because she always gives me that extra encouragement I need to do well. Another reason is because she provides me with every thing I need. She is also a great role model and if you met her you would soon find out she is a very sophisticated woman. That is why I dedicate this book to my mom.

Sara Everman

I'd like to dedicate this book to all of the teachers and anyone who had a hand in helping us succeed. And to my favorite author, Joseph Delany. He showed me how to write like you were in another time.

Mark Hamner

I'd like to dedicate my writing to all those who helped me create and work on my blog and blog entries. I also want to dedicate my writing to my parents who helped me so much at home when I was writing and revising my blog entries. Those people that I dedicate my work to are: Mom, Dad, Ms. Weimer, Ms. Wilfong, Mr. Schutte.

Tori Hernandez

I would like to dedicate this book to my amazingly awesome teachers. They helped any time that I needed help, and they never gave up on me. Also, I would like to dedicate this book to my great friends who were here for me when I needed them. Hunter Kay, Vanessa Mashushire, Maria Jared, Dara Turner, Sarah Crouch, Samantha McDonald, Haley Napier, and a lot more. I couldn't have done this without my family's support. They push me to do my best, and I really appreciate that. So, I would just like to say thank you!

Lara Hoaglan

I dedicate this to Ms. Weimer, my favorite teacher, for supporting me until the very last word. I also want to thank Grandma, Karlee, Bekah, Lindsey, Ashley, Vanessa, and Kylee for having the faith in me like real friends. That got me through this crisis of a project.

Tyler Hoffman

I am going to dedicate this book to my mom. My mom has always been there for me when ever I needed comfort. She helped me when ever I had problems. She can be hard sometimes but she never lets me down when I need her.

Devin Hubbard

I dedicate this book to all my friends and family, especially my Mom for all the support she has given me since I was born. I would also like to thank my teacher Mr. Schutte for giving me the chance to do this. I want to thank Cedrych Davis for being a good friend and always being there for me.

Reed Jaynes

I dedicate this story to Neil Toth for teaching me so much about so many things. I'd also like to dedicate this to Debra Jaynes and Sommer Toth for being so nice and setting me in the right direction. Thanks for being such good role models....

Calin Johnson

I would like to thank my mom and dad for their support in my project. I would also like to thank my teachers, Ms. Weimer, Ms. Wilfong, and Mr. Schutte.

Maurice Jones

I'd like to dedicate this to my friends that help me fix things. Also my parents for helping me with this.

Hunter Kay

I dedicate my story to my Uncle David Kay. He is also a writer. He inspired me write whenever and whatever I want. He has so many short stories and I love to sit down and read them. I love him with all my heart and I couldn't live without him. Thank you unkie Davie. I would also like to dedicate this book to my best friend Dara Turner. She is the one who kept me on track the entire writing process. If I was off track she would yell at me to get back on track. Thank you so much Dara. There is also my mother. She has done everything for me throughout my life. She is the one who tells me to follow my dreams. This is for you mom. Thanks!

Austin Keith

I dedicate this to my dog Jester because I was on the couch eating food and he started to drool and he reminded me of a dog with rabies and that helped me a lot. But don't forget the most important person me for writing.

Emily Kirchenbauer

I dedicate my chapter of this book to my teachers and my closest friends. My teachers have been a wonderful encouragement and awesome critics of my work. My friends have also been great inspirations. Many of the details of my character and the different aspects of her life were based off of them. So thanks be to: Sam, Daniel, Brian, Derek, Johann, Blaine, Savannah, Emily, Ms. Weimer, Mr. Schutte, Ms. Wilfong, Mr. B, and Jim. I also would like to thank my buddies at school: Lara, Karlee, Vanessa, and Bekah.

Vanessa Mashushire

I would like for my dedications to go to all the people who were there for me and encouraged me not to give up during this writing process, Ms. Weimer, Ms. Wilfong, and Mr. Schutte. You guys encouraged me that even though things seem difficult right now, as long as I do my best, that's all that counts. And Momma, Daddy, Tendai, and Cj, I love you guys so much! You're the reason I wake up every day! And also I dedicate this to my Uncle David and Aunty Amilia, and all my family in Zimbabwe.

Also, to all my friends at school, just seeing you guys everyday made my day: Bitty , Kylee, Karlee, Lara, Emily, Lindsey, Rabekah, Hunter, Dara, Tori, Jenna, Heather, Courtney, Brooke, Kimi, Stephanie, Katie, Mercedes, Read, Jonathan, yes, I guess Kevin, Austin, Ashley, Kaitlin, Cassidy, Bre-Aja, Morgan, Natalie, Kat, Melissa, Anna, Both Saras, and everybody. Even though there are so many of you that I can't name all of you, you are all the reason why I come to school everyday (other than my education). And I also dedicate this to my friends that don't go to my school, Khensane, Haley, Sheunopa, and Britney. You all also inspire me everyday and I love you guys!

Lamarcus McClain

I would like to give a dedication to John Smith. I say this because he has done a lot for the Virginia colony. He is also the leader of the Virginia colony. If it was not for him that colony would have suffered and died. He came and brought them food and water. He practically brought the life. That man was a savior.

Samantha McDonald

I dedicate this book to all the people who helped me out and encouraged me to do it. The people who I really want to dedicate this to are Heather, Jenna, and Breaja they told me never give up because I was going to on this book we are writing. I am glad they are my friends they complete me. I don't know what I would do with out them. So thanks guys for being there for me and helping me out with this.

Katie McKinney

I would like to dedicate this book to all of the people reading it. It is because of you that we are able to raise money for our school and get the things we need to get to have a better education, a better chance at getting a good job, and a better lifestyle. Thank you from the bottom of our hearts, from all the kids at DDA.

Johnathan Miers

I dedicate my writing to Ms. Weimer, Ms. Wilfong, Mr. Schutte, and Mr. Weimer. They all helped me to get them perfect.

Haley Napier

I dedicate this page to Abby Wilfong and Bob Schutte for making me do my work, I like to goof off a lot.

Karlee Nielsen-Baker

I would like to dedicate my small chapter to my teachers who helped me, to my mother, my father, my stepdad, and the rest of my family. I also dedicate this to my friends who had to suffer in working on this book: Kylee, Lara, Kat, Emily, Rebekah, Lindsey, Vanessa, Bitty, and anyone else I didn't mention who is a friend. I would also like to dedicate it to my best friend, my sister Kristine Storms, who offered to help me even though she hadn't hardly any clue about what the topic of these journal entries were about. Thanks... and I love you , peoples!

Katelyn Parton

I want to thank everyone who helped me and believed n me. Without you I would not be here. Thanks!

Darrell Plymate

I would like to dedicate my writing to Ms. Wilfong for helping me keep writing my blogs that I did write. She also helped me write the best I could on the blogs. I would also like to dedicate Ms. Weimer for talking to me about my blogs and edging me to write.

Mercedes Preston

I dedicate this book to my mom Lisa, my dad Jimmy, my stepdad John, my stepmom Misty, my bother Isaiah, my sister Raeleigh, and my other brother Christian.

Makuela Rader

I would like to thank my Expedition teachers and my friends and family for supporting me. It has been a long, fascinating journey.

Bobby Rose

I'd like to thank my facilitators for the support and pressure to get my blogs done. Also, Rebekah Loss You make me laugh you have always been there for me .Thank you for all of your support and not for hitting me when I tried to push you to do your work too. I love you. Lindsey Krucuz, You're a good friend you always made me smile every time I was in a bad mood. Thank you for pushing me to get all this done. I love you. Nate, you've been my good friend for a long time you've made me laugh with those stupid phrases you got from movies and TV or just made up. I love getting in trouble in Band with you. Thank you for all of your friendship and lessons on the Piano.

Heather Skaggs

I dedicate this book to my mom, Ms. Weimer, and my friends. These are the people who have helped me believe in myself. I have no clue where I would be with out them. They are my heroes.

Anna Scott

I dedicate this to my aunt and cousin for their inspiration.

Kevin Simison

I dedicate my work to Harley Davison motorcycles. My Dad has a Harley Davison. I based a character off of him. He would want me to dedicate to them.

Kaitlin Spears

I dedicate all my work to all the wonderful teachers at DDA. I'm also dedicating my work to all my family and friends.

Kylee Standish

I would like to dedicate my book to my friends, family, teachers, and school. If not for them I would not have finished it. So, thank you!

Jon Stumpf

I dedicate this to my parents for being loving and caring. I give thanks to Mr. Schutte, Ms. Wilfong, and Ms. Weimer for their help.

Hunter Thompson

I dedicate my part of the book to my mom and my teachers because they are the ones that helped me and stuck with me until the end of all this and they still believed in me.

Audrey Traylor

I would like to dedicate my part of the story to my teachers for helping me, my family for reading all my stories, and my best, best friend Alex for letting me base my story on her. Thank you everyone!

Dara Turner

I'd like to dedicate my portion of the book to my mom, Pam. When ever I need help or advice you're there. You lovingly contribute to my colonial obsession and support me in anything I do.

I'd like to give a shout out to a few people also. To my dad, Bill, for the tremendous amount of help he provided, night or day. To my teacher Ms. Weimer for welcoming any question I had, and helping me through this whole process. To Sandy Lady for selling me my first authentic tea cups (That was the beginning of my colonial obsession), and to my best friend, Hunter Kay, for all her support, ideas, opinions and help.

Thanks for everything, everyone!

Eric Turner

I dedicate my blogs to my family for pushing me over my limit, especially my parents Donna and Terry.

Taylor Vanover

I would like to dedicate this book to all of my friends, family, and teachers. I would most like to thank Ms. Weimer and Mr. Leineweber because they have been there fore me ever since I started DDA and I will always thank them for that.

Anthony Vaughn

I would like to dedicate my part of the book to all of the facilitators who helped me: Mr. Schutte, Ms. Wilfong, and Ms. Weimer. I would also like to dedicate my part of the book to my friends and family.

Kimi Wood

I dedicate this book to Shelby Ellis. The reason is because she is always encouraging me to do more than I want to. She's always there for me, and I'm always there for her. If I didn't have her in my life then I'm not sure what I would do. She means the world to me. She is like my other half. She's the peanut to my butter.

www.ingramcontent.com/pod-product-compliance
Lightning Source LLC
Chambersburg PA
CBHW020244030726
47499CB00001B/45